Mistress of Dartington Hall

To Kath

Best wishes

Rosemary

Mistress of Dartington Hall

ROSEMARY GRIGGS

DAUGHTERS OF DEVON

The manufacturer's authorised representative in the EU
for product safety is Authorised Rep Compliance Ltd,
71 Lower Baggot Street, Dublin D02 P593 Ireland (www.arccompliance.com)

This is a work of fiction. Names, characters, businesses, places, events and incidents are either the products of the author's imagination or used in a fictitious manner.

Cover design and cover artwork by Bob Cooper.

Troubador Publishing Ltd
Unit E2 Airfield Business Park,
Harrison Road, Market Harborough,
Leicestershire. LE16 7UL
Tel: 0116 2792299
Email: books@troubador.co.uk
Web: www.troubador.co.uk

ISBN 978 1836283 799

British Library Cataloguing in Publication Data.
A catalogue record for this book is available from the British Library.

Printed and bound by CPI Group (UK) Ltd, Croydon, CR0 4YY
Typeset in 11pt Adobe Garamond Pro by Troubador Publishing Ltd, Leicester, UK

Chapter One

The Spanish Are Coming

November 1587, Dartington Hall

'The church bell… Dear God…it can't be?…Not the church bell?'

It came again, as menacing as a thunderclap on a scorching summer day. There was no mistaking it. St Mary's Church, nestled so close to Dartington Hall, you could almost lean out of the window and touch it. Even on a misty autumn afternoon, the tolling bell boomed loud as a cannon shot. It's deep tones rolled round the walls of my chamber. Yet I fought against it, willing it away.

Clotilde whirled round to face me. As her fear-filled eyes met mine, the green-glazed pitcher slipped from her shaking hand and crashed onto the unyielding wooden floor. Broken shards glinted in the dim light as she dropped to her knees, scrabbling to gather the scattered fragments.

'Listen!' I put a hand to my ear and waited. 'It's quiet now. Perhaps someone pulled the bell-rope by mistake.' I wanted to reassure her, though my heart was thumping against my ribcage.

On her knees, Clotilde tried to grasp the splinters of my beloved pot with weathered fingers worn by years of toil. It was a fine piece, a valued gift, and a bittersweet reminder of my brief stay at Queen Elizabeth's court after my wedding. Yet, seeing the distress in my old nurse's eyes, I forced a smile and bent to help her collect the broken shards into her apron.

'Don't worry, Clotilde. It was just a pot. It's lucky it was empty, or it would have soaked you!' With a nervous little laugh, I straightened up and stepped gingerly across the creaking boards to the tall casement window Gawen's father had been so proud of. I forced it open a crack, gasping as the cold air brushed my face. I pushed the window wide, leant out, and listened again.

I shifted my weight, trying to find a comfortable position, fiddling with the window catch, my mind racing. It was only a matter of time until Philip of Spain's formidable ships packed to the gunwales with fierce soldiers would land on our shores. But not yet – not on a foggy day in November. I held my breath, waiting at the window, and hope sprang as the silence lengthened.

The brief respite came to a sudden end when the bell tolled again, a strident clanging that made me jump back from the window.

Frantic footsteps thundered up the stairs, accompanied by piercing shouts from below. The heavy oak door burst open, and Alice Blackaller, the kitchen maid, tumbled through it. Her wide eyes darted around and her breath came in ragged gasps. Alice was normally such a placid girl, but as she stood trembling in the doorway, her plain features had arranged themselves into a white mask of terror.

'The Spanish are coming. They'll murder us in our beds,' Alice shrieked. With a pained groan, Clotilde hauled herself to her feet, hugging the broken pieces in her apron close to her stomach.

'Mon Dieu! They are coming! I blame the Queen of England! To think she sent her cousin to her death! I remember poor Mary, the one the English call the Queen of Scots, when we were at court in Paris. When your father was captain of King Henri's Scots guards.'

'Hush, Clotilde! There's no time for that sort of talk!' I cut her off mid-flow and felt a rush of adrenaline as I pushed Alice aside, knocking her off her feet. Ignoring her howls, I picked up my skirts and sprinted down the stairs. I almost collided with William Putt at the bottom. That steadied me. There was something reassuring about William Putt. He was as different from Hugh Rist, his shifty predecessor as steward of my household, as a faithful hound is from a rat. With his open, honest face, clear grey eyes and wide welcoming grin, William was a man in whom anyone might place their trust. But, for once, William was not smiling.

'Ma'am, you must stay in the parlour! Gather all the children and the servants there. I'll go see what's amiss.' With those words, he shot out of the door.

The commotion had already roused them, so it took no time for me to usher everyone into the cosy room where everything was in its usual place. The old settle, drawn up close to a blazing fire, had bright embroidered cushions spread across it. A comforting smell of wood smoke lingered in the air, just as it always did. It all seemed reassuringly normal, inviting, safe. Yet my skin crawled as I paced the floor while the bell continued its relentless tolling. While we waited, the air in the parlour became heavy and oppressive, almost as if I could cut through it with a sharp sword.

Seven-year-old Arthur, eyes round as meat platters, tugged at my sleeve with trembling fingers.

'Mother? Is it the alarm? Shall I fetch my sword to defend you? When he went to Ireland, Father told me to look after you all.' I put my hand on his fair curls, marvelling at their soft silkiness, and smiled a reassurance I didn't feel.

'No, Arthur, there's no need. It's nothing. Someone practising at ringing the bell, I expect.'

My eldest daughter, Lisbeth, threw me a scornful look and tossed her head, setting her auburn hair dancing.

'Where is your cap, Lisbeth? It's not seemly for you to go about bareheaded.' I tapped my foot and pursed my lips. It was a familiar argument. The girl would not be told. Even in such a moment of alarm, she must test my patience. With another disdainful glare, Lisbeth turned away. The other girls sat upright on the old wooden settle, their hands entwined, faces set and white. At last William returned to stand before me, rocking back and forth on his heels.

'I'm almost certain it's a false alarm. There's one come from Totnes with a tale that Spanish ships are upon us. But we've had no confirmation from the constables, and in this cursed fog no one can make out the Yarner beacon. I doubt we'll find it lit. We can't be sure, but I'd wager the Spanish won't bother us in this season.' I could see the sense of that. 'But that damn fool of a rector had the bells rung. Begging your pardon, ma'am, but he should have waited. Terrified people are swarming into the church from all over the estate like angry bees when the hive is threatened. You must come and settle them down, ma'am.'

Gawen was far away, likely still in Ireland attending to the Queen's affairs. After his farcical attempt to divorce me was overturned, and the Queen herself instructed him to treat me better, he'd made himself scarce. To my amazement, he'd trusted me to manage his affairs in his absence. Feeling the weight of responsibility settle on my shoulders, I ignored the fluttery feeling in my chest and summoned all my courage. Somehow, I must suppress the rising panic that had sent the people of Dartington rushing headlong to the church.

I wrapped a warm woollen cloak around my shoulders and stepped out into the damp atmosphere to make my way along the mossy path. The harsh croaking cries of the rooks jarred on my nerves as they soared above the old yew tree. Their raucous cawing competed with St Mary's church bells to add to the doom-filled atmosphere as I struggled to keep my feet on the slippery cobbles. I told myself there was nothing sinister about the black-winged shapes circling high above in the murky mist-laden air. They were just birds disturbed from their roosts in the tall trees beyond the graveyard, upset by all the frightened people running towards the church.

I ducked into the porch behind William and with a hefty shove, he forced the ancient wooden door to yield with a loud protesting creak from the hinges. A blast of noise from the gloomy depths beyond the doorway hit me. Swaying on my feet, I reached out a desperate hand to grasp the doorjamb for support. At first it was hard to make any sense of the women's shrill voices rising in a discordant descant above the deep, rumbling undertones of cursing men. Then, amidst all the din, a single voice rang out, clear and powerful. Her words echoed like a clap of doom round the ancient walls of St Mary's Church.

'The Spanish are coming... God save us all! The Spanish are coming!'

I dithered on the threshold, telling myself I needed time to adjust to the darkness. In truth, I was trying to fight off haunting memories of my childhood, of dark, disturbing days filled with terror in Rouen, a city besieged. I glanced up at the star-shaped vault of the porch roof above my head. Those solid stones, the face carved long ago into the central boss, had welcomed the people of Dartington for generations.

Where better for them to come to shelter from the invaders, to find comfort in this darkest hour?

Knowing I must follow William inside, I braced myself for the familiar musty hint of dying flowers mingled with a grim odour of death and decay. No amount of beeswax could mask it. I fixed my eyes on William's broad shoulders as he set his mouth in a grim line and motioned for me to follow him. People huddled together as close as sheep penned in the fold, blocking the aisle in front of him. Elbowing them aside, he pushed his way through the wall of bodies.

'Make way! Make way!' Heads turned. A sibilant hiss, only just audible, snaked through the crowd, carrying the words:

'The mistress... 'tis the mistress!' It died away as quickly as it had started, and a deathly silence fell. If a pin had dropped from a woman's head covering, it would have echoed as loud as a hammer in the smithy.

William marched forward, and the crowd parted before him like the waters of the Red Sea in the Bible story. I followed close at his heels, my black silk gown swishing against the dusty paving. The sharp click of William's boots beat out a rhythm while, behind me, Clotilde's worn wooden pattens clacked on the floor. Her laboured breathing sounded harsh in the chilling stillness that filled the little church.

I came to a halt beside Griffin Jones, the young rector, who wavered in an agony of uncertainty by the pulpit. Beads of sweat glistened on a face as white as the crisp collar peeking out above his dark cassock. With restless fingers, he fiddled with the folds of cloth draped over his skinny frame, looking for all the world like a startled rabbit about to bolt.

It took all my determination to turn and face my terrified estate workers and servants. Every instinct in my body screamed at me to turn and flee. But the image of my formidable mother, Isabeau de la Touche, Comtesse, de Montgomery, flashed into my mind. She would not have flinched from the task. Nor would I.

I turned, but before I could speak, a woman's anxious shout rose from somewhere in the dark recesses of the church.

'Mistress, the beacon was lit.'

Another took up the cry, and another.

'They say the Yarner beacon was lit. That means the Spanish are coming. The Spanish are coming.'

Another hoarse voice screamed, 'They'll bring the torments of their Inquisition on all us poor folk.'

Yet another yelled, 'They'll murder us all in our beds!'

A thickset man, a shepherd by his dress, stepped forward, held up his hand and called for quiet. His deep bass voice fell into the commotion like a pebble dropping into a deep well as the crowd fell silent.

'What must we do, ma'am?' he asked. I looked from face to imploring face and saw the hope in their eyes. They thought I, Mistress of Dartington Hall, could somehow make it all go away. To stop my hands fluttering and waving in my French way, I clasped them tight together in front of me and threw my shoulders back.

'I stand before you, mistress of this household...' I started in a voice that rang out, confident and firm, sounding much stronger than I felt. 'You all know me.' The hush was deafening. Eyes full of fear sought my face as they hung on my next words. 'Now, tell me – who has said the beacons are lit?' No one spoke. 'Has anyone seen the Yarner beacon alight?' A few shook their heads. The only sound was a child's whimper. 'Has anyone here seen a light from any beacon? Blackawton, Marldon, Denbury, or Dean?'

This question was met with some muttering. A few shuffled their feet and nudged their neighbours, but no one spoke up. 'Can any say with certainty the beacons are aflame?' At last, some men shook their heads. I glanced at William and he nodded.

'No! I thought not! And the master has sent no word,' I went on. Even now, even at this vital time, I could not name him husband. 'Nor have we heard anything from Lord Lieutenant Bourchier, or any of his deputies. There has been no warning signal. There have been no sightings of enemy ships off Devon's coast. Whatever you have heard, the Spanish are not coming today.'

I was not at all sure that we could rely on the Deputy Lieutenant's to send word to us if there was a genuine alarm. But the mention of Bourchier seemed to have hit the right note. Suppressing a flicker of annoyance, I swallowed the bitter pill that Queen Elizabeth's council had appointed William Bourchier as Lord Lieutenant of the county. I snapped my lips together and reminded myself that now was not the time to dwell on Bourchier's triumph in obtaining an annulment of his first marriage to poor Mary Cornwallis. I suspected Bourchier's success might have encouraged my husband's cruel attempt to abandon me. But that was all in the past. Now I must concentrate on the anxious people of Dartington.

A few men turned to their wives, patted their arms, nodded encouragement. But the women's faces did not relax as they clutched their children by the hand. Perhaps some felt reassured that Bourchier was in control. But that alone would not still all their fears.

'What you have heard is born of idle talk and grown large out of mistaken intelligence.' My voice rose, clear and imperious, just like my mother's. 'Acting on rumours makes fools of wise men. Hear me well – until we see for ourselves that the beacons be lit, until we have confirmation from the constables, there is no attack. It is just as it was in August when unfounded reports of Spanish ships upset us while we were busy with the harvest. That time it proved false and so it will now. We must go about our business.'

There was a more general shuffling of feet, a few murmurs, but I could see I had not yet convinced them. I tried another tack, feeling I was clutching at wisps in the wind.

'It was a wise thing that you all came here to the church.' That brought a few feeble smiles. 'We can all pray together that the good Lord will deliver us from the threat of our enemies.' I shot another look at William and could see that he was as worried as I was that praying would not be enough to calm them. I must try again. 'Sir Francis gathers his squadron of ships in Plymouth, ready to defend us.' That met with a few nods. Francis Drake was popular in Devon, lauded for his audacious raid on Cadiz earlier that year.

'We will be safe here. The chain at Dartmouth stops invaders finding a safe harbour. If they are ever foolish enough to make landfall anywhere on our coast, then we will repel them. The trained bands stand ready.'

A snicker of bitter laughter rippled round the church, and they raised their voices again. 'Trained bands? What use are they? Are we supposed to believe they can stand up to the might of Spain? They've only had a few sessions of learning how to use muskets! Most have no weapons at all!'

The atmosphere was suffocating, as if the heavy fog gathering outside had already found its way into the church. I glanced up at the roof and locked eyes with a Green Man. He was an unsettling sight, his face painted in the most garish colours, staring at me from one of the roof bosses. I felt my ribs tighten and raised my head as I refused to wither under that creepy stare.

At last, a spark of inspiration came. A plan took shape, a glimmer of hope. If we could keep them occupied, engage their minds with useful tasks, we might quell their fears for a time. I squared my jaw.

'First, we will hear the word of God.' My voice bounced back at me from the walls to hang in the air in the hushed church, but still I persevered. 'Then, we will rehearse our preparations as if it were a genuine warning while we wait for more certain news. Are you with me?' I scanned their faces, which looked sombre and fearful in the eerie light. At last, the shepherd, the man with the commanding voice, nodded and spoke up.

'That we are, Mistress Champernowne.' Others followed his lead, and I let out a long breath.

'Raise your hands those who will guard the weapons here in the church.' A flurry of hands went up. 'You six,' I said, waving the men to the side. 'Stay behind. Look to the culverins and shot we keep hidden here. Check the supply of powder and match. Have all ready, just in case.'

'Aye, aye!' Their faces shone with relief. I searched the crowd, looking for the portly little man who served as churchwarden.

'Where is the churchwarden?'

'Here, Mistress Champernowne! I'll watch over the armour – it had a good polish only a few weeks ago.' I smiled as he waved an arm.

'Good! Are there any men of the trained bands here today?' Silence, then heads turned as a tall, ruddy-faced young man pushed his way through the crowd.

'Edward Mann, Yeoman of Staverton, ma'am,' he said, clicking together the heels of a rather fine pair of leather boots. He then gestured to his three companions. 'We four came to see if there was any truth in the rumours that the Spanish fleet was upon us. We stand ready.' The others nodded in unison. They were all well dressed, though not showy.

'If the Deputy Lieutenant's call a general muster, many others will have to serve. Yet the men are unprepared and ill-equipped. Do you know the drills, Edward Mann? Could you give instruction, tell them the commands?'

'That I can, ma'am. They promoted me to corporal at the Michaelmas training.' The young man puffed out his chest. I considered his firm chin and steady hazel eyes. Satisfied, I made my decision.

'Well, then, Edward Mann, set them to check their weapons and to practise the drills, if you will. Be ready for my inspection later today.' A surprised, rather respectful look spread across his homely face, and he nodded his assent.

'You others, go with Master Mann. Find your staves, pick up your pikes and billhooks. Take whatever weapons you can find and assemble in the courtyard. Where are you, William?' I was now in full flow.

'Here, ma'am!' He nodded with a flicker of his usual grin, like a ray of sunshine breaking through thick, gloomy clouds.

'Send men to the beacon house we built last year on Yarner Hill. We don't keep it tended in this season and I'm sure it has not been lit as a warning. But we can check that there is sufficient dry kindling and furze, and that no passing vagabond or foolish knave has set it afire.' Three men stepped forward without William needing to ask. I recognised the aged gardener and his two sons.

'We'll go,' the old man said, doffing his cap. They turned and hurried away.

The door had no sooner closed behind their departing figures when a woman with wild, terrified eyes and a child at her hip shouted out, 'But what about us poor women? What must we do when the Spaniards come?' Her question made me shudder. The frightened women sheltering within the solid walls of St Mary's Church on that autumn afternoon could have no inkling of what utter devastation might come to them if an invading army rampaged through our lands. I'd seen it in France – burnt-out villages, ravaged fields, and women and children without food or shelter. The women of Devon would be in the front line if the invaders came. I knew only too well how they would suffer.

'If you wish, you women and children, any men beyond the age of sixty or below sixteen, you may all come into the hall to await more news. Master Putt will set you to work to check our stores.' William nodded his approval. He knew it would keep most of them busy for a while and likely quell the panic. I turned to the rector.

'Now, Sir Griffin, let us hear the word of God in the English tongue.' The nervous young man edged forward and picked up his Bible in shaking hands. 'We'll have no Latin mumbling, nor any service to Rome here,' I went on. 'We are true English subjects of Her Sovereign Lady, Queen Elizabeth. The Spanish and their Inquisition shall not touch us.' A weak cheer went up as Rector Griffin climbed the steps to the wine-glass-shaped pulpit.

'Come, warden, bring a light that he may read to us from the good book.'

Soon a soft glow lit young Griffin Jones' cadaverous face and picked out the intricate carvings of the pulpit as he led us in prayer. His reedy voice grew stronger as he took comfort from the familiar words. 'We will begin with Psalm 121. I will lift up mine eyes unto the hills, from whence cometh my help. My help cometh from the Lord…'

Chapter Two

Rehearsal

The same day in late November 1587, Dartington Hall

Later, in the hall, Mary read aloud from a book while Katherine, who everyone called Kate, and Ursula huddled close together on a pile of soft cushions. I watched Mary struggling to make out the words in the fading light filtering in through one of the towering windows. When she lifted her head, I gave her an encouraging nod. I could always rely on Mary to look after her younger sisters. Ursula cradled Diane the doll in her lap, her chubby little fingers stroking the doll's garish gown, taking comfort from the soft fabric just as I had years ago.

On that autumn afternoon, my younger daughters, obedient and well-behaved, made little fuss. Yet, now and then, they glanced at the door, catching the frisson of anxiety that hung in the smoky atmosphere. Meanwhile, Arthur grinned as he kicked a pig's bladder around. It was his favourite game. The ball danced between his feet, but the constant rhythmic thudding played on my nerves.

'Not inside the hall, Arthur! Foolish boy! Do you have nothing better to do?' I scolded him more sharply than I intended, but soon my frustration melted away. I couldn't help but smile when I saw the familiar pout appear on his lip like a fat caterpillar.

'Come here, Master Arthur.' Marie patted the seat beside her. 'See what I have for you.' She drew a piece of gingerbread from beneath her apron and picked up a well-worn book. Arthur's face lit up. He was not a studious boy, much happier outside, often found hanging around the stables or down at the mews, bending the falconer's ear. Yet Marie had a way of coaxing him to study.

'You be such a fine scholar. Will you read it out to me? For I can't make it out at all!' Without demur, he settled to the task. Running his finger along the line of text, he faltered only a few times.

I nodded my thanks, and as Marie raised her head, she smiled. She had become a cheerful soul after her daughter Joan came to Dartington to serve as Lisbeth's maid. But where were Lisbeth and Joan? I scanned the crowded hall, searching in vain. My chest tightened as if caught in a vice as panic surged through me. I couldn't find them. False alarm or no, those two should be in the hall with everyone else. It was not safe for them to be roaming about all over the countryside. As usual, my eldest daughter was playing up.

'William! William!' My shriek caused the girls to look up and the book slipped from Mary's fingers, landing on the floor with a thud. 'Please, send some men to search for Miss Lisbeth. Hurry, William, we must find her.' Without even picking up a cloak, he rushed to the door.

'No doubt she's gone walking in the gardens,' Clotilde whispered, laying a soothing hand on mine as the door banged shut behind the steward. 'Or she'll be hiding up by the holy well, as usual.'

I paced up and down until William reappeared at the door. His boots thudded over the hard stone floor, leaving a trail of muddy footprints as he led them in. Joan followed my daughter, meek as a lamb, though she cast an anxious look at her mother. Lisbeth trailed behind William, throwing me a belligerent glare over her shoulder. Radiating defiance, she slumped onto the cushions beside her sisters. The daggers aimed at me from Lisbeth's flashing eyes found their mark, piercing the thin skin of my relief. I felt the weight of her gaze settling on me like the swirling mist gathering outside, cold, heavy, and unforgiving.

Agnes Searle, the midwife's sister who tended my physick garden, set down a basket brimful of dried herbs and pushed a stray lock of grey hair from her face.

'Mistress, I could use some help in the still room.' Agnes spoke loud enough for all to hear. 'With all this talk of the Spanish, I thought to replenish our supply of salves and potions. They might come in handy if, may God forbid, anyone gets injured. I've brought extra ingredients from my store, but I'll not finish grinding in the pestle and mortar before dark without more willing hands to the task. The two girls work hard, but there's a lot to do.'

She gave me a steady stare, unnerving me for a moment. Then I realised she was sending me a coded message. Clever Agnes had picked up the need to keep the watching women occupied and was offering a task they would relish. Agnes's healing skills were well-respected, and she had worked wonders with my still room girls. There wasn't a plant or herb she couldn't find a use for. Medicines would be useful if the men were ever called up to fight.

'You're the answer to a prayer,' I whispered. Then louder, 'Take as many as you wish and teach them how to prepare ointments that might be useful.' With a knowing smile, Agnes went off to lead them to the still room.

It was almost dark by the time William and I stepped into the courtyard. An earthy smell hung in the mist, mingling with the smoke from a nearby chimney. Damp seeped through my clothes, chilling me to the bone, but I pressed on. As Edward Mann gave the order, the men scrambled to stand at attention, brandishing an unexpected assortment of weapons, everything from firearms, billhooks, axes, and sickles to simple staves. William drew me aside, keeping his voice low.

'Don't inspire confidence, do they? What's the use of snatching these ordinary folk from their daily tasks for a general muster? They won't stand a chance!'

'I fear you're right, William.' I scanned the ragged line of working men. Compared to the soldiers my father had commanded in France, they were a shambling crew. A few had donned the old-fashioned armour from the church. Well-polished and maintained by the wardens, it gleamed in the torchlight. But most of the others wore tattered cloaks over russet tunics. A few men had sturdy leather doublets that glistened with moisture. One man stood out. Over a woollen tunic, he wore a stained linen jerkin that seemed to weigh him down. I stopped before him and peered at his unusual outfit.

'Master Mann? What is this garment? Does it give protection to the wearer?' I reached out a hand to feel the cloth of the man's jerkin and traced a line of stitches in the shape of a square.

'We call 'em jack-o'-plates. The metal pieces sewn inside do act like armour if you're under attack. But a jack allows a lot more movement, especially if you need to fire a shot. See – I wear one, though mine is of stronger cloth.' He pulled back his short cloak to reveal a protective doublet beneath.

'That sounds sensible.' I frowned and ran my eye along the line of men again. 'But one or two among so many? Russet and woollen cloaks will give no protection at all.'

'They have issued some jacks to the trained bands, ma'am.' Edward stopped before a broad-shouldered man with a grizzled beard. 'Others, like this man, still have them from their time as fighting men in France... er... begging your pardon, ma'am... or in the Low Countries.' His face flushed as he remembered I was French. 'But most of the men who'll be called to general muster will have to make shift for themselves.'

'I see... thank you, Master Mann.' I gave him a nod and moved along, then paused. 'Tell me, do I have this correct? All the men must bring rations with them for twenty days if the call to muster comes?' The corporal's mouth dropped open, as though he could not credit that a woman would know such a thing.

'It is so, though I doubt many will bring enough ... er... food that won't spoil ...' His voice trailed off, and he looked down at his boots, leaving me to wonder if he had brought any provisions with him when he left Staverton that morning.

'Then you must reinforce the requirement to keep enough in store. Each man must have his ration pack always ready against the call to arms. Dried peas, grain, hard biscuits and salt fish, perhaps? I'll give it some thought and instruct the women.' Edward Mann nodded. 'Thank you,' I added more gently. 'You have done well today.' His grin widened, and he stood to attention as I went on. 'I am in no doubt it is a false alarm, but keep the men here until we have certain news.' I returned to the hall with much to ponder.

Chapter Three

A Visitor

The same evening in late November 1587, Dartington Hall

Dusk fell, the candles were lit, casting dancing shadows on the walls, as with sagging shoulders I dragged my clumsy feet up the stairs. As night descended, men lingered outside while women and children murmured in the Great Hall. No one wanted to return to their cottages until word came to reassure them it was indeed a false rumour. I left it to William to see them all housed for the night. I could do no more that day.

As I stumbled into the little antechamber, I yawned, ready to fall into the soft, inviting warmth of my bed. A smiling Clotilde greeted me in French.

'*Bravo! Bien joué!* ''Twas well done, Mistress Roberda. Your mother, Madame la Comtesse, she would be so proud of you.'

'I'm afraid I've done little to ease their minds. For once, I wish my husband was here.'

Clotilde let out a disapproving tsk. I could feel the tension in her fingers as she loosened the laces of my gown. Suddenly, she froze, and her face went white. A shout rang out across the courtyard.

'Ho! Who comes there?'

'A friend!' came the muffled reply.

Clotilde fumbled to put my gown to rights, and insides quivering, I flew down the stairs and raced across the hall. William beat me to the door. I felt a rush of cold, damp air hit me as it swung open and I stepped into the porch.

'Who can it be, William? Who comes so late to my door?'

'Have no fear, Mistress, they've identified as friend. The guards would not let them through otherwise,' came the reassuring reply.

Hugging my cloak round me, I waited beneath the White Hart badge, squinting through the darkness until I felt the strain in my temples. Dense and ghost-grey, the fog had crept up from the River Dart, blotting everything out. All I could make out was the fuzzy outline of the archway on the other side.

At last, a solitary pinpoint of light danced and shimmered, only to be snuffed out once again. William dashed forward, sending a forgotten pail flying with a clatter, while I waited in the doorway, fidgeting from foot to foot. Men emerged from their makeshift billets, their silhouettes distorted and grotesque. The light from the torches they held aloft cast eerie shadows on their anxious faces as horses' hooves clattered on the cobblestones. Two shapes emerged from the gloom under the arch. As they came nearer, the lanterns caught a trail of steam rising from the beasts' heaving, sweat-drenched flanks. The realisation hit me like a hammer blow. Whoever they were, they had come at a gallop. They might be bringing news of an imminent invasion.

The first rider hauled his mount to a standstill, and with practised ease, he swung his leg over the saddle. Standing head and shoulders above the crowd, half armour glinting in the torchlight as his cloak parted, he commanded the space. For a heartbeat, until he swept off his feathered cap, I thought it might be Gawen.

The waiting men called out as they jostled each other for a clearer view.

'Sir! Are the Spanish coming indeed?'

'No! Not today! Have no fear. Their ships will not dare to worry us at this season,' came the clear reply. 'They remain where they belong – in Spain!' A nervous cheer went up, sounding brittle and uncertain in the damp night air. 'That is the ones Drake didn't scupper in his raid on Cadiz last spring!' At that, the cheers grew louder. The man turned and surveyed the ranks of men with their cudgels and pitchforks, pikes and billhooks at the ready.

'I can see they would receive the welcome they deserve here!' he said. Then, in the tones of one well accustomed to authority, 'Now, you may all disperse to your homes.' I heard no more, for the cheering drowned him out. Men stepped forward to lead the horses away while others wandered off to collect their belongings.

Sir Walter Raleigh swaggered towards me. Behind him, a burly fellow, presumably a servant, scuttled along, carrying a bag. Even dressed for action, Sir Walter had not abandoned his finery. A huge pearl danced beneath one ear, catching the light as he marched out of the mist. To my amazement, a pang of disappointment washed over me. I dare not acknowledge it, but I think, in that moment, I wished it was my husband who had brought relief from all our fears.

'Sir Walter, you are welcome.' I kept my tone icily formal. 'Step inside if you please.' As he walked in, a hushed silence fell. The women stood, mouths agape, as if dazzled by a God who had dropped from the skies.

'Good mistresses all! Return to your homes,' he said, ''Twas a false warning! You have nothing to fear. The Spaniards' ships are nowhere near our shores!' At the sound of his reassuring voice, the women's faces relaxed into smiles. I am sure many a girlish heart skipped a beat as he threw back his head and laughed. 'You may all rest easy in your beds this night. The Spanish will not bother you!'

'Hurrah, hurrah. We knew as much all along. Hurrah!' The women giggled as they hurried off to greet their menfolk and make their way home. Many threw admiring glances over their shoulders as they went.

Dashing Sir Walter turned and gave me an exaggerated bow, sending his short cape dancing behind him as he dipped his head.

'Mistress Champernowne! It is many years since I last had the pleasure of your company,' he murmured as he took my hand and raised it to his lips.

'Indeed it is, sir.' Irritated, I turned away. I had no patience with his courtly games. 'You are most welcome, as is any good news you bear. Have you travelled far?' Brisk as a wasp in sunshine, I led the way to the parlour, throwing the question over my shoulder as I went.

The manservant followed, leaving a second set of wet footprints on the floor. With a swift motion, Sir Walter threw off his dripping cloak, sending droplets of water scattering. Standing before the blazing logs, he looked as though he owned the place.

'I'm near soaked to the skin with this cursed fog. Come here, man! Take my wet clothes and boots from me.' His servant obliged, removing the boots and easing off the half armour. He took the sopping cloak and hung it before the blaze before offering dry clothes from a weathered oilskin bag he carried. I looked away as, without a hint of self-consciousness, his master stripped down to his shirt and donned a fashionable doublet, running his hands over the fine velvet. He turned his back to the fire, seeking its warmth, and soon the pungent smell of damp woollen cloth mingled with the acrid smoke. Turning a smiling face on me, he spoke again. 'Ah, that's good! Ease for my aching bones! I'm come from Exeter. Called on my good mother while I was there.'

'How is your mother?' I asked. Relaxing a little, I cocked my head to one side. Fond memories of the gentlewoman who had been such a dear friend to me during Lisbeth's birth flooded into my mind.

'Losing my father took its toll. She fares better now.' A broad grin spread across his handsome face. 'Seeing herself named at the top of the tax list for the district of St Mary Major gave her quite a boost!' The idea of Katherine Raleigh, a wealthy woman in her own right after years of marriage, made me chuckle. Although she had been happy with her second husband, I knew she would relish being a 'femme sole' with her own rights to property.

'Ah, yes! I can well imagine! Your mother was a friend to me when first I came to England. And she helped me find places for the young French women I brought to Devon, women left destitute in the aftermath of those bitter wars, fought in the name of religion.' My smile faded as I remembered how Katherine and my father-in-law, Sir Arthur, had supported my refugee scheme. Until my jealous husband put a stop to it! In my mind, I heard Gawen's voice again, like a smothering wet blanket, snuffing out the wavering spark of my compassion.

'I will visit her in Exeter when I can.' My voice wobbled a little as I swallowed down painful memories that threatened to engulf me. 'I would have gone sooner, but I have been hard-pressed to keep matters well in hand here at Dartington in my husband's absence.'

He shot me a quizzical look, which I ignored. Then he waved a hand towards Clotilde and Marie, who sat by the fireside. They had set aside their stitching; poor light makes hard work for old eyes. I had no need to instruct them to stay. They understood that I could never find myself alone with a man.

'My people will remain. They have already eaten, but your man can find something in the kitchens.' At that moment, Alice staggered in, ogling my visitor and balancing a steaming pot of mutton stew on a tray. As she set the bubbling pot on the table, she slopped some onto the boards. After trying to mop it with a cloth, breathing heavily, she wiped her hands on her apron, then retreated to a seat in the corner.

'Now, while you eat, you can tell me what's really happening. As you have seen, my people were much alarmed. Have you told them the truth? Is there ought to fear? Will we soon come under attack?' I rapped out a string of anxious questions, and to his credit, his fine features took on a more serious cast.

'For today, we are safe. But in time they will come. Be in no doubt, they will come.' He stared into the flames for a long moment, then took the proffered seat. Once settled in his chair, he busied himself heaping the rich, meaty stew onto a platter before he spoke again. 'You have done well to calm the fears of your people, Roberda.' I let his familiar use of my given name pass. 'You have kept them well occupied. Stilled the panic. I've come across many running scared from their homes on my way from Exeter. The whole county walks on a knife edge. It doesn't take much to set them off. Your steward – that likely fellow who met me outside – he has told me how you reassured them. It was well done.'

Walter cut himself a hunk of bread from the loaf, scattering crumbs across the board. Between mouthfuls, he gave me the full story.

'Yesterday, the twenty-ninth day of this month, Bourchier had intelligence that Plymouth was to be the target of an attack. It's ideal as a harbour for Spanish ships. So he ordered a muster and assigned more of our forces to Plymouth. That news spread and tales grew in the telling until people believed the enemy was already upon us. The false news spread like wildfire. Of course, the Spaniards won't come in this season.' He paused and his knife hit the table, making a sharp sound echo through the room. He retrieved the knife and set it down beside the empty platter. His piercing eyes met mine, and I saw the unshakeable assurance of a man who knew the sea. 'They would not risk the venture in this season. Not once the autumn gales raged in the Western approaches. But the word was out, and once started, a rumour's hard to quell.'

Marie and Clotilde exchanged an anxious look, while Alice squirmed in her seat by the door.

'Indeed it is, Walter!' I said. 'The Lord Lieutenant should be more careful in his communication! Someone brought the story to Dartington. Thinking they had fired the beacon, the men all came to the church.' I had his full attention as I continued. 'The women packed into the church with them, being afraid to remain at home.' Lost in his own thoughts, Walter spooned more of the savoury stew onto his platter.

'You must understand,' I said. 'Even a trail of smoke coming from a bonfire of autumn leaves is enough to terrify my people. Any rumour of invasion brings abject panic.' At last, he raised his head.

'They need not worry.' He spoke with the arrogance of a man who had the whole world at his fingertips. 'The fleet is well prepared. The men stand ready. Our commanders will see off any threat, and they will find glory in the deed.'

With no sign that the plight of the women had entered his head, Walter mopped his plate with the bread and wiped a dribble of gravy from his chin with a napkin. I felt a surge of irritation that made the hairs rise on the back of my neck. Leaping up, I seized the poker, its cold weight firm in my grip. Burning with frustration, I thrust it into the fire, prodding and poking at the flaming log, which had no need of such attention. A stream of bright sparks flitted up the chimney and one spat out onto the hem of Marie's kirtle. Clotilde shot from her seat to throw the last dregs from her mug of ale onto the glowing speck of ash that had already burnt a tiny hole in the cloth.

Clotilde's hands were gentle but firm as she prized the fire iron from my grasp and returned it to its place. She turned and laid a steadying hand on my arm. But I was too angry to heed the silent warning in her eyes. The thought of the terrified women huddled together in the church clutching their babies made me bold.

Whirling around, I fixed my eyes on my guest, determined to ignore the unpleasant smell of singed wool.

'You men! You're so taken up with your warships and weapons – aye, and your hopes of glory and plunder!' He grinned and shook his head in mock contrition. That did it.

'I believe you men relish the thought of this war. You don't consider the women at all! What will happen to us when the invaders come? Have you taken us into account in your planning?' I jabbed an angry finger at his chest. 'Have you? Do you expect we women to wait for the Spanish to rape us and pillage our homes, to burn our crops and kill our children?'

Walter raised his hands in a parody of horror.

'Do not mock me, sir! I have seen war at its worst in France. I know how the women will be treated.' I closed my eyes. I saw the devastated city of Rouen in ruins, saw the widows with no homes to go to, saw the fields laid waste, the empty granaries, the children with huge hungry eyes. His noble forehead wrinkled, and his eyes widened.

'In truth, I had not thought of it, Roberda. Some are moving women away from the coast to ensure their safety. Perhaps you would rather go to some relative elsewhere? I'm sure Gawen could arrange it.'

I stood over him and banged my fist down on the board so hard that the platter and mugs jumped.

'You misjudge me, sir! I do not seek a cowardly retreat for myself. Wealthy women like me may have that option, but I will never take it. My concern is for all the others. What of the working women?'

His jaw tightened, and he raised his hand to finger the pearl earring. But I had not finished.

'When you call up the muster, the men leave their womenfolk unprotected. Their wives and daughters will have to toil in the fields and bring in the harvest. But no one considers the women's safety. Is it any wonder they panic? The men at least have a purpose. They can prepare to fight. But what are the women to do?' My hands fluttered, like a pair of wild birds caught in a trap. But when I saw Walter regarding me with an amused, sardonic look on his face, my fists clenched into balls of wrath.

'Ah, I see!' he said with a grin. 'With nothing they can do, the women will run around in terror like chickens, headless but not dispatched? They will impede our soldiers?' He dipped another piece of bread into the gravy that remained on the platter, then scoffed it down, licking his lips as he savoured each last mouthful. He looked so self-satisfied, so arrogant, I could not help myself. A furious snarl erupted from my throat, carrying not only anger but also all the anxiety that had built within in me during that long day.

Walter's brow furrowed. Leaning across the table, he reached for my hand and said, 'I am sorry, Roberda. I have been teasing you. You're glorious in all your righteous anger! But you are right. I will think on it.'

'You'd do well to think about how to better equip the men too,' I muttered, yanking my hand away to brush an angry tear from my eye.

'What do you mean?' he asked. I had his full attention now.

'All men summoned to battle need protective clothing. Yet today's courtyard gathering revealed that most lack even an old, worn-out jack-o'-plates to protect them. The armour in the church will serve for a few of them. The rest must make do with their workaday clothes. They will be easy prey for Spanish swords.'

'Jack-o'-plates, you say? Men attending the general muster must provide for themselves. I've heard of an armourer in Bodmin who can cut metal pieces from discarded out-of-fashion armour. There's a linen armourer in Plymouth who knows how to stitch the plates into the linings. Thank you for drawing it to my attention. I will enquire.'

I would not let him off the hook lightly.

'Time is short. Our men will be called to fight. The least we can do is give them some clothing that will protect them.'

'I hear you! You are both wise and beautiful, good Mistress Champernowne.' He chuckled, emphasising the formality of my title. 'You take after your mother, and that's no mistake; like her, you are a wise and valiant woman. Others might learn from your example.' Then his face grew more serious as he stared into the fire, which, after my attention with the poker, was blazing. 'This time it was a false alarm, but they will come. In February, when Mary of Scotland met her end, that sealed matters. You may be sure of it. Philip of Spain has his sights set on England.'

'It must have been an agonising decision for the Queen.' I said. 'To do away with her own cousin!' My voice was calmer, carrying both disbelief and sympathy.

He hesitated before he replied and for once all humour drained from his face. 'Cecil was out of favour for a while – she put the blame on him. But she needs him now.'

His shoulders dropped, and a grim expression twisted his mouth as I asked, my voice quivering. 'Will they try to seize Plymouth? To establish a secure refuge for their ships? It seems to me a wise plan. Plymouth or Falmouth? Somewhere along the coast?'

Walter's head went up as though he had just remembered something. 'Make sure all your people attend church on Sundays. Your man, Jones, isn't it? The Queen's council will send words for him, words that will bolster our people's resolve to stand strong for England.'

'We are all good churchgoers here. I'll be glad if they issue some words for that snivelling fool of a rector. I can't think why Gawen preferred him to the living. He's a lily-livered sort and might spread his own fears if he's not well directed.'

Walter burst out laughing, dissolving the tension between us. For all his grandeur and fancy clothes, I could still see a hint of the boy I'd first met so many years ago at Ducey. I couldn't help grinning at the memory.

'Monsieur L'eau!' It was the name I'd given him because his Devon drawl made his name sound like the English word 'water'. 'Do you remember when we first met? We've both come a long way since then.'

'How could I forget?' He laughed, and I felt my face burning.

'Hmm! We were children then.' Even as we laughed, I struggled to keep the bitterness from my voice. 'I was green in the ways of the world. You were only a boy, in the train of your famous cousin, Henry Champernowne. Who would have thought that Monsieur L'eau would become the favourite of our glittering Queen, knighted and appointed Lord Lieutenant of Cornwall, while my husband would attempt to cast me off, sullying my reputation forever?'

'I am sorry for your troubles,' he said with a rueful grin.

'Yet you did not speak up for me when my husband took me to court and set me aside, did you? He might have listened to you instead of those scurrilous fools.' Walter had the decency to blush a little.

'I was in Ireland, as was your husband for a time.' A cloud crossed his face, but I snorted. Walter must have had plenty of opportunities to speak to Gawen and warn him away from his folly. He went on in a voice as smooth as silk, 'I'm glad you survived the ordeal. Your family came to your aid, I believe? My mother spoke for you when she heard of your plight; my brother John Gilbert too. Anyway, in the end, they overturned the sentence, so all's well again.'

'I doubt if the matrons of Devon view it so,' I said. 'They already had their suspicions about me; called me "that flighty French piece". I expect they thought all the nonsense with the church court proved them right.'

'Hmm… they are a formidable lot, the women of Devon!' He lapsed into silence. After a while, he looked me in the eye.

'Listen, Roberda, I'm sure Gawen is truly sorry for what happened.' The words came out pat, as though he had rehearsed the line. 'He had concerns about your dowry. He tells me that, even now, it remains unpaid. That money is now lost to the French Crown, I suppose?'

'Indeed it is! They took everything from my father when he went to the scaffold on the orders of the Queen Mother of France. They said it was a fine summer's day in Paris. My brothers have had to fight to regain any part of their inheritance. My mother lives near penniless at Pontorson. And as you say, the wretched dowry remains unpaid.' I folded my arms across my chest. 'None of that gave Gawen licence to treat me in such a fashion!'

Walter shook his head, reached over and made to pat my hand, but I batted him away. I was not ready for his sympathy.

'I hear your brothers are rallying to Henri of Navarre,' he said. 'Mayhap his time will come. You know that my uncle, Sir Arthur, set much store by the dowry money and lands agreed on your marriage? Gawen was angry, yes, and misguided too, but I'm sure he regrets it all now.' I narrowed my eyes and studied his face. His portrayal of Gawen as a penitent husband seemed suspicious.

'Well, he has a strange way of showing it. On the few occasions he's been here during the last three years, he hasn't even bothered to speak to me.' Walter's next words threw me into confusion.

'He's in Exeter. He will soon be here, so you may have your reunion.' For an instant, I thought I might swoon.

'Gawen comes here? He seeks a reunion?'

'Yes, he thinks it is time. Expect him in a day or two.' He shrugged his shoulders, as if relieved to have delivered the message. 'Now, Roberda, the hour is late. Will you offer lodging for a weary traveller? I may stay for one night only.'

'It will be my pleasure. We always have rooms made up for important visitors like you.' I managed a feeble smile as his grin widened.

'I now serve on the Queen's council and am sent to check our state of readiness in the West. Dartington's a handy stop on my way. At first light, I'll be gone. I must meet Lord Bourchier and the Deputy Lieutenants in Exeter. Your husband waits there to receive his commission.' I stared at him, open-mouthed, wondering whether Dartington was really such a handy stop. It occurred to me that Gawen may have sent his charming cousin to soften me up and prepare the ground for his return.

'I hope you'll take a turn in the gardens with me before you leave,' I suggested, going through the motions of courtesy. 'Will you take more refreshment before you retire?' I signalled to Alice, who stood beside the door, gaping like a landed fish. Her rosy face grew even more red as she scurried around setting more platters on the table while I sat by, deep in thought.

I watched Walter wolfing down meat pasties and apple tartlets. As he ate, he threw back the best part of a pitcher of our best red wine. With a shaking hand, Alice hurried to refill his glass.

Replete and completely at ease, Walter spread himself out on the settle, yawned and stretched his feet to the fire. Perhaps he spoke of Drake and the Queen; perhaps of the designs of Philip of Spain, the supposed strength of his forces, or of how the deputies all had differing ideas as to the right way to defend Devon. I cannot be certain, for my mind was spinning. I struggled to stay still and quiet in my seat while he droned on. It had been three long years since Gawen and I parted in anger. Now I must prepare to meet my husband.

Chapter Four

Courage Comes in the Morning

Early next morning, late November 1587, Dartington Hall

My eyes snapped open. A strangled scream clawed its way into my throat, a harsh, raspy shriek slicing through the pressing darkness. Despair smothered me, weighing me down like a heavy blanket.

The bed I had shared with Gawen was a suffocating prison cell, solid walls closing in, allowing no glimmer of hope. The feather mattress was an impenetrable granite slab. The carved tester pressed down as my frenzied fingers clutched at the silk bedcover. The nightmare trapped me, holding me in its unrelenting grip.

Clotilde shattered the spell when she pulled the sumptuous red velvet curtains aside with a loud, impatient swish. Bleary-eyed, I shrank into a ball under the covers. I curled my knees up tight, trying to stop shaking. The familiar scent of lily of the valley and clean linen clung to her as she leant over me, holding my hand in a warm, comforting grip.

'The dream?' Her voice was little more than a breath in the silent room. I managed a weary nod and clasped her fingers tight, noticing the swollen knuckles, the painful testament to a long life of toil. Soothed by the reassuring sight of a face I knew better than my own, I snuggled under the covers.

'Yes... it has left me undisturbed for so long. I had all but forgotten its terrors.'

'It is not yet light. Should I remain while you attempt to sleep?' Her gentle voice came as a soothing balm.

'What would I do without you, Clotilde?' I whispered. 'I couldn't bear it when he sent you back to France.'

'Well, I'm here now, and he isn't!' With the slightest dip of her head, she gave my hand a squeeze. I sat up and struggled to get my arms into the velvet robe she offered.

'At this hour, after the nightmare, I know I won't be able to sleep. Fetch me that casket.' I pointed to a carved box perched on a chest beside the door and, with a frown, she brought it to me.

With gentle fingers, I lifted the lid, and a gentle waft of sandalwood-scented air whooshed out, soft yet laced with a subtle hint of exotic spice. The folded pages stacked inside held many memories, moments of both joy and sorrow. In the dim candlelight, I turned the packages over, feeling the weight of the wax seals.

I put the first to one side – I could not bear to read the note sent by my half-sister Béatrice after our papa's cruel death on the scaffold in Paris.

'After all these years, I still can't imagine stunning Béatrice, with her glorious auburn hair, as an abbess in charge of a wealthy convent in France,' I said. Clotilde picked up the doll from the bed where I had discarded her during my night terrors.

'Ah, I remember! You had a rare fight with Béatrice in Rouen, didn't you? Jealous little minx that you were.' Clotilde's throaty chuckle echoed around the room, making me smile.

'Yet it was Béatrice who helped secure my release. And when they captured my father, she went to the Queen Mother to plead for Papa's life. But against the wrath of Queen Catherine, she didn't stand a chance.' I didn't want reminders of that time of grief. With a heavy sigh, I set Béatrice's missive aside, along with several others in my sister Charlotte's careful hand, and more bearing my mother's businesslike script.

When I came to a handful of letters from Anne Cecil, I paused. Anne had befriended me when I first came to Queen Elizabeth's Court and we had kept in touch ever since Opening her last letter, I found, folded inside, a copy of the poignant verse she composed after she lost her baby son, Lord Bulbecke. Reading the words my friend had penned in her sorrow, stirred up painful memories of my own lost child. Baby Philip lay beside his grandfather in the cold grave in Dartington's church.

'It was after our boy died, Gawen began false proceedings against me,' I said. 'Poor Gawen, it was his pain that drove him to it.'

'Pah! Resentment, and his jealous nature, more like. It might have been different if your father had paid the dowry.'

Clotilde tutted and fussed with the bedcovers, leaving me in no doubt of her disapproval. As I turned to the next letter, she placed Diane the doll on the bedside coffer and took a deep breath.

'Why must you do this? It will only make you more upset.'

'But, Clotilde, he will be here in a day or two. I have to decide what to do.' I wilted a little under her scrutiny but went on searching in the sandalwood box. Clotilde pursed her lips and went on with her tidying, moving round my bed, busy as a flea in a fur collar.

Setting my mouth in a determined line, I peered into the box. A flimsy slip lay crumpled at the bottom. I smoothed out the paper until the inked strokes of the lawyer's pen stood out as clear as a row of stakes in the deer park fence. Once again I read aloud Gawen's message, the last words I had from him.

'Madame. The sentence against you has been reviewed. It seems I was misinformed. I am instructed that I must treat you better. That will best be served by my absence.
I am bound for Ireland again, in the service of my queen.
You are reinstated as my wife and mother of my children.
You will have charge of the household and estate in my absence.
Trosse will assist.'

I traced my finger over the signature Gawen had scrawled beneath the writing. It looked angry and defiant.

'I may be speaking out of turn,' Clotilde started in a strident voice, quite unlike her usual purr, 'but I will say my piece. It's a good thing you dispensed with that dried-out cadaver of a man, that lawyer Trosse. Much better that you took it on yourself. You have done well.

Everything's in order and all the servants are happy in their duties. Don't let the thought of your husband's return throw you off balance. You have nothing to be ashamed of.' The candle's wavering light reflected in Clotilde's glistening eyes as she straightened up. 'I beg you. You are not thinking straight. These are perilous days. Strong winds could soon carry the might of Spain to plague us… don't let those same winds blow you off course. Even in these dangerous times, you do not need help from the man who wronged you.'

'Clotilde, when all is said and done, he is still my husband.'

'Ha! I see it now. You miss having a man in your bed. You think he'll change and be kind to you!'

'Now you have gone too far! I have no choice. If he returns to claim me, as is his right, the children must come first.'

'I doubt his return will make Miss Lisbeth the joyful and carefree girl she was before he took her away. You always held that girl a bit too close, if you ask me. The separation damaged her more than the others.'

That touched a raw nerve. Lisbeth, my firstborn child, my bright, beautiful, biddable girl, came back a stranger after our enforced separation.

'And now she's impossible! She won't speak to me at all!' The words burst from me as I gripped the casket so tight that my fingers hurt. 'Perhaps having her father back would not be such a bad thing. I must consider it.'

I folded Gawen's terse note and placed it on top of the one from Anne, and with a defiant shrug, I looked Clotilde in the eye.

'Despite the shameful things he did, Anne Cecil reconciled with Edward de Vere.' Clotilde's lips pulled into a tight line as she brushed imaginary dust from the coverlet, and spoke up again. .

'Lady Anne – she has her father to stand by her. Your mother, your brothers and Madame de Beaufort, your sister – they are all far away. There is no comparison.'

'Poor Anne! Lord Burghley couldn't do much to curb the evil excesses of that dreadful man,' I said. 'Edward de Vere is notorious as a brutal philanderer who preyed on young girls and on boys, too, not to mention the debts he racked up. To think he had the gall to accuse Anne of infidelity and deny their Elizabeth was his child.'

Clotilde's eyes flashed as she took the box from me.

'Well, perhaps I spoke in error when I said there's no comparison. Gawen Champernowne may not be as evil as de Vere... I mean my Lord of Oxford... but he ruined your reputation with his false allegations against you.' She put the box down on the oak chest with a thump.

'Was it all his fault?' I asked. 'Those blackguards who hated me fed him a pack of lies. All because I am French.' Clotilde pulled a face, and I said no more. I wouldn't admit it, but a nagging thought plagued me. Gawen had believed them.

A cock crowed, its brash, raucous trumpet call piercing the morning air.

'If I am to walk with Sir Walter before he is on his way, it's time I was up. There are things I would ask him.' Still huffing and puffing, Clotilde laid out my clothes.

Once dressed, I hurried down and caught up with Walter in the hall. He was ready to take his leave, his cloak already draped over one shoulder and his man waiting outside with two saddled horses.

'Do you have time for a walk in the gardens?' I asked, putting on my brightest smile. 'I've questions for you.' He returned my smile, and with a gracious bow, offered his arm.

'I can always spare a moment or two in the company of so lovely a lady.'

Wrapped up warm against the cold, we picked our way along paths glistening with a delicate touch of frost. Clotilde and Marie followed, for the sake of propriety. They were both huddled in layers of thick winter clothes.

After the previous day's dense and dismal fog, a radiant sun shone from a clear blue sky, lifting my spirits. Spiders had festooned the holly bushes with fragile webs where dewdrops sparkled. Clusters of bright red berries nestled amongst the spiky dark green leaves, which would soon deck our hall at Christmastide.

Walter rubbed his gloved hands together and pulled his cloak tighter.

'You have made a delightful garden here, Roberda. It would have pleased my uncle to see it so. He had so many plans. Never built that banqueting house, did he?' We had reached the close-clipped expanse of the bowling green, which overlooked a dip in the ground beyond the wall. 'Over there, where the land lies low' – he gave an expansive wave – 'that's where I'd put a water feature. A lake and fountains would be just the thing.'

'That would be a costly venture? I doubt Gawen would think it the best use of his coin,' I replied.

The walk had warmed me, but the ice-cold air still tingled against my skin, carrying with it the sharp piney tang of the majestic yew tree near the church. Walter's eyes misted over, his gaze taking in the distant green hills, forming a perfect backdrop to my gardens.

'Devon's a fine place on a morning like this. I should spend more time here,' he said, and a sad smile touched his lips.

'Ah, but Queen Elizabeth would miss you!' My laughter sounded brittle in my ears. I wondered if it masked a little spark of envy I hadn't realised lurked within me.

We retraced our steps to my physick garden and watched a robin hop onto the stone placed there in memory of my father's faithful sergeant at arms, Alain du Bois. While the proud little bird puffed out his bright breast and sang a wistful air, I plucked up the courage to ask a burning question.

'Have you heard anything about the commission Gawen will receive? Will he captain the Phoenix of Dartmouth?'

Walter shook his head.

'I believe he'll have a more important job to do; he'll lead two hundred horsemen. They'll harry the enemy should they land; slow down their advance.'

'Ah… I know what that means. I've seen it in France. Mounted soldiers will try to delay them. But when they can't stop the Spaniards, our gallant soldiers will burn the fields and barns, the crops and granaries. They'll leave nothing for the invaders to plunder. The country folk will have to evacuate or starve! How can I prepare my people for that?'

'You speak of war like a seasoned general,' he said. I smiled and inclined my head as he sought to reassure me. 'It may not come to that.'

'I pray it does not.' I studied the path beneath my feet, trying to find the right words. 'Drake and Lord Admiral Howard will need

Gawen's ship, the *Phoenix*. I'm afraid he'll be upset if he can't be on board when the alarm comes, no matter how you dress up his role as leader of the cavalry.' Walter was silent as we strolled towards the house. He paused by the door.

'You'll find Gawen changed. Ireland changes us all.' It was rare to see the flamboyant Sir Walter with sagging shoulders and his mouth turned down. I caught the regret in his eyes. 'When we come home, we are not as we were before.'

'I suppose war does that to most men.'

'Hmm… Did you know your father-in-law had lands in Ireland?' That was news to me. 'And I believe Gawen's cousin of Modbury is keen to set up there.'

'Richard? I wonder what his wife, Judge Popham's daughter, has to say about that! And you? Do you have your eye on lands over there?' His melancholy air vanished as easily as a snake sheds its skin and he gave me the most outrageous wink.

'Perhaps!' he said. I couldn't help but titter. Yet, although I was standing next to one of the handsomest men in England, I felt no flicker of attraction.

Just at that moment, Lisbeth burst into our path, slamming a door behind her. I withdrew my hand from Walter's arm, feeling suddenly hot. Lisbeth's lip curled with contempt and the chilling intensity of her stare hit me like a blizzard wind. Without uttering a single word, she turned and marched off towards the kitchen.

I shook my head slowly and looked away. To his credit, Walter did not press me for an explanation.

Our footsteps echoed into the silence as we crossed the screens passage. By the time we reached the porch, my thoughts had returned to preparations for imminent invasion. Determined not to let my defiant daughter distract me, I seized my last chance to speak up for the women of Dartington.

'I hope you will remember we womenfolk in your discussions with the Lord Lieutenant. Give us work to do. Let us play our part in your preparations – we won't be a hindrance.' Walter clicked his heels and gave a mock salute.

'Indeed, Madame, I heed you well!'

Smiling, I continued. 'As I mentioned yesterday, I've noticed that few of our men have suitable clothing to protect them. Could women stitch new quilted jacks for the pikemen?'

'My goodness! I can see how determined you are. I suppose the guild of linen armourers might object.'

'Do you mean to tell me you'd hold the profits of the guilds above the need to equip our men as we face the invaders?' He avoided my eye.

'I'm not sure women would be equal to the task...' But seeing the stony determination in my face, he sighed. 'Very well. I'll enquire. If it's possible to cut canvas or fustian or even sturdy linen according to the armourer's design, I will send some to you. You might also get your women to provide suitable rations to sustain their men while on duty.'

'Exactly so! I remember how my mother always had plenty set by. Provisions we could carry with us, should we need to leave our home at short notice. During yesterday's alarm I set the women to checking our stores.'

'I've always said Gawen didn't realise what a jewel he had in his keeping,' he said with a grin. 'A woman like you – her worth is far above rubies! I hope you'll receive Gawen kindly when he returns.' His words sent me into a frenzy, for I couldn't think how I would greet my estranged husband.

Walter, ever gallant, bowed his head to kiss my hand. Then, in a fluid motion, he was up on his horse.

'God go with you, Sir Walter,' I called, adding formality to my farewell for the benefit of any onlookers. He reined back and came alongside me again.

'And may God be with you also, Mistress Champernowne!' With a cheery wave, he set his heels to the horse's flank and clattered under the arch. Throwing decorum to the winds, I called out after his retreating figure.

'Remember the womenfolk!' Laughing, I wandered back to the hall to prepare for Gawen's return.

Chapter Five

A Reunion

December 1587, Dartington Hall

The girls' heads were bent low over their stitching, their brows furrowed in deep concentration as the dim light from the rain-lashed windows fell on their faces. I watched as their determined fingers pushed glittering needles through the fabric, while the downpour drummed out a relentless rhythm against the glass. My own hands were still in my lap, resting on tangled skeins of silk and crumpled linen. My mind churned in a whirlwind of emotions as fierce as the tempest raging outside.

Perched on the edge of my seat, I strained my ears for the sound of my husband's footsteps over the fierce wind that howled through the trees beyond the garden wall. My pulse was racing, and I found it hard to breathe as I waited in the suffocating atmosphere of the parlour at Dartington Hall.

Three years had passed since he left me. I could hardly believe he was in the chamber above, changing out of his wet clothes. How clever I had been to engineer a slight delay by despatching William to fetch him a dry doublet and hose. But I knew I could not put off our reunion any longer. As the door opened, I felt shivers running between my shoulder blades. But it was William who entered, out of breath from carrying a bulging pack, which he set down with a groan. A faint damp smell reached me as he peeled off the oilcloth covering.

'Master Gawen has arrived,' William announced, shooting an anxious glance in my direction. I stood up abruptly, and my needlework slipped from my lap, followed by a pair of shears, which landed with a sharp tinny clatter. Swallowing hard, I scanned the doorway, holding my hands clasped tight together in front of me.

I had rehearsed countless versions of my greeting, from a stinging reproach to a loving, wifely welcome. But when he bowed his head to pass under the lintel, all the words froze on my lips. My heart cartwheeled in my chest, turning over and over like the tumblers who entertained us at Christmastide.

Five years had changed him. He seemed more assured as he ran a hand through his springy, dark hair as he took in the scene. I had forgotten just how handsome he was; the stern lines etched on his face added a new air of maturity. Despite all the cruelty he had shown me, I couldn't deny the tiny spark of affection that still burnt within me. He was my husband, and I his wife.

All of a tremor, I reached out to him, hoping to bridge the divide that had torn us apart. My uncertain hands hovered for a moment, only to fall to my sides as Gawen crossed the room in a few purposeful strides, turned and stood before the blazing fire.

I stole a quick glance at my children. Mary, Kate, and Ursula had set aside their stitching and sat close together, wide-eyed, as if mesmerised by the rare sight of both their parents in the same room. Lisbeth stood apart from the others, her back turned on me. As for Arthur, Marie had been doing her best to keep him entertained. From the sticky smudge around his mouth, it seemed likely that he had charmed more than a few treats from her. Just as I turned my head, Arthur's book crashed to the floor. He wriggled free and hurled himself towards Gawen, skidding to a sudden halt, his new leather boots squeaking on the floor. Arthur clicked his heels and gave his idea of a salute, which his father returned with a warm smile. The boy had forgotten all about the formal greeting I had taught him.

'Father! Father! I put my horse at a fence yesterday and we sailed over.' Arthur's face flushed pink and his high-pitched voice rang out loud and clear. Even amid the tension, a tiny smile flirted around my mouth. It didn't matter at all to a seven-year-old that the horse was a small pony and the fence just a broom placed across two upturned flowerpots. To my relief, Gawen beamed down on our son, who was jiggling around, squirming like an excited puppy.

'Why, young man, that is quite an achievement! Well done!'

'Ned the falconer's training a new goshawk! Would you like to come to the mews to see him, sir?'

Hungry affection shone from Gawen's eyes as he patted Arthur's head.

'A capital plan! We shall go together when the rain stops. But first, perhaps you are wondering what I have for you in my pack?' Gawen waved an arm and in no time at all Arthur was on the floor, fumbling with the straps. His delighted squeals when he drew out a set of balls like the ones jugglers use drew the girls to their feet. Mary cast an anxious look in my direction, waiting for my approval before she led her sisters to join Arthur. They dipped into neat curtseys, and Gawen beamed as he motioned them to the pack. Soon a profusion of silks and ribbons, a line of peg dolls, books, and a fine feather quill scattered the floor. Only Lisbeth stood apart, with her shoulders set and rigid.

'Lisbeth, come and greet your father,' I summoned her, praying that for once she would drop her belligerent attitude and behave herself.

I could hardly believe my eyes when my eldest daughter turned around and glided across the parlour, graceful as a swan, her gown swishing like the gentle rustle of leaves in a summer breeze. Her eyes remained cast down – she was all sweet, demure modesty – until she rose from a faultless curtsy to favour her father with a dazzling smile. It was like watching the sun breaking through on a grey winter's morn.

'Welcome home, Father!' Gawen basked in the glow of her greeting, while Lisbeth peeped up at him from under her lovely lashes. It was obvious she directed no animosity towards her father, although I hadn't felt the warmth of a smile from her in ages. I frowned at her and pressed my lips tight together. The girl was a puzzle.

'Can this be Lisbeth?' he said, a fond expression lighting his usually stern features. 'Why, you have grown into quite a beauty, my dear! I have brought you a bolt of silk damask for a new gown. The colour will suit you well. I hope the rain has not seeped in to damage the cloth. And there's some of that new lace too.'

'Thank you, Father. That was a kind thought.' Her answer carried such maturity I had to look twice to be sure it was my Lisbeth speaking. She joined the other girls and was soon smoothing out a rippling length of carnation coloured silk and trying the lace against it.

There was no doubting Gawen's joy in seeing his children again, and he covered any embarrassment he had at our first meeting by responding to their chatter. As I watched him, jumbled memories, fragments of our life together, danced through my mind. I could never forget the splendour of our glittering wedding, the shimmering lights reflecting off the jewels and gowns of all the ladies as we exchanged vows before the Queen herself. The hurt when he left me a maid on our wedding night still stung. Yet, despite our shaky start, I had been relieved and thankful when he came home from France unharmed after the horrors of St Bartholomew's Day.

I remembered how his disappointment grew as each daughter was born. Even when at last Arthur, the longed-for son, arrived, it was not enough. I understood his fear that one son might succumb to some childhood illness, leaving him without an heir. But it was more than that. Gawen wanted to outdo his illustrious cousin, Henry Champernowne, who had left two sons when he died a hero in France. We had lost our second boy. I had given him only Arthur and a parcel of girls. Above all, Gawen was furious about the dowry my family promised but never paid. Bitter and disillusioned, he'd taken out his anger on me in a false divorce.

Yet, seeing him there in my parlour with the children, I remembered happier days, times in the bedchamber we had shared, times when he let down his guard and allowed me to glimpse his deepest hopes and fears. Alas, his misplaced jealousy always resurfaced to smother all hope of love growing between us.

The rhythmic clicking of Gawen's boots brought me back into the room. Startled, I glanced up and saw him standing just a few steps away. Like a nervous student facing a formidable schoolmaster, he twisted his hat in his hands, eyes fixed on the ground, avoiding any connection with mine. The air that separated us grew frigid, as if a solid wall of ice stood in our way, keeping us apart.

'My Aunt Raleigh advised what gifts I should bring.' A timid smile flickered on his lips, only to vanish in an instant. To my surprise, my voice sounded light and warm when I answered.

'It was well done, Gawen. It is a long time since the children have seen their father.' Gawen's cheeks turned rosy and he shook his head as though he could not quite believe his ears. The expression of pleasure and relief on his chiselled features moved me beyond measure. It made him look years younger.

'The gifts will help ease your return,' I said, and a tiny patch of the ice wall melted.

'Roberda…' He was staring at the cap as he continued to turn it round and round. 'Roberda… I…'

'*Pas devant les enfants!*' I spoke without thinking, resorting to my mother tongue as I often did in moments of stress. In a flash, I remembered they had once used my speaking French with my brother's tutor as proof of my infidelity. I switched to English. 'Welcome home!' The cap was still at last. 'Let us talk later, husband. Will you sup with me?' Another chink in the wall thawed when he raised his head and nodded.

In a reprise of the scene with Walter days earlier, Alice set the dish down with a thump.

'That will be all, Alice. I will serve. You may go.' The plump maid scurried through the door, casting a puzzled look over her shoulder as she went.

'Clotilde? Marie? You may retire too. Master Gawen and I have much to discuss. I will call you when I need you to help me prepare for bed.' Marie turned without a second glance, but Clotilde held her ground, her anxious eyes searching my face.

'Are you sure, *ma petite?*' she whispered.

'Yes, Clotilde, I have made up my mind. Please leave us.' With a curt nod, she threw a venomous glare at Gawen and, eyes flashing, made for the door.

I ladled a generous portion onto Gawen's plate, sending a rich, meaty smell wafting round us. On that early December day, a warming dish of chicken baked in a pie with malmsey wine was just what we needed. I was thankful that we were not bound by the Advent fast. Fish alone would not have been so satisfying for this special reunion supper.

The crackling fire danced behind him, bright ribbons of light reflecting off our best Venetian glass. I poured the rich, ruby-coloured Rhenish wine and took my place opposite Gawen at the board. As we enjoyed our meal, we spoke of King Philip of Spain's forces and the likelihood of an invasion. We discussed Drake's raid on Cadiz and even talked about the Queen. At first, we both weighed each word with great care before speaking. Gradually the cosy warmth, the wholesome dinner and aromatic wine had its effect. As we relished the taste of stewed apples, flavoured with cinnamon, and served with caraway biscuits, we spoke more freely. Although we both kept to topics we considered safe – the harvest, the unfavourable weather, the children's progress – it felt like the distance between us was shrinking.

Settling himself on the oak settle, Gawen undid his doublet and stretched his legs out before the comforting flames. The twinkling candlelight burnished his features with a tinge of copper, giving him a strikingly handsome appearance – or at least it would have if it were not for the tight pinched look about his lips. Many a woman would find him attractive, yet, unlike most men of his class, to my knowledge, he had never taken a mistress. Even in the dark days of our separation, he never suggested he wanted to replace me with another. I settled into my seat, mirroring his pose and leaning back with my elegant slippers poking out from the hem of my silk gown.

Before I knew it, the words tumbled from my lips.

'I am glad to see you, Gawen. I give thanks you came to no harm in Ireland.' He closed his eyes and drew in a heavy breath.

'My brother George is still there, he said, his voice cracking with emotion. God alone knows if he will return. I hope and pray I never have to go to that benighted place again. I'll not tell you of the dreadful things I've witnessed, sights I can't describe, sounds not fit for a lady's ear.' I bit my lip. Even though I sat close beside him, even though we talked together, any reminder of the past might plunge us into the cold depths of our differences. I held my breath and waited.

'I heard from Walter that you did well to reassure our people when rumours of an attack on Plymouth were rife.' His voice was gruff and gravelly and he did not look at me. 'I am grateful for that and for your care of our children.'

'There is no need to thank me. I did but do my duty as your wife. Since…' Just in time, I stopped myself from mentioning his cruel behaviour or our last meeting. 'During these last years, I have devoted myself to the children and to setting the household and estate in good order.'

'You have managed everything very well.'

'I have my mother to thank for that. When my father was fighting for the Huguenot cause he gave her full power of attorney and she ruled over his lands, not in his stead but in her own right. I watched her well, learnt how to act with fairness and firmness. I set out to win the trust of our people here at Dartington. And I believe I have.'

'Yes, you have, and I'm glad of it.' The words sounded sincere, but I could see the vein at his temple pulsing – a telltale sign Gawen was getting agitated. His next words confirmed it. 'But are you suggesting that you don't want to relinquish control of this place now that I'm here?'

I cursed inwardly. I should not have mentioned my mother, for that was sure to remind him of the missing dowry. To avoid setting his back up any further, I gave him a swift reassurance.

'No! No! You mistake me. I will step in only when you must be away. And God knows, Gawen, they may send you off with no notice if the Spanish come.'

I rose from my seat to pour a fresh glass of wine and handed it to him. Fixing my eyes on his, I dived into the frigid waters that swirled between us. 'Husband, we speak of politics and of Spain and the war that will soon be upon us. We discuss the household. We discuss our children. But there is another topic we have both been avoiding with the greatest care. We dance around it on tiptoes, afraid of the pain it will unleash. But it is time to acknowledge what is past and discuss our future.'

Gawen leapt up from his seat and marched up and down, plucking at his doublet with restless fingers. In that moment, I glimpsed the old angry Gawen. As the silence grew ominous, cold fear slithered through my veins, its grip tightening like a snake. Doubt crashed over me like a wave on a desolate shore.

When he broke the silence at last, his voice caught me off guard with its unexpected gentleness and genuine concern.

'I can't see any way forward for us. It is done. All the people in Devon know. Most of them point the finger at me.'

'No, Gawen, they lay all the blame at my door. They still hold me responsible for everything. To them, I'm an adulterous foreigner, while you, Gawen, are a wronged Devon gentleman. Despite that, we have to bring it out into the light. For the sake of our children, we must find a way forward.' As I spoke, his face flushed, and he bit his lip.

'Roberda, I am sorry. I don't know what to say... I... they deceived me. So many gave witness against you.' His anguished eyes sought mine.

'What has happened is done. You cannot undo it. I cannot forget, nor yet in truth forgive. But let us try to put the past behind us and go forward for the good of the children who waited so eagerly to meet their father. They are going to need both their parents as we face the Spaniards.'

'What must we do?' He felt for the seat behind him and sat down, shaking his head.

'I will take you back as my husband, if that is your wish.' I got the words out at last. I wasn't at all sure that it would ever be his choice. We had not spoken of it. I had not quizzed him, had not asked if he now accepted my innocence of the demeaning charges laid against me before the Bishop's representative at Staverton church. I had not demanded that he obey the Queen's command to treat me well. 'All I ask is that you think on it,' I said. I made my way to the door, leaving him staring into the flames, and spent a restless night in my lonely bed.

When I met him early the next morning, he was already booted and spurred for his journey, eyes following Arthur's retreating figure.

'As I promised, I've been with him to see the goshawk. He's a good lad. Famished, I'll warrant. Boys his age are always hungry. He's gone to find something in the kitchens. Now I must be gone.'

'What will be the role of your regiment of light horse should they come?' I asked while he fumbled to fasten a warm cloak over his shoulder. 'Will you be in danger?'

'I'm not sure if I should tell you any more of how the council thinks to deploy our cavalry.'

'What? Do you fear there are spies here?'

'No, not here... I hope not... I wouldn't want to alarm you, but there are some who harbour a love of the Catholic way. We must be watchful that there's no one among us who might give away our plans to our enemies. That is all.' The fresh morning air made me shiver as Gawen took the reins from the groom and swung his leg over the saddle. He gave a rueful chuckle as he gathered the reins. 'I'm appointed a captain because of my experience in France with cousin Henry. But I will have two hundred men behind me, when Henry led only a hundred soldiers in France.'

I smiled, thinking how good it was to see him no longer consumed with jealousy. Henry Champernowne, the brave soldier his father had doted on, had cast a long shadow over the younger, less confident Gawen.

'There are few enough men with battle experience,' he said. 'I've seen action in Ireland, too, so I'm the one to lead our mounted forces. I'll also need to provision my ship, the *Phoenix*.' There was no hint of resentment in his voice.

I gathered my courage to bid him farewell.

'Gawen, I meant what I said last night. May God bring you home safe.' He nodded and rode off through the arch without a backward look.

Chapter Six

Preparations

December 1587, Dartington Hall

'Miss Lisbeth, if you keep fidgeting like that, how on earth can we take your measurements for the tailor?' Pinching her lips together, Marie extended the end of the tape towards her daughter Joan. 'Please, just a little more patience.'

I fixed Lisbeth with a stern glare to reinforce the reasonable request. She made a silly face before regaining her composure to help the two women finish the task to the tailor's satisfaction. He stroked his wispy white beard and looked up from a well-worn black book, where he had noted down the last measurement. He ran a wrinkled hand over his gleaming bald head, then spread the carnation damask fabric out on the table. With years of experience, he assessed it, feeling every intricate detail between his aged fingertips.

'Hmm… I'm told the ladies of the court all prefer the French style these days. Is that what you'd like?' he said, raising his head.

'Yes – I don't suppose anyone would want anything Spanish in these times. Perhaps you could add some of this delicate lace?' I replied. 'What do you think, Lisbeth?' The girl shrugged her shoulders, making a show of her indifference. However, from Joan's nod and the excited look on her face, it was obvious she and Lisbeth had already discussed ways to embellish the new gown.

'If it pleases you, mistress' – Joan piped up in a voice so small I could hardly catch her words – 'my mother could edge the cuffs with lace. We could add some to the ruff too – Clotilde knows how to set a ruff, don't you, Clotilde? Ooh! It will look so pretty.' The girl flushed bright red and slipped behind Lisbeth, trying to hide. Marie sighed, her round face wreathed in smiles.

'That Holland linen we've been saving will be perfect,' Clotilde said. 'It's so fine you can almost see through it. We'll make the cuffs and ruff collar if Master Tailor can supply the gown. She'll look pretty as a picture.' I ignored another grimace from Lisbeth and turned to the tailor.

'It was good of you to come from Totnes at such short notice. I'm sure you're busy. Can you finish it in time?' The tailor hunched his shoulders, looked down at his scuffed boots, and dredged up a heavy sigh.

'I can have it done before Christmas. Business is slow. Most of my customers think of nothing but the coming war.'

'Ah, yes, I understand. But I had expected your son, for he made up the last set of gowns for us.'

'He's called to the muster,' the old man replied in a gruff voice. His eyes flitted round the room anxiously as he clasped his hands together.

'It is but a rehearsal,' I said. 'Perhaps they won't come.' The words sounded trite, but I wanted to offer some comfort.

The old man wiped his eyes with a clean kerchief he had spirited from his doublet.

'I hope Lord Bourchier knows what he's about,' he said with a shrug. I took a moment to consider my reply. Gawen had warned about spies, but I knew hardly anything about troop movements and defences, so could give nothing away.

'I am sure Lord Bourchier has matters in hand.' I said it more in hope than genuine belief as he rose to leave.

'This is not the first time we've faced such a threat. My family, we come from Dartmouth, ma'am,' he said. 'When I was a boy, I would go to St Saviour's Church and admire John Hawley's brass. You've heard of him, no doubt?' I nodded. He puffed out his scrawny chest and went on. 'A great man, he was. Ship owner and merchant, mayor of Dartmouth, and a noble soldier too.' At that, the old man's cheeks suddenly reddened and he swallowed hard. 'Begging you pardon, ma'am, for it was the French that tried to invade our shores in John Hawley's time. Oh, he saw them off, he did. They didn't assault the town of Dartmouth but landed on the undefended beach at Blackpool Sands. Bourchier should make plans to repel King Philip's forces from such places.'

'I am sure all is in hand,' I replied evenly, but I made a mental note to ask Gawen when he returned. I thought the tailor had a valid point.

'Well, Hawley fought them off and so shall we should they dare to come.' He bowed and slipped the weathered book into his pouch. The silk fabric rustled softly as he gathered it up before he stomped to the door. 'I will send word when it is ready for fitting, ma'am.'

After he had gone, Lisbeth turned to Joan with an exaggerated shrug.

'What's the point, anyway? My father won't be here for Christmas, and nor will anyone else. Why bother making a new gown?' She stomped out with Joan, her shadow, following behind.

Throughout the month of December, the kitchens were as bustling as usual as the servants prepared our holiday feasts. The smell of exotic spices – nutmeg, cinnamon, and cloves – drifted through the house to tickle our tastebuds. With the men called to the muster, the women had to shoulder additional work. Most did not complain. They were glad to be busy. It stopped them thinking of the worst.

I missed William's reassuring presence when he joined the men who responded to the call to muster, saying every man must do his duty. When he came home with the others, they all bore tales of poor kit, lack of weapons, and confusion, which did nothing to ease the fears of the remaining servants.

'It seems there are differing views amongst the deputies.' William crossed his arms over his chest and rubbed the back of his neck with one hand as he stood before me. 'The talk was that it was the cost of it all that plagued our Devon worthies. Trade through our ports has fallen away in the last year or so for fear of the Spanish; they feel the loss of their coin.'

'That I understand.'

'The local gentry and all the rich merchants say they can't afford to pay. They're angling for the Queen to stump up more to pay the trained bands and send more weapons. God's teeth, if you'll pardon me, ma'am, we are in sore need.'

'I know, William. If they come, I'm afraid Devon will be the first target.'

'Aye, Plymouth is likely the closest safe harbour to Spain. But our leaders don't seem able to agree on a plan. We all turned out as instructed. Lots of 'em from the trained bands of Devon and Cornwall and more besides. Waste of time, that was! On the thirteenth of the month, they countermanded the order to muster. So here we are! Home again. I can tell you, the men aren't pleased!'

'Well, I'm glad to have you back William. I'm sure they will devise a sensible plan,' I said, trying to sound more confident than I actually felt. 'Sir Walter was clear that they're unlikely to attack in midwinter. Let us look to our stores, in case we need to leave at short notice, and let us prepare for Christmas.'

Even though we couldn't have the elaborate feasts we had in happier days, I was determined to celebrate the season. With fewer people at our table, there would be an abundance of delicious dishes. With the prospect of impending conflict at the front of my mind, I went to the kitchen to give instructions that more beef joints be salted than was usual.

The cook, a stout man past the first flush of youth, scratched his bald head as I explained.

'We can include dried and salted beef in ration packs for the men summoned to duty. Or, heaven forbid, in the event of an urgent evacuation, we can take it along with us.' When he crossed his arms across his chest and scowled, I thought he might resist. Then he picked up a meat cleaver and nodded his head.

'Yes, ma'am! I'll see to it. It will save fodder for the winter if we cull a few more beasts than usual. We started on the pigs a month since.'

A week later, I returned to the kitchens to cast a satisfied eye over the rows of hams hanging in the lofty kitchen, where the smoke infused the meat with flavour. Beyond, in the dairy, a trough filled with salt held huge joints of beef.

'That's better,' I said. 'It will stand us in good stead against emergencies and still leave plenty for our Christmas feast. We brought in a better harvest this year,' I went on, trying to sound positive. 'Much better than the year before.'

Alice flashed me an anxious glance. She was on the far side of the large table, measuring flour into an earthenware bowl to make a pie crust. As she worked, a film of white spread over the board, and a larger pile fell from her spoon onto the kitchen floor.

The fat cook's down-turned mouth told its own story. With slow deliberation he wiped blood from a knife, spreading a red stain on his apron.

'That's true, ma'am,' he said. 'But the price of wheat's shot up. It'll get worse when they need rations for the sailors that will man our ships. They'll need feeding if we're to have any chance of sending the Spanish back where they belong.'

'Best keep a close watch on our supply of flour and dried peas, then.' I glared at Alice, who was scraping up the spilt flour. 'And make sure there's no waste!' The girl cringed under my scrutiny. Addressing the cook once more, I said, 'Do your best with our Christmas fare, but be sure to keep back plenty.'

'I'll do my best, ma'am,' he said, turning his attention back to the rabbit he was jointing. As I picked my way between the barrels of flour, he called over his shoulder. 'It's good to have all the men back.'

'Indeed, master cook. It is.'

Gawen was not with the men who came back to Dartington, cursing the deputies as loudly as they cursed the Spanish.

Chapter Seven

Once Upon a Christmastide

Christmas 1587, Dartington Hall

William stamped the snow from his boots, scattering a cloud of powdery white over the floor. Smiling, he set down an armful of greenery, releasing an invigorating evergreen scent. Arthur's rosy cheeks were aglow as he scampered in and signalled to three burly estate workers. The men grunted and groaned as they struggled to manoeuvre an enormous tree trunk into the hall from the screens passage. After several attempts, they hauled the massive piece of lumber towards the waiting fireplace. Following behind, more servants struggled to carry huge bunches of holly and ivy.

Mary clapped her hands, her homely face pink with excitement. She was always the most mild-mannered and helpful among my girls. I could rely on Mary to obey instructions without question. Seeing Lisbeth holding herself aloof as usual made me hope Mary wouldn't change as she grew older.

The eager girls cut pieces of greenery to wrap around candles in every window, laughter bubbling from them as they vied to outdo each other. Agnes arrived carrying a large basket. Shaking off her damp cloak, she settled down on the floor with the girls, showing them how to twine dried flowers, rosemary sprigs and bright red berries into the foliage. While the girls worked, Agnes reached into the basket and drew out an enormous bunch of mistletoe, which with deft fingers, she wove into a kissing bough to hang inside our door.

Lisbeth joined her, seated on the floor, counting the white berries.

At William's direction, two stable boys raised a ladder.

'Have a care! Don't fall!' I called as one boy balanced atop to string the evergreen garlands amongst the magnificent carved oak beams. Meanwhile, William prodded the smouldering cinders in the hearth with a sturdy metal poker before adding pieces of charred wood from a basket, tossing them into the flames that soon flickered in the cavernous fireplace.

'There!' He said, standing back to survey his efforts with satisfaction. 'The remains of last year's Yule log are already alight. Soon this year's will send sparks up the chimney and bring warmth and light to our Christmastide.'

'Thank you, William!' I stretched my face muscles into a warm smile and felt the tension drop away. 'Following the old customs will steady us all,' I said. The steward's answering grin lit up his face, and his eyes twinkled as he took in the crowd of chattering servants who worked with the children to create a wonderful display of festive cheer.

'Aye, Mistress! 'Twill be good to forget our enemies for a few days. May God send us a peaceful holiday.'

'Amen to that,' I said, giving Arthur's shoulder a squeeze. We stood side by side, spellbound by the first tiny flickers, which soon grew bolder and became vivid tongues of light as they licked round the wood. Our Yule log, stripped of its bark and left to dry for months, promised a cheering blaze.

'I wish Father were here,' the boy whispered. 'Oh, how I wish he were here for Christmas.'

'I know, Arthur, I know.' I hugged him close as a fleeting spasm of fear threatened to snuff out the joy of the moment. Arthur blinked fast, trying to hold back his tears. 'Your father has important work to do. He is with Sir Francis. They count our ships, ready to fight the Spaniards if they appear.' I turned to see Mary placing a green garland on little Ursula's head.

'Lisbeth, Kate? Won't you wear one?' she called. Soon they all had crowns of green and danced about, light-footed as laughing wood nymphs.

'Boys can dance too.' Mary chuckled, snatching off Arthur's

cap and replacing it with a ring of foliage. 'Come, Mother, won't you show us how you danced at Queen Elizabeth's court when you were young?' Mary grabbed my hand, and I soon felt my linen coif knocked from my head and a wreath set in its place. Caught up in their laughter, I showed them the steps of a courtly dance. Even Lisbeth joined in, shrieking with laughter as she trod on Arthur's toe.

'We must have music,' Kate cried, clapping her hands together. I stared at my feet. We could no longer afford the minstrels who had once played for Gawen's father. All of them had gone to Modbury to join Pierre, the talented French boy I had rescued from starvation so many years ago. Perhaps William noticed the disappointment on my face because he stepped forward.

'I have no lute, but I can sing.' With that he launched into one of the age-old English songs of Christmas, his rich baritone voice echoing to the rafters. As he reached the chorus, Agnes, Alice, and Marie joined in, their voices harmonising to create a glorious wall of sound. Meanwhile, Clotilde stood to the side, humming along and tapping her feet to the rhythm, while other servants added their voices to the impromptu choir. The children and I, caught up in the merriment, danced faster and faster. We abandoned the formal steps and instead, hand in hand, we pranced round and round in a gleeful circle, hoots of laughter mingling with the singing. It was a mad moment of freedom and hilarity, a brief respite from the midwinter gloom.

Our dancing feet froze when William broke off in mid-flow, stood to attention and made a stiff bow. Pushing back a lock of my fair curling hair, I whirled round, expecting to see the rector frowning at us for such behaviour on the holy eve of Christ's birth.

I gasped and let go my grip on Arthur's warm fingers as my hand flew to my mouth. It was not the rector. It was Gawen whose broad shoulders filled the doorway.

To my amazement, my husband was looking at me with such a rapt expression it made me feel weak at the knees. The room seemed to hold its breath as Gawen's gaze locked with mine, an unblinking connection that sent a shiver of excitement through me. In a surprising, graceful motion, he removed his cap and approached me, leaving a trail of wet footprints on the floor. My heart thudded so loud in my chest, I thought he must hear it as he reached for my hand. When he pressed his lips to each of my fingers, I felt light-headed.

Arthur's shrill voice broke the spell of the moment.

'Father, Father, I knew you'd come home for Christmas!' Arthur's face was shining with joy as he tugged at his father's arm. I felt the heat in my cheeks as I retrieved my hand from Gawen's grasp. His eyes never left my face as he ruffled Arthur's hair.

'Sir Francis and the others have left Plymouth and gone to Mount Edgecumbe. I expect they will continue their planning there or at Buckland during the holiday. They suggested I join them, but I needed to come home.' All the time, butterflies tumbled inside me as his eyes held fast to mine.

Arthur came between us, hopping from foot to foot, and determined to get his father's attention.

'I was only joining in their silly dance to make them happy. I'd much rather hear all about where you've been, Father!' With one last look at me, Gawen turned to our impatient son.

'Well, my boy, they have appointed me captain of the light cavalry. Men and horses drawn from all over South Devon. We were all called to the muster, trained bands and those of the general muster, too, as Lord Bourchier ordered.' Arthur's sparkling eyes never wavered from his father's face, as he absorbed every single word. 'Some of my horsemen didn't even turn up. I'll have to roust them up after Christmas if we're to be ready to fight off an attack. I'll call 'em out for a pack of gutless fools, shall I?' He gave Arthur a playful poke in the ribs, causing him to collapse into a heap, laughing fit to burst his sides. Gawen joined in and their mirth was so infectious soon the girls were giggling.

'I hope the muster was useful,' I said. By now I was laughing, too, feeling as if a coiled spring had unwound inside me.

'It's given us a better idea of how many men we can rely on, yes. My good friend Francis, along with cousin John Gilbert, John Hawkins, and Grenville, they've ordered work to improve the defences in the ports.'

'That's reassuring!' I don't think I grasped his meaning. In truth, I was still feeling dizzy.

'Yes, and high time too,' Gawen went on in a more serious tone. 'Dartmouth defences are out of date. Designed to deny enemy ships safe harbour, not to repel a landing force. Plymouth needs strengthening too. They'll rope in some of our men to help top the ramparts and set up sharpened stakes to reinforce the barriers. As soon as the twelve days are done, they'll be called up.'

Brimful of excitement, Arthur skipped off on a joyful circuit of the hall. Turning to Gawen I dropped my voice low.

'I fear it will not be such a feast as we had in your father's time. The tenants will come, but most of our neighbours are away, or else they won't come on account of me.'

'No matter! Everything I need is here.' I gasped as his eyes found mine again.

From the corner of my eye I saw Clotilde squinting at me with her arms crossed across her chest. A tremor of disbelief shot through me as I looked back at my husband.

Arthur bounced up to us again, clamouring for his father's attention.

'Our men practise at the butts every Sunday, Father. I count 'em to be sure they're all there.' Arthur's huge, round eyes shone as Gawen gave him a mock salute.

'You'll make a fine general one day, lad.' He gave Arthur a gentle pat on the behind. 'Off you go. Help your sisters. They need your strength to hang the final garland over the door. Then we'll visit the mews to see how that hawk's progressing. It's stopped snowing, so as long as you put your stout boots on, we may go together.'

Reassured to see Gawen playing the fond father, I smiled as our son trotted off, grinning from ear to ear. 'It means a lot to him to have you take notice of him. He's missed having a man he can look up to.' Gawen took my hand.

'I'm willing to play my part as a father and, if you'll have me, as a husband. I've given much thought to your words. You are right. We must put the past behind us – and not just for the sake of these children.' The hopeful look in his eyes melted the last blocks of ice between us. Light-headed and speechless, all I could do was nod.

After supper, the children went smiling to their beds to dream of the feast we would enjoy on the morrow. I climbed the stair to my chamber, where the candles cast a soft light, transforming the room into a snug and inviting bower. I rocked on my feet beside the bed – the one we had shared as man and wife – rubbing my hands on my arms, eyes darting towards the door.

My velvet slippers were silent on the boards as, with the merest sigh of silk, I walked the length of the room to stand before the mirror in its gilded frame. Fine Venetian glass – Gawen's father, Sir Arthur, had spared no expense. The flickering candles cast a kind light on the woman looking back at me. I saw a face little lined, with no need of paint or artifice, nor touch of cinnabar to brighten the rosy lips. I set my head to one side and saw my father's cool blue eyes looking back at me. Perhaps mine were brighter, warmer than his, with sparkling lights undimmed, but the likeness was there for all who knew him to remark. A few silver threads now nestled amongst the golden waves teased up into the latest style to frame my face beneath the frippery of feathers and ribbon that passed for a headdress. I fancied my waist looked slim as a girl's above the farthingale.

With her lips clamped tight together, Clotilde watched me turning this way and that as I preened before the glass. Her disapproval hung in the air like a dark cloud in a summer sky as she looked me up and down. With a heavy sigh, she took my best smock from the chest where it had lain so long amongst bags of fragrant herbs. She traced the embroidery with a finger and shook her head.

'You've decided then?' Her voice crackled, and I swallowed hard.

'I have, Clotilde. I am sure he has changed. I am certain of it. All will be well. Did you see how he looked at me?'

'Harrumph! Many a woman has come to rue the day she thought a man had changed his ways.' Tutting softly, Clotilde helped me undress, then held out the shift. A heady scent of summer freshness clung to the linen, lifting my spirits as it fell over my head. Still tutting, Clotilde withdrew.

I climbed up onto the bed and lay there, plucking at the velvet bedcover. I hugged my arms across my chest as doubts raced through my mind. Perhaps Clotilde was right and I would be foolish to give him another chance. Anne Cecil had taken her wayward spouse back, but it had brought her little joy. Even though Gawen wasn't as much of a blackguard as Edward de Vere, yet false accusations of my infidelity were no small matter. I wondered for the hundredth time whether a man like Gawen could change. Clotilde was always telling me he was like the leopard cat that, try as he might, could never change his spots.

Squeezing my eyes tight shut, I thought again. False alarms were a sharp reminder that enemy ships would soon bear down on Devon. Time was not on our side. For the sake of my children, I must decide.

Feeling dizzy, I clambered down from the bed, shivered as my feet touched the cold floor. In my haste, I upset a ewer of water placed on the coffer for my morning toilette. Hearing the crash, Clotilde flew in and mopped up the spillage. I shivered again, and without a word, she handed me a warm nightgown to wear over my smock. I slipped my arms into its cosy embrace, relishing in the soft caress of its velvety folds. The silvery moonlight filtered through the window as I weighed my options.

A tiny flame of love still flickered somewhere deep within me. When I saw desire kindle in his shining eyes, I couldn't help but hope that through kindness and love we could allow the flames to flare up again. I hung onto that belief and exhaled slowly through my parted lips.

'Clotilde, I am decided. My husband and I must make our new beginning before they whisk him away to fight. For fight he will; he's appointed captain of a regiment of horse.' She pursed her lips as I ploughed on, determined to convince her. 'I've seen many battles in France and know the dangers only too well. I couldn't bear to lose him without healing the rift between us. I am determined. We must resume our life together this night, not just with an outward show, but with a full marriage.'

Clotilde's lips remained clamped together in a tight line. At last she gave a little shrug, made for the door and cleared her throat. Her sharp voice sliced through the gathering shadows like a scythe taking down long grass.

'It is your decision and you must bear the consequences,' she said. 'I hope you will not live to regret it.' Love and concern shone from her eyes, as she shuffled out, wringing her hands in her apron.

The candles had burnt low by the time the door creaked open. Gawen stumbled in. Without hesitation, I stepped forward and took his hand.

'Roberda! I did not dare to hope for this.' I reached out and touched his lips with my finger.

'Hush. Gawen, this is not the time for words.'

Chapter Eight

The Season to Be Merry

Christmas 1587, Dartington Hall

As we gathered in the garden, the sun's rays danced on the glistening surface of a delicate blanket of snow, startlingly white under a clear blue sky. The crisp air filled my lungs with a refreshing chill and, as I glanced up, I saw wisps of smoke rising from the chimney, carrying a faint smell of burning wood. Our Yule log was already blazing on that snowy Christmas morn.

Gawen offered me his arm, and matching my steps to his purposeful stride, we set off together towards the church. The children followed us in a neat line, Arthur bouncing along in front.

'I can't wait to try some of cook's sweetmeats,' he said, his tremulous voice overloud in the frosty air. 'Sugared almonds, and marchpane, gingerbread!'

'It'll be such a feast,' Mary said, making her sisters giggle as she rubbed her hand over her tummy. 'Did you see the Christmas pie? You're the youngest, Arthur, so you'll get the first slice. Then you can make a wish.'

'I know what I'll wish for,' Arthur said, weaving between the girls to run alongside his father and me. He left a trail of zig-zag footprints in the snow as he jiggled along, so excited he couldn't keep still. A pang shot through me to see the hope in his bright face as he looked at us, his parents, walking together for the first time in years.

I beamed up at Gawen and convinced myself that his grey eyes had lost their flinty edge. In a warm, husky voice, he said, 'My wish has already come true.' I caught my breath. My usually distant husband sounded like a gallant lover.

Lisbeth shot me a poisonous look, but even her scowl could not stop me from wanting to sing for joy. I tripped along, light as air, while Lisbeth thumped her feet down with every step. She seemed oblivious to the delicate drops of melted snow that splashed onto the hem of her beautiful carnation gown where it peeped from beneath a scarlet cloak.

William Putt grinned as he marched along at the head of the household servants. Behind him, Clotilde and Marie walked arm in arm, Marie grinning, eyes crinkling with merriment. Clotilde's answering smile was strained, as if the frost had touched her lips.

My nostrils twitched as we passed under the vaulted porch into the church. Burning beeswax candles all but dispelled the usual musty odour and their flickering flames lit up great bunches of greenery. Our little church was transformed, much more welcoming than the cold refuge we'd rushed to in panic a few weeks earlier.

'Why's the plough here?' Arthur asked as we filed past. Brought from the nearby hamlet, it was festooned with holly and ivy, as in ancient custom. I kept my voice low as I answered.

'It's reminding everyone that it's a holiday. Unless they have to feed the animals or put food on the table, no one does any work for twelve days.'

'Does that mean I don't have any lessons?'

I nodded, tousling his curls as he danced along, grinning from ear to ear. Asking Arthur to sit still on Christmas Day was like asking the fire not to burn. He wriggled in his seat, constantly on the move. He looked as if he might burst with the effort of keeping all the happy thoughts in his mind from coming out of his mouth during the long service.

Arthur was not the only one who fidgeted while Griffin Jones, the weedy little rector, droned on. The stable boys elbowed each other, sniggering at some secret jest, while Kate and Ursula preened in their best gowns, turning this way and that, hoping the light would catch their best side. The rector's reedy voice quavered, and, at times, I struggled to hear him. In contrast, Gawen's low voice was full of conviction as he responded to the familiar prayers. I wondered if it was his time in Ireland or on the battlefields of the Low Countries that had brought him to a newfound and deeper connection with his God.

In conclusion, Jones recited a message from the queen's privy council. It was meant to instil a sense of patriotic resolve in the congregation, but his words sent a ripple of unease through the crowd of tenants and servants. William frowned while Alice shook her head. The cook shuffled his feet, and the gardeners scowled.

I put up a hand to loosen the ruff at my throat, threw back my shoulders, and raised my voice.

'It's Christmas morning. No attack will come in this season. The seas are far too rough. I'm sure we may enjoy our holiday without fear.' Gawen's jaw clenched and his hand tightened on my arm.

'The rector obeys the Queen's instructions,' he said. With the vein at his temple throbbing, his eyes flashed a challenge at me. Then he turned to the rector. 'You are right to remind us, Sir Griffin. Even on this day we must not let down our guard.'

I tapped my foot and opened my mouth to remonstrate, but another furious glare from Gawen made me swallow my words. Out of the tail of my eye, I saw Clotilde sneer and nod, as if saying, 'See, he hasn't changed.'

Beside me on the bench, Arthur's limbs seemed to loosen and collapse, and he bit his lip. Turning on a bright smile, I gave him a hug.

By the time we reached the hall, Gawen was smiling at me again. But that flash of the old angry Gawen in the church left a bitter taste. It brought home to me the nature of the bargain I had struck with him.

'Delicious,' I said to the cook, who beamed as he carved succulent slices of beef from a huge joint. 'Thank you. There's plenty left for you to take to the kitchens. I never saw such an array of shred pies.'

'Don't eat too much marchpane, Arthur. You'll be sick,' Mary cautioned as Arthur stuffed another sweet morsel into his mouth.

I watched Gawen throwing back another glass of spiced hippocras. It was a cosy scene, my husband home, my children's smiling faces, the wine glinting within the sparkling crystal glass. I listened to their happy laughter, breathed in the warm cinnamon aroma with its woody overtones and tried to put aside my worries.

On St Stephen's Day, Gawen surprised me with a bundle of letters.

'I almost forgot I had them in my bag when I came from Exeter. From your family in France and one from Anne Cecil, I believe.' He handed them to me with a smile.

Seeing the red wax seals still intact, I shot a triumphant glance over my shoulder at Clotilde. She squinted back at me through narrowed eyes. Like me, she was remembering how Gawen used to open any messages addressed to me. But the look on her face told me that unopened letters would not be enough to convince Clotilde he had left his controlling ways behind.

As I read Anne's letter, I shared my concerns with Gawen.

'She's not well... a persistent cough that she can't shake. Her unhappiness shouts out from these pages.' Gawen gave me an odd look.

'Poor Anne.' I sighed, tracing my finger along the line of writing. 'If it weren't for your cousin Walter and her father, who both pleaded with the Queen, I doubt de Vere would ever have received permission to return to court. But even that hasn't brought Anne any joy. She seems so unhappy.' I read on. 'Ah, but that's good... another daughter born last May... but what's this? Oh no! She says she has lost another child, one of the older girls, in September.' It came to my mind that, like me, Anne had been more successful in providing daughters to her wayward husband than sons. 'You remember? She lost her son a few years ago. Losing a child is the worst burden for us women to bear.'

'And for men too...' I glanced up and saw Gawen's lips tremble. His voice dropped low, as if the words were squeezed from somewhere deep within. 'I still think of our poor boy who lies in St Mary's Church beside his grandfather.' As I reached out to take his hand, I yearned to comfort him.

'I know. It's hard to bear,' I said. 'But we have Arthur and the girls, and perhaps God will grant us other sons.' I couldn't read the pained expression on his face as he withdrew his hand from mine.

More Christmas visitors arrived for the Twelfth Night revels, including the Seymours of nearby Berry Pomeroy. Young Edward

Seymour was closeted in Gawen's study, leaving me to entertain Bess. The dark rings beneath her bright blue eyes made Gawen's sister look haggard and older than her years. I watched her pushing a slice of warden pie round her plate without interest.

'Are you well, Bess?' I asked as soon as we were alone.

'I lost a baby, that's all. Miscarried at three months.' Her eyes filled with tears, but she choked them down. 'It happens to us all. There will be others.'

'But, my dear Bess' – I put my arms around her – 'I'm so sorry. As you say, few of us escape that pain. It's natural to feel sad and grieve.' I patted her hand and offered her a clean kerchief.

'At least I've shed some of the fat I put on after the others were born! Edward complains it's costing a fortune, what with my tailor's bills as I have my gowns altered again!' A little of her usual sparkle returned. 'Now, Roberda, to cheer me up a bit more, tell how things are with my dear brother?' I felt my cheeks flaming and gave a nervous chuckle.

'He's a changed man, dear Bess! We are together as man and wife once more.' Bess's eyes widened in disbelief, and she cocked her head to one side.

'I hope you're right, Roberda. You look happy, but be careful. Do men like Gawen really change their ways?'

'You're as bad as Clotilde. If I'm prepared to give him another chance, everyone else should do the same.' I set my jaw, and burying an uneasy qualm, I ignored Bess's incredulous stare. 'Now tell me all the gossip. What do you think of Drake's new wife? She sounds very different from poor Mary Newman.' Bess gave me another searching glance before she accepted my attempt to change the subject with a slight shrug of her shoulders.

'Yes, indeed, Mary Newman was a God-fearing little body, patience itself through all Drake's long absences. I was surprised that, after she died, he married a young woman like Elizabeth Sydenham. But she's wealthy, daughter of a judge, and like all men, I suppose he wants sons.' She moved closer and whispered in my ear. 'But I can't help but wonder if our courageous sea captain has embarked on a more challenging journey in marriage than his most daring adventure at sea. They say he's fast running out of patience with her. All she cares about is entertaining her neighbours, attending great civic receptions and that sort of thing, while he's preparing our defences against Spain. I'm hoping for an invitation to Buckland Abbey soon so I can judge for myself.'

'It's so good to see you, dear Bess. It feels like Christmas now you're here,' I said.

But her visit was a short one. I waved Bess and Edward off early on Plough Monday as the village women removed the greenery from their spinning wheels, signalling their return to work.

That same morning, with heavy feet, I stomped across the courtyard where an attentive groom held the horse's head. I took care to avoid flashing hooves that sent sparks flying. Gawen swung his leg over the black stallion's back and bent from the saddle to plant a light kiss on the top of my head. A jealous spasm ran through me, causing me to see spots before my eyes.

Driven by ambition and a wish to make a name for himself, Gawen was determined to join Sir Francis Drake, the man whose friendship he valued above all others. It was unreasonable, but I couldn't help it. Knowing he preferred following his hero to staying with me at Dartington struck me like a blow to the ribs. With a bitter taste in my mouth, I waved him off and returned to my duties.

Snow rarely lingers long in Devon, and the magic of Christmas morning soon melted away. Persistent winter drizzle set in, but bad weather and treacherous squelching mud did not keep Gawen at home. During the dreary months of January and February, I never knew where he was. Sometimes he would turn up without warning, return to my bed, and stay for a day or two before disappearing once more. Everyone was on edge, haunted by the fear that Catholic spies lurked among us. Perhaps it was for the best that I remained ignorant of Gawen's movements. What I didn't know, I couldn't reveal.

Chapter Nine

Useful Work for Anxious Hands

February 1587/88, Dartington Hall

I gave a loud snort and held my sewing up to the light, glaring at the pristine row of stitches on the crisp linen. The children turned their heads, their eyes widening, as my mounting frustration reached its boiling point. With another dissatisfied huff, I tossed the sewing into my workbasket, where it landed with a dull thud.

Jumping up from my seat, I paced around the room. It was no use. Marching up and down didn't make me feel any better. I flopped onto the settle, tapping my fingers on the oak seat beside me.

'There must be something more we women can do... stitching blackwork patterns onto a new collar will not keep the Spaniards at bay!' Marie raised her head from her sewing.

'I was wondering, ma'am... might the women stitch shirts for their menfolk? We have linen a-plenty set aside, and the men would be glad of extra clothing when called to the muster. Who knows how long they'll be gone.'

'What a good idea! Why didn't I think of it? They can sit together, here in the warm, and sew. Clotilde, please go with Marie and check how much fabric remains from the Dartmouth merchant's roll.'

Smiling for the first time in days, I watched as the two women hurried off. It was not long before I heard heavy footsteps returning. My maids staggered back into the parlour, their faces flushed with exertion as they struggled under the burden of a bulky package. Sweat glistened on their foreheads as, panting, they hauled it into the room. With one last collective push, they placed the bulging parcel on the floor in front of me. Marie straightened up, rubbing her aching back, and let out a groan.

'Phew! It's so heavy! A messenger left it at the door. Whatever can it be?' The excited children crowded round, elbowing each other aside for a good look. With nimble fingers, Marie untied the string, and the package fell open.

'I was hoping for more toys from Father,' Arthur exclaimed, pulling a face. 'Even a few books would be better! It's just a pile of old canvas.' He scuttled off and soon the wooden clink of the gaming pieces sounded as he played a lively game of Nine-Men's-Morris with Kate. Ursula and Mary picked up their sewing, only raising their heads when Arthur crowed with delight when he got the better of his sister. As usual, Lisbeth was nowhere to be seen.

Clotilde bent over the parcel, examining the unexpected delivery.

'Ugh! This material is coarse. I wouldn't like to use it for my smock.' She held up a piece of musty-smelling fabric. 'Look, it's already cut to form a tunic, with marked squares on each piece. There's a paper here.' I snatched the folded sheet of crinkled paper from her hand, and my smile broadened as I read.

Right Excellent Lady
 This is the best I could find, but perhaps your women can create something to protect their men. I cannot supply the armour plate to make a true jack-o'-plates, but you, my lady, are resourceful. You will find a way.
 Your ladyship's to be commanded.
 W Ralegh

I held up two identical pieces of canvas.

'From Sir Walter! Look! It's for making jack-o'-plates for the men that have none. See, we'll need to sew these together, stitch padding and some metal between, then add linings. If we stitch around each square, it will hold the metal pieces in place, and we'll have a sturdy jerkin.' Marie stared at me, a study in bewilderment as I went on.

'Don't you see? The metal plates will protect the wearer. Now… let me think… what could we use? Nothing too heavy, or he won't be able to move.' An ancient suit of armour that had been collecting dust in the corner for years caught my eye, It must have belonged to some long-dead Champernowne ancestor.

'William,' I called out, but he was not within earshot. 'Find him, Marie.' She shot me another puzzled look but trundled off in search of my long-suffering steward. I continued to turn the canvas in my hand until, slightly breathless, William hurried from the kitchen, bringing an enticing smell of roasting meat with him.

'Ah, William! Here's useful employment to help us prepare against invasion. Go fetch the blacksmith and gather a few women as well.' I explained our task, and with a weary smile, he retraced his steps. Clotilde cleared her throat.

'Best be careful. Master Gawen may not wish it to be used so, nor you to act without his consent. Remember how angry he was about your refugee women?'

'Nonsense, Clotilde, you fret too much!' Clotilde's once merry hazel eyes were clouded, brimming over with genuine concern. I knew she meant well. But I was blinded by my desperate need for happiness with my husband.

'He's a changed man, Clotilde. He won't hinder my honest work for the war effort.'

'Very well.' She looked as prim as a Latin master. 'Are you certain that rusty breastplate shouldn't be kept with the other pieces stored in the church?' I poked it, puffed out my cheeks and blew. A cloud of dust flew into the air, settling on Clotilde's clean apron.

'If it was any use at all, it would already be in the church,'I said. 'See, the rust has eaten away the buckles. I expect Sir Arthur kept it for the coat of arms engraved on the front.' After she had brushed the dust from her clothes Clotilde turned her attention to the fabric Walter had sent.

'We'll need to punch holes with a leather worker's awl before we can stitch through this stiff stuff!'

'We'll see. Let's tackle it now,' I said, impatient to begin.

The parcel of canvas was the start of our small enterprise. At last I felt we were doing something useful. But trying to stitch through the stiff canvas made my fingers sore. I threw the needle down and pounded my fist on the tabletop.

'It's no use. It's too hard!' Alice crossed the room and peeped over my shoulder.

'Why, it's just like the stuff my uncle uses.'

'Your uncle?'

'Aye, ma'am... he has a loft by the quay in Brixham. He is a sailmaker. He'll know how to stitch this.' I could have kissed her chubby cheeks, regardless of the sticky remains of her breakfast pottage that lingered there.

'Send for him then. Bid him come to help us. I'll pay him well.'

A few days later, Ned the sailmaker, a wizened little man with deep wrinkles etched across his face, sat cross-legged on the creaky wooden floor in the parlour.

'Not so stiff as the new sails I've made for the *Phoenix*,' he said. With expert hands, he guided the sharp point of a massive curved needle into the stubborn cloth. 'There... see... like a knife through butter.' Grinning broadly, he held up the sewn-in armour plate for our inspection.

Having the perfect tool for the task made all the difference. How we cheered as William tried the first jack and declared it comfortable. That success gave us the confidence to make swift progress with a second.

On a bright morning we were muttering and groaning with grim determination as we strained to push the stout needles through the canvas and layers of felt lining. Nearby, a pile of metal plates, cut to size by the blacksmith, lay waiting.

The shining metal surfaces glinted in the dim light of candles set close to the stitchers to aid their work. Nearby, another group sewed shirts for soldiers. Save for the faint crackle of canvas, the occasional clash of shears as they dropped to the floor, no sound disturbed our peaceful morning.

I picked up the heavy needle once more, determined to lead by example. Its rigid, cold metal touch made me shiver and the rough fabric rubbed my skin. As I tried to focus on the task, loud voices caught my attention. The needle fell from my hand, landed with a metallic tinkle and skittered across the stone floor. Startled, I turned to find Gawen standing in the doorway.

'What's this? Whatever are you doing?' he demanded as his eyes roved round the room and came to rest on the pile of metal plates. 'What's all this?' His voice rose. 'Not the armour! It belonged to my great-great-grandfather, the one that lies in Modbury Church, or at least that's what my father used to say. Roberda? Explain yourself!'

I caught Clotilde's smirk as I rapped back a sharp reply.

'Well, he won't be needing it now, will he? Anyone can see it's out of date, useless for the battles of today. Cut up, it can serve as jack-o'-plates for men who can't afford their own.' A flush of heat spread across my cheeks as I held up the completed jack for his inspection. 'Would you have our people go naked into battle when the Spanish come?'

Gawen towered over me as he took the padded jerkin from my hand. I could feel the tension in him as he examined the garment. He walked to the remaining pile of metal plates, picked one up and felt the weight of it in his hands. The sight of the pulsing vein on his temple made me bite my lip as the silence in the room stretched on.

At last Gawen's mouth opened, and I braced myself for an onslaught of criticism. But to my astonishment, he threw his head back and let out a belly laugh.

'You're right. Better to put the metal to use. These poor women will have raw fingers and no mistake.' He picked up the completed jack once more. 'Hmm... it's not too heavy... it will serve them well.' He set it down, and I thought I saw love shining in his eyes. 'Roberda, I did not mean to disturb you. Home for a brief visit with Richard and John, wanted to let you know.'

It wasn't unusual for Gawen to entertain visitors. I was used to hearing their voices raised in an animated discussion as they revised and refined their plans in the light of the latest intelligence from Walsingham's spies.

'Ah, here they are,' he said 'You know Richard?' I nodded to Gawen's cousin and extended my hand. Richard took it, and as he bent his head, I noticed the petulant turn of his lip. 'He's just returned from Ireland.'

'I trust all is well at Modbury?' I asked. 'Are you finding time for your musicians?' Before he could answer, another man pushed past the pasty-faced Richard. Gawen stood aside to make way for the dark-haired stranger.

'This is John Harte from Yarnacombe, near to Modbury. Come to speak with us on our best strategy as we prepare to face the Spaniards, and other legal matters.' Gawen's voice boomed, overloud, full of bluster, but I thought nothing of it.

Although clad in lawyer's black, there was a swagger about John Harte as he ducked his head under the lintel. Swarthy, with hair black as a raven's wing, Harte exuded a sense of arrogant confidence as he leant against the doorpost with his head tilted back. A faint smell of horse mingled with a musky perfume from the pomander at his waist. Although heavy drooping eyelids shaded his eyes, I didn't miss the flash of scorn dancing in the pools of darkness as he stared at me.

'John... my wife.' Gawen waved an arm in introduction.

'Ah... the French wife! *Enchanté!*' Harte's atrocious Devon drawl grated on my ears. He flashed a false smile, and those dark eyes lingered on my gown with a brazen impertinence, giving me the unsettling sensation of an army of spiders crawling across my skin. I responded with a curt nod.

'I'll send a tray to your study, Gawen.'

'Thank you.' Gawen acknowledged me with a fleeting smile as he and his visitors left us. I could hear their laughter as Gawen followed them out. He called over his shoulder, 'Do continue with your work.' The women's voices rose, chattering like starlings as they wondered what news the men had brought.

I shot Clotilde a defiant look. With my hands on my hips and a gleam of triumph in my eyes I drew her away from the other women.

'You see, he did not seek to criticise or curtail my work. He is a changed man!' Clotilde's face went white as she glared at me.

'Hmph, there are more ways than one for a man to control his wife. A wife always with child has little energy to act on her own initiative.' That stopped me mid-stride. I stared at her, open-mouthed. As I saw the hurt in her eyes, I winced.

'Tsk! Did you think I'd have to ask the laundress? I know your courses have stopped.'

'I was going to tell you.' My chin quivered as I turned away.

'It's a fine time for you to be bearing another child. The forces of Spain are about to rain down on us!' Clotilde threw her hands up into the air. There was an uneasy silence before she spoke again. 'But it is only to be expected after your joyful reunion at Christmas.' The derision in her voice cut me to the quick. She went on, turning the knife in a raw wound. 'I don't suppose it will be the last. Mark me well! Bearing his children will wear you down. It is the best way for a man to keep his wife in her place.' She picked up her skirts and bustled away like a hen with ruffled feathers, leaving me speechless.

After Clotilde's comments, I knew I must tell my husband about the baby. The hour was late and shadows danced on the parlour walls when I approached him. He sprawled on the settle, relaxed after a satisfying dinner, his visitors gone.

'More wine before we go to bed?' The smell of the rich red liquid was making me feel queasy, but I hoped another drink might put him in good humour to hear my news.

'Hmm... why not? I need not leave too early tomorrow.' Gawen sounded weary as he gave me a weak smile.

'What? Away again? So soon?' My voice dropped low.

'I'm headed for Plymouth tomorrow,' he said. 'There are reports that the Spanish commander, Santa Cruz, has died. Some believe that may delay or prevent them. Francis believes that King Philip will appoint another leader. According to our spies, they only wait for better weather. They will come.' He fidgeted on the settle, hunching his shoulders.

'And Master Harte? Does he go with you?' The two seemed to spend a lot of time together, yet Gawen had never explained why. His reply was evasive, as usual.

'Perhaps... He's a useful friend to have in these times.' I put a hand over my mouth to cover a yawn. There was no point pressing Gawen, and I had other weighty matters to discuss.

I reached for the wine glass. The smooth surface felt cool against my fingertips as I handed it to my dispirited husband. He took a sip, savouring it slowly, swishing the liquid round, before he gave me an enquiring look.

The timing may not have been perfect, but he had to know.

Gawen clicked his fingernails on the polished oak boards of the seat beside him. 'What is it? Do you have something to say?'

I took a breath. The air felt heavy and oppressive weighing down on my chest. Yet, despite the suffocating feeling that threatened to overcome me, I knew I had to press on.

'I'm sorry. It's the worst timing, but I must tell you. There will be another baby in the nursery before the summer is out.'

His eyes held mine and I noticed him licking his lips – perhaps it was in cautious hope.

'You are certain?' he asked, his voice so warm it felt like a velvet caress. 'A brother for Arthur!' Yet, as his lips curved into a smile, I caught a fleeting glimpse of something else. I tried to convince myself it was pure delight, but I could not ignore the subtle hint of triumph lurking beneath Gawen's outward joy.

Chapter Ten

Mistress of Dartington Hall?

Lady Day, March 1588, Dartington Hall

On Lady Day, a dark sky hung low, heavy as a millstone, crushing any vitality the coming of spring might have promised. The Dartington tenants trudged into the Great Hall, carrying with them the unmistakable fusty odour of damp wool. It clung to their sodden clothes, never quite overpowered by the ever-present sharp smoky smell. Clutching their drenched cloaks, they shuffled in, worn boots leaving muddy imprints with each step. A few inched closer to the fire, drawn to its warmth like moths to a flame, hoping for some small respite from the chilly, all-pervading dampness. Wisps of steam rose from those fortunate few closest to the hearth. Amongst all the men, a handful of women in dark robes chatted together. They were widows able to hold land in their own right.

They had all come to settle their rights, to sign new agreements, to pay their dues and to hear the latest gossip. Neighbours greeted each other, but their voices were hushed, as if smothered by an unnerving atmosphere of foreboding.

I shivered and huddled into the thick cloak of Devon serge Clotilde had wrapped around my shoulders. A glance through the open door told me that the weather had not improved. Day in, day out, for more than a month, we had endured this deluge. There was no refreshing beauty in the rain that poured from leaden skies onto the no-longer-grateful earth. Puddles of murky water collected in every depression, making the courtyard look like a pockmarked face. The river swelled beyond its banks, turning the waterlogged meadows into great lakes, where mournful herons perched in submerged trees, hoping to snatch a meal from the waters. Rutted lanes became a treacherous quagmire.

Perhaps it was just the relentless rain that spread a brooding, gloomy atmosphere over everything on that dismal day. I saw it mirrored in sombre expressions on every face. Even William, usually so cheerful and reassuring, looked down in the mouth as he waited beside me.

'We'd best make a start, ma'am,' he said. With a nod, I made my way through the throng. As I moved among them, smiling a greeting here, prompted by William to offer congratulations or condolences there, I took in snippets of conversation.

'Ground's sodden… Sowing time long past… Too wet to get the seed in… Poor harvest… if there's any harvest at all… Gone to the trained bands… Who will till the fields?… Murrain in the cattle… Foot-rot in the sheep… And then there's the Spanish… the Spanish!'

By the fireplace, a well-dressed man with a grey beard and flushed face rested his hands on his enormous rotund belly. He faced the company, warming his backside. His voice carried over the rest.

'All this fuss about the Spanish! Pah! Santa Cruz, Commander of the King of Spain's forces, is dead. Without him in charge, I doubt they'll come to bother us at all.' Heads shot up and the low hum of voices died away. The red-faced man stood up straight, like a preacher on Sunday, relishing the attention he was getting.

I stared at him, sure I'd come across the braggart before, yet unable to put a name to the face. The memory came to me with the strident ring of his voice. Rowe, by name, a bothersome man, full of self-importance. He held tenements in Totnes and lands in Staverton. Ah, yes – the previous year, he had taken exception to my decision in a dispute with his neighbour. Even my iciest glare did not silence him. He went on with his tirade.

'They say King Philip has given up the attempt. It's time to stop all this nonsense and move on, if you ask me.' A wizened, white-haired farmer spoke up in reply, but amongst the muttering crowd, I couldn't quite catch his muffled words. The orator's next words cut through the buzz of voices, even louder than before.

'That Francis Drake! Pah! He's just a warmonger! He's only interested in the rich prizes he can take. No wonder he keeps telling us all the Spanish are coming. Took my men to Plymouth to build defences. No hands to sow the seed. It'll be a poor harvest and no mistake.'

I looked at William, who narrowed his eyes, shaking his head slightly.

'Best you speak to them, ma'am. That sort of talk doesn't help anyone.'

'No indeed! My husband tells me there's no doubt the Spanish ships will come. Everyone must remain vigilant. You don't think he's a Papist sympathiser, do you? A spy, trying to make us drop our guard?' William frowned and studied the man.

'It's possible. Thomas Rowe is a bad-tempered sort and, if memory serves, I think some of his family supported the protests against the prayer book years ago.'

'Um… What did you say? Uh… a rebellion about a prayer book?' Frowning, I raked through my memory, trying to remember whether Sir Arthur had told me about this uprising. 'Tell me more, William. Remember, I'm not a Devon woman born and bred. I thought England had avoided vicious civil wars of religion like those in France.'

'It was when young King Edward was on the throne. Some Devon men joined those of Cornwall. Took up arms. Said they were complaining about the prayer book in English. There was some bloody fighting outside Exeter. Sir Arthur played his part to quell the rebellion. At least that's the tale I had from my father.' He nodded again towards the pompous man who was still expounding his ideas to any who would listen. 'I'll get the constables to investigate, just in case Rowe favours the Papists.'

As William finished speaking, John Blatchford, the bailiff, a man built like a mountain, joined us. It was his responsibility to oversee the tenancy agreements alongside William. His imposing presence would be useful if any disputes arose. Flanked by my two trusted assistants, with skirts swishing, I glided through the throng. I stopped only once to greet Edward Mann, the well-turned-out young lieutenant of the trained bands. He doffed a velvet cap and made a confident bow.

'How fares the training, Master Mann?'

'Fair to middling, my lady! We lack provisions and armaments, as ever. They say the Queen is loath to part with more money. Perhaps she believes they won't invade.'

'Whatever the Queen may think, my husband is sure they will come, Master Mann. You must stand ready and train your men well.' His eyes met mine for an instant before he nodded his agreement.

I stepped forward, ready to play my part in the day's business. Crisp-edged papers and parchments lay in neat piles on the table before me. Inkhorn and quills were prepared, ready for use. William's clenched fist pounded against the polished wooden table, causing the inkhorn to jump. A few drops splashed onto the gleaming surface. Catching the tang of ink, with its hint of iron, I swayed on my feet. It reminded me of the smell of blood.

Shaken, I took my seat and gulped in a few lungfuls of air, hoping to quell the inconvenient nausea that threatened to overtake me. It wasn't the time to succumb to any feminine frailty. My mother had never let pregnancy stand in her way as she followed my father to war. No more must I allow it to hamper my duties as Mistress of Dartington Hall.

Ever vigilant, Clotilde peered into my face.

'Is all well, *ma petite*?' I waved her aside with a flick of my fingers, as though shooing away a bothersome insect.

The sharp bang on the board cut through the murmurs and commanded their attention. Just as in the church during the false alarm, they looked to me for leadership. Yet something had changed. Instead of urgent, lively panic, I saw weariness and despair. They had lost the will to fight.

I thought of my mother as I rose to my feet. Standing solid before the assembled tenants, I was ready to carry the weight of responsibility that once again lay on my shoulders.

'Welcome, one and all. I am glad to see you here. In these hard times, it is right and proper that we carry on with our business as usual. We should not let the threat of Spain put a stop to our lives.' In the silent hall, I could not help but hear Rowe's triumphant chortle.

'I told you so! No need to worry about the Spanish!' He looked around, expecting applause, like an actor taking his bow.

'We have heard quite enough from you, Master Rowe. Please continue to warm yourself.' I waved my hand in front of my face, as if warding off a bad smell. 'But be careful. You don't want to scorch that fine doublet, do you?' A titter trickled round the room, lightening the depressing atmosphere. With a deliberate movement, I turned my back on Rowe and addressed the crowd.

'Now, hear me well! We are all brought low by this miserable wet springtime. This terrible weather is in God's hands. But the defence of our land is in our own. Don't let false rumours deceive you. My husband has intelligence from the watchers. Philip of Spain will not abandon his Enterprise of England. The Spanish fleet waits for a fair wind in Lisbon harbour. Be assured. They will come. We must be ready for them. Sir Francis gathers all our ships in Plymouth. With God's will, we shall defeat them.'

Behind my back, the fat man had the impertinence to let out a braying laugh. 'All vessels ordered to Plymouth, do you say? So why has Sir John Gilbert let his ships set sail from Dartmouth, bound for the Americas?'

I turned and gave him a stare cold enough to freeze milk in the pail. 'No doubt Sir John has his reasons, Master Rowe. It makes no difference. Our task remains clear. We must secure sufficient supplies to withstand whatever comes and keep our weapons ready. We must…' A movement in the screens passage stopped me in mid-flow. Heads turned to see my husband framed in the doorway, an imposing figure in his worn leather jerkin and swirling black cloak. With a clatter that rang out round the walls, Gawen dropped his sword to the floor and marched in, throwing aside a dripping broad-brimmed hat as he went.

A welcoming smile froze on my lips, and I clenched my jaw. John Harte was at Gawen's side, sidling in with his black cap pulled down over his eyes. A young man trailed behind, struggling with a worn leather bag bulging with documents and maps, which he dumped in front of me. Clasping my hands before me until the knuckles turned white, I took a furtive peek at the slippery John Harte, who raised his head and gave me a slow, condescending grin.

But then my husband favoured me with a dazzling smile and all my irritation melted like thin ice on a winter puddle in the sunshine.

I shot a gloating look Clotilde's way as Gawen took my hand. He held it just a little longer than was necessary for a brief show of courtesy, then turned to the crowd.

'My wife is right. Don't doubt it. The Spanish will come.' Gawen spoke with such authority, he had them all gawping. 'King Philip has already replaced Santa Cruz as commander. It's the Duke de Medina Sidonia who's in charge now. Word is he was reluctant to take it on. He has little experience of the sea, which may be to our advantage. But when the storms abate, he will set sail. And we will be ready for them.' Gawen paused, then his voice came out loud and slow. 'What say you all? Are you ready?' He raised his arms, and the crowd responded with a cheer. I had to admit Gawen was skilful at stirring what remained of their patriotic fervour.

'I am just returned from Dartmouth where I've been provisioning the *Phoenix*. She'll sail for Plymouth to join Drake's fleet,' he went on. 'The trained bands stand ready. Men keep watch at the Yarner beacon and all along the coast. Messengers are ready with post horses to carry news and messages to the Queen and her council. All is in hand. We must all play our part and you must all keep watch, for when this foul weather eases. Believe me, they will come.'

A few men cast disparaging looks at Master Rowe, who took a step backwards and tried to fade into the crowd. Gawen was by now in full command.

'Now, let us get to business. I'll take over and hear any disputes. Blatchford, who is first?' The bailiff pushed up his sleeves and thrust a paper in front of my husband.

Watching them, I bit my lip and crossed my arms over my chest, feeling my features tighten. Clotilde shook her head, telling me she'd noticed, so I painted on a smile.

'You look very pale, my lady,' she said, her voice laced with concern. 'Come away and rest. Master Champernowne has taken your place here.' My faithful maid glared at Gawen, eyes narrowed, mouth set. She hustled me up to my bedchamber, clucking behind me like a flustered hen.

I rejected Clotilde's gentle urging as she attempted to settle me on my bed for a rest. Instead, I stood rigid as the iron poker she used to stir life into the fire. Reborn, it hissed and sizzled as flames licked up the chimney until a sudden gust of wind made acrid smoke swirl back into the room, making me cough. My hands curled into tight fists as I scowled at the relentless rain that lashed the windows.

'He has usurped me as Mistress of Dartington. Undermined my authority with the tenants. He even did it with a smile on his lips!' Clotilde dropped the poker with a clatter and squared up to me.

'By all means, vent your anger. But you have made your bed, now you must lie on it. Think of the child you carry.'

She led me to the bed, and with a pouting lip, I surrendered to her tender ministrations. As she removed my shoes, she looked up at me, swallowing before she spoke in a low voice.

'Rest for a while, *ma petite*. I will be at your side.' The wind howled in the chimney, filling the room with its eerie wailing. Safe within the thick bed hangings, I festered for a long time, jumbled thoughts tumbling through my mind. At last exhaustion took hold, pulling me into restless slumber, broken by disturbing dreams.

Chapter Eleven

Drake Swaggers In

Spring, 1588, Dartington Hall

Sudden sprays of rain, as hard as volleys of sharp arrows, pelted the window and shook me from slumber. Rubbing the sleep from my eyes, I realised Gawen was leaning over me as I lay on our marriage bed. I scrambled to sit up and saw that the sky had grown even darker. I must have slept through the afternoon.

'Good to see you resting. Take good care of the little knave you carry!' He reached over and patted the mound of my swelling stomach through the embroidered coverlet. Gawen had been all solicitude for my welfare since I told him about the child I carried. I tried to persuade myself it was love that made him so caring, not just the prospect of another boy in the nursery.

With a groan, I levered myself into a more comfortable position. 'Are the tenants all gone? Is all in hand?'

'No need to concern yourself, my dear. All is well.'

'What was all that about your cousin, Gilbert? Did he send his ships out from Dartmouth against orders? I thought you told me all shipping must stay in port in case better weather brought them upon us?'

'Yes, that's so. Walter says he wrote advising against it. But he's a pig-headed customer, is John Gilbert, and even the Spanish won't get between him and a likely profit! He's not the only one. They say some of the Bristol merchants have also gone against the order.'

'Well, it doesn't set a good example, does it? If the likes of Sir John, the very men who are supposed to be in charge of our defences, flout orders, how can I keep everyone here busy making preparations for invasion?'

'No, you're right. But there's no need for you to worry. Are the children well?' The change of topic was swift. Soon we were talking of Arthur's progress in his studies, the girls' proficiency in needlework, Lisbeth's talent for playing the lute. I didn't notice how smoothly he steered me towards domestic matters, away from estate business and preparations for war. I could hear Clotilde, just beyond the door, muttering under her breath as she folded fresh clean linen. But I paid no heed. Instead, I basked in Gawen's attention, telling myself it was a sign of his true affection for me.

The month of May brought with it the long-awaited arrival of glorious spring. Despite the constant fear of invasion that hung over us, I stole away one morning to stroll in my gardens. The gravel crunched under my feet as I set out along the path that led me through neat beds lined with budding lavender. I smiled as the sweet, intoxicating fragrance of apple blossoms lifted my spirits. No longer plagued by the morning sickness of the early months, I felt energised, ready for anything. That was just as well. I couldn't afford to linger for too long that morning. The warm sun served as a reminder that the better weather meant calmer seas. The Spanish fleet might soon lurk in the waters off Devon's coast. There was much to be done.

Making a mental tally of the barrels of dried fish we could set aside in case of an urgent evacuation, I bustled to the kitchens to see if the flour was still usable. Dark and humid conditions were a perfect breeding ground for weevils, so I'd ordered the barrels moved from the damp storeroom to stand near the kitchen fire.

I had only just removed my light cloak when Sir Francis Drake himself swaggered in. Following close on his clicking heels came Gawen, his face flushed with admiration, in awe of his friend. Completing the party was the ever-present John Harte, accompanied by his scribe, a young man with arresting blue eyes.

I felt Harte scrutinising me and suppressed a shudder. Dressed all in black, he melted into the shadows, yet his presence made my skin creep. I knew Gawen was keeping some estate accounts from me, and I suspected Harte had lent him money. Even William, my trusty steward, was tight-lipped when I asked him about Harte's business.

Ignoring Harte, I greeted Drake with a beaming smile to overcome the instant irritation the pompous sea captain always provoked in me. He made a perfunctory bow and strutted past me into the hall. I was sure I could detect a salty tang about him, an essence of the briny sea where he felt most at home, as he brushed me aside. I stifled another burst of anger as my hackles rose once more. Recovering myself, I followed the men.

'It has been quite some time since we last welcomed you to Dartington, Sir Francis.'

Brusque as ever, Drake answered, 'I am on my way to London.'

'I hope you can stay long enough to take refreshment,' I said. 'Won't you come into the parlour?'

Despite being dressed in a weathered leather jerkin, battered by many voyages, Drake's mere presence had the power to turn Dartington into a bustling hub of activity. William appeared with a bevy of serving maids at his elbow. I signalled to Alice, whose mouth was hanging open.

'Perhaps you'll take a mug of our finest ale, Sir Francis?' I said, ushering him through the hall, where drafts stirred papers on one of the long tables. While the maid scuttled off in search of a fresh flagon, Gawen guided our guest to a comfortable seat near the parlour fireplace. Despite the morning being warmer than of late, a log still smouldered in the grate. However, Sir Francis declined to sit near the fire. Instead he fretted and fumed, bristling with pent-up energy as he paced up and down. I tried to distract him with conversation about his young wife.

'How fares Lady Drake at Buckland, Sir Francis?'

'She is well enough!' was the terse reply. I tilted my head to one side and watched him striding round and round my parlour, his sea-boots tapping on the floor. Remembering my conversation with Bess at Christmastide, I wondered how he and Elizabeth got on together. Somehow I couldn't imagine Sir Francis having much time for socialising. It was clear he had no interest in discussing his wife that morning.

'How can I convince the Queen, Champernowne?' he asked, his voice rising. 'Reliable reports tell us the Spanish fleet is still in Lisbon. We could be upon them within days. A swift strike, like Cadiz. Why can't she understand it would eliminate the threat to us on English soil?'

'Speak to Cecil. If anyone can convince her, he can. He's back in favour after that spell away from court. He's the one to persuade her. Get Walsingham on our side, too, and she'll reconsider.'

Drake nodded but went on pacing the floor. He reeled off the preparations needed to strike the Spanish fleet in Lisbon harbour. As I listened, I saw through the bluster to the clever and resourceful soldier beneath. His plan to take the war to the Spanish, rather than sit in England waiting, sounded a good one to me. My father always said that surprise was the most valuable asset in any battle. As I listened to his reasoned arguments, I reassessed Sir Francis Drake and found a new respect for Gawen's hero. I hoped he would persuade Queen Elizabeth. But I kept my thoughts to myself.

'I'll come with you if you like,' Gawen said. 'Harte can stay here and deal with some paperwork I need prepared for my return.' Harte's hooded eyes seemed to me to bear a sinister weight as he nodded without saying a word.

Chapter Twelve

Lisbeth

Late Spring, 1588, Dartington Hall

A few days later, a wheezing Clotilde came puffing into my chamber as I was rising from a brief afternoon nap. I raised my head from the pillow to see her stumbling into the room. In her haste, she knocked a ewer of water flying, leaving a puddle on the boards. A dark wet stain spread on Clotilde's skirt, but she hardly seemed to notice as she slumped onto the cushions in the window seat. Still groggy from sleep, I slipped from the bed, fumbled until I found a linen shift waiting for the laundry maid and mopped up the spillage.

'Whatever is it, Clotilde?'

''Tis Miss Lisbeth!'

'What? What has she been up to now?'

I held Clotilde's hand as she struggled to get her breath back and waited for her to calm down.

'I was searching for Agnes to ask if she could make up another batch of her potion. All this wet weather plays havoc with my knuckles and knees.' She paused for a moment, rubbing her hands together, and I noticed how gnarled her finger joints had become. 'Thinking she might be in the church, I went out and followed the path. There I found that silly girl Joan blocking my way. I could tell something was afoot. The girl's face turned red as my best flannel petticoat!'

Clotilde paused, fanning herself with the page of a letter she'd picked up from where it lay on my writing desk.

'Go on.'

'Joan did her best to detain me with foolish talk. But she did not deceive me. I pushed by her and then I saw Miss Lisbeth! Oh, it pains me to tell you! She was in the arms of that young man that comes with Master Harte. Under the yew tree, they were. Anyone might have seen them!'

'No!… Oh… no… Whatever did you do?'

A sly smile crossed Clotilde's wrinkled face, making her look like a fox loitering outside the henhouse.

'Now, as to that young man, I should think he has expanded his French vocabulary! May God forgive me, for I cursed him with every French oath I could think of. I sent him on his way with a rare flea in his ear.' Clotilde's smile faded as she smoothed down her damp skirt. 'Miss Lisbeth, she screamed and shouted like a fishwife on Dartmouth quay until she ran off.'

'So… where is she now?' I struggled to keep my voice calm.

'Locked herself in her bedchamber, sobbing.'

'Do you think it's gone any further?' It was dawning on me how grave a situation this might be. 'A well-born girl's worth is all in her reputation. Has it gone any further, Clotilde?'

'I don't think so.' The old woman shook her head. 'But we must put an end to this budding love, even if we find ourselves tangled in the thorns of Miss Lisbeth's anger. The boy is a mere scribe for Master Hart. He is not suitable.'

'I despair! Has she taken leave of her senses? Where is the dear sweet child who clung so close to me? These past months Lisbeth has become such a surly little minx, I hardly know her.' I thumped my fists down hard on the desktop until Clotilde, calmer now, grasped my hands.

'She is no longer a child,' she said, holding my eyes. 'You were no older than Miss Lisbeth that day I came upon you standing much too close to a young man. Have you forgotten how it feels?'

'Why, there was nothing between me and young Sir Walter! There is no comparison.'

'Only because you were so besotted with his cousin, the dashing Henry Champernowne!'

I sighed. She was right. I was not so old I could not recall the delicious, exciting, terrifying moment when a young man's eyes first met mine.

'What shall I do? I know I've neglected her, left her to her own devices too often.'The sigh that escaped me held all the frustration and guilt of motherhood. 'I did my best. I was not the one who took her away.'

'Indeed! The master should take his share of any blame. But that is in the past. We must deal with this at once.'

'I must talk to her, but Clotilde... speaking to that girl, it's like poking a stick into a wasp's nest. Her vicious words fly at me and their sting finds its mark.'

'Yet it must be done, and only you can do it. Leave her to calm down a bit. She'll come out when she's hungry.' She rose to leave me and on an impulse I threw my arms around her and gave her a hug.

'Thank you, Clotilde, you have done well. The problem is now all mine.'

I slept little that night, tossing and turning as thoughts came yapping and growling at me like a pack of snarling hounds with a stag at bay. These last weeks and months, preoccupied with rekindled hopes of happiness in my marriage, I'd made little time for Lisbeth, my firstborn, dearest child. Had I left it too late to mend matters with my daughter?

The next morning, Lisbeth emerged from her chamber, slamming the door shut behind her and stomping down the stairs. Halfway down, I caught up with her. She hesitated, hanging her head and twisting a kerchief in fidgety fingers. Her eyes were red and swollen, clear evidence of a miserable sleepless night.

'It's a glorious morning, Lisbeth,' I said, keeping my voice light without a hint of reproach. 'Will you walk with me in the gardens?' To my amazement, she nodded her assent, and we went down together. As we strolled side by side through the formal gardens, I allowed the silence to linger between us.

Lisbeth trudged along beside me, her eyes fixed on the ground beneath her feet, deaf to the joyous chirping song of the blackbird and the insistent cooing of amorous pigeons. She passed the flourishing herb beds in my physick garden without so much as a glance; the breathtaking carpet of bluebells nodding beneath the majestic trees beyond the wall might as well have been an arid desert. My daughter shuffled along, head down, blind to the enchanting beauty of that radiant May morning.

In silence we went on towards the holy well, where I settled onto the weathered bench, feeling its coolness through my light gown. Time seemed to stand still as I waited, watching the light dancing on ripples on the surface of the pool as the water bubbled merrily up from the ancient spring below. At last, with eyes flashing anger and defiance, she spat out the words.

'I suppose the old crone has blabbed?'

'Now, Lisbeth, Clotilde only wants what's best for you. Oh, my dear child, if anyone saw you there, it will ruin your reputation. Clotilde was right to send that young man on his way. She was right to tell me.' The way her lip stuck out was just like the face she would pull as a child when caught out in some small mischief. How I wished she was still that happy little girl.

'Joan was supposed to keep everyone away.'

'You must not lay the blame on that poor girl's shoulders. You should never have involved her so.' A mottled flush crept up Lisbeth's dimpled cheeks. She turned to me and rolled her shoulders, as though squaring up for a fight.

'Will you tell my father?' Her tone was more defiant than fearful.

'Do you think I should? Do you think I must?'

As I heard her mutter, 'No... yes... I don't know...' halting and hesitant, I thought there might be a glimmer of hope. Perhaps I could reason with her.

'Lisbeth, I understand much more than you realise,' I said, giving her a hesitant smile and leaning towards her. She shifted away from me, but I went on, 'I was young once. I remember well the feelings a young man can stir.'

'Oh yes, no doubt you do, Mother!'

I reeled a little at that, seeing her pretty mouth twisted with scorn. Swallowing hard, I began again.

'It cannot be. He is not for you. Accept it and let us keep all this foolery between ourselves. Your father has enough to worry about as we prepare against the coming invasion. If I were to tell your father, then Master Harte must also know, and the young man will lose his position. You wouldn't want that, would you?'

'I can't give him up. I love him! Matthew's so clever, all set to study in Cambridge, if Harte will sponsor him. He writes such wonderful verses. He wrote a sonnet to my eyes!' Even faced with her belligerence, I found it hard to suppress a smile at that.

'Lisbeth, I am sorry, but you know that for all his good looks and charm, despite his excellent education, you cannot marry this boy. Your father and I will find a suitable match for you when the time is right. It is the way of our world.' That did it. She shot up from the bench beside me and stomped to the edge of the pool before turning to face me. With an angry broken roar, like crashing billows on a desolate rocky shore, the waves of Lisbeth's fury broke over me.

'It's a horrible world! I hate it! Do you think you can make me a pawn in your chess game, marry me off to some horrible man just because it will put money in the family coffers? I don't care what my father says. Nor do I care what you say. You can't make me give him up!' Her clenched fists, knuckles white with rage, pounded against her sides as her feet thudded on the mossy grass, releasing an earthy smell.

'Lisbeth, please be reasonable. This behaviour will not help you. No one wants to wed a tiresome girl, certainly not one who has disobeyed her father.'

'You don't care about me. You let them take me away. Now all you care about is keeping my father happy. After your behaviour with those men, too!' I recoiled, swaying on the seat as if she'd hit me. It took a shaky breath or two before I had enough command of my voice to answer.

'Lisbeth! I was blameless! There was nothing between me and those men. Evil people misled your father. The accusations were false. He is sorry now.'

'Is he? Is he? You might think so, but is he? He just wants you to breed another son. If you don't, he'll wish he'd set you aside for good.' She landed her blows with precision on the tender bruise of Gawen's past rejection. Shaken to the core, I tried to rise, but my legs refused to hold me. Having done her worst, Lisbeth turned, picked up her skirts and pelted down the path towards the house.

It took what felt like an eternity for my rapid breathing to return to normal. Doubts swirled in my mind, menacing as an impending storm. Images of Gawen's rare affectionate gestures flitted through my mind. Lisbeth's cruel words made me wonder anew whether his outward display was a genuine transformation, that he had in truth accepted me as his rightful wife, that he cared for me. Or, as Clotilde supposed, perhaps it was all a facade, concealing his true intentions of merely using me to bear his sons. After all, he was always talking about giving Arthur brothers.

A dark cloud snuffed out the bright sun, and a chill little wind stirred my skirts. I could smell the rain in the air. Yet, despite the damp seeping up from the grass through the soles of my leather shoes, I remained seated, one hand on my belly, until I felt the baby stir. Sitting there beneath the trees, I listened to the rustling leaves and prayed for a healthy boy. The second son Gawen longed for above all else.

As the first drops of rain fell a sharp sound disturbed me. I looked up to see Marie pounding down the path, sending gravel flying with her every step.

'You must come at once, my lady. William's back from Dartmouth, and he bears the worst news. Come, ma'am! Come!'

I allowed her to wrap a warm cloak round my shoulders, wondering what could be worse than the troubles caused by my wayward daughter. A single glance at Marie's pale face and her wide eyes returned me to reality with a jolt. William must have brought the news we had been dreading for weeks. I squeezed my eyes shut for a moment and took a few controlled breaths before I followed my maid.

As I entered the hall, I felt my hackles rise. There was John Harte, interrogating my steward for all the world as though he, Gawen's puffed-up lawyer friend, were the master of my household. The young scribe, Lisbeth's beau, sat hunched over a stack of documents, not daring to raise his head. The scratching sound of the nib as he covered papers in neat secretary-hand cut through the air, setting my nerves even more on edge.

A crowd of house servants gathered around William with bated breath, eager for the latest news, however bad it might be. To my intense annoyance, William stood before Harte, cap in hand, as if he were seeking his approval.

Adopting my mother's most impressive stance, I commanded William to give me his report. To my secret delight, he turned to me.

'There's word in Dartmouth that the Spaniards have put to sea, Mistress.'

A fearful gasp, a desperate rasping hiss, burst from the assembled servants, and cries of 'No! No! God save us all!' Even William, usually calm in a crisis, looked rattled.

'A Dartmouth man came from Saint Malo; he had heard it from a Frenchman who'd come all the way by land from Spain. He'd seen them leave the port. There's no doubt. They're on their way. More ships than you could count, he said. For all this little squall, the weather seems set fair for their passage. I fear we will have to put our plans into action soon.'

Harte intervened in a lordly voice.

'Master Champernowne will be here this afternoon to take control.' I tugged at my cuff, and with a shake of my head, I flicked my eyes up to the roof beams. Harte had heard from my husband while I had not. He started to question William once again, as though trying to catch him out, but I cut him off.

'That is good news, Master Harte. I trust you have completed everything my husband requested. Once done, you will be free to depart.' I did not wait for his response but turned on my heel and headed towards the kitchens. 'I need to check our supplies. Come along, William!'

Harte was right. Gawen arrived before I had completed my rounds. He greeted me with an absent-minded peck on the cheek.

'Where's Harte? Has he prepared the papers?' I ignored his question, determined to hold his attention at least for a short time before he went to ground in his study with the loathsome Harte. I put my hand on his arm.

'How did things go for Sir Francis? Has he persuaded the Queen to support his plan?' Gawen spluttered and let out a foul oath. He acknowledged my raised eyebrows with a brief apology.

'I'm sorry. I shouldn't speak so before you, Roberda, but the Spanish fleet of one hundred and thirty vessels has sailed. They've packed their ships with thirty thousand well-armed soldiers, yet still she prevaricates! Pah! However much the Queen wants to believe it, there's no hope that Philip of Spain will give up his holy crusade!' I felt my jaw clench and reached out to grip his arm, my fingers digging in as a spike of fear shot through me.

'Are they coming? Coming here?'

He took my hand and gave it a reassuring squeeze, though the callouses on his hardened fingers merely reminded me he might soon be called upon to wield his sword in our defence.

'Word is that they won't attempt a landfall here but will sail on to rendezvous with the Duke of Palma in Flanders. Then they'll launch their attack. They know we have Dover well protected, so who knows where they'll strike. Might even have the audacity to sail up the Thames itself.'

I sank down onto a bench, welcoming the comfort of the familiar polished surface of the oak boards.

'So they won't invade Devon after all? We are safe?'

He gave the briefest nod, as though he hadn't taken in my question. Gawen's next words set another chilling prospect before me.

'Drake will watch 'em. He'll chase 'em up the Channel, provided he can afford to man his ships. But we'll muster in case the intelligence is wrong.' He threw his shoulders back. 'I'll lead the mounted forces of Devon. Now, where's Harte?' As he turned to leave, I called out.

'He's finished your papers, so he can go.'

That evening, Marie released my long tresses from their tight braids with a rough tug and took up the brush. She worked on my hair until it shone, then plaited it anew, letting the braids fall over my shoulders. Clotilde, sitting beside me, clenched her teeth and winced as she rubbed her throbbing knuckles.

'You've missed a few strands, Marie,' Clotilde said. 'Here, let me show you.' As she tried to take the brush from Marie's hand, it slipped from her grip and dropped to the floor with a dull thud. Clotilde sank back into her seat and held her head in her hands.

'It's all right, Clotilde.' I knelt beside her.

'It's my hands, you see.' She held them up for my inspection.

'I know. It doesn't matter. There are plenty of people who can brush my hair, but there's no one else I can rely on for wise counsel. Don't fret.' I put my arms around her, and gradually, her shoulders ceased their shaking.

I dismissed Marie to prepare a warm posset for me, hoping that the velvety concoction, cream infused with sweet ale and fragrant lemon, would ward off the chill that had been creeping through me since Gawen's return. Marie's heavy footsteps thudded on the boards as she made her way through the door and up the stairs. I turned to my elderly nurse.

'Lisbeth is quite beyond control, Clotilde. Whatever shall I do with this foolish daughter? Should I tell my husband?' She moved her seat a little closer and held my gaze, her blue eyes pools of sympathy, glinting in the dim light.

'All will be in confusion as he prepares to meet the Spaniards. He has enough on his mind. I would let it lie. Master Harte and his scribe have gone. There is no immediate danger that she will defy you. I've made enquiries. The boy's as meek as a mouse!'

'Ah! Perhaps that is part of the attraction! That wilful girl thinks she can bend him to her will!'

'It's nought but a girlish fancy,' Clotilde said, motioning me to sit. 'Absence will soon mend it. Leave her to stew. We have more important concerns now.' She took my hand in hers. The roughened skin felt cool and somehow comforting as Marie bumbled into the room bearing a steaming mug.

'I wasn't sorry to see the back of that odious man, Harte. He left as soon as Gawen had signed off whatever deals they had been hatching between them. Gawen boasted, said he had all set in hand. Whatever did he mean?' I ran my restless fingers through my hair, tugging at the plait Marie had so carefully arranged. Patient and discreet to a fault, Marie took up the brush again.

'Don't upset yourself, ma'am,' she said, her voice as soothing as honey dripping from the spoon. 'Drink this and then rest. You must care for yourself and the babe.'

Chapter Thirteen

Call to Muster

Summer 1588, Dartington Hall

The first brood of noisy swallows left the nest, and the grass stood high in the meadows, ready for the scythe. In any other year, everyone would be busy in the fields, cutting the hay and working late into balmy summer evenings. However, that June, many of the men were already called away to help shore up Plymouth's defences. It fell to the elderly, the very young, and the women to keep the usual farming calendar turning. The task became even harder when the spell of better weather broke, and furious storms raged across our land.

For over two weeks, the hungry, beleaguered sailors aboard Drake's ships waited for supplies. When Gawen stormed in, the pulse at his temple was throbbing.

'She won't put up the money needed to feed the crew of Drake's ships waiting in Plymouth Harbour. Howard has joined him. He, too, was in favour of striking the Spanish before they reached our shores. But because of these damned storms, that chance has gone. The same Westerly gales that hold our ships in port will carry the Spanish into our waters.' He slammed his clenched fist down on the oaken tabletop with a thump. 'We just sit and wait like rats in a trap while our Queen refuses to pay for provisions and arms that we need to defend her!'

'William tells me a man came wanting to buy cattle for more salt beef.'

'That would be Marmaduke Darrell. Fat lot of use it will be. It takes eighteen days to kill an ox and cure the beef. That will be too late. Drake's sailors are going down like flies. They're hungry, and diseases are spreading.' I poured him a mug of ale, which he took with little grace.

'How does your friend Drake like taking orders from Lord Howard?' I asked, seeking to turn the conversation. But he soon reverted to the problem of inadequate provisions.

'He's focussed on the task. I don't think he likes Howard being above him. But he says it is to be expected. They seem as one on the lack of supplies. Drake will have to put his sailors on half rations if victuals don't soon come through. And all I can do is wait for the call to muster!' He paced round the bedchamber, like a dog confined to the kennel when the hunt was out. Then, spinning round to face me, he stared at my growing belly. 'Will you not reconsider, Roberda? There's no shame in going to a place of safety well inland. It's doubtful now they'll land here, but just in case. Better for you and the boy.'

'We have discussed this. I won't leave my people when they need me, Gawen. Don't forget, I am French, classed by many as a foreigner, though you'd have a hard job finding anyone more Protestant than me in all of Queen Elizabeth's England. I don't want to risk being apprehended on the road, mistaken for a Papist-lover or a Spaniard. The children and I will remain at Dartington.'

'Harrumph. Speaking of the children, what ails Lisbeth? She used to flash me a smile as bright as sunlight on a spring morning and greet me with a voice as blithe as a lark. Now she mutters and mumbles, refuses to even look at me. Despondency clings to the girl like a wet cloak. What's amiss?'

'Girls her age are prone to such fits of melancholy. It will pass.' Gawen's eyes bore into me, probing, insistent. 'Is that all?'

Determined that I would not reveal Lisbeth's secret dalliance with an unsuitable scribe, I kept my voice steady.

'I'm sure there is nothing for you to worry about. But she is growing up, Gawen. When this alarm is done, we must find a husband for her.'

His face turned fiery red.

'There is no money for a dowry.' Slamming down his mug, he stormed off, cursing as he went, leaving me chewing my lip. I did not tell him about John Harte's man as we waited and prayed for deliverance from our enemies.

Dawn comes early a month past midsummer. That sultry morning, I woke with the sun to find the clammy linen sheet clinging about me. I shifted to free myself, longing for a few moments of peace before the house was astir. But the child within me had other ideas. He was squirming and kicking with such force the feather mattress beneath me jumped. I heaved myself into a more comfortable position and sighed as Clotilde bustled in.

'To carry a child in summer's heat is tiresome indeed, Clotilde.'

'There's not long to wait now. Drink this.' Clotilde's hand quivered a little as I accepted the cup from her. I studied her face, searching for any traces of pain amidst the lines etched there by the passing years. Yet, all I found was affection shining from her worn eyes.

A pleasant herby aroma floated up from the drink.

'Agnes has added a hint of musk, along with her herbs and spices, and mixed them all in a syrup of elderflowers. She says this cordial's excellent protection against swooning,' Clotilde said. As I sipped the refreshing drink, Clotilde peered out from the window.

'This oppressive weather must break soon. We'll have storms today if I'm not mistaken.' I struggled to rise, but she laid a hand on my arm.

'Why not rest awhile longer while you can? Save your strength for what is to come,' she soothed. I yielded to the comfort of down-filled pillows and drifted back to sleep.

The jarring sound of St Mary's bells jolted me awake, their urgent and discordant peels piercing my sleepy haze like sharp swords. Marie's voice, shrill and trembling with fear, reached me from the antechamber.

'The beacons are lit. The Spanish are coming. This is no false alarm. The Spanish are coming!'

Cursing my heavy belly, I clambered from the bed as quickly as I could and called for Clotilde. As she laced me into my gown with clumsy fingers, my thoughts were with Gawen. I laid a hand on my belly and offered a silent prayer that he would return unharmed to see his son born.

'He's gone to his cousin's house, Greenway, by the River Dart,' I said. Clotilde pursed her lips, and with a brisk movement, set a linen cap on my head.

'Reports from Burleigh's spies suggest a landing in Devon is unlikely.' It was not the thought of Gawen making a stand with Sir John Gilbert and his ragged band of mustered men that made the hairs on my arms to stand on end.

'I know. I'm sure he'll be safe enough here in Devon. I'm concerned about him getting caught up in fighting nearer to London. It makes me feel sick to think of it,' I said. With a groan, my elderly maid bent to pick up a pin and frowned, looking round for Marie, hoping she might take over. But Marie was not in evidence. With a grimace, Clotilde fumbled to attach the crisp starched cuffs at my wrists.

'Please keep still,' she said. 'I am trying to send you down dressed as befits the lady of this house.'

'Oh, Clotilde! His deepest desire is to lead his cavalry to join the Earl of Leicester and protect the Queen's person.' I felt even more queasy when I remembered Gawen's radiant face bidding me farewell. 'He was brimming with excitement, eager for action in defence of his sovereign. By now, he may already be on the road to Tilbury, leading a group of armed riders. And the best trained soldiers in the world may even now be marching through Kent, intent on capturing Queen Elizabeth. May God protect him!'

Clotilde gave me another hard smile.

My dressing complete, she faced me and set her hands on my shoulders.

'Wasting your energy worrying about your husband will help no one. The people here need your guidance. Think of your mother. What would she do? Go down and do your duty.' Only Clotilde would dare speak to me so. I knew she was right.

I descended with a firm step to find Griffin Jones, the rector, hovering at the foot of the stairs, blinking like an owl wakened in the afternoon. He shuffled his restless feet and picked at the lace on his sleeve.

'The churchwarden's released arms from the church, and the men have set off for Galmpton to join Sir John Gilbert at Warrebeck. There's funds set aside to pay them, ma'am.' The spineless young rector glanced from one door to the other as though searching in vain for a swift escape.

By Warrebeck, he meant the windswept plain above the village of Galmpton, that some called Warborough Common. Not far from John Gilbert's house, it commanded views right across Torbay. It was an obvious vantage point for Gawen's cousin to rally the militia against the possibility of attack.

I gave the rector a withering stare, wondering why he should think paying our people mattered at such a vital time. But when I saw his panic-stricken eyes wavering in a face as white as whey in the dairy, I took pity on him. I even managed a smile as I bit back a swift retort.

'That is all in order, Sir Griffin. They all know their tasks.'

'What if the Spanish should land, ma'am? They say they've crammed those great ships with fierce soldiers, ready to put us all to the sword!'

'Now then, Sir Griffin! It is most unlikely they will land. All the intelligence suggests that they are heading for Flanders to meet the Duke of Palma.' He shuffled his feet and clutched at his prayer book as I went on. 'Sir John will stand ready until he is sure they've passed us by. Go to the church and pray for our deliverance, Sir Griffin. Beyond that, all we can do is wait.'

I let out a sigh as the nervous young man, so ill-suited to such an alarm, scuttled off.

Throughout the entire day, I kept myself occupied, giving orders to the remaining servants to keep them busy. The sky grew inky black and ominous, hinting at more storms to come. The winter wheat was ready for the scythe. I pondered the risks of sending out elderly men and young boys to cut the golden corn and women to gather the sheaves into stooks.

As we waited in suspense, more days – three, then four – turned into a week. I missed William's reassuring presence. He had answered Sir John's call to the muster with the others.

Clotilde and Marie went about their duties with heads down. I ignored their pleas that I should rest. The children crept around or huddled together in the parlour.

'Where is my father? Is there news?' Arthur asked the same questions twenty times each day. Lisbeth, who had put away her defiance, sat meek as milk, stitching with her sisters. I gave her short shrift when she plied me with questions about the whereabouts of Harte and his man.

None of us voiced the nagging fear that grew more insistent as each day passed. What if the Spanish had not sailed on up the Channel? What if Walsingham and Lord Burleigh's informers had got it wrong? My blood ran cold in my veins when I imagined Spanish soldiers armed to the teeth wading through the shallow waters of Torbay. Perhaps they were already swarming towards the rag-tag army on the common.

The storms abated, and a dazzling sun shone from a clear blue sky. I took the risk of ordering that the wheat be cut. The activity seemed to boost everyone's spirits. I called Alice from the kitchens.

'Fill mugs with small ale and cider and carry them to the wheat fields. Take meat pasties as well for those who toil in this scorching heat.' Alice trotted off with a smile, happy to have something constructive to do.

Late in the evening, as the bats flitted under the eaves in the dimpsy light, I heard singing and laughter echoing round the courtyard. Thinking it was the workers back from the fields, I paid no heed until William poked his head round the door, a grin stretching from ear to ear. They had ignored the curfew, and made for home, and they were in good spirits.

The next morning, somewhat refreshed, we gathered in the parlour, eager to hear William's account.

'You should have seen Sir John on his white horse! We stood in ranks across the common. Over a thousand of us, there were. Though we weren't all well equipped, we all stood ready to fight. The lucky few wearing your jack-o'-plates were the envy of them all, ma'am.'

'Did you see them, William? Did you see the Spanish ships?' Arthur's eager face shone, but in stark contrast, William's expression turned grave. He gave a slow, deliberate nod.

'That I did, young master. That I did. I hope I never see anything so terrifying again.' He shook his head from side to side.

'Did you see my husband?' Clotilde gave me a black look but I couldn't contain my anxiety any longer. William shrugged his shoulders.

'He was beside Sir John at the start. But then a messenger came – oh my, there were so many of them flying around at such a rate! Post horses commandeered and ready for the riders to change everywhere from here to London and back again. They carry word almost as fast as the beacons.' I scowled and set my hands on my hips.

'But what of my husband?'

'Once the threat of a landing was over, Master Gawen led all his mounted men away. Bound for Tilbury, where Lord Leicester assembles his forces in case the Spanish should succeed and join up with Parma. There's concern they may launch an attack from Kent or Essex. Or so I believe, ma'am.'

'As I feared! May God protect him!' Feeling light-headed, I sank onto the settle, waving Marie away as she thrust a cushion behind me. Margery Searle, the midwife, on hand as my time drew near, gave me a long stare as she took Marie's place at my side. I ignored her pursed lips and furrowed brow.

'Tell us more about the ships, William. Arthur piped up. 'What colour were their sails? Could you see the guns?' Arthur's cheeks had a feverish glow.

'Their sails are black as the night sky – like an endless line of black ants, they came crawling across the horizon – all the way from Berry Head to way beyond Hope's Nose, as far as I could see. They say they sail in convoy, all grouped tight together in a shape like the horns of the new moon. Each of their great ships protects another.' He took a long draught from the mug and wiped his mouth on his sleeve before he went on.

'Another rider came from Plymouth, said he'd heard the guns. Sir Francis and Lord Howard had to wait for the tide before they could give chase. They engaged the enemy in fierce fighting. It sounds like they harried the Spanish fleet, but could not stay them, nor break their formation. Those great galleons sailed on to meet the Duke of Palma and his army. Then they'll likely unleash a multitude of Papist soldiers on our shores.'

Even Arthur fell silent when he heard the chilling truth confirmed by William's words. While imminent danger no longer threatened Devon, the war was far from done. My mouth was dry with fear as the child wriggled and squiggled inside me.

'So they sail on to threaten our land!' I said, my voice shrill. 'I pray they will keep a close guard on our Queen. God alone knows what world this boy will be born into!' Margery's scrutiny bore into me, noticing every detail, until her eyes came to rest on my feet.

'It would be best if you would sit down, ma'am,' she said, eyeing my ankles.

'Nonsense... William has more to tell us. Go on.' He set down his empty mug with a sigh.

'Our Devon men have come home. I doubt Sir John could have kept them any longer – they drifted away as soon as those devilish ships had passed Torbay. There's a lot of muttering about pay – or the lack of it! Yet our English soldiers must still stand ready at Dover or Tilbury or wherever they gather. Begging your pardon, ma'am, but I pray the Queen has the sense to pay those men and see them well fed.'

We were all quiet, digesting the depressing news. At last William spoke in a more encouraging tone.

'Yet there's some cause for hope. Our English ships are faster and can turn about. They're nimble and they can tack into the wind. And we have the finest commanders. Perhaps they'll catch them before they reach Flanders.'

'So we have captured no prizes yet, William? Not put any of those Papist fools to the sword?' Arthur asked. William shook his head, and Arthur collapsed onto a bench, his young face twisted into a frown.

'Well, now, that's not quite true, young master,' William said, and the boy sat up, a glimmer of hope shining in his eyes. 'There's one of them won't trouble us any more. The *Nuestra Senora del Rosario*, flagship of Don Pedro de Valdés, who had command of some other great ship.'

'What do you mean? Has Sir Francis blasted her out of the water?' Arthur's face brightened at the prospect.

'They say Sir Francis took her – but not before some of the damned English Papists she had on board had slipped away! Traitors, the lot of 'em!'

'Amen to that!' The words burst out from Marie as she snapped her sewing basket shut. She stared at William as he continued his tale.

'Sir Francis had the Rosario brought into Torbay. Saw it myself, I did. They say Don Pedro's taken up and any Spaniards that might fetch a ransom. They took a few more of the crew and some English Papists up to London. May they hang and rot!' That brought out a ripple of agreement amongst the servants.

'The Spaniards they didn't take to London – well, Lord alone knows what they'll do with them. Taken 'em to Torre Abbey, I heard. Locked 'em up in the barn.'

Although my back ached from standing so long, I rallied my dwindling store of strength and spoke up to cheer them all.

'The prisoners are not our problem. William, I'm glad to have you back and the other men too! Let us all go about our business as we await more news.'

Most people at Dartington Hall breathed a little easier, slept a little better. Yet I tossed on the feather mattress, fighting off demons. Thoughts of Gawen plagued me.

'How could I bear it if fate snatched him from me so soon after our reunion?' I asked one morning as Clotilde laid out my clothes. She pulled a face and huffed, as she did, every time I mentioned him.

Margery, who had seen most of my children born, moved into the antechamber next to my room, pushing her truckle bed up close to Marie's. A few days later, she found me forcing my feet into my slippers.

'They are so tight, Margery. I must have eaten too much and put on weight. I've had a rare fancy for cook's gooseberry tart.' Margery sat on the floor and took both of my feet into her lap. She lifted my skirt to reveal my swollen ankles.

'This is not from eating too many sweet tarts. I have seen it before in a woman near her time. You must take to your bed now if you would bring this child safe into the world.' And so, in the sweltering heat of a stormy August, my confinement began.

Chapter Fourteen

From Our Greatest Joys, Our Greatest Sorrows Flow

September 1588, Dartington Hall

With the utmost care, Clotilde placed the delicate, swaddled bundle into my trembling arms. Despite the waves of exhaustion washing over me, I mustered the strength to cradle him, marvelling at his tiny fingers and inhaling his sweet baby fragrance. Lost in wonder, I watched the oh-so-fragile rise and fall of his little chest, the only sound the faint whisper of his breathing.

Margery's weary voice, rough and raspy, shattered the stillness.

'A boy, ma'am!' Margery offered none of the usual words of praise for his health and vigour. She didn't say, 'You have a fine son,' or 'He's a lusty fellow.' She just mouthed the words 'A boy.'

'Thank God,' I murmured. 'It's a boy for Gawen.' Too weak to do more, I handed him to Clotilde. A feeble smile tugged at my lips as I allowed my heavy eyelids to close.

Sleep came in ragged snatches. At times, drenched in sweat, I writhed on the bed, casting off the covers with frantic hands. Then the grip of my childhood terrors held me trapped in a terrifying cycle of false awakenings. Every time I thought I had escaped, the haunting image of an old woman falling from Rouen's towering walls would come back, her screams growing louder. In the dream, I was on tiptoes, peering through the shattered glass, smelling blood, as I saw again and again the soldier's face explode, before he, too, tumbled.

The touch of the plush velvet coverlet against my fingertips reassured me that this time I was awake. Yet still I kept my eyes shut, unwilling to trust in another illusion.

The faint swishing of women's skirts and their hushed whispers fluttered into my ears. I pried my eyelids apart and lifted my head. Three women stood as silhouettes against the golden sunlight pouring in through the open window. I tried to speak, but the effort was too much for me. Bone-weary, I lay back, listening to their soft voices.

'Margery? What have you to say? Will she recover?'

'I hope she will, Mistress Seymour. It's a blessing for her that the babe came before his time. For the child, it may prove a different story.'

'*Le pauvre petit...*' Relief surged through me when I heard Clotilde's voice! 'He will need our prayers, and so will she.'

'With God's help and careful nursing, she will recover.'

'But the child, Margery? What of the child?' Bess asked.

'Where there is life, there is hope, Mistress Seymour.' A heavy sigh, then, Bess answered, only just loud enough for me to hear.

'If my brother doesn't come soon, he may be too late.'

I could contain myself no longer. Pushing myself up on wobbling arms, I called out.

'Bess? Is that you?'

The three women spun around in a confusion of shining silk, homely wool and crisp, clean linen.

'You're awake at last! Thank God, you're awake. I've been watching you toss on that bed for three days.' A refreshing hint of musky perfume clung to Bess's skirts as she rushed to my bedside, soon overpowered by the flowery perfume of lily of the valley as Clotilde leant over me. She fussed with the bedcovers as I gathered what little strength I had left to ask about my husband.

'Is Gawen here?' Bess tossed her head.

'My brother has yet to return from Tilbury.'

'But, Bess, the Spanish ships are long gone, aren't they? Or was it all just a dream?' I asked. Bess laid a comforting hand on mine.

'All is well on that score,' she said. 'Rest easy. Drake's fireships scattered them to the mercy of the winds, and God sent such a powerful gale that it blew what remained of King Philip's fleet clean away. The Queen is safe, the country is safe. We are safe.'

'If that's the case, the Queen doesn't need protection anymore. So why is Gawen not back?'

Bess pursed her lips and clenched her teeth. Alarmed, I shifted on the bed. The effort sent shards of searing pain shooting through my battered body.

'Bess? You must tell me. Where is he?' I whispered.

'That I cannot answer, for I don't know!'

Clotilde gave an extra pillow a firm thump before she shoved it behind my head. I had no time to quiz them further as Margery bustled up to the bedside, and pushing Clotilde aside, she offered me a steaming bowl.

'Come. Ma'am. Eat. You must build up your strength,' she urged. Though it was tasty, well seasoned with herbs, a few spoonfuls of the nourishing broth was all I could manage before fitful sleep claimed me once again.

The next day, the first day of September, they took my baby to the church to welcome him into God's family. They dared wait no longer. As I lay near senseless in my bed, they named my boy Alexander, a family name, Bess said. Some long-dead Champernowne ancestor had carried that name somewhere in Devon. Perhaps it was Tawton, I couldn't recall. Gawen had ordered it before he rode off, and so it would be.

Later that day, I lifted my head to see Margery leading an apple-cheeked young woman into my chamber.

'This is Lucy, Alice Blackaller's younger sister, who's been nursing your boy.' I squinted at the buxom girl, raised a hand and let it fall. Lucy looked a clean and healthy girl, who would make a good wet nurse. It was all I could do to steal a furtive glance at my son, cradled in her arms.

'Thank you, Lucy.' I didn't want to prolong a conversation, but she was a talkative girl.

'Poor little mite! Born before his time. He needs to build up his strength. It's a good thing I'm here, for my little maid's ready for weaning. I eat well. Ma'am, good healthy food from my father's little farm. He'll not want.' She looked down at the baby. 'There now! Shall I take him so you may rest?'

'Yes, please do.' I waved her away and fell into a deep sleep.

For days Margery shook her head and fussed over me, coaxing me to eat. 'Can you take a spoon or two, ma'am?'

'I have no appetite.' I turned my head away, asking 'Is there no word from my husband?' But always she shook her head.

The servants kept their victory celebrations muted at Dartington Hall. Mindful of baby Alexander's fragile grip on life and my slow recovery, they kept their carousing hushed. The children paid me a visit and sat in silence, eyeing the door. I sent them away. I lost count of the days.

'He's here! Father's here!' Dependable Mary, my second daughter, screamed the news at the top of her voice as she blew into my chamber like a whirlwind. 'Now you'll feel better, Mother.' I felt the tension leave my weak muscles. He was home!

'You're a good girl, Mary. Will you be my tiring woman? I must look my best for your father.' Mary picked up a brush and drew it through my fair locks until they shone like gold, braided my hair with gentle fingers, then fixed it around my head with a linen ribbon.

'Here, Mother, put this on. ' She set a pretty cap embroidered with flowers on my head and held the glass for me. 'You look so much better!' I couldn't fathom how that could be. What could be worse than the haggard face staring at me from the glass? My cheeks were white as parchment, my staring eyes sunk into dark pits.

Clotilde rushed in, her face like thunder.

'He's only gone to the nursery rather than come first to you! He's brought that man Harte with him. I suppose that scribe's here too.' She lowered her voice. 'We must watch Miss Lisbeth.'

'All will be well, Clotilde. My husband is home, and I have given him a son.'

As dusk was falling, he came to my bedside, his footsteps soft on the polished wooden floor. I took some comfort as he held my hand, yet when I looked into his face, I saw a storm brewing within Gawen's steel-grey eyes, anger and sorrow battling it out.

'Gawen! Welcome home!' He released my hand and sat down with a thump, as though the ground beneath his feet had given way.

'I have seen him,' he said.

'The boy? How is he?'

'He looks frail… as though a puff of wind would blow him away.' Gawen rubbed his hand across his forehead and his lips twisted. 'He looks just like our other boy, like Philip, who lies in St Mary's Church beside my father.'

'Gawen, this baby is our Alexander. It's a good name. I've read about a general who lived long ago who had that name. He will be strong and brave, like his namesake.'

'Then we must pray that he has a soldier's strength. He will need to fight hard if he is to survive.' He lapsed into a brooding silence, his shoulders slumped as he studied the floorboards. I searched in vain for words that could reach him.

'Lucy is a healthy girl. She tends him well. He has the best of care.' When this elicited no response I tired a change of tack. 'Did you go to Tilbury? Did you see the Queen? Thank God the Spanish army never made landfall.'

His head went up at that, and his lip curled. 'Once again, they denied me the chance to prove myself in battle! We rode all that way to Tilbury at breakneck speed. What a waste of time and effort that was!'

He half rose from his seat, then sank down again.

'By the time we got there, everyone already knew the wind had driven the Spanish fleet far to the North.' Gawen ran a hand through his dark curling hair and gave a bitter laugh. 'God's Blood! I'd wager the wind had already blown them all the way to Scotland. And yet she must put on a show, addressing her loyal soldiers as the valiant warrior queen. Leicester had the arranging of it!'

'So the soldiers were all disbanded?'

'With no pay and meagre rations, they would not wait long! We turned and rode away.'

I couldn't help it. I had to know.

'Why has it taken so long for you to come home? I've been in sore need of you!' The vein at his temple was pulsating as he let out a weary sigh.

'There were reports that the winds blew the Spaniards clear round Scotland. The Queen's advisers were worried they might seek succour in Ireland. I went to Bristol to aid those provisioning ships bound for

Ireland to bolster our defences. My cousin Denny is at Tralee.' I tried to remember which of his many cousins this Denny might be. He must have noticed my confusion, for he continued. 'Edward Denny, you remember him? His mother was my father's sister.' In a flash, I saw it. Gawen felt he had been thwarted yet again. With an understanding nod, I reached for his hand, but his fingers felt stiff in my grip and soon slipped away.

'We heard that many drowned in the storms. Some escaping shipwreck swam ashore. The Queen's forces soon rounded them up and sent them to Tralee, where Denny's wife ordered them all hanged at the gibbet! She's an Edgecumbe.' My mouth fell open.

'I was too late,' he went on. 'So, when Bess sent word of your confinement, I came home. And here I am. Home, only to find my boy's life hanging by a thread.' With another deep sigh, he stood up and stomped from the room.

I was out of bed, standing at the window, mesmerised by the rain-lashed trees swaying in the rough wind. A musty autumnal smell crept in through a crack in the casement, making me shiver. Exhausted after another sleepless night, tossing and turning, worrying about my baby boy, I rubbed the back of my neck.

Joan burst in, feet clattering on the boards, and I whirled round, fearing the worst. Her face was as white as a bedsheet, her voice all a-tremble.

'Ma'am, ma'am... a Spaniard! He's here, at Dartington, come to murder us in our beds!'

'Calm down, Joan. What are you talking about?' As I spoke, William knocked at the chamber door and dipped his head beneath the lintel.

'Sorry to disturb you, ma'am, but I thought I should reassure you all is well.' He glared at Joan, who was cowering behind my chair, whimpering like a frightened puppy.

'What nonsense is this about a Spaniard?' I asked, heart thumping. William's steady gaze, his open face showing his simple strength and loyalty, soon had my pulse slowing down to a more normal rhythm.

'Nothing to alarm you, ma'am, for all's under control. They

caught him on the road from Totnes, down by the mill, and brought him here. In a sorry state he was and not fit to harm anyone.' He jutted out his chin as Joan peeped out from behind me.

'Stop your snivelling, Joan!' William said with another furious glare. 'There's no need for anyone to be alarmed. Master Gawen questioned him. Seems he was one of them from that Rosario Ship – the one Sir Francis captured. They've kept the prisoners at Torre Abbey, but Sir John Gilbert's had some of 'em over to Greenway. Put 'em to work in his garden, or some such. This man slipped away at night-time. He says he fell in the river and got caught up in a thicket, though how anyone can make sense of his gibbering, I don't know. His clothes are all ripped to shreds. But here he is.'

'You're sure it's just one man? Not some ruse to allow others to find us here?'

William flashed me a reassuring grin, and my hands relaxed as the tension melted away. 'No, ma'am. Don't you fret, 'tis just the one. We've got him held safe in the church until Sir John can send men to fetch him away.' Footsteps echoed on the stair and Gawen stalked in, puffing a little.

'What's this, William? Not frightening my wife, I hope?' He poked an accusing finger towards William's chest and the steward's face drained of colour as he took a step backwards.

'Quite the reverse,' I said, my voice sharp. 'William's here to put my mind at rest about some poor Spanish soul who's found his way here.' Gawen's lips twisted into a cruel grimace.

'I'd have put him to the sword if it weren't for that weakling rector. Said it's our Christian duty to treat the blackguard well.'

'And so it is!' I said firmly. 'He's no more than a poor soldier doing his duty for his country, even though that country is our enemy. William, who is watching him?'

'Churchwarden's got it all in hand, though he's complaining he'll have to pay someone to keep the rascal under lock and key.' Gawen cursed under his breath and raising his arms, he unleashed a tirade of criticism in a voice so full of venom I'm sure it would have left Sir John wilting had he been in the room.

'I told cousin John he was playing with fire when he took them to Greenway! We can't have the Spaniards running about all over

Devon. Any Catholic sympathisers hereabouts will be only too happy to shield them.'

Ignoring Gawen's snort, I stepped between him and William.

'Send the churchwarden to me, William.' The steward hurried out to do my bidding, while Gawen's face grew even darker, threatening as a thundery sky. After pacing round the room a few more times, he let out an exasperated sigh and stomped off.

At that moment, I didn't care at all about my husband's anger. I was resolved to make sure the Spanish prisoner received compassionate treatment while at Dartington. After all, I knew what it was to be a stranger in a strange land, suspected because I spoke in a foreign tongue.

The portly churchwarden's face was red as a cockscomb when he sidled in.

'You have the Spaniard secure?' I asked.

'We do, ma'am, and we've sent a messenger to Sir John to fetch him away. I'll have to dig deep to find the coin to pay for his watching.'

'I'm sure you'll manage. Tell me, have you given him fresh clothes?' He bit his lip.

'Er… no… er… him being an enemy, we left him to suffer.'

'Do you not know your scripture, man?' The man flinched as I snapped at him. 'The Lord said, "Love your enemies, bless them that curse you, do good to them that hate you".'

The churchwarden shuffled his feet and looked at the floor as I went on.

'Have shoes, shirt, stockings and whatever the poor man needs provided.' He looked up.

'But, ma'am! He's a Spaniard!'

I threw up my hands. 'Do as I say. Go!'

He scuttled out, narrowly avoiding knocking Clotilde from her feet as she came in.

'Whatever has put the master in such a temper?' she asked. I turned back to the window.

'He's just taking out his pain on others, Clotilde. He's worried about our boy, just as I am. The arrival of that poor Spaniard gives him a chance to vent his fury. I've ordered the man be cared for until Sir John fetches him away.'

'You did right, *ma petite*.' Her voice, with its French lilt, was soft and comforting as she reached out to touch my arm. 'I'm come from the nursery. There's no change. He still clings on.'

A few more days passed, as I held onto the vain hope that my boy would grow stronger. One morning, I gazed listlessly from the window while Clotilde went about her duties like a furious whirlwind.

'Didn't he tell you?' Clotilde asked, at last, slamming the lid shut on a chest without bothering to set the folded linens neatly inside. As she straightened up, she left a shift peeking from the lid and caps and aprons in a heap on the floor. It was not like Clotilde to preside over such confusion. Hands on hips, she continued to berate my husband.

'He's known all this time but didn't tell you! Anne Cecil was your friend at court! Oh, I know I should not speak of him so. But he must have known long ago? Even before they saw the black sails of the enemy off the coast. Long before he went to join Sir John's forces at that place with a strange name. Ah... these English names! That's it! Warrebeck, they call it, don't they?'

'What are you rambling on about, Clotilde? I haven't heard from Anne in ages.' Clotilde huffed and puffed as she bent to pick up the linen she had dropped.

'I wouldn't know even now if I hadn't overheard him talking with that Master Harte,' she muttered.

'Overheard what?' I asked. The anger melted from her eyes.

'*Pardonne-moi!* I beg forgiveness for my anger, but he should have told you. Now it falls to me to bring you more sad news.'

'News of Anne?' She hesitated, as though gathering her strength. Weighing her words with care, she delivered the heaviest blow of all.

'There's no easy way to tell it. Anne Cecil died in June.' Her words dropped like pebbles falling into a deep well. 'Everything was in confusion here with us all thinking the Spanish were coming. It seems no one thought to tell you. I am so sorry.'

'When?'

'They say she died on the fifth day of June, at Greenwich. Her poor father, Lord Burghley, he's had no time to grieve, what with defending the country and seeing to the Queen's wishes.'

'And my husband knew of this?' I let out a roar, frightening a lingering swallow beyond the window. The little bird swooped away to join his fellows gathering in the branches as they prepared to leave us. With my hands balled into fists, I beat on the windowsill. 'Pah! He was so intent on making a name for himself fighting the enemy on our shores, he didn't even tell me my friend was dead!'

A memory floated into my head. Anne in the splendour of Westminster Abbey, on her wedding day, standing beside that popinjay Edward de Vere. How she idolised him, even though he treated her with such contempt.

'Where is the justice in this world? How could God allow a good woman like Anne to suffer, die, and never witness her children grown? She was the daughter of a powerful man, born into a life of comfort. Yet everything turned to dust.' My shoulders heaved, and Clotilde held me close.

On a fine morning with a touch of autumn chill in the air, Bess found me staring out of the window. With her usual radiant smile, she offered me a pretty posy of flowers. Fresh-picked from the garden, with shimmering droplets of dew clinging to the velvety petals, the late rose buds were flushed with the merest hint of pink.

'I thought they would brighten your chamber. Clotilde's gone in search of a pot to put them in. Cheer up! I know. He's in a foul temper, but that will pass.' She patted my hand and bit her lip. 'Dearest Roberda, I fear I must leave you. Edward wants me at home.'

I turned my head, and through the window, I caught sight of a sudden burst of vivid scarlet, dancing like a flame amongst the clipped hedges of the knot garden. Lisbeth had not troubled to hide her scarlet partlet as she vanished from my sight, making for the holy well. I twiddled the gold chain pinned to my gown and fingered the miniature of my husband that dangled from it.

'Is Harte with Gawen?' I asked. Bess nodded.

'Can I confide in you, Bess?' I recounted the unfortunate story of Lisbeth's ill-advised involvement with Harte's scribe.

'Bess, what can I do? She might be with him at this very moment.'

Before Bess could reply, Clotilde burst into the room, panting for breath. Pulling Joan behind her, she slammed the heavy door with a bang.

'Tell the mistress what you told me, Joan.' The girl blinked like an owl caught unawares by a lantern's beam.

'You may speak freely, Joan,' I said. 'We have no secrets from Mistress Seymour. Tell me. Is it about Lisbeth?'

'Yes, ma'am, it is. She's been chasing Master Harte's man, but he'll have none of her. She caught him by the door, and he told her straight. Said his place was worth more to him than an idle dalliance.'

'So that boy has some good sense! He has heeded my words!' Clotilde said. Joan's face was by now the colour of Lisbeth's partlet as she shrank back against the closed door. Clotilde gave an impatient click of her fingers. 'Go on, girl, tell the mistress all.'

'Miss Lisbeth… she railed at him, shouting and hollering, but he just left her standing there! Oh, she went off in a rare state, ma'am, screaming at me to leave her alone.'

'Thank you, Joan. You have done well to tell us. Go now and seek her out. I expect she'll be at the holy well.' Joan turned and fled through the door. As soon as her footsteps ceased to echo on the wooden stairs, I turned to Bess, wringing my hands in my gown.

'You see, Bess! With Gawen in a bad mood and my baby so frail, I can't take any chances that he'll find out about Lisbeth's behaviour. Oh, Bess! I don't know how to deal with her!' To my amazement, a wide smile broke on Bess's lips.

'Well, the solution is simple. I'll take her with me. I'm sure Gawen will agree. She'll be company for me and it will do her good.'

Lisbeth couldn't help grinning when I told her. In that moment, I caught a flash of the little girl she used to be. She called for Joan to pack her things, picked up her skirts and took the stairs two at a time.

After Bess and Lisbeth left I saw little of Gawen. Alexander grew no stronger.

A month after the baby's birth, a distraught Lucy grabbed my arm as I was leaving the nursery one morning. Her shoulders sagged, and she kept clutching at the kerchief at her throat, twisting it between restless fingers. Poor Lucy seemed to have shrunk and lost all her bounce and vigour since she first became a wet nurse to my sickly baby.

''Tis a struggle to get him to take more than a tiny feed now, Mistress! I've done my best. Truly, I have.'

'I know, Lucy,' I said, trying to comfort her. She dabbed her eyes with a cloth.

'I'm afeared the master may blame me.'

'None of us lay the blame on you, Lucy. Master Gawen understands. Alexander's life is in God's hands.'

Later that morning, I knelt on the frigid, unyielding stone floor in our church. I felt the bitter cold seeping into my bones as I tried to pray. But no words or prayer came. I shot up from my knees and fled from the desolate, echo-filled church. The stench of decay followed me out.

Two more days crawled by. Two more nights when I bent over the cradle, willing each breath into those tiny lungs. That morning, Clotilde insisted I take a break from my vigil and rest. I made my way to the garden, my favourite sanctuary. But even there I found no solace. Sitting in the arbour, basking in the warm late September sun, I had an open book resting on my lap, forgotten and untouched.

I knew before she uttered a single word. The sombre expression on Clotilde's wrinkled old face confirmed my deepest fears. Little Alexander, despite his courageous name, had fought his last battle.

Gawen came to me then. We clung together in our shared grief, and in my arms, he let down his haughty guard. I held him close, my lips brushing against his ear as I whispered, 'We will have other sons, Gawen.'

Those words set my life's pattern for the years to come. The nursery filled with more girls. First came Jane, then the twins, Frances and Susan. Pregnancy and childbirth consumed me.

To her credit, as the years passed, Clotilde forbore to say, 'I told you so.'

Chapter Fifteen

The Accident

March 1592, Dartington Hall

Arthur's cheeks were as rosy as a September apple as he set the slender rapier on the table with a jubilant grin. The glint of sunlight danced off the polished blade, casting a shimmering reflection on the walls.

'My fencing lesson's done for today, Mother!' The excitement in his voice was unmistakable. 'Father says I may accompany him on an afternoon's hunting.'

'You should eat before you go, my boy. A growling belly might frighten the game!' It was a joke between us that Arthur was always hungry. He would soon be twelve years old and was growing as fast as a weed in the onion patch. Every time I looked at his long, sinewy limbs, I gave thanks to God that I had this one healthy son.

'William says it'll rain soon and put a damper on our sport. Grumpy old fool!'

I took a quick look at the sky through the towering window. The once benign fluffy white clouds were now gathering together. A sudden breeze stirred the banners hanging in Dartington's splendid Great Hall. In the fireplace, orange and blue ghosts danced along a log, pirouetting and prancing, their phantom feet sending sparks flying up the chimney.

'He may be right this time. Showers and rough winds can come on fast in this season.'

'We'll take shelter if we need to,' he said, with all the confidence of youth. 'I'm not going to pass up the chance. Father's waiting for me! The grooms already have the horses saddled.' He raised his arm in a cheery salute and marched away.

I followed him to the door, eager to wave my son off on his adventure. Gawen was on his favourite black stallion, a magnificent beast with powerful muscles that rippled under a coat that shone like polished ebony. As Arthur prepared to mount his more sedate chestnut gelding, Gawen's horse tossed its head and snorted, causing white specks of foam to spatter the cobbles. I thanked God that my husband was such a skilled and daring rider.

Clotilde was panting as she joined me in the porch, sixteen-year-old Mary at her side.

'A magnificent sight, is it not?' She nodded towards the black horse. 'Puts me in mind of a certain knight who once came to Ducey!' Mary gaped at me.

'Tsk, Clotilde! Be quiet! That was long ago.' The memories of my girlhood infatuation with Gawen's cousin, Henry, made my cheeks burn with embarrassment. 'I was but a child!' I turned to Mary, 'Please go to the nursery and check on your baby sisters.' Mary, always obedient, gave me another questioning look before heading inside. Clotilde went on as though I had not spoken.

'It's a wish to be as good as his cousin Henry that drives him still! All this time hoping for a second son so he can equal Henry's tally.' I sighed. She was right, but it did no good to dwell on it. I tried again to distract her.

'Look, they're ready to move off.'

Making up the hunting party was John Harte on a rangy grey. The odious man always seemed to be by Gawen's side.

Calling to his two best hounds, Gawen led the cavalcade through the archway. I raised my hand in salute, but he didn't even turn his head. Clotilde made no comment, but I knew what she was thinking. She made no secret of her distrust of Gawen's transformation into a loving husband.

I waited until they were out of sight then sought refuge in the cosy parlour where I took up my sewing. We settled into a companionable silence until the fading light caused me to call for Marie to light the candles. With surprising agility, she manoeuvred her considerable weight round the room, shielding the glowing taper with her hand. Soon, gentle light filled the room again. As Marie threw another log on the fire, she gave it a good poke. This violent action sent armies of sparks marching up the sooty fireback, while a pungent whiff of smoke swirled around the parlour. Rubbing her back, Marie straightened up.

'There's no word from the hunting party, ma'am. William's taken an ox cart out to see if they need help to carry their prizes home. The weather's turning nasty, so I shouldn't think they'll be long now.' As my eyes darted to the door, a tightening in my chest threatened to overwhelm me.

'You go to bed, Clotilde,' I said, trying to control the tremor in my voice. 'I'll wait for them. Marie will stay with me. They won't be long.'

Clotilde hesitated for a moment and gave me a hard stare, then shuffled towards the stairs. Outside, the storm still raged.

After a while I sent a protesting Marie to her bed.

I sat for so long it felt like my seat bones were sticking out, right into the uncomfortable settle, and I ached all over. Another pregnancy was sapping my energy. Pacing round the room, I tried to get the blood flowing again.

The moon hung high in the night sky, its eerie light flooding the parlour, when I heard hoofbeats in the courtyard, muffled voices and the faint creaking of the cart's wheels. I rushed to the door, to find William was already there, out of breath, having raced across the courtyard. He stood on the threshold, panting, head down, cap in hand.

'Ma'am? Please, will you sit down?'

'Sit, William? That I won't. What on earth is wrong with you? I'll hear whatever you have to say as easy on my feet.' Still, he did not meet my eye but stood, shoulders hunched over, twisting the woollen cap in his fingers.

'William?'

'Ma'am, I'm sorry to tell you. There's been an accident.' Arthur's shining face, flushed with excitement, flashed before my eyes. I thought my chest would explode.

'Not my boy!'

'No, ma'am, it's not Arthur. He's come to no harm. It's the master.'

A moan slipped through my lips.

'You're sure? Arthur is unharmed?' I rocked back on my heels and failed to take in his other words. 'What's that? What did you say?'

William explained again, with infinite patience, that it was Gawen who had suffered a terrible injury that March afternoon.

It took four of them to carry him in, each step bringing a groan from the makeshift stretcher, a rough canvas cloth fixed on poles. I couldn't drag my eyes away from the blood seeping through the cloth, the dark stain spreading while a trail of red drops spattered the floor. A sharp coppery smell filled the parlour, cloying and overpowering. The child started turning somersaults within me.

William took charge of practicalities, leaving me pale and numb, a mere bystander in a horrific scene. With careful hands, they laid Gawen on a truckle bed, spirited from the room above.

I half turned to see Arthur, frozen in the doorway, his mouth hanging open. Marie appeared beside him, her kirtle awry and unlaced, donned in haste over her shift. She wrapped her arms around the boy, pressing his head against her warm, comforting bosom. Arthur's shoulders trembled with each sob as he choked out the words,

'A hart, a white hart... broke from cover right in front of the stallion... reared up... close beneath a tree. A branch... Father fell... horse bolted... foot still in the stirrup. He'll be all right, won't he?'

I remained motionless, locked in my horrified stupor, unable to reply. Somewhere in the deepest recesses of my brain, I recognised it should have been me comforting my boy, not Marie. Rooted to the spot, numb and empty, I couldn't take it in.

'Now then, Master Arthur! Come along with me.' Arthur seemed to rally at Marie's calm voice. 'Master Putt has sent for the physician from Totnes... Agnes Searle's on her way. He's in the best of hands.' Taking him by the hand, she led him away.

Agnes arrived, calling for hot water and clean linen cloths, and the men around the bed moved to make way for her. Her face blanched, and she stood stock still for an instant. Then, setting her mouth in a determined line, she examined the injured man. I watched, mesmerised, yet feeling no connection to the scene unfolding before me as she took a twist of cloth from her basket.

'Master Putt! Take this to the kitchen. Have them boil water, scald a cup and fill it with wine, then dissolve this powder of ground bark and leaves of the willow tree. If we can get him to drink, it may ease his pain.' She turned to the bed. 'Now I must wash the wounds so that we may tell the true extent of his injury. You say the physician comes?' William nodded and hurried off to the kitchen.

I was close enough to see Agnes reach out her gentle fingers towards the wound. As the cloth she held touched the mangled flesh, a piercing, high-pitched scream cut through my brain fog. The anguished shriek reverberated around the walls, leaving an unearthly chill in the air. I could not connect that sound, more animal than human, with Gawen, my husband, who writhed on the truckle bed.

My legs turned to jelly and I would have fallen had Clotilde, who had suddenly appeared, not reached out and caught me, her frail frame providing unexpected support. She guided me away, into the darkened hall, where no one had bothered to light the candles. As in a dream, I collapsed onto the hard bench and, with a tender touch, Clotilde put a glass of wine in my trembling hand. Someone had rekindled the embers in the fireplace and a feeble flame lit the blood-red liquid. I swallowed a mouthful; it tasted like ashes.

'No! No! This cannot be!' I cried as Clotilde wrapped her arms round me.

'Think of the babe,' she said. 'You must keep your strength. Leave it to the others to tend to him. Ah, here's Master Percival, the physician!'

Alice, hands shaking, held the light for a corpulent man carrying a bulging bag. He crossed the room with swift strides, and on shaking limbs, I rose, rushed to him, took his arm.

'Please. I beg you. Do all you can to save my husband.' He gave me a curt nod and went on into the parlour, where the piercing screams had subsided to low groans. As I watched him go, I noticed John Harte lurking behind the door.

Chapter Sixteen

Allies or Enemies?

Late March 1592, Dartington Hall

The physician's eyes, magnified by the eyeglasses perched on the bridge of his red, bulbous nose, glinted in the light of a single candle. I braced myself, feeling quite sick, as he prepared to deliver his verdict on my husband's chances.

'I am afraid the damage is severe,' he said, his deep voice heavy with concern. 'He's strong and fit, but you should understand... the horse ran on for some time before they could bring him to a halt. I fear your husband's life lies in the balance, Mistress Champernowne.'

The image of the black stallion careering between the dense trees raced through my mind. I imagined the beast's ebony coat glistening in dappled sunlight as it dragged poor Gawen behind. I could almost hear the sickening thwack of his head against the unyielding tree trunks and the thundering hoofbeats echoing in the stillness of Chase Grove Wood. The blood in my ears throbbed, as if in rhythm with those relentless hooves.

The physician's florid face, etched with worry lines, swam before my tear-filled eyes. Clotilde's arm wrapped around my waist, giving me a steady anchor. After a moment, I gathered myself, found my voice and asked him to continue, though every fibre of my being trembled with dread.

'He's lost a lot of blood from the head, and he has many cuts on his chest and arms. I've done my best to bandage him. It is the leg that concerns me most, ma'am. The bone is crushed. I've removed a few splinters and I've set the leg. But the humours have been disturbed. We must be alert, Mistress Champernowne. We must be alert. The next two days will decide it.'

'Thank you, Master Percival.' I said, staring at him with unseeing eyes. I was oblivious to the firelight dancing on his bald head as he bent to gather his instruments into his threadbare tapestry bag. He collected up his glass bottles and vials, along with his bowls and jars filled with mysterious dark ointment, thrusting them higgledy-piggledy into the depths of the bag.

Percival straightened up, red-faced from the effort of lifting his heavy burden. He cocked his head to one side as a soft moan escaped from the small bed where Gawen lay. Gradually, the moaning ceased, replaced by heavy breathing. The physician's worried expression softened and a faint smile played about his lips.

'Ah! That's good! He will sleep now. The woman, Agnes, has good sense. She knows what drafts will give him some relief.' He nodded to Agnes. Her eyes never strayed from her patient, who at last lay still, cocooned in layers of bandages. The physician let out a contented grunt.

'I will return on the morrow, and with your permission I will bring a surgeon with me.' The ominous words hung in the air, while their import sank into the depths of my consciousness like an anchor finding purchase at the bottom of the ocean. A wave of nausea washed over me as the acrid taste of bile rose in my throat.

'What? A surgeon? Surely there is no need for a surgeon?'

The idea of Gawen at the hands of a barber-surgeon horrified me. I had heard enough tales of their gruesome work on the battlefields of France.

'A precaution, ma'am, that is all. I fear we must face the possibility, however remote, that we may not save the leg.' With that, he took his leave.

I sat down heavily, head in hands, as I tried to digest it all. A sudden movement alerted me. Someone was hiding beyond the open door.

'Well, Master Harte? What are you doing skulking there? I have enough troubles without you adding to them.' I waved a hand as though swatting away an irritating fly. He stepped forward and made a perfunctory bow.

'I pray you, Mistress Champernowne, do not distrust me now. I'm not the one you should fear. I've been a good friend to your husband and would be to you too. Especially at this time, which may be your greatest need.' Startled by the urgency in his voice, I stared into his brooding eyes. To my surprise, I was sure I saw genuine concern there, not malice. His gaze shifted to the open laces of my gown, loosened to accommodate my expanding girth.

'Be assured, should your husband's condition worsen, I will do all I can for you and all your children... even the child you carry... should the worst befall.' A lump swelled in my throat, and shaking my head from side to side, I rounded on him.

'How dare you, sir! How dare you suggest my husband will not recover? He is strong and healthy. He will come through this ordeal. Why would I turn to you for help?' Harte ducked his head and took a step back as though I'd hit him. Clotilde, always by my side, steadied me with her hand on my arm. Her hushed whisper cut through my irritation like a sharp blade.

'Madame! *Je vous en prie!* I beg you! Hear him out. We all pray that Master Gawen will make a swift recovery, yet his injuries... they are terrible. His life is in God's hands. You must be prepared for whatever may come. It will do no harm to listen.'

'Perhaps... Oh... very well... What do you have to say?'

'Only this; your husband made his last will some time ago. I have it in my keeping. Call me if he is in danger. We must implore him to reconsider before it is too late.' I could feel the beads of sweat gathering on my forehead as I exchanged a nervous glance with Clotilde.

'What do you mean, sir?' Harte fixed me with an unnerving stare.

'I must warn you that the will he has signed leaves you and your unborn child without protection. Worse still, there is one who may seek to dispossess you further.' I gaped at him, left speechless by his words. He had not finished. 'I beg you to think on it. When you are ready, I will bring the will so that you can see for yourself. For now, I will leave you to the good offices of your maid. I will be here when you need me.' With that, he bowed and walked away. Clotilde narrowed her eyes as she watched him go.

'Well, that was unexpected. Whatever can he mean?' I asked. I hardly expected Clotilde to answer, and she gave me none, but sat down beside me, deep in thought. For a long time, my old nurse stayed quiet. At last she took my hand in hers, her roughened fingers comforting as they wrapped round mine.

'From what the physician told you, I fear you must brace yourself and prepare for the worst,' she said. 'I will speak bluntly. Master Harte means that should your husband die, you will have to fight to secure your children's inheritance. I think he is offering his assistance, and in your situation, you'd do well at least to consider his offer.'

The light dawned at last. If Gawen did not recover, I would be left a widow with an underage son and seven daughters, all in want of a dowry. Not to mention a baby due in three months' time.

As that uncomfortable thought settled in my mind, I took a turn in the garden to clear my head. I sought solace amongst the vibrant spring green of new furled leaves and lemon-yellow primroses turning their pretty faces to the sun. But all the colours of Devon in springtime could do little to cheer me. With dragging feet I turned and headed for the house to confront the tragic scene within.

A musty odour of sweat, iron-tinged from the blood, clung to every object in my parlour. It mixed with the acrid bite of brandy, wine, and vinegar used to cleanse the wounds. That smell reminded me that a fierce battle must be waged to keep my husband alive.

The tormented figure sprawled on the makeshift bed bore no resemblance to Gawen. In the early morning light, tiny droplets of perspiration shimmered on his forehead as he mustered every ounce of strength to sit up and greet me, cursing his weakness. It proved too much for him. Gasping, he allowed Agnes to lay his head down again. As I reached out to grasp his hand in an attempt to comfort him, his bandaged palm flinched. Pain contorted his face as he tried to hold up his torn hands.

'Have a care!' The agony in his voice was unbearable.

'Sorry… oh, Gawen!'

Seeing my proud husband brought to such despair and helplessness broke the damn of my sorrow. At last I allowed hot angry tears to fall unchecked, landing on the linen sheet to spread a dark wet stain on its crisp white surface.

'Do you see the state I'm brought to… Can't even lift my head to greet my wife…'

'No, no! You look better.' I was desperate to bring him some comfort. 'Agnes says you've taken some broth. It will strengthen you.'

'Roberda, I'm no fool! There is only one ending to this. I've seen many a shattered leg on the battlefield.' His frantic eyes darted around the room until they settled on Agnes. 'Woman, where are you? Show her.'

Without a word, Agnes pulled back the sheet. I flinched as she revealed the horrifying sight of his bloodstained left leg. Though I gagged, I couldn't look away. With the gentlest touch, Agnes replaced the covers, causing him to swear again as the light linen sheet brushed his wound. Gawen's eyes blazed with anger and fear, pinpoints of fiery light amidst the bandages that enveloped his battered head. As he drifted out of consciousness, his last words were bitter.

'Percival will return with the surgeon. What use am I without a leg?'

I stayed at his bedside that whole day and the next night. I dozed fitfully, only to wake with a jolt to check that his chest still rose and fell. As dawn broke on the second day, his breathing seemed more regular, and I felt able to accept Agnes's offer to take my place at his bedside. With heavy feet, I dragged myself up the stair and fell into a deep, dreamless slumber. The sun was high when Clotilde woke me.

'The surgeon has come with Master Percival. I'm sorry… their faces tell a painful story. They're watching to see if fever takes hold. They stand ready to intervene.'

I felt exhausted, hollowed out, an empty vessel, drained of all energy. Seeking confirmation I did not need, my voice cracked with emotion as I ground out the words.

'You mean the leg?'

'Yes, I think it's time to speak with Master Harte.'

'But can I trust him? That man! He's forever in the way, always hanging around Gawen! Why should I believe he's on my side?' Clotilde threw up her hands.

'If I speak out of turn, not as a servant, but as your true friend, will you listen to me?'

I looked into her face. A tapestry woven by years of love and devotion was there, amongst all the lines and wrinkles. If there was one person on God's earth I could have faith in, it was Clotilde.

'Go on, Clotilde. I am listening.'

'You wanted to believe your husband cares for you, just as you care for him. Am I correct?'

'Yes, I suppose so.'

'It has made you resent anyone else who claims the attention of Gawen Champernowne.' I shook my head. 'No... don't deny it. You see Master Harte as an enemy because you think he has taken your husband's attention from you.' I gaped at her. 'It was the same with Sir Francis until you realised he was the best sailor to save England.' Those words hit the mark.

'I see what you mean, Clotilde. Yes, I did resent Sir Francis, but then came to recognise his worth.' Perhaps she was right and I had been jealous of anyone who claimed Gawen's time. Now I thought of it, it had even come between me and my beloved daughter, Lisbeth.

Clotilde waited, giving me time to think, judging when it was the right time to go on.

'I beg you, give Harte the benefit of the doubt. This is a time that will test you more than anything you've faced before.' I bridled at that.

'Pah! What could be worse than a husband who locks you up and tries to divorce you?'

She threw up her hands.

'And yet you cling to the belief that he has changed!'

'He has!'

'Admit it. It's as I predicted. You are his means to another son and getting his hands on that dowry your parents promised. He's been clever enough to deceive you into thinking he cares for you. But to him you're no more than a brood mare.'

Her harsh words felt like a thousand tiny needles pricking me. But amidst the sting, I couldn't ignore her. The flame of her unstinting love for me blazed from her eyes amid her brutal honesty.

'Don't be a fool. Face up to it. Listen to Master Harte,' she said. Her voice was pitched low, but it carried with it the weight of conviction.

All those times I'd convinced myself he loved me flashed through my mind. How I wanted to cling to that belief. But, as Clotilde watched me, I forced myself to remember the times he'd ridden away without a farewell, stayed away longer than was needful. Could it be true? Had I really been such a fool?

'You are right, Clotilde. I'll hear what Harte has to say.'

I met him in the Great Hall, where pungent smoke from a new-lit fire pricked my eyes. Harte opened a small box and took out a rolled document. He unfurled it across the heavy oak table, his slender fingers gliding over the surface, easing out every crease.

'I've kept it safe since he signed it. I fear it will not make easy reading for you.'

Seated on an unforgiving wooden bench in the sunlit hall, I studied the document Harte had retrieved from the box.

'Impossible… it cannot be.' My hands carved through the air as if to ward off the truth written in black ink on that hateful paper. 'He makes no mention of me! Not a word! How can this be?… Since his return we have lived as man and wife.' I reached out for Clotilde's hand. 'I thought after all our troubles, he cared for me.'

Clotilde closed her eyes and pressed her lips together but said nothing. Harte's grating voice cut through my misery.

'I am sorry… do you see it now? You must implore him to add a codicil. He's made no provision for you or the unborn child.'

I read the will again. I scanned the bequests to the poor of the local town and to his servants. He didn't forget his brother Edward, nor his cousins, He even specified a ring, to be engraved with the words 'in remembrance of a friend' for cousin Arthur, and one for Sir Francis Drake! Gawen doled out basins and ewers (my basins and ewers) to his four overseers. But he left nothing for me!

Fury and disappointment fought with disbelief. White-hot anger won the battle, and I fumed as I re-read his words about our daughters.

'How can Gawen leave our daughters a share of that wretched dowry, the root cause of our differences? No one in my family in France has the means to pay it. So how can that provide for my girls? Why it's high time Lisbeth, Mary, Kate and Ursula were married. But he has never stirred himself to provide for them!' I read on.

'He makes Arthur his executor, yet Arthur is only twelve years old. What does this mean, Master Harte? What does it mean?'

Harte explained how Arthur would likely become a ward of the royal court, how one of the overseers might attempt to claim his wardship for themselves. How that would give them the management and income from all my husband's properties and leave me destitute.

'There is no mention of a widow's jointure,' he said, his voice now clipped and condescending.

My mouth opened and closed, but no words came. Harte continued.

'He's charged four of us to see his wishes carried out. Sir Edward Denny is returned from Ireland but kept busy on the Queen's business. Edward Seymour, his sister's husband, will not trouble you. But Richard Champernowne of Modbury is another matter. He's in debt up to his ears and he has a temper, as I'm sure you know. You must act fast to thwart his ambitions.'

'Richard? My husband's cousin? Are you sure?'

'I am. Richard has let down his guard to me on more than one occasion. Showed me he's resentful, envious that your father-in-law held Dartington. He will snatch what he can from you and your children.'

I knew Richard had a reputation for seeking quarrels and mistreating people. He spent heavily on maintaining his musicians and singers and living beyond his means. Pierre, the boy I brought with me from France, was one of them. Momentarily distracted, I shot a question at Clotilde.

'Have you heard from Pierre recently, Clotilde?'

'Have no fear. He's well, and such a talented musician, his master can't afford to upset him. But from what I hear, he's lucky to be in that position!'

The full force of it hit me then. I realised I had been ignoring the dangerous currents swirling around me. All the while, I was producing all those healthy baby girls, oblivious to everything else. Yes, I had held Dartington together when we were in great peril, managed the household and won our tenants' respect. But after Alexander died, I was caught in Gawen's trap. Consumed by constant childbearing, I had buried my true self. It was as if I had fallen into a deep sleep. It took the appalling accident to wake me up.

'What must we do?'

Still suspicious, nonetheless, I allowed John Harte to take control.

'We must get him to sign a codicil while he has the strength to do so. It's no use hoping he'll change the first will, but such a codicil could provide for the child you carry.'

Harte was right.

It took every ounce of my strength and self-control to watch my husband grappling with the pen. My jaw hurt from grinding my teeth together, as once again, he failed to acknowledge me in his last wishes. Gawen refused outright to do more than acknowledge that my unborn child, whether boy or girl, should have the same share as our other daughters – a share of my unpaid dowry – a share of nothing, for that money was not in our coffers.

His hands trembled as he attempted to sign the codicil. The sound of his laboured breathing filled the room, the only other sound the scratching of pen on paper. At last it was done.

Master Percival, the physician, John Fell, the surgeon and John Harte looked on. Percival squinted through his eyeglasses. Fell, a brawny, squat little man wearing a leather apron, stood at his elbow. With solemn deliberation, each took up the pen and set down their names, bearing witness to Gawen's signature.

It was near midnight on the nineteenth day of March. I shuddered as shafts of silver moonlight glinted on the surgeon's tools. Agnes stood ready, wringing her hands in her apron, with the ghastly array of knives and saws lined up on the table behind her. Without a word, I gathered my skirts and left the room.

Chapter Seventeen

Heartbreak

March 1592, Dartington Hall

In the early hours of the morning, unable to sleep, I lay fretting, fully clothed, on my bed. The child inside me was as restless as I, squirming and shifting, fluttering inside me like a captive bird.

I slipped from the bed and began pacing around. My chamber felt suffocating, the walls pressing in on me. I walked round and round like a caged lion. In my frustration, I grabbed the heavy iron poker and swung it at the bed hangings. I cried out, shouting words that would have shocked even the most battle-hardened soldier. This desperate attempt to rid myself of the bitter taste of his betrayal brought no relief. Frustrated, I pummelled my hands against the bed-post and hurled a pot against the wall, watching the shattered pieces scatter.

Clotilde tiptoed into the chamber and closed the door behind her with a gentle click.

'You must rest. Who knows what we must face tomorrow?'

'Rest? How can I rest? How could he do it? Even now, he refuses to include me in his will. He has never loved me as I love him! What a fool I've been!'

'Hush now. You will wake the children.' She tried to take my hand, but I yanked it away and resumed my stalking round the room. I didn't even notice the pain when my fingernails dug into my palms. In my despair, I lashed out at poor faithful Clotilde with vicious words, wanting her to feel my hurt.

'I suppose you feel smug! You always said he would not change! How does it feel, being so clever?' My thoughts careened wildly, a tempest of blistering anger aimed at my deceitful husband, followed by waves of self-loathing for my own foolish belief in his love. Amid it all, I dared not face the hideous reality that Gawen might die, leaving me a penniless widow, while his overseers fought like dogs over a bone to see who would have control of my son and his inheritance. Clotilde tried to calm me.

'Think of the child you carry. You must not punish yourself so. Come.' She drew me to the bed, and we sank down together to perch on the soft feather mattress, so close my knees touched hers. Clotilde opened her arms, and I clung to her. In time, my shoulders were still and Clotilde gave me one last hug.

'You will not sleep this night. Let's go down and wait together.'

Throughout the long night hours, Gawen drifted in and out of consciousness amidst sweat-soaked sheets. Sitting just beyond the door, I could hear the rickety truckle bed rattling as he shuddered when the violent shaking that the physician called 'rigor' possessed him.

As the sky grew lighter, Percival came to me in the hall, Harte a few steps behind.

'The fever advances,' the physician said. 'His only hope now rests upon the surgeon's knife. It must be done.' In an agony of indecision, I looked around in panic, seeking for someone else to take responsibility. Clotilde gave me a firm nod.

'Do what you must, Master Percival.' I said the words, though my voice seemed to come from somewhere far away.

Piercing, bone-chilling screams followed me as I staggered back to my chamber. Unearthly howls, sounds no human soul could make, continued all through the darkest hours of that interminable night. Those screams seared into my memory haunting me long after the harrowing ordeal was over.

Once Gawen emerged from his drug and alcohol-induced stupor, Percival reported surprising signs of improvement. Agnes tended to my husband's needs patiently and, despite the loss of his limb, Gawen's spirit rallied.

Several days went by. His voice boomed from the parlour, shouts, curses, and demands for attention day and night. He called for me, but I couldn't bridge the chasm of his betrayal. My wound was deep, as if one of Master Fell's formidable knives had sliced into the depths of my soul.

Days turned into a week, and Percival grew more optimistic about Gawen's recovery. Yet still, I couldn't bring myself to face him. Instead, I turned to Arthur and my daughters. It was all I could do to restrain myself from complaining about how their father had treated me. But I forced myself to swallow down the bitter taste of resentment. He was their father. Even now, I didn't want them to think ill of him.

The girls trailed around, not knowing what they should do, taking refuge in the comforting surroundings of the nursery with their baby sisters whenever they could. Poor Arthur sat for hours, gazing into the fire, with faithful Marie by his side. I tried to still their fears, put on a brave face, told them he was improving every day. I don't think any of them believed me.

Bess arrived from Berry Pomeroy, and I was glad of her support. Whenever the weather was fine, we took to walking in my physick garden side by side, as we had years before when I first came to Dartington, a young bride full of hope. Returning from one of these walks, I found Clotilde waiting for me

'Ah, there you are, *ma petite*. I've been searching for you.'

'What is it?'

'I have been thinking. It's of no use to regret what's past. No use to blame yourself. What's done is done. That's why I wanted to speak to you. It's time for you to think of the future. Do you still have the will and the paper he signed that night?'

'I do. Some instinct warned me to keep hold of them.' The will Harte gave me was locked in a secret compartment at the bottom of my sewing box. I'd secured the codicil too. Harte hadn't asked me to return them to him. 'Master Harte may seem genuine, but Clotilde, can I trust him?'

'That has been troubling me. He speaks of Master Richard as your enemy, but he himself is also one of the overseers named in the will. I have made enquiries. John Harte has a reputation as a money lender who puts his own profit before other people's concerns. He seems to befriend you, but can you be sure he will not seek to take what should be your son's? I wouldn't put all your faith in him. Better to seek advice from one you can trust. Master Bridgeman, the lawyer who acted for you before, is a man of honour. Write to him without delay!'

I looked deep into her rheumy old eyes and knew she spoke true. Should Gawen die, I knew my situation would be grave. In a sudden rush of energy, I spun round to face Clotilde.

'You are right. My mother would not sit here wailing and wilting and castigating herself. No more shall I. He may yet recover, but let me think… yes, Bridgeman will know.' She nodded and the muscles round her mouth relaxed as she gave me one last look before leaving me.

Writing was not a skill in which I excelled, but I could trust no one else with the task. I took out my pen and laboured hard to make a copy of the will and codicil. Many blots and crossings out littered the page. But it was readable. Next I scribed a letter to Bridgeman. Later that day, at my request, Clotilde brought William to me. Amongst all my people, I knew I could rely on him.

He stood to attention as I rattled off my instructions, then asked me to confirm.

'So you'd have me ride for Exeter and seek Master Bridgeman?'

'Yes, Jasper Bridgeman is an honest man, and he's a lawyer.'

William grinned. 'Ah, a rare man indeed, then.'

I allowed my lips to twitch a little at that. 'He is indeed. He served me well during my troubles with the church courts. It was not his fault matters went against me. I have written my request to him. Bring me his answer as soon as you can.' His forehead creased as he took the documents from me and secured them in a leather pouch.

'People may notice my absence. I'll put it out that my uncle that lives in the city has called me to witness his will as he lies on his deathbed. That should throw any nosey types off the scent! I'll go with all speed.'

Clotilde gave him a broad smile as he hurried away. She smoothed her apron and gave me a crisp nod of approval.

'Bridgeman will tell you what the law will allow.'

I did not visit the sickroom, leaving his care to others. Until one day, Agnes came to me. Her face drained of all colour, and her hands shaking as she gasped out the news I'd been dreading.

'I thought the danger passed,' she said. 'I left him sleeping, went to the kitchen for another bowl of pottage to strengthen him when he woke. When I got back, I noticed the change in him. The fever is on him again. The wound to his leg – it looks angry and red. Mistress, you must come to him. We must send for Master Percival.'

'Yes, Agnes. See to it. Send a boy to Totnes for the physician.' But I did not go with her to my husband's bedside.

Lady Day came, the twenty-fifth day of March, the day tenants came to pay their dues – a reminder that time did not stand still though my world was in confusion. They would all come, knowing that Gawen's life hung in the balance, wondering how his death would leave their agreements. With William away on my secret errand, it would fall to me to sit beside the bailiff.

I felt a little of the tension leave me when I met Blatchford early that morning under the White Hart badge. He was a reassuring sight, his broad shoulders all but blotting out the view of the courtyard. He carried the rent books beneath his arm and his businesslike air stilled some of my qualms. Before I could speak, an anguished shriek from the sickroom split the still morning air. A shudder ran through me, leaving me shaking. I looked up at the frowning bailiff.

'How is he, ma'am?' he asked.

'Worse, I fear. Every movement brings my husband searing pain. We must not allow the tenants in the hall where they'll hear his moans and screams.'

'I've set up the old schoolroom on the west side of the courtyard,' he said. His deep, firm voice steadied me. I shot him a grateful look, and we crossed the slippery cobbles, where a thin film of dampness lingered from overnight rain. It felt good to be outside, and I paused to inhale the earthy smell before I followed the bailiff, who ducked under the lintel and climbed the stairs. The room held many fond memories for me. The table was still there, the hard benches where my refugee women had sat, wide-eyed and fearful, as they learnt enough of the English tongue to get them by. I sniffed, and with a brisk nod, I turned my attention to the task at hand.

'Can I rely on you to deal with what is needful? Give no indication of the master's health, even though they will pry and suspect.' His brisk nod gave me all the reassurance I needed. I hardly noticed the stream of men in their worn breeches and woollen coats or the women with hoods pulled down, who sidled up to Blatchford with purses ready. True to his promise, he gave short shrift to any question about my husband, and we completed the business at speed.

Feeling drained, I rested all that afternoon, trying to shut my ears to the gruesome sounds coming from the room below. The physician arrived. Another day passed. Agnes called me again.

'He's asking for you, ma'am. If you don't go now you'll always regret it.' I nodded and swallowed hard. Her meaning was clear.

It was all I could do not to gag when the overpowering stench hit me. I thought it would overwhelm me as I settled into the seat beside him. I could see that Agnes had tended him well. The linen sheets were fresh, and she had spread aromatic herbs on the floor beneath the makeshift bed. Yet the pungent odour of decaying flesh was too strong for rosemary and thyme to blot it out.

Percival shook his head.

'That young rector of yours has just left us. There's no more to be done. It will not be long.' I leant over the bed, searching the skeletal face for a glimpse of the handsome man who had been my husband – the man I loved. In that moment, none of the bad times mattered – his cruel treatment, his attempt to put me aside, his arrogant, controlling ways, not even his omission of my name from his last will. The memories that flitted through my tortured mind were of happier times – Gawen, the loving father, patting a young Arthur on the head as they watched a hawk stoop for the kill; Gawen, the soldier riding off to fight the Spanish; that Christmas when our eyes met, and I was sure he loved me. If only God had given us more time.

A tear rolled down my cheek as I placed my hand over his. I felt a slight tremor, a fluttering touch, light as a sparrow's wing.

'Can he hear me? Will he know me?'

'Perhaps,' Percival answered.

'I would tell him that despite all, I forgive him.'

'Whisper in his ear.'

I bent over the emaciated figure and told him I loved him. His words in reply were soft as a breath of breeze across a summer meadow. I had to bend my ear close to his mouth to hear him murmur.

'Roberda… Ah… Ah… Roberda!'

I watched the light fade from his eyes.

Chapter Eighteen

A Widow

March 1592, Dartington Hall and Exeter

William thrust the creased paper into my hand and stood back. As I studied Bridgeman's response, my maids held their breath, making no effort to pretend they were working on their sewing. My hand trembled as I clutched the page.

'I must act without delay. Is everything ready for the funeral?' Clotilde and Marie exchanged a worried look. Steady, dependable William stood before me, arms relaxed at his sides, ready to do my bidding.

'It's set for the day after tomorrow... the twenty-ninth day of March. We've sent out to everyone who needs to know. The rector stands ready and we've hung the hatchments at the gate.'

'Hmm... hatchments?' The black strokes of Bridgeman's pen looked like lines of debris left on a deserted beach by the waves of a stormy sea. With my mind in turmoil, trying to decide how to put the lawyer's advice into practice, William's words floated away.

'Yes, hatchments, ma'am! It's customary.' I knew I'd heard that term before when Sir Arthur died but couldn't bring to mind the meaning. William tried to explain further. 'Painted boards with all the master's achievements. His coat of arms, ma'am. So everyone can know what manner of man has passed away.'

'Ah, yes! Like those that still hang within the church for his father? I remember now. We were supposed to replace them with a fine monument.' A shudder racked my body, and I felt suddenly sick as the horror of it all hit me anew. We were talking about my husband, strong, vital, bad-tempered Gawen, who now lay in the cold church, awaiting burial. Despite all his many faults, his last whispered words had been for me. In my grief, I clung to the hope he had cared for me a little.

A deafening silence pressed around us all, as loud as thunder. My thoughts drifted until I came back to the room with a start when Marie's stitching fell to the floor. William cleared his throat. I read the lawyer's instructions again and made my decision. I must act. For Arthur's sake, my grief would have to wait. I pressed my lips together and clenched my fists as though preparing for a fight and looked my steward in the eye.

'Thank you, William. Master Harte has already written to the overseers of my husband's will, I believe?' I swallowed the acid bile that rose into my mouth as I remembered he had done so without consulting me.

'He has. Master Richard Champernowne is here. He's come from Modbury with all his train.' William's lips turned down in a scowl. 'You'd think he was some high-born lord going to a king's banquet. It'll cost us a pretty penny to house all his people. He even has a minstrel with him.'

For the first time since Gawen's accident, I allowed a smile to creep over my lips. It felt strange, my skin tight as if it had set like cold pottage left too long in the skillet.

'Pierre is here? It's been years since I last saw him.' William gave me a blank look. 'Ah, you never knew him. It was before your time here. He's an orphan boy I brought from France, now a musician at Modbury. I must speak with him before I retire. But first, to business!'

I motioned for Marie to close the door. With a puzzled look, she trundled over the creaking boards and slammed it shut with a thud.

'Are you sure no one listens beyond the door, Marie?' I asked. With eyes wide, she opened the door a crack and peeped out. The latch fell again with a satisfying click as she nodded.

'There is no one there.'

'Good! What I'm about to say is for your ears only. No one else must know. William, have my horse saddled and ready before it is light, if you please. I must leave before anyone stirs.'

'Leave? What? In your condition... is this wise?' Clotilde's voice cracked. 'Think of the child.' The veins stood out on her neck as my old nurse turned to William for support. 'Tell her, Master William. Roaming the country with a baby on the way! It cannot be sensible.'

William's face flushed, but he said nothing. Clotilde looked at me, heaved a sigh, and her voice dropped low. 'Where do you need to go? What's the rush?'

'Master Bridgeman advises I must make haste to prove the will. He says that as the widow, with my son a minor, it is within the law. But I must beware, for Harte and other overseers will battle for my boy's wardship. Pah! They are in for a disappointment. There's not much in our coffers worth fighting over.'

William shifted from foot to foot, as he weighed up the situation.

'Ah, yes, I see, ma'am. There may be little to spare now. Yet with good management, the estate could yield a tidy sum. That's what they'll be after. That and a nice fat dowry when they find Master Arthur a bride from some wealthy Devon family.'

'Bridgeman says I must get there first. Prove the will so that I keep control.'

He shook his head. 'That I understand. But as she says... in your condition... is it wise?'

I cut him off with sharp words. 'Like my mother, I'll not flinch from doing what is needful.'

Clotilde shook her head, and her nervous fingers chafed at the kerchief at her neck. She had not given up. Her protests became more shrill. 'As I recall it, your mother travelled in a carriage or a litter. She did not ride through the rough country lanes of Devon on horseback. It's too dangerous. What if you should fall?'

William nodded and frowned. He was silent for a moment, pondering the options, until a slow grin spread over his homely features. 'I have it! I'll arrange it all! You'll only need to ride as far as Staverton. I'll have a carriage waiting there to take you all the way to Exeter. And no one will know you've gone.'

'What? Are you sure?' I couldn't help but smile as Clotilde, my valiant protectress, squared up to him and jabbed a finger at his chest. 'How can you arrange it? Where will you find a carriage?'

William shrugged off her derision and turned to me. 'Remember Master Rowe – the one who kicked up a fuss that time on Lady Day years ago, when we were all in fear of the Spanish?'

'A fat man who hogged the fire? We thought him a Papist!'

'The same! Papist he is, and a puffed-up fellow, full of his own self-importance. He's done well for himself and has a carriage of sorts. And he owes a debt to me.'

'How so?'

'I warned him when they were seeking recusants. He kept a priest, so they'd have taken him if I hadn't given him the nod to hide the man in time. I didn't do it for his sake, you understand, but he has a young wife and children.'

'Can we trust him?'

'In these times, he's even more in fear of being discovered. He'll not speak of it for fear I'll reveal his Papist ways.' He paused, and I waited. 'This is how we'll manage it. I will ride with you. I'll tell everyone the old man has died in Exeter.' I gulped. William, the most honest man I'd ever met, never told untruths. I couldn't believe he would do such a thing for me.

'I hate to have you lie on my behalf!'

'It is nothing! If it helps, if you can set things right for you and Master Arthur, I don't mind making a little pretence. But there will be an almighty row when they realise you are missing.'

William's fierce loyalty left me speechless for a moment.

'Thank you, William… er… let me think… well, they will not expect me to attend the funeral. It is not the custom,' I said. 'Tell them I am distraught and ill, overtaken by grief, and will not leave my chamber or see anyone. Clotilde, you must bring food as if I am here. Keep up the pretence as long as you can.'

Clotilde looked as though she didn't know whether to laugh or cry! In the end, pride overcame her concern for my welfare.

'That I will! It puts iron back into my veins to hear this fighting talk. You're like your mother, Madame la Comtesse, fit and strong. The child will survive.'

And so we arranged it all. I dismissed them to their tasks, yet still a nagging worry played at the back of my mind. Richard's prying eyes might spot something. When Clotilde brought my supper tray, I asked her to send Pierre to me.

'Tell him to come. But he must slip away unnoticed.'

Later that evening, in my chamber, Clotilde stuffed clothes into a worn leather bag. She opened her eyes wide and pushed the bag under the bed out of sight when a tap sounded on the door.

'Don't worry,' I said as I lifted the latch with a loud click and peeped out. 'It's Pierre.' I resisted the urge to wrap my arms round the young musician, who stood hesitating on the threshold. I knew that would only embarrass him. Pierre had always been self-conscious, aware that I was far above him. His bright face was as good as any tonic as he held out a bunch of pretty, pale yellow flowers.

'Daffodils, Madame. They grow deep in the woods. It is too early for lilies!' His shy grin was infectious, and I soon found myself laughing with him at the memory of the bunch of lilies of the valley he had brought to me one May morning long ago.

'You and I have travelled a long journey since then, Pierre. You, a famed musician, play for all the nobles of the West at Modbury. While I, alas, am now a widow. Does he treat you well?'

'My music is his pleasure. He treats me well enough. It's not always so for everyone in his employ. On the whole, he is a fair master, but he's given to fits of melancholy.'

'Ah!... I have heard of it. But your place is secure?'

'It is. But how may I serve you?'

With no more delay, I told him of my mission. 'We must keep it from them as long as possible. They will not expect to see me at the funeral but may seek me afterwards. Can you find some way to detain your master?'

'That's easy enough! I have a new composition. He has yet to hear it. If he runs true to form, it will entrance him. He'll not give a thought to you until he has the tune himself. It is his passion. That and making himself seem the highest, the most cultured, in all the land. And falling out with all his neighbours over money!'

I dared not probe further, though I could hear the bitterness in his voice. 'Thank you, Pierre. Do nothing that will endanger your position. If you can keep him occupied a day or two, it will suffice. Now you'd best be gone.' I took his hand and a rosy blush warmed his cheeks, still rounded as a girl's, although so many years had passed.

'God speed your journey and bring you home safe,' he said, his clear blue eyes clouded with concern.

I slept little that night. No more did my maids.

In the early hours, Marie was hard at work. The silver thimble on her finger caught the faltering light of a candle as she knelt on the hard boards at my feet. I smiled, remembering how pleased she'd been when I gave her that thimble a few New Year's past. She puffed out her cheeks and sighed with satisfaction as she drew the needle through the heavy woollen cloth of my riding gown.

'That's it! The last stitch is in. If you're challenged, no one will suspect you have anything hidden in your gown.' I smiled my thanks as the skirt fell about my feet, already clad in my finest leather boots. Treading softly, I went to my coffer where Diane the doll sat, as she always did. Ignoring the memories her painted face always stirred, I turned the key of the small sandalwood box. The lid gave a protesting creak as I lifted it to reveal the contents, making me throw an anxious glance towards the door. The sight of Gawen's signature on the curt note he'd left all those years ago brought me up short. For an instant my hand hovered, fingers shaking. I gathered myself, threw back my shoulders and reached into the box, flinging the contents aside until I revealed the shining wood below. Tripping the secret lever that concealed the hidden compartment, I drew out a velvet pouch, setting the coins inside clinking.

'My mother left this store of coins when she went home to France, after my release. Maman never trusted Gawen would stick to his bargain and reinstate me. She left this against some emergency that would leave me destitute. I've not touched it since. Now it must be sufficient for any costs I may incur on this secret journey.'

Marie's voice was soft and urgent. 'Hide it beneath your skirts, ma'am.'

I fixed the purse onto my girdle, hung it inside my gown and felt its comforting weight at my hip beneath the heavy fabric. With my finger pressed against my lips, I said farewell to my loyal maids.

Dawn had yet to break when, stepping to the left to avoid the creaky board, I crept down the stairs. In the vast cavern of the hall, the molten core of the dying fire cast only a dim light, making it hard to find my way. In the darkness, I bumped into a bench, sending it tumbling with a fearful clatter. Frozen to the spot I waited, not daring to exhale until I was sure no one was coming, then hurried on my way. Once outside, the feeble early light revealed the courtyard's grey stone walls, wrapping round the ancient buildings. A flutter of fear made me pause and wonder if I was right to leave this familiar haven. The thought of the avaricious Richard made me square my shoulders. It must be done, for Arthur's sake. That man would squander my boy's inheritance in a six-month if he got his hands on it.

I walked gingerly, as though the courtyard was paved with eggshells, with the papers secreted amongst my clothes, the purse hidden beneath my skirts.

As agreed, William had horses waiting beyond the arch, out of sight. I scurried to the heavy-legged mare, chosen for her imperturbable temperament. William helped me mount, and I manoeuvred myself into as comfortable a position as I could. Without a word, we were away. What followed was the hardest journey I ever made.

The mare proved placid, and we reached Staverton with no mishap. I hauled myself into Rowe's carriage with relief, only to find jolting over rough roads almost as uncomfortable as riding side-saddle. A night's rest at an inn, keeping my hood drawn over my face, did little to ease my aching joints.

After a torturous journey, we arrived in Exeter, where the hubbub on the bustling streets was deafening. I followed Bridgeman's directions and soon arrived at a house built of the local red stone in Cathedral Close. There we found the public notary Alexander Searle, in a cramped room that smelt of dust and ink. He peered at me from behind a table littered with books and legal documents, sucking his teeth, a sound that set my nerves even more on edge. Searle ran a hand through straggly hair as grey as a badger's pelt while I shifted my weight from one foot to the other. The baby fluttered and wriggled inside me, making me feel queasy.

'I can see to it,' the notary said in a nasal drawl. 'But you must swear an oath that you will manage affairs properly on behalf of your son until he is of age. And you'll need to pay me a fee!' He rubbed his hands together, and I wondered if I could trust him. As if reading my thoughts, he drew himself up to his full height, his eyes on a level with my shoulders. The irascible little man planted his hands on his hips, stuck his chin out and answered me with an edge in his voice.

'It's within my powers as the notary appointed by the Church Authorities. I can grant administration in this estate and see it registered. If anyone contests it, there'll have to be a hearing; otherwise, you will receive letters of confirmation.'

'No one contests my husband's last wishes as set down in this his true will. I will swear it.' I drew out my purse and paid the sum he demanded, then took the Bible in my hand to swear my oath.

At last it was done, and I had the probate signed and secure.

Leaving William to secure a few days' lodging for the carriage and horses, I made my way to the familiar house near the Cathedral's Palace Gate and knocked hard on the door.

Katherine Raleigh remained seated as her maid, a pretty girl in a spotless apron, ushered me into her parlour. I gasped and put a hand to my mouth to hide my shock. Walter's mother had changed beyond recognition since the last time I saw her. Her once bright hair, peeping from beneath a linen cap, now had streaks of white. It framed a face as wrinkled as a walnut. Only her sharp eyes were unchanged as she studied me. Wilting under her scrutiny, I stuttered, trying to find the right words of greeting. But there was no need to worry. Katherine's voice boomed out from her frail body.

'So he's gone! My nephew was ever a troubled soul, God rest him. I can guess why you're here in Exeter. You mean to take the administration of his affairs in hand?' I nodded, wondering how the news of Gawen's death had reached her so soon. 'Good for you!' she said. 'Dartington will benefit from a woman's management!' Despite her broken body, Katherine's wit and humour remained as sharp as ever. I took the hand she offered, feeling the paper-thin skin that covered gnarled, bony knuckles. Her grip was firm as I sat down beside her.

'Life as a widow can be hard, my dear. Your task won't be easy as the crows gather to pick his estate clean. But you'll manage, as all we women do. You're more powerful in widowhood than ever you were as a wife.'

I dared remain with Katherine in Exeter for only one day. A day to treasure as my strength returned. We talked of the past, of the refugee women we had helped, of her boys, of Sir Arthur, and of my children. I even told her about my wayward daughter.

'Once I had such a girl,' she said, her unfocussed gaze drifting away. 'Reach her if you can.'

'I'm sorry to have upset you,' I said, as she brushed away a tear..

'It is long ago, too late for me. But for you, there is time. Your Lisbeth may find happiness and come back into your life.'

'I fear I have failed her.'

The old lady leant towards me.

'Ah, the curse of motherhood! All mothers recognise that feeling!' she said. I could feel the warmth of her touch as she took my hand, drawing me nearer.

'I know. It's a hard cross to bear. We mothers, we feel it's our fault when our children step out of line or do things we wouldn't advise. A dismal refrain plays forever in our minds, reminding us of what we could have done differently, how we could have prepared them better for the world. We are never truly free from this burden, even though we know they are old enough to make their own decisions.'

Wondering if she was thinking of Walter, I asked how he fared at court.

'Pah! That boy has flown too high. He's about to get his wings clipped.' The old lady winced and shifted in her seat. Panic flickered across her wrinkled face as she realised she had spoken in haste. 'Don't breathe a word. It's not reached the Queen's ears yet.'

'Dearest Mistress Raleigh, your secret is safe with me. I'm unlikely to see anyone when I return to Dartington, let alone tell them any secrets. Whatever has he done?'

Katherine Raleigh's knuckles turned pale as she gripped the carved arms of her chair. The smell of beeswax polish wafted round us as she fidgeted in her uncomfortable seat. It was a fine piece of furniture, of the latest design. Yet even a pile of plush cushions heaped upon the rigid oak seat gave her no relief. With a sense of foreboding, she whispered, 'Married without the Queen's consent. Worse still, it's one of her ladies, Bess Throckmorton. It will not end well.'

'But he is Queen Elizabeth's favourite. Will she not forgive him in time?'

'Oh, the arrogant puppy thinks so. But he doesn't understand the depth of Elizabeth's jealousy. It won't help that they already have a child.'

'So you have a grandchild? Is it a boy?' I bit my lip and wondered why that must always be the first question.

'Yes, a boy, though I've not seen him. But then, I have other grandchildren a-plenty. The Queen has a long memory! It may be even worse for the Throckmorton girl. Remember how Queen Elizabeth treated Lettice Knollys after she married Robert Dudley?'

'Ah, yes, I remember. Lettice was my mother's friend. Is she still not reconciled with the Queen?'

'No, nor likely to be.'

The maid breezed in with a tray bearing fine crystal glasses, which she filled with canary wine. I took a sip, feeling it tingling on my tongue, and realised how tired I was. Katherine wasted no time and gulped down a mouthful before turning to me again.

'Boys are no easier than girls, you see. A mother never ceases to worry about her children. They are more precious to us than any jewel.'

The warm, stuffy atmosphere in Katherine's parlour made me drowsy. I stifled a yawn, but as the daunting truth of my situation hit me, I lingered, seeking comfort from the old lady who had always been a friend to me.

'I'm burdened with a string of daughters and lack the means to provide them with dowries,' I said. 'I have only one son, and I must safeguard his inheritance. Others are intent on seizing everything that remains of my husband's estate.' She took my hand and gave it a squeeze and waited.

'They gather in a pack like the wolves that used to haunt the woods in France. They think me vulnerable as a lamb, easy prey,' I said, putting my hand up to finger the necklace at my throat, feeling the smooth, rounded surface of each pearl. At least I had that in my possession.

'Who do you fear most?' she asked.

'If I am honest, it's Gawen's cousin of Modbury,' I blurted out, wanting so much to confide in someone I could trust. Katherine frowned and narrowed her eyes.

'You must mean Richard!' She let out a cackling laugh and the wrinkled lines on her face deepened. When next she spoke it was with the licence old people feel they have to speak outrageously. Her voice carried both mischief and amusement. It was clear, both in her words and her expression, what she thought of Richard Champernowne.

'He's a moody and troublesome man who can't resist meddling in other people's affairs. You've bought some time. No doubt Gawen held lands of the Queen?' I nodded. 'There will be an Inquisition. After that, no doubt he'll seek to buy the wardship of your boy.' I nodded.

A sly smile crossed her face. 'Let me think on it. Richard of Modbury married one of the Popham girls, didn't he? Hmm... Thomas Horner married the other sister... She died last year... Hmm...' Her voice trailed away, and she sat staring into the flames. I retired to my chamber, dismissing her words as the ramblings of an elderly woman. For the rest of my stay, we spoke of other things.

On the third day, I set out on the arduous journey to Dartington.

Chapter Nineteen

Duty

April 1592, Dartington Hall

As the coach lurched to a standstill, I slammed into the stiff, unyielding leather-covered board behind my seat. Struggling to right myself, I breathed a heavy sigh as William drew his horse alongside and gave me a reassuring smile.

'Only a couple more miles to Staverton, ma'am! I can see riders approaching. Looks like Master Harte and his men. Come from Dartington, I'd wager.'

I leaned forward and lifted the iron catch. When the coach door swung open, a rush of fresh air whooshed into the confined space, reviving me. In a frantic attempt to tidy my appearance, I pushed stray tendrils of hair away from my face, righted my hood and arranged my skirts in a more decorous manner.

I had only just settled myself on the seat when John Harte hailed me through the open door. He sat his fine grey mount with all the assurance of a seasoned rider, while the gelding pawed the ground and tossed a flowing mane.

With heart pounding, I scanned Harte's inscrutable face as he removed his broad-brimmed hat with a flourish.

'I take my hat off to you, my lady Champernowne! No doubt you've been to Exeter? It's easy to guess your mission.' I inclined my head and mustered a feeble smile. The urgency of his voice sent a chill through me.

'You need to be careful. Richard Champernowne will become High Sheriff of Devon next year. He won't hesitate to wield the power that comes with his position.' The force of those words hit me and my head drooped, like a daisy wilting in the sun.

'Look, Gawen was my friend,' he said, still staring at me. 'Trust me when I tell you, I stand ready to help you secure the future for his boy.'

I bit the inside of my lip. 'So, you have ridden all this way to tell me that? Really?' I said, shooting a look at him through narrowed eyes. He plonked his hat back on his head and gathered the reins with rough hands. The sharp movement disturbed his horse making it flare its nostrils, show the whites of its eyes and lay its ears back.

'Richard awaits your return,' he called as, without waiting for my reply, Harte set his heels into horse's flanks. With a wave of his gloved hand, he vanished in a cloud of dust which settled on the felted wool of my travelling gown like flour falling from the cook's sieve when he prepared a pie crust. Unsettled, I flapped my hands to brush away the dust, as if to remove every trace of my encounter with the man I dared not trust.

'All right, ma'am?' William asked, blocking the light in the doorway.

'Yes, yes! I'm surprised they've lingered at Dartington. I will face a stern reception.' The child wriggled like a butterfly trapped inside me. The movement added to the fluttery feeling in my chest, making me nauseous. But I swallowed hard and summoned my firmest voice. 'Let us head for home.'

When we arrived in Staverton, with William's help, I mounted up to finish the last leg on horseback. With the placid mare leading the way, I tried to work out how to deal with Richard. The mare plodded along the well-worn track beneath trees bursting with spring green. I stared straight ahead.

An unexpected downpour drenched us during the last stretch and my cloak clung as if it were a lead weight at my shoulders. Desperate to escape the mingling smells of damp wool and horse, my aching limbs drove me to seek William's aid at the mounting block. I slid down from the saddle in a graceless tumble, and straightened my skirts.

'You all right, ma'am?' William asked in a low voice as he peered into my face. I nodded, and not for the first time gave thanks that

I had such a kind and loyal steward. While I was recovering my dignity, Marie raced across the wet cobbles, her ample bosom rising and falling rapidly as she struggled to catch her breath.

'Oh! Thank goodness you've come, ma'am!' She took my travelling bag in her hand. 'There's ever so many waiting inside. We've been at our wit's end to keep 'em all fed.'

'I'm sure you've all done well, Marie.'

'We've done our best. But seeing to their needs isn't the worst of it, ma'am. That Master Champernowne, the one from Modbury, is in a rare temper. Then there's young Arthur, poor lamb. He doesn't know what to do, with so many fine gentlemen all asking him questions. And on top of all that, since they discovered you were missing, Clotilde's taken to her bed with a fever!'

Despite the nagging pain in my back, I dragged my reluctant feet over the worn cobbles behind her.

The distant hum of men's voices, interspersed with boisterous bursts of laughter, reached my ears well before I approached the porch. The notes of a lute rose above the hubbub while I shrugged off my sopping cloak. Marie passed it to her daughter Joan, whose hands trembled as she took it.

'Thank you, Joan. I trust all is well? Where are my girls?' A hesitant smile lit her plain face.

'All up in the nursery. Miss Mary takes care of the little ones. Kate and Ursula sit and talk about clothes. They try to peep at all the gentlemen whenever they get a chance.' Her face coloured, and she bit her lip.

'As well they might,' I said. 'At their age, my mind was also full of such things. But what of Lisbeth?' Joan shifted the weight of the cloak onto her arm and looked at the floor.

'She sits with an open book on her lap for hours but never turns a page. She's so upset about her father, ma'am,' she said. That did nothing to bolster my confidence. Lisbeth had been distant enough before Gawen's death. Now I feared she might have slipped well beyond my reach.

'Go now, Joan. Don't draw attention. Tell the girls I will speak with them all tomorrow.'

In the passage, I almost bumped into a maid carrying a flagon of ale from the buttery. She dipped a clumsy curtsy, spilling a few drops onto the well-scrubbed floor, before rushing off to refill mugs for the men who thronged the hall. I did not follow her but hesitated on the threshold, out of sight.

Griffin Jones, the weedy young rector, hurried along the screens passage.

'M-Mistress Champernowne, I hope I d-d-d-id as you would wish. They all came for the b-b-burying. We've laid him to rest, ma'am. I've just c-c-come from the church.' He swayed on his feet as a cough raked his slight frame. Although I had heard he was ailing, my eyes widened to see his hollow cheeks and pallid looks.

'You did well. Now, go find a drink, sir, before you splutter your last. Don't mention you've seen me. I'll be down to meet them once I've changed.'

At that moment Agnes appeared, nodded to me and produced a bottle from the folds of her skirt. She emptied the medicine into a cup and then took the rector's arm. 'I was looking for you, sir. Drink this. It will ease the cough.' He gulped down the dose, and Agnes ushered him into the crowded hall.

I forced myself to peep through the hangings and spotted Gawen's brother, cousins, friends, and familiar faces amongst the local gentry, all true Devon men. 'What will they think of me, Marie? The French widow who had feigned distress and grief, unable to leave her chamber, when in fact she had gone missing!'

'I'm sure you only did what was right and proper, ma'am,' she said. 'Whatever's right for Master Arthur.'

I sighed. 'Hmm… some of them may not see it that way.' I took one last peep at Richard who had his back to me, stiff shoulders, rigid posture betraying his state of mind.

'I must change my gown before I face them. Marie, hurry to Clotilde. Have her lay out my best black silk. I'll come round by the garden door and up the stairs so they don't see me.' She bustled away, wheezing. I followed her out into the garden at a more leisurely pace, careful not to leave muddy prints with my wet leather boots.

Outside, the rain had eased, though the air was damp and cool enough to make me regret handing my cloak to Joan. With the smell of wet grass in the air, I glanced at the tower of St Mary's Church.

The sight pulled me up short as I remembered Gawen lay there in the cold church beside his father and our two lost boys. With another heavy sigh, I hauled myself up the oak stairs to my chamber, where Clotilde waited, clutching her hands together in front of her.

'I'm pleased to see you have no fever, Clotilde! You did well!'

'I had no fever. Telling untruths goes against the grain, but it was expedient to say I had. Did all go as planned in Exeter?'

'I have accomplished it, for now.'

'The child?' she puffed as she bent to remove my mud-caked footwear.

'Is well – seems to wear even heavier boots than I do. Many a kick tells me the little maid or fellow is in fine fettle!' The wrinkles on her face melted into a faltering smile as she helped me out of my clothes.

'They buried him with all due pomp, though the rector is on his last legs. I can't see him lasting the year out,' she said.

'Yes, the poor man looks like a skeleton walking. That will be another problem to add to my list. I'll need to find a replacement.'

'That is tomorrow's problem. You have other concerns at present. Let me help you dress.'

I wriggled into petticoats, farthingale and gown and waited for her to tie the laces. As I ran my hand down the length of the skirt, my courage returned. Despite the gown's sombre black hue, the lustre of the shimmering silk marked me out as a woman of noble birth.

Clotilde took the last pin from her mouth and, with deft fingers, fastened the velvet stomacher in front.

'The plain one, I think. The blackwork embroidery is stylish, but the other looks more formal,' she advised, standing back to assess the overall look.

'Yes, and I'll wear the ruff. It gives an air of authority.' A glance in the glass confirmed it. I gave a slight shrug and threw my shoulders back. Armed in rustling silk, with my head held high, I went down to make my entrance.

The clamour of voices ceased, swallowed up by a bone-chilling hush as menacing as that which follows the sudden end of a mosquito's high-pitched whine before its sting.

Every head turned. The silence sucked the air from the room as I hesitated, scanning for a friendly face. I found one in Pierre, seated by the fireplace, his lute resting on his knee as though he waited for the cue to resume playing. Beside Pierre stood a boy with a cascade of blond curls and eyes as blue as the sky on a clear May morning.

Sir Francis Drake swaggered up to me and shattered the strained silence with a resounding click of his heels.

'Mistress Champernowne! I'm sorry for your loss. We will miss him.' I rallied my forces to greet him with a bright smile.

'Sir Francis! It is good of you to come. It would have meant a lot to Gawen.'

'Hmph!' He opened and shut his mouth, looking like a fish out of water as he twiddled the gold buttons on a fine doublet embroidered all over with gleaming pearls. The brave hero's discomfort made me want to laugh.

'I am grateful for Dartington's hospitality, though I wish it wasn't this sorry errand that brought me here. It's a sad business.' He waved his arm round the assembled men. 'It's given us a chance to talk. We need to refine our strategy against the Spanish.' That shook me and I felt frosty fingers of fear chasing a path down my spine.

'But surely all threat of invasion is long gone?' Drake's face took on a puce hue and his frown deepened.

'I wish that were so. There are reports of Spanish soldiers gathering in Brittany. Even now, King Philip is building another armada.' He shuffled his feet, glancing round the room as if seeking support.

'Do my people need to prepare for the worst once more?' I took a step backwards. 'Will we have to live on a knife's edge again, jumping at every false rumour?'

Sir John Gilbert's face was flushed and perspiration glistened on his forehead as he stood beside Drake. He wiped his brow with a lace-edged kerchief and, with a grunt, stuffed it into the sleeve of his over-tight jacket, the rich fabric straining against his added weight.

'No need to worry overmuch, Roberda,' he said in a voice as sour as vinegar. 'Drake always overplays it!'

Sir Francis shot a poisonous glare at Gawen's cousin and called for his horse.

'I don't bury my head beneath the sand like that fantastic bird they call an ostrich. Our attacks on the Spaniards in their home ports have not done enough. There aren't enough sailors, nowhere near enough trained men. Our harbour defences need strengthening. We must persuade the Queen to provide more money.' As he spoke, Sir Francis scanned the faces ranged about him and got a few nods of approval. 'I'll bid you farewell. I must return to Plymouth to check how the fortifications are going.' He turned on his heel and a serving man held out a woollen cloak to cover his elegant attire on the journey.

'But wait. Sir Francis!' I caught his arm. 'Gawen has left you a ring. I would discharge my husband's wishes. Will you wait while I fetch it?' I said it loud and clear and heads turned.

'Send it on to Buckland. My wife will deal with it.'

As Sir Francis swept out, John Gilbert grinned.

'Champernowne's musicians have kept us entertained.' He nodded to Richard, who looked like a bull confined in the pen, straining for the chance to break free. He crossed the room in a few short strides and loomed over me, casting a shadow as dark as the Devil himself.

'So you're back! I see you're not lamenting in your chamber after all! Your French servant has been deceiving us for days.' His voice rose, and like a pot over-boiling, he sputtered. So much so that a speck of spittle flew from his mouth, just missing my shoulder, when he spat the word 'French' at me.

'Clotilde was following my instructions. I had an urgent errand in Exeter.' I could almost see his hackles rising.

'Pah! What devious plans have you been hatching? I'm named overseer in his will. Harte tells me it is in your keeping. Deliver it now, that I may prove it and manage my cousin's affairs.' He towered above me, and I sensed everyone holding their breath, eager to see the outcome of this skirmish, the first battle of what might become a protracted war.

'Master Harte is correct. I have the will. But you need not trouble yourself with its proving. It is done. I am granted administration until my boy comes of age.' A hush fell, as complete as the silence that falls in a woodland glade when the fox is near. No one moved a muscle as they craned their necks to see what Richard would do. He just gaped at me, fists clenched, so I went on in my best imperious voice.

'I will assume control of this household and estate and manage my husband's affairs for the benefit of our son, Arthur.' The starched folds of my finest ruff collar helped me hold my chin high as I looked steadfastly at my son. 'Gawen placed great trust in our boy, naming him his executor. He will take up that role as soon as he reaches his majority. I will ensure he gets an excellent education and all the support he needs, that he may be competent to take over in due time.'

Richard's mouth hung open as the force of my frosty smile hit him.

'Pray tell me, Richard, will it fall to you to work with the escheator – Master Woodley, is it not? Will he convene an Inquisition to discover my late husband's land holdings?' He jerked his head back.

'So, you know the law?'

'I am well advised.'

'Well, you are correct. I will sit on the Inquisition. I will contact Woodley with the utmost speed! Then we shall see!'

I turned my back. 'Ah, Cousin Adrian, thank you for coming.' Adrian Gilbert lolled on a bench with the handle of a large mug clasped in his pudgy fist. 'I hope we shall have time to walk in my garden later. I would seek your advice on some new planting. Is your brother Raleigh not here? Your mother told me he has more pressing matters to attend to.'

Adrian let out a loud guffaw, and his ample belly jiggled, putting pressure on a doublet much too snug for comfort. Like his brother John, Adrian had a tendency to gain weight.

'Hah! Walt, you mean! Hah! He'll be in hot water! Aye, right up to his elbow, when the Queen finds out! The fool married without her consent.' People nudged each other as Adrian's booming tones caught their attention. Muttered exchanges broke out, and everyone forgot about the flash point of Richard's anger.

'I'll stay a day or two more, if I may,' Adrian said. 'You have one of the best cooks in the county here at Dartington, and old Gawen kept an excellent cellar!'

As I moved around the room, thanking everyone, a stark realisation hit me: Gawen was gone. The whispered condolences and weak smiles offered by these people could never heal the gaping rent in my world. Yet I moved amongst them, fulfilling my duty as the grieving widow.

Richard's brother, another Arthur, was engaged in a deep discussion with a well-dressed man I recognised but could not place.

'I'll see that you have the ring he bequeathed to you,' I said. But he was soon discussing the strength of the Plymouth harbour wall, the ideal position for bastions, and how best to arm defenders.

Edward Champernowne, Gawen's brother, gave short shrift to my enquiries of his wife. Instead, he insisted lawyers draft documents for the annuity my late husband had promised him without delay.

'I will set it in hand and will fulfil his wishes to the letter.' I gave him a brief nod and moved on.

Pierre's keen eye noticed the flicker of uncertainty on my face, and he took up his lute once more. He played a haunting melody; I guessed it was of his own devising. A hush fell in the hall when the boy beside him began to sing. His angelic voice soared up to the roof beams, transfixing us all. I cocked my head to one side to listen as the beauty of the refrain overwhelmed me.

As the last notes died away, the boy bowed, and a ripple of applause grew louder, with calls of 'Encore! Encore!' Richard's manner transformed. Proud as a peacock on the farmyard wall, he smiled and bowed, as if taking credit for the astounding performance himself.

While the musicians held everyone's attention, I slipped away, leaving my trusted servants to move among them with more refreshments.

I willed my feet to climb the stairs once more to find Clotilde waiting to help me disrobe. We exchanged no words and soon I slipped between the crisp white sheets, drinking in the delicate lavender fragrance from a bag she pushed under my pillow. The soft embrace of a feather mattress had never felt better.

Chapter Twenty

An Olive Branch?

Summer 1592, Dartington Hall

Summer followed spring, and the swallows' first brood fledged, but I had no time to enjoy my abundant gardens. Closeted in the office where Sir Arthur had often composed letters to the Queen, I tried to deal with the financial mess Gawen had left behind.

On a sunny June morning, I slumped back in my seat and tossed the quill pen aside, spattering a few drops of ink over the piles of papers scattered in confusion over the disordered desk. Ledgers and rent returns, parchments and indentures – none of them helped. Glaring at the documents, I let out an angry roar. No matter how many times I tallied the numbers, the answer was always the same. Gawen had left me nothing but empty coffers and a growing list of debts.

I was squinting at yet another set of numbers in the vain hope I might find some chink of light amongst the dark discoveries when Clotilde crept in bearing a ewer of ale.

'Can you believe it? He hasn't paid all the bills for kitting out the *Phoenix* during the Armada time. There were eighteen officers on that bark, as well as ordinary seamen. Their pay amounts to a tidy sum, and even now, it's not paid. Then there's the shot and powder and victuals. Tell me, Clotilde, how can peas and beef and fish and cheese and biscuit and beer, together with powder and tallow candles and nails come to thirty-eight pounds?'

'No? Surely not?' Her eyebrows shot up, giving her the look of a startled rabbit. For once, she defended Gawen. 'In that time of great peril, the Queen was unwilling to foot the bill. Devon's men had to ready their ships. So I suppose his spending was justified.'

'Well, I can't justify keeping those poor sailors waiting for their pay all this time. And that's not all! I've discovered Gawen sunk a lot of our money into work on the weir at Totnes. He bought the lease of the town mill about the same time as he pursued that ridiculous case against me.' My voice rose to an angry squawk. Clotilde wrinkled her forehead.

'So he held the lease of the town mill? Wasn't that a good thing? The past few years we've had plentiful harvests. Plenty of wheat for the miller to grind. Plenty of money for the mill owner!'

'That might have been so. But he sold the lease of the mill. Whatever would his father have thought?' I pushed back my sleeves and thumped a mug down on the table. A dark stain of wasted ale spread, encroaching on the papers strewn across the polished wood.

Clotilde scrambled to mop up the spillage as I continued my rant. I picked up a paper and waved it under her nose. 'See! Here! As we waited for the Spanish to come and lay waste to our land, my fool of a husband sold the lease of the mill to Jeffrey Babb. He's the one who will take any profits in the future, not us!'

She refilled my mug and handed it to me.

'Drink and try to stay calm. Anger solves nothing.'

I gulped down a few mouthfuls, then set to work again. Another document tied with faded linen tape caught my eye. As I lifted it, the red wax seals danced. I smoothed out the crumpled paper and pored over the writing.

'This is even worse! The deal Sir Arthur struck to secure Dartington is by no means complete. I'll need to take advice and I've no money to pay lawyers.'

'You will find a solution. Think of your mother and what she achieved.'

'She didn't have to contend with a husband like mine! Leave me alone, Clotilde. There's no more you can do. There's no more anyone can do!' Throwing a last anxious look over her shoulder, she left me, closing the door with a soft click.

I tallied the numbers again, trying to find a glint of hope. However I ordered the accounts, they told the same sorry tale.

Some time later, a light tap on the door announced Marie, bearing a platter of meat pies and a mug of ale.

'Cook sent these for you,' she said, looking for a space to set down her burden. Finding no other room, she rested the plate on top of a stack of dusty household account books, handed me the mug, and rubbed her hands on her apron.

'Clotilde says you've shut yourself up in here far too long. She begs you to eat and then take a turn around the gardens.'

'I have much to do, Marie.'

'Won't you join us, ma'am? It's such a lovely sunny evening.' The look in Marie's eyes reminded me of Gawen's hounds when they thought a bone was in the offing. With a brisk nod, I shooed her out of the door.

I forced myself to swallow a few sips of the ale, but despite the enticing smell of nutmeg and cinnamon wafting from the cook's delicious mutton pies, I couldn't bring myself to eat.

Leaving the untouched pies behind, I wandered through the silent hall, my faltering footsteps soft on the boards, and out into the garden. Bathed in the soft, golden rays of the evening sun, delicate snapdragons, carnations, and sweet williams created a stunning tapestry of pale pink hues. The drowsy fragrance of roses filled the air, the only sound a steady hum of the bees.

Clotilde was in her favourite spot in the arbour near the memorial to her friend Alain du Bois. She patted the seat beside her, inviting me to join her. I sat down, relieved to ease my aching back and settle into a comfortable position on the worn woodwork. Sunlight warmed my face as, squinting through half-closed lids, I watched Marie bend to pick a bunch of my favourite heartsease flowers. With a broad smile that showed the gaps between her front teeth, she offered them to me.

'Do you remember how we were picking these that day your mother came from France to release you?' I smiled and nodded. The posy did indeed bring a vivid memory of Maman, come to save me from Gawen's foolishness.

A burst of laughter and lively chatter floated over the clipped hedges as the girls gathered behind the yew hedge. The colourful beds where marigolds and pinks vied to outshine each other amongst thyme and sage blurred and I closed my eyes.

Clotilde's question woke me.

'May I enquire how your task progresses?' She conveyed a wealth of genuine concern in those few words.

'Not well at all, Clotilde! As I told you, my husband has run up debts. I can't see how we can repay them.'

She patted my hand. 'I'm sure you'll find a way.'

I threw up my hands. 'I should have kept a closer eye on things. You warned me about Gawen, but I didn't listen. You were right all along.'

She went on patting my hand. 'Being right brings me no joy,' she said.

'Sorry, Clotilde, it's my fault. I was so wrapped up in my hopes of love. Cocooned in motherhood, I let him take over everything – the household and the estate. Oh, he kept me busy giving birth to his children, just as you said.' Clotilde squeezed my hand, but I batted her kindness away as my smouldering anger burst into flame.

'I know I should not speak ill of the dead! But how could he leave me with nothing? I can't believe it! In that will, he relies on what he calls "the marriage money due to me" to provide for my girls. That accursed unpaid dowry!' Beside the hedge, Marie raised her head at my raised voice, and fumbled with the bowl of fresh-picked strawberries she was holding. A few luscious red fruits spilt onto the grass, and she groaned as she stooped to retrieve them while I ranted on.

'He's gone and left me alone to manage it all. Left me with a string of daughters with no money for their dowries. While that vulture Richard waits to pick my bones.'

'There, now! Richard of Modbury's not all bad – Pierre says he's a good man at heart.'

'But, Clotilde! I'm in despair. What will become of my girls? They will never find husbands! And what will remain for Arthur?' She let a little puff of air slip through her teeth. Her voice was soft and consoling.

'It's not your fault your family never paid the dowry owing for your marriage. Have they set a date for the Inquisition?'

'They have. It will be on the seventeenth day of July, in Totnes. Cousin Richard will be in charge, of course, with Woodley at his side.'

Clotilde waved a hand towards my swelling belly. 'By then, you'll have other concerns.'

'Indeed! I've had a strange approach from Richard's wife, Elizabeth. She offers to bear me company as my gossip when my time comes. Whatever would she know of childbirth? They've been married for ten years with no sign of a baby.'

'If I may suggest it,' Clotilde said, 'I think you should accept her offer. It may be an olive branch in your troubled times.'

And so while I fretted about the future, spare-boned Elizabeth, with her long face and frizzy hair, arrived to see me bring Gawen's last child into the world.

On a sultry afternoon, the midwife stood with her hands on hips and smiled. Margery had seen me through another labour.

'Your pains were soon over this time. You have another beautiful daughter,' she said.

I held the baby close, tempted to put her to my breast as I had my firstborn. But thoughts of Lisbeth pulled me up short.

'Call for a wet nurse, Margery. I'm sure there's one of the Blackaller girls ready and willing.'

Clotilde searched my face. 'There's no need this time. You may choose. There's no husband clamouring for another son.'

'I'm glad it's a girl. What cruel irony had it been a boy and him in his grave!' Margery gave me a sharp look as my voice rose. 'I have to solve our money problems. I can't spend months tied to a nursing chair. She'll do well enough with a wet nurse.'

'Are you sure?' Clotilde said, her brow creased. As exhaustion and strain welled up within me, angry words exploded from my mouth.

'Pah! You'd think when I fed Lisbeth myself all those months… you'd think that would have forged a bond between us that would last forever. But look at her now! Get the wet nurse!'

The two women exchanged glances as I passed the baby to Clotilde, who bent over her, cooing like a turtle dove.

'As you wish,' Margery said, gathering her things. She studied my face for a moment longer, then hurried off to do my bidding.

As she left the room, I heard her call. 'You may go in now, Mistress Champernowne. It's all over. All's well.'

'Quick, Clotilde! It's Elizabeth. Her husband has sent her from Modbury to spy on me. Hold the glass for me! She mustn't see me this way.'

But it was too late. She was already advancing towards my bed. I gritted my teeth.

'Well, Elizabeth. There you are! We were wondering what had become of you while I was toiling away.'

Elizabeth had not proved the most useful of companions during my confinement. As soon as my pains began, she retreated, leaving it to the midwife and Clotilde to bear me company.

She sidled up to Clotilde. The look on her face suggested she'd just caught a whiff or a foul smell coming from the garderobe.

'Would you like to hold her?' Clotilde asked, cradling the child in gentle hands. The woman's face blanched, and she trembled as she took the baby.

'I have little practice in such matters, I'm afraid. My sister was in Somerset when her babies came. Poor Jane! After losing her last boy just months after his birth, she never recovered.'

That remark hit a raw nerve. I exploded with a sharp reply.

'It is the lot of many women to lose their precious ones. Two of mine lie in the church next to their father.' She had the decency to look contrite and muttered an apology as, with an awkward movement, she returned the baby to me.

'Have you chosen a name?' she asked.

'Bridget. She shall be Bridget. Have you heard from your husband, Elizabeth?' I was eager to know if they had held the Inquisition into Gawen's land holdings.

'He is in Totnes. He asked me to tell you he and Master Woodley have completed their task. The matter will now go to Her Majesty's Court of Wards.'

'Ha! Well, if he plans to sue to have Arthur's wardship, you'd better warn him there's no money to go along with it. He'll be buying my husband's debts, not getting a slice of a lucrative estate.'

Elizabeth mustered a thin smile that seemed to stretch her sallow skin tight over cheekbones as sharp as daggers.

'My dear, after your ordeal, it's not surprising you're overwrought. Richard seeks only what is best for you and your boy. We can discuss this when you're on your feet again.'

She stalked off, her back held as stiff as a pike staff. It took all my self-control not to hurl my empty mug after her. So much for the olive branch!

Chapter Twenty-One

A Surprise Invitation

December 1592, Dartington Hall

'Me too! Me too!' Susan and Frances clung to my skirts, tiny fingers gripping the folds and kicking up a frightful din. No longer the youngest in the nursery since Bridget's arrival, the twins had transformed overnight from contented babies into terrible toddlers. Not to be outdone, three-year-old Jane joined the commotion, lisping, 'Why can't we come too?'

'No, girls, I'm sorry, you're too young to come to Modbury for Christmas this time. When you're older, there will be lots of Christmases. This year I'm sure Marie and William will arrange it all so that everyone at Dartington has the best holiday ever.' Marie nodded, and William, grinning from ear to ear, lifted the little girl into his arms, tossing her high above his head until she squealed with laughter.

'Of course we will, little one,' William said. 'The mummers will come to the door. There will be more marchpane and sugared plums than you can eat. We'll have carols and games every day until Twelfth Night.'

Mary, my dutiful second daughter, took Jane from William's arms, set her down and shooed the girls off to the nursery. Their giggles and laughter danced behind them, each vying to shout the loudest that they would be Princess of the Pea. As Mary neared the door, she paused and glanced at me. A gentle beam of winter sunlight seeped through the ancient glass of the tall window, highlighting her plain face. Her jaw was firm, set and determined.

'I'll stay here with them, Mother. I don't like parties, anyway.' It was typical of selfless Mary to put younger sisters first. A knot of regret tightened in my belly. Mary was more of a mother to them than I would ever be.

'Are you sure, Mary? There's no need...'

'I'd enjoy it more here, Mother, and you will be much happier knowing they are in my care.'

So, only Lisbeth, Kate, Ursula, and Arthur prepared to join me for Christmas at the Court House with Richard, sour-faced Elizabeth, and all their fancy guests.

'Whatever are we to wear?' Ursula caught my arm as I handed my reply to the waiting messenger. 'Our clothes are old and worn out. We'll look like country mice amidst all the cats in the county.'

I sighed.

'Given Dartington's finances, having new clothes made is out of the question. We must make do with what we have.' Ursula blanched at my tart reply. 'That's the least of my worries. I'd like to know what lies behind this unexpected invitation.'

A few days later, I summoned my girls to gather in the parlour. With anticipation painted on their faces, they crowded round the door, their lips slightly parted. Unusual noises, banging and the occasional muffled curse, announced the surprise I had planned.

With much grunting and groaning, four brawny stable lads bumped two weighty wooden chests down the stairs. It took two of them to lift each of the heavy coffers, with beads of sweat forming on their brows, as they set each chest down with an echoing thud.

'Thank you. But two? I asked for only one. This one,' I said, eyeing the familiar tooled leather top on the chest I had brought from France so many years ago.

The tallest of the four, a boy with carroty hair and freckles, rubbed his fingers where the iron handle had dug into his flesh. 'Us didn't know which to bring, so us brought 'em both.'

I thanked them and despatched them with a brief smile. Their laughter trailed behind them as they made a quick exit, no doubt hoping to avoid further requests to move anything else from the jumble in the loft above the nursery.

'Is this it? What's inside?' Unable to keep still, Ursula shoved me aside as I pointed to the smaller chest.

'I thought we might find something in this one to kit you out with new clothes, girls.' I studied the second battered coffer, which was covered in bat droppings and cobwebs. Its rusted hinges sprinkled a residue of red dust over the scrubbed floor. 'I don't know what's inside the other one. Get a cloth and clean it, Marie.'

The hinges creaked, and it took some force to lift the lid, but it was soon apparent that the chest was full of folded clothing, women's clothing. Kate and Ursula were on it in seconds, pulling out silk kirtles and velvet gowns, fur-trimmed cloaks and faded linen shifts with elaborate blackwork embroidery. Even at a cursory glance, the rich fabrics and bright colours emerging from shrouds of crumpled linen were of the highest quality.

The girls tossed the chest's contents across the floor, creating a pool of vibrant blues and greens against luxurious black velvet. The addition of pink and yellow sleeves added highlights, creating a breathtaking effect. In a whimsical moment, I thought it looked like a sparkling sea. I imagined the areas of darker cloth hiding mysterious shallows where fearsome sea serpents lurked. Ursula's delighted squeal brought me back into the room. She reached deep into the near-empty box and pulled out an old-fashioned gable hood; she plonked it on her head and paraded round the room, making Kate dissolve into hysterical giggles.

'Why did women wear such ugly headdresses? It's like having a church roof perched on your head.' That was when I realised who had worn the sumptuous garments stowed away to lie forgotten in our attic.

'These must be your grandmother's court clothes. Lady Mary, your grandmother, you know – she was Sir Arthur's wife – she served King Henry's queens.'

'Oooh – which one? Was she lady-in-waiting for the one who got her head chopped off?' A ghoulish grin spread over Kate's pretty lips as she pretended to wield an axe.

'I know she served the last one, Queen Katherine Parr. I'm not sure about the others,' I replied. 'These must be all the clothes she used to wear at court.'

Clotilde stepped forward with a broad smile.

'Then they are a godsend.' She held up a kirtle of shimmering rose-pink silk stamped with a pattern of Fleur de Lys. 'If we cut round the mildew patches, we can find enough fine cloth here to add new sleeves to your gowns.'

I fingered the soft silky fabric in wonder, thinking of the conversation I'd had with Bess last time she visited. 'Bess says big sleeves are the latest thing.'

Clotilde turned to Marie, whose face was aglow. 'What do you think, Marie? Can we turn out some fashionable ladies for the Christmas season?'

Marie bubbled over with bustling energy as she held a crimson gown up to the light. 'Fancy! All this hidden away all those years! Just look at this fine stitching. Oh, yes! I can dress you finer than any lady in all of Devon with this fine stuff!' Despite her heavy frame, Marie moved with an unexpected grace as she bounced from foot to foot. Clutching the red fabric in her eager fingers, she twirled the gown around as if she were dancing. 'Joan, help me lay these out so we can see what we can do.' Joan burst into giggles as she grabbed a damask gown from the heap to help her mother.

Everyone laughed except Lisbeth, who, as usual, held herself aloof with a scornful smirk on her face. As the titters died down, snakelike, she glided across to the other chest.

'So, what's in this one?' she asked, her voice dripping with menace. I followed her steely eyes, so like her father's, to the battered chest that had once cradled all my hopes of happiness. A lump rose in my throat and the room faded as the memories of my arrival at the gilded court of Queen Elizabeth flooded back.

My hand trembled as I lifted the lid. It gave much more easily than the other and there it was, wrapped in fine gauzy stuff, blue-green damask still bright as the day it was last worn – my wedding gown! As I sat down with a bump, a rush of lost dreams flitted through my mind, stirred up by the memories that beautiful gown had rekindled.

'Hah! I know what this is! You used to show it to me when I was little. It's your wedding dress, isn't it?' Lisbeth's voice was harsh as a diamond scratching on a windowpane. Deaf to the laughter and chatter as the others crowded round Marie, I crumbled under my daughter's harsh scrutiny. My head dropped as I remembered Gawen's stiff shoulders, his disdain for the ceremony forced on him in the Queen's chapel at Greenwich. Even on that first day, Gawen had shunned me.

I dragged a terse reply through gritted teeth.

'Yes, it's the gown I wore at Queen Elizabeth's court when I married your father. Cut it up if you need it.'

In three weeks, Marie and her team of skilled seamstresses, drawn from the house servants and estate workers' wives, wrought miracles with our outfits. Their lively chatter cheered the gloomy days of December as their nimble fingers danced over the sumptuous fabrics crafting wonderful new gowns for us all. Soon our Christmas finery was ready to be packed into sturdy chests and taken to Modbury on a rickety ox cart.

The girls' breath hung like a white mist in the chilly morning air as they clutched fur-lined cloaks about them. Even Lisbeth had braved the cold to say farewell to their favourite aunt. Summoned from Berry Pomeroy for a brief visit to advise on the latest cut of sleeves and ruffs, Bess was about to leave us. She chuckled as she clambered onto her grey mare to return to her family. As she settled herself into the creaking saddle, Bess bent down to whisper to Kate.

'I almost wish I was going to Modbury for Christmas, too.'

'Oh, can't you come too, Aunt Bess?' Ursula called. 'It's going to be such fun! I can't wait for Christmas Eve! We'll be there in time to see all the fine guests arrive.' Her cheeks glowed as she clutched her arms round her chest, wrapping the folds of the woollen cloak tight, as if she couldn't hold her excitement inside her a moment longer. 'Do come with us, Aunt Bess! It's going to be such a wonderful Christmas,' she begged, jiggling from one foot to the other.

'I'm afraid my husband has other plans.' Bess's grimace as she gathered the reins did not escape my notice. I was well aware of the strained relationship between Edward Seymour and Richard of Modbury. She put on her brightest smile. 'We have a grand gathering to attend at Longleat with the Thynnes.'

'We are in awe of you, my Lady Bess,' I said, dipping my head in a pretend curtsey.

Bess chuckled. 'Well, I'm sure you young ladies will turn all heads this holiday season. A Merry Christmas to you all!' With a wave of her exquisitely gloved hand, she steered the mare over the frosty cobbles. As the hoofbeats died away, Lisbeth raised her voice.

'What's the use of us turning heads, Mother? With no money for our dowries, it will do us no good.' With an angry toss of her head, she turned and headed for the hall.

Lisbeth marched ahead of me, taking exaggerated strides, her bright green cloak swishing with each step. Inside, I found Clotilde folding the last of my shifts, ready to send all our clothes on to Modbury.

'Lisbeth's right, of course,' I said as I flopped down onto the window seat. Clotilde shut the coffer lid with a snap and took a seat beside me.

'What do you mean?' she asked.

'She's right. Fine gowns are a welcome distraction, but my girls won't find husbands at the yuletide celebrations. We all know that!'

She put a hand on mine. 'Worrying won't solve anything.'

'You're always such a comfort, dear Clotilde. But I'm at my wit's end to know how to provide for my girls. And I'm worried about Arthur's inheritance, too. I don't trust Richard.'

'Do you know if he's sent a request to the Court of Wards?'

'I don't think so, not yet. But I can't believe that he would let any opportunity to profit from Gawen's lands slip away.'

Clotilde's arm crept round my shoulder while I twisted the ring round and round on my finger. The plain gold band was an unwelcome reminder that Gawen had left no fine jewels to me. 'Can you believe it, Clotilde? He bequeathed rings to Francis Drake and Arthur of Modbury. He left nothing for me but a pile of debts!'

Clotilde turned to face me, tilted her head back and looked me straight in the eye. 'Courage, *ma petite*. Go to Modbury. Let the young people enjoy themselves. Listen well. He may drop his guard.'

'Will you come with me?'

'I'm too old to ride such a long distance. You do not need me. Use your own good sense. At worst, you will eat well and enjoy the festivities. At best, you'll return with a better idea of what the future holds.'

Exhausted with the worry of it all, I rested my head on Clotilde's bony shoulder. We sat together until the light faded and she got up to light the candles. The air in my chamber was soon thick with a rank smell. I pulled a face.

'I'm regretting ordering we use tallow candles to save money!'

'No doubt we'll survive it,' she said, with a grin and an exaggerated sniff. Feeling much better, I squeezed her hand. Renewed energy surged through me.

'After all Marie's efforts, at least we will look our best amongst all the high-flown ladies and gentlemen of Devon!' I said. 'I couldn't have born it to have those women look down their aristocratic noses at me.'

Clotilde clapped her hands together. 'Remember, you are the daughter of the Comte de Montgomery and Isabeau de La Touche. You're far above these overblown women of Devon.' Her words put steel into my bones. I drew myself up, chin high, and paraded round the chamber.

'I am, and Richard Champernowne better beware. I'll fight for my children as fiercely as any lioness defends her cubs.'

Chapter Twenty-Two

Unsettling Encounters

Christmas 1592, The Court House, Modbury

At last, dawn broke on a crisp and frosty Christmas Eve. We mounted up, wrapped in Lady Mary's furs against the bitter cold. Calling out our farewells to the little ones who stood forlorn beneath the porch, we set off in high spirits.

A delicate layer of sugary frost coated the frozen grass under the hedgerows, where it lay still untouched by the feeble winter sunlight. Each deep breath sent frigid air searing through me. As I gathered the reins, I felt invigorated, brimming with energy. Although still apprehensive, I was determined to enjoy the holiday.

Urging their horses forward, Ursula and Kate kept up a stream of excited chatter. Arthur joined in from time to time with a quip that had them all giggling. I followed, then came a more sedate Lisbeth, although even she could not quite hide her excitement. Bringing up the rear of our small party were two strapping serving men, Joan hanging on for dear life behind the younger lad.

After a bone-chilling ride, it was a relief to see the battlements of the towering wall that protected the Court House. Grooms waited to lead our tired horses away as we dismounted, the clatter of their hooves fading as we entered though a doorway with the Champernowne arms carved in stone above our heads.

As I crossed the threshold, Richard stood stiff and formal. I inclined my head, though his words of welcome sounded hollow in my ears. Just then, Arthur of Modbury, my son's namesake and Richard's brother, appeared, framed in a doorway. I'd seen little of this other cousin who, years ago, had taken over Gawen's role as spy in France. When not fighting in the Low Countries he spent much of his time at his wife's estate at Crewkerne in Somerset. Unlike Richard, he had inherited the family's dark good looks. Every inch a soldier, he ducked under a low beam and extended a package bound in stained oilskin.

'Ah! Well met! My man brought this from France. There's no need for me to send it on to Dartington now. I can hand it to you.' His jovial manner was so unlike his brother's haughty words of welcome, I burst out laughing. I thanked him for his kindness and handed the parcel to Joan, whose flushed cheeks and shining eyes showed how excited she was to be chosen to accompany us.

'My people will show you to your rooms,' Richard said, flapping a hand at an old crone who took our cloaks, then led us up a winding stair. When we caught the hubbub of lively conversation coming from the room below, Ursula and Kate looked ready to bolt for cover.

'There's ever so many fine ladies and gentlemen here already,' Ursula said, fingering the delicate necklace she always wore at her throat. With a pang of guilt, I realised it had been a long time since they had been in polite company.

'No need to worry, girls. You'll look wonderful in your new gowns and I'll be there with you.' Lisbeth rolled her eyes, as if to say having me there might make their ordeal worse.

Dressed in all our splendour we descended together to meet the cream of Devon society. Glasses of warming hippocras awaited in the softly lit parlour, where a delightful combination of fragrant beeswax mingled with enticing spicy smells wafting through an open door. Richard spared no expense for the yuletide entertainment.

'Come, take a glass, warm yourselves.' Richard's welcome just about included us, though he appeared more interested in the well-dressed couple behind me. Weaving our way through a group of gentlemen who were rubbing their hands together before the blaze, we found Richard's wife.

'Ah, Roberda, Arthur, girls, there you are,' Elizabeth said, eyes bulging as she noted Kate's blue-green damask gown and Lisbeth's fashionable puffed sleeves. 'How nice you look… and you too, Arthur, how you've grown.' As her eyes rested on my boy, she swallowed, and something about her forced smile put me on my guard. Her thin lips turned up, but no warmth reached her eyes. Once again, I wondered what lay behind this unexpected invitation.

Pushing her way through the crowd, a middle-aged lady grandly swathed in widow's black bore down on me.

'I'm Elizabeth Stretchleigh. Which is Katherine?' She raised an arched eyebrow as she sized up my girls. I gave her a tentative smile as I pointed to Kate.

'Ah… yes,' she said with a brisk nod. 'A relative of my late husband's sent a gift when she was born, thinking in due time she would be of suitable age for my son, her godson. Perhaps you do not remember?'

Her condescending air put me on edge and I had no memory of any gift. I could only think that Gawen had failed to pass on this piece of information. The last thing I wanted was to begin discussions about a marriage. Hawklike, Richard watched me as, couching my reply in the vaguest of terms, I moved on to speak to others before she could quiz me further. The conversation was an unwelcome reminder of my girls' plight.

On Christmas morning, dressed in all our finery, we walked the short distance to St George's Church, entering through an ornate carved doorway Richard had installed at great expense.

I felt a surge of pride when Arthur offered me his arm and leant in to whisper in my ear. 'Come on, Mother, let's show them that the Champernownes of Dartington can hold our heads high.'

'That's well said, Arthur! You cut a fine figure in that doublet. I don't think Marie has had to alter it much to fit you, for you're almost as tall as your father was. He would be so proud of you.' Arthur's face turned pink, and he seemed to grow another inch as I took his arm.

Moving on, I acknowledged John Harte with a brief dip of my head. He gave me a wry grin and doffed his cap in response before he stood aside to let us pass.

The hushed church welcomed us in, the sweet scent of rosemary mixing with the piney scent of greenery that adorned every available surface. We passed tombs I took to be Arthur's ancestors, and as Richard's choristers lifted their voices in a glorious anthem, I glimpsed a smiling Pierre amongst the musicians.

After the solemn church service, the grand feast began. In Modbury's imposing hall, the air was thick with the mouthwatering smell of savoury meats, freshly baked bread, and exotic spices. The opulent spread, a magnificent assortment of dishes, was intended to dazzle the assembled company of Devon gentry, neighbours, and tenants invited to share Richard's largesse. After they removed each course, liveried servants waited with bowls for us to rinse our fingers and refilled our glasses and mugs with ale or wine.

Thankful for my position well above the salt, I exchanged pleasantries with a matronly merchant's wife and a jovial gentleman from Cornwall, seated on either side.

The Totnes matron regaled me with the latest achievements of her growing brood.

'...He's only four and he already knows his letters... and then there's our Meg, such a pretty maid...' I nodded now and then as she continued her monologue and let my attention wander.

Richard sat at the top table, Lord of all he surveyed, making the most of his exalted position. He was in deep discussion with Harte, who was tucking into a platter of shred pies with gusto. Every few moments, they flicked a glance my way. I was sure they were talking about me. But I couldn't catch a word of their conversation from where I was sitting. Elizabeth, demure as a mouse, picked at her food and kept silent by Richard's side.

As I sat at the board, my eyelids heavy, the buzz of conversation and laughter grew louder and the musicians' tunes more and more lively. Richard ordered his servants to push the tables aside to make space for dancing and games.

A little later I popped another morsel of gingerbread into my mouth, savouring its cloying sweetness on my tongue, and wondered again when Richard would show his hand. I couldn't believe he didn't have some ulterior motive for inviting us.

Seeking distraction, I pointed out my children to my companion, whose name I had discovered was Jane Hayman.

'It's a rare treat for my girls. Just look at them dancing with the Prideaux boys.' She followed my gaze to Kate and Ursula, who were blossoming and dimpling as the young men cast admiring looks in their direction.

'And is that another daughter?' she asked, pointing to a glum-faced Lisbeth, steadfastly declining all offers to step a measure.

'Yes, that's Lisbeth. She prefers to spend her time in quiet pursuits, like reading. She's not fond of the dance,' I said, trying to deflect attention from my eldest girl's sullen looks. 'Oh, and there's my boy, Arthur. Oh my goodness, it looks like he and those boys are about to start a wrestling match!'

'Ah well, Christmas is the time for games and such high jinks,' Jane said, sucking on a sugared almond. 'Let them have their fun.' I nodded, watching Arthur shrug off his doublet and in his shirtsleeves, give his all against an older boy.

'It's a joy to see the broad grin on his face,' I said. 'He took his father's death badly. It's the first time I've seen him carefree in months.'

'Ah, yes, I am sorry for your loss. I heard of it, of course. It must have been a difficult time.' Jane held my gaze, clearly hoping I would reveal something of my sad situation, which was no doubt the talk of Totnes. I stuffed my mouth full of marchpane to prevent further conversation.

As the evening wore on, Pierre and his companions played haunting melodies. A little unsteady on my feet, I went to my bed feeling bloated and heavy. Despite all the joy of Christmastide, nagging worries plagued me all night long.

On St Stephen's Day, Elizabeth cornered me on the stair.

'My husband wants to talk to you,' she said, her voice sharp and cold as the falling snow outside. I searched for an escape but found none. This was it. I followed her into a book-lined study where a dog lay stretched before a roaring blaze. Richard sat behind a large desk, with notebooks and sheets of music arranged in neat piles, an inkhorn and quill close at hand. He invited me to sit, but I declined.

'Well, Richard?' I said with an ice-cold edge to my voice.

'I hope you're enjoying the holiday? Arthur is a fine boy, is he not?' he said. I ground my teeth but said nothing. Faced with my silence, he tapped his fingers on the desktop and came straight to the point.

'I have written to the Court of Wards and await a reply. It's best for everyone if Arthur is under my care.'

I stood my ground and pushed back my cuffs as if squaring up to fight him. 'Better for you, you mean, since you will then tap into the income from his lands until he is of age! I know how this works! You'll marry him off and keep the marriage money, so that you can spend it on glorifying your magnificence even more.'

'Be reasonable, Roberda.' His patronising voice grated on my ears. 'How can you, a woman, manage his affairs?'

That did it. I exploded. 'I managed Gawen's estate successfully for years while he was serving the Queen in the Low Countries and in Ireland. Everything was better run under my stewardship than it has been since he returned. Had I been in charge, we'd have more to live on now.'

His jaw dropped. 'Whatever are you talking about? It's a valuable estate.' He was all bluster, but I could see I had him rattled. Perhaps it would help if he had some inkling of the dire state of the lands he coveted so much.

'Our coffers are empty.'

'But I believe the French have reinstated your brothers' estates,' he said, looking over the eyeglasses perched on the bridge of his long nose. Every word he spoke was like a sharp dagger, pricking me, goading me to anger. It was easy to see how his calculating mind was working; he wanted the wretched unpaid dowry that had caused all my woes.

'Their titles, my ruined home at Ducey, perhaps so. But none of the money that the French Crown took. My mother lives in penury at Pontorson. While the fighting continues over there, that will not change.'

He adjusted his glasses, then raised his voice. 'Look, be reasonable, Roberda. Arthur can come here.' He nodded to his wife, who seemed to shrink in her seat. 'Elizabeth would love to have him here. She'll be a mother to him.'

I gave the woman my most withering stare. 'Arthur already has a mother. He needs no other,' I said, icily polite.

Richard's patience broke. He stood up, pushing his chair back with a clatter. 'Roberda. You must see what is best for the boy!'

I did not deign to reply. Across his desk we faced off against each other like men sizing each other up at the start of a wrestling match. An uncomfortable silence stretched between us, neither of us wishing to give ground. At last he spoke. 'We'll return to this. But now I have more important matters to discuss with others.' He turned away, giving a disdainful flick of his hand to dismiss me as he would a servant.

In a great whirl of silk, I flounced round and shot out of the door. How I reached the chamber allotted to us, I'll never know. I threw myself down on the bed and beat my fists on the pillow.

I slept little that night, tossing in the bed I shared with Lisbeth. In a moment of madness, I imagined taking Arthur and the girls to France and throwing myself at the mercy of my family. But the last I'd heard, my brothers, Jacques, Giles, Gedeon, and young Gabriel, were all embroiled in the fighting that continued to tear the country of my birth apart. My mother, so far as I knew still lived poor as a church mouse at Pontorson, and my sisters were all busy with their own families. It was only then that I remembered the package of letters.

On the next day, while everyone was revelling in the festivities of the Feast of St John, I slipped away to a secluded corner in the solar with the oilskin-wrapped package in my hands. I dared not hope that what Arthur of Modbury's man had brought from France would offer me a solution.

Seated on a cushioned bench, bathed in the watery winter sunlight filtering in through the solar window, I listened to the faint echoes of music and merriment drifting up from below. Deep in thought, I traced my fingertips over the package's glossy oilskin covering, which bore many stains from its long journey to Modbury. With slow, deliberate fingers, I peeled it away to reveal a stack of battered letters that had taken weeks, months, some even years, to reach me.

An unfamiliar clerkly hand had scrawled across the front of the first I picked up, though it bore Maman's seal. I bit my lip, wondering if this meant my mother, who had always taken such pride in wielding her pen, could no longer write her own letters.

I read them all, a jumbled mixture bearing confused news, some recent, most long overtaken by new events. Amongst it all, one horrific fact stood out. As my chest tightened, I threw up my hands, causing the pages to scatter on the rush matting near my toes. The anguished wail that echoed around the empty room didn't seem to come from my own lips.

His footsteps on the stairs must have been as soft as a whisper. Only when his rich baritone voice sliced through the silence did I jump from my seat and whirl around to confront the intruder.

'May I be of assistance?' he said. 'You seem distraught.'

I found myself facing a commanding figure, tall and broad-shouldered, with hair that caught the light like a shimmering silver moonbeam.

I didn't recognise the suave gentleman who clasped my fingers in a gentle grip. But his warm touch was comforting as he guided me back to my seat. As soon as our eyes met, a surprising wave of trust washed over me.

Without releasing my hand, he settled himself and waited. A splutter of words came from my mouth in an incoherent stream.

'News of my family in France! I should have noticed... it's been so long since I heard from them... too much absorbed in my small world... I didn't know...'

'Is it bad news?' he asked as the black edge of the letter from my sister caught his eye. 'Ah, I see it is. It can be so hard to bear, can't it?'

I nodded. 'I didn't even know... my brother Giles died in battle.' I felt dizzy as the shock sank in. 'Giles was such a handsome boy. We grew up together but I haven't seen him for years. I can't believe he's gone.'

My companion said nothing but kept his eyes on my face as he patted my hand. My voice broke as an angry flame flared hot amongst my sorrow. 'He was fighting to secure the French Throne for the Protestant king, Henri of Navarre. Why can't they all agree that by his blood he's the rightful king? But the Catholics, the Guise family, want one of their own to rule. Pah! All for religion and power. Those wars blighted my childhood! Will they never end!'

With infinite patience, he drew a silk kerchief from his elegant, tailored cuff and handed it to me. With shaking hands, I mopped at my cheeks, thankful I had put no rouge or cinnabar on my face. As if released from a vow of silence, I poured out all my troubles.

'I'm sorry. It is all too much! One brother is dead, others still fight for the Huguenot cause. My mother is too ill to write in her own hand. My husband is dead, leaving me penniless, my daughters without hope of marriage, and my son is about to lose his inheritance.'

'If it pleases you, if it eases your mind to tell it, I will listen,' he said.

I shook my head. 'I fear you will think me foolish, sir.' There was a glint in his calm grey eyes.

'I see only a valiant and beautiful lady in distress,' he said. I stole a cautious glance at him. 'Let me introduce myself, Mistress Champernowne. I am Thomas Horner of Mells in the County of Somerset.' My head lifted. I had heard that name before? It came to me. Katherine Raleigh had mentioned him when we sat together in her cosy Exeter house.

'Oh no! Forgive me. I should not have spoken so!'

'Have no fear. Anything you say will go no further.' His voice was kind and gentle as a caress. 'As I think perhaps you realise, my late wife was a sister to Richard's wife, Elizabeth. Richard is not the easiest of men. Believe me, I understand Elizabeth's situation well, and yours too. Mistress Raleigh speaks so well of you.'

I felt over-hot all of a sudden, and with an abrupt movement, I stood up, snatching my hand from his.

'Sir, I thank you for your kindness.'

'It is nothing. I hope when you feel more composed, you will permit me to speak to you again. If I may, I would like to help you get more certain news of your family in France.'

With panic guiding me, I fled, heading for the door. As I reached for the handle, I turned. He was gazing at me with such a strange longing while that wistful smile played on his lips. To my amazement, a gentle flutter danced somewhere deep inside me, a faint spark kindling a sensation I had not felt in years.

Chapter Twenty-Three

A Hunting We Will Go

Christmas 1592, The Court House, Modbury

Arthur turned his back on me. By the window, my son shuffled from foot to foot, fidgeting with the leather-bound volume he held in his hand. I waited. It seemed a long time before he cleared his throat and spoke up.

'I don't think I'll hunt today. I'd rather finish this book.'

Moving closer, I put my hand on his shoulder.

'But, Arthur, it's the last day of December! It's such a fine morning. See, the snow has all melted.' I pointed to the grassy lawn beyond the knot garden. 'It's a lovely day for hunting, and all the other boys are going. It's traditional at Yuletide.'

'No thanks. I'll stay with my book.'

I stepped between him and the window and took the book from him. I turned it over, ran my fingers over the embossed lettering, and opened it. The faint, musty odour of aged paper hinted that Arthur had not turned a page for some time. Richard, a man of cultured aspirations, had a well-stocked library, and I suspected my son had plucked the book from its shelves.

'An intriguing tale, no doubt. But, Arthur, this is not like you. No one would call you a studious fellow.'

A blush crept over his beardless cheeks and he looked at his feet. I noticed his scuffed leather shoes, something I had failed to consider when we kitted ourselves out for the Christmas visit.

'I understand, my boy. Mothers know these things.' Arthur blinked hard, trying his best not to cry. As I took his hand in mine, I marvelled to see his fingers were now longer than my own. My little boy was on the brink of manhood.

'Have you ridden out to hunt at all since your father's accident?' I put the question as gently as I could, but still it unnerved him. His cheeks were now the colour of my best red silk petticoat.

'Er... um... no.' He shook his head. 'I can't forget it.'

My grip tightened on his hand before I released it. The image of Gawen's fall replayed in my mind, the horse dragging his father through the dense woods, his body bouncing off roots and tree trunks. The horror of that moment must have left an indelible mark on Arthur's memory.

My motherly instincts took over.

'How would it be if I came along with you? We could face it together.'

'Would you?' he said, his face brightening.

Neither of us had heard Lisbeth creeping into the room behind us. Startled, we both jumped when she spoke.

'I'll come too. We'll give you company, brother. It's time you got out and enjoyed such things again. Just give Mother and me time to change into our riding gowns.' Her helpful offer surprised me and I flashed her a grateful smile as we hurried to find Joan to help us prepare.

Joan had come out of her shell and was enjoying her new status as our lady's maid. She was soon pinning a veil onto Lisbeth's hat. With a grin, she turned to me. 'Oooh, ma'am! That green riding gown suits you so well.' Her hand flew to her mouth, and she gasped. 'I didn't mean to speak out of turn, ma'am, but it does. That colour is just right.'

'Do you think so?' I said, preening before the glass she held. The image I saw reflected there surprised me, for my cheeks looked rosy, my eyes bright. 'Do you think they'll criticise me for not being in deepest black, like that haughty woman Elizabeth Stretchleigh? Her husband's been dead for years!' Joan looked doubtful but didn't venture an opinion.

'Well, it's the only thing I have for riding, so they must think what they will,' I said, running my hand over the velvet lapels. Lisbeth smirked while Joan bent over the coffer, all but disappearing into it as she rummaged around amongst the remaining shifts and sleeves.

'All you need is a cap to set it off. Ah! Here it is! From Lady Mary's chest!' She held up an old-fashioned gentleman's bonnet of sumptuous green velvet with a bobbing white plume. I turned the cap in my hand and noticed letters embroidered into the silk lining.

'G.C.? Now, who can that be? Not Gawen, for I've never seen him wear such a hat.'

Lisbeth, impatient to join the others, snapped at me. 'My grandmother's first husband, the famous George Carew, of course! He went down with that ship in old King Henry's time. When England was at war with the French.' She put a nasty emphasis on the last word. With a poisonous glare at me, Lisbeth rolled her eyes and muttered an aside to Arthur, just loud enough for me to hear,

'Tsk! Do you see our mother? She's acting like a lovesick girl. And what about that feather? I suppose it's the French way. Just like her!' With that she marched out of the open door.

For a moment, I forgot to breathe as disappointment and anger battled within me. How could my own daughter still believe the wicked lies told about me so long ago? Anger won the contest for my emotions. I swallowed the sting of her hurtful words, rammed the bonnet onto my head, set the feather at a jaunty angle and marched after her. As I tripped down the stairs it did occur to me that there might be a grain of truth in what Lisbeth had said. I dare not own the feelings kindled by my meeting with Thomas Horner.

When I met Richard's wife on the stairs, curiosity overcame prudence.

'Ah, Elizabeth, you're not joining the hunt?' I took in her fine gown of dark tawny velvet, which would certainly not be suitable for riding.

'No, I prefer to stay within,' she said. 'You, though, seem ready for the chase!' She squinted at my bright green outfit, yet I did not waver under her disparaging scrutiny.

'I think I met your late sister's husband yesterday,' I said, fishing for information.

'Thomas Horner, you mean?' she asked, giving me a condescending glare. 'He arrived late yesterday. He's been busy with some business – he's a wealthy man, in the cloth trade, of course, but I expect it was his duties as a justice of the peace in Somerset, or some parliamentary business that delayed him. Oh, yes, Thomas is an important man.' Her tone implied he would have no time for the likes of me. I nodded and moved on, hoping she had not noticed the colour rising in my cheeks.

In the crowded courtyard, riders hurried from the house as horses champed at the bit. Richard's hounds milled around, straining at leashes. Soon they were getting under the horses' hooves, yelping when a well-aimed kick hit the mark.

As I waited, seated on a patient grey mare, I noticed a tall figure striding towards a magnificent bay stallion. He might not be a young man, but Thomas moved with the energy and grace of a man half his age as he climbed lightly into the saddle. The beast's nostrils flared as it pawed the ground, sending sparks flying from the cobbles, but in no time, he had the fiery animal under control and looked about him. A delicious prickle ran down the back of my neck when he glanced my way and raised his whip in greeting.

The terrain beyond the Court House was a striking contrast to the wooded slopes around Dartington. It stretched out, more open and expansive, perfect for the chase.

At first I rode beside Arthur, whose rigid posture set his mount prancing. But when the brassy notes of the horn sounded shrill on the frosty air, he let go. A wide grin spread across his face and he gave the horse its head, leaving Lisbeth and me far behind. Horses thundered over the hillside and the hounds gave voice, and I caught the thrill of the chase too. But on my stolid mare, I couldn't keep pace with Arthur. He was among the first at the kill, calling out to the others and revelling in his moment. By the time I reached them, he was bubbling over with excitement. I doubted he would ever be reluctant to hunt again.

I turned away, not wanting to see the last moments of so proud a creature. The huntsman dispatched the graceful hart, and his men butchered the animal. Lisbeth remained captivated, transfixed by the grisly scene. She watched, fascinated, as they cut out the liver and lights, while a metallic smell tainted the crisp air.

'They call it the umbles. They'll take it to the kitchens to make umble pie for the poor. Do you think our insides look like that?'

she asked. Horrified, I stared at her with my mouth open. Arthur chuckled and drew his horse between ours.

'What a thing to ask! How should I know? Why not ask your physician friend? I'm sure he'll tell you, Lisbeth,' he said. Dripping pure disdain, Lisbeth kicked her mount into a trot and rode away.

'What was that about?' I asked.

'Haven't you noticed? She's forever talking to that fat doctor. What's his name... the one with the bald head?' I swayed in the saddle and had to right myself.

'You don't mean she's taken a fancy to him?'

Arthur laughed again. 'No, it's nothing like that. She's just obsessed with medicine and potions and doctoring and stuff. She spends hours and hours in the still room with Agnes. Ever since Father...' His voice trailed away, and he turned for home.

I followed more sedately, wondering how I had missed Lisbeth's interest in matters medical. Working with Agnes in the still room was one thing, but it wasn't proper for a girl to be delving into the gory details of how bodies worked.

But I soon forgot all about my daughter when Thomas caught up with me and matched his horse stride for stride with mine.

'It's good to see you enjoying the hunt,' he said, holding my gaze. 'It's brought roses to your cheeks.' According to Joan, my cheeks had been shining even before I set out from the cosy house into the chilly December air. I didn't want to admit to myself the true reason. I had lain awake all night, replaying my conversation with the silver-haired gentleman the day before.

A stinging breeze whistled and whipped through the trees, driving us to seek refuge beneath the spreading branches of a mighty oak. Stripped of its leafy canopy, stark winter twigs pointing skywards, the majestic tree offered little shelter from the icy blast. And yet I felt a warm glow spreading from the core of my being.

Thomas stirred a whirlwind of emotions in me, an intoxicating mixture of guilt, apprehension, and excitement. To hide my confusion, I made to turn away, but he steered his horse alongside. A strong gust whipped at my skirts and the horses tossed their heads.

'Further down we'll come under the lea of the hill. Shall we go on? May I accompany you on the ride home?' I nodded my assent and tugged my green hat down low. I didn't miss the playful twinkle in his eye as he raised his voice over the blustery wind. 'If I may say so, you look very well and that is a fine hat.'

At the bottom of the slope, sheltered from the worst of the weather, we slowed our mounts to a walk. We chatted about inconsequential matters – I know not what – and I felt a spring release inside me, as though I was waking from a long sleep. I felt light as air when we reached the courtyard and Thomas helped me from the saddle. His warm hand against mine sent a thrill through me, as though my insides were vibrating.

Over his shoulder I saw Lisbeth watching me from the step and I yanked my hand from his. Flustered, I fled, not sure I was ready for the feelings that Thomas Horner had wakened in me.

The remaining days of the holiday passed in a haze of festive jollity. Mummers entertained us with their plays and songs, and I laughed as loud as any at the antics of the fool Richard had appointed his Lord of Misrule. Pierre and the musicians performed new airs to delight us all. Yet I felt detached from the merriment, as, in my panic, I tried to avoid Thomas.

He kept his distance, only exchanging a few innocuous words now and then as he moved amongst the revellers. I wondered if I was mistaken. I had squandered my love on Gawen, who had not even cared enough for me to make proper provision in his will. Perhaps once again, I was looking for something that was not there. I wished Clotilde was with me to give me her good counsel.

On Twelfth Night, the noise level rose another notch, and the dancing was fast and furious. I declined all offers to join the dance, lest I give Lisbeth an excuse to judge me frivolous. She was always talking to the fat physician, but I dared not risk a scene in front of Richard's guests. I would have to tackle it when we were home.

The Modbury cook, a man of generous proportions, beamed as he wheeled in the Twelfth cake, and Kate giggled when she found the dried bean in her slice.

'You are Queen of the Bean. Your wish is our command,' the Lord of Misrule announced amid great hilarity. I left them to their fun, and collecting the letters from France, I made my way to the solar. We would return to Dartington on the morrow, and I wanted to read them again. Most of all, I needed time to think.

A little later Thomas found me in the empty room, plucking at my kerchief and pacing up and down, the letters thrown down on Richard's upholstered window seat. Thomas's voice was soft and earnest.

'I would not presume upon you. But I must tell you this. I would do anything in my power to help you, Roberda.' My fingers wouldn't keep still, twisting the lace-edged kerchief round and round until I had wrapped my hand up in it as tight as a bandage. I couldn't frame the words to give him any reply.

'Could your brothers come to your aid?' he asked, pointing to the letters lying on the velvet cushions.

Suddenly wary, I swallowed hard. His question echoed Richard's. Could his interest in me be nothing but a ploy to help his dead wife's sister? I threw my head up and stuck out my chin.

'My French relations lack the means to provide dowries for my daughters. Why, my own is still outstanding! Thank you, sir, but there is nothing you can do.' He staggered backwards a pace and shook his head, as if my formal tone had struck him a mortal blow.

Silence hung in the air like a fog, thick and oppressive, sucking all the energy from the room. I studied the lines on the palms of my hands, as if expecting to find some great revelation written there. At last, he dredged up a heavy sigh.

'That may be so at this time but matters change rapidly in France. If Henri of Navarre prevails over the Catholics, then your brothers may have their inheritance restored. What news you have is old, I believe.'

Hating myself, I persisted. I had to flush out any hint of conspiracy. 'Richard would be glad to get his hands on any money that may come from my family in France! I hope you are not enquiring on his behalf?' I said, watching his reaction. He recoiled again, reeling from my fresh attack.

'Roberda… may I even call you so? I am at a loss for words.' A long moment passed as he gathered himself. 'Was I mistaken? I hoped you understood. I speak from care for your well-being.' He returned my searching gaze without flinching. I could have no doubt of his honesty.

'Are you aware of my past?' I asked. The women of Devon still talk about me. That French woman whose husband wanted to set her aside. Many still believe me guilty.'

'I'm not concerned about any of that. I judge only by what I see before me.' He took a step closer, sought my hand, but still I held back. 'Roberda? I respect your need for time. The need to protect your reputation too. But please, will you let me help?'

'But what can you do?' This time I sensed the relief in his sigh. I had not refused him out of hand.

'I can at least find out how your brothers fare and how the war in France progresses. Queen Elizabeth blows hot and cold. She sent the Earl of Essex with forces to aid the Huguenots, but he failed to relieve Rouen. Norris remains. It's all wrapped up with the Low Countries. She seeks the best way to damage Spain at least cost to her exchequer.'

My head went up. 'Rouen?'

'There was a siege. Essex lost his own brother in a skirmish.'

I felt the blood drain from my cheeks as I saw again the old woman falling from Rouen's battered walls. I felt the strength in Thomas's arm as he supported me, settling me on the seat. Running his fingers through his hair, he asked, 'Are you unwell? Would you like me to call your maid?'

I gripped my hands tight together to stop them shaking. 'No… it will pass. A memory, that is all. I was in Rouen as a child.' Tender understanding flashed across his face. I allowed him to take my hand.

'Ah! During an earlier siege?'

'Yes, my father led the defence of the city long ago. Poor Rouen! Ravaged again, you say?' I shuddered. 'I had no idea there had been another siege. My husband saw fit to confine me to a small world. I have lost track of affairs beyond Dartington's gates. Aye, in truth, since we lost baby Alexander, I've known little beyond my own chamber and the nursery.'

I gave my shoulders a determined shake.

'Thomas?' I tried out the feel of his name on my lips and liked the sensation. 'Did you say Essex was there? Do you mean Robert Devereux?'

'The same! Roberda, if you could have more regular word from your family, would that ease your mind a little?' His desperation to help me shone through.

'Robert Devereux is my brother Gabriel's friend. They were at Cambridge together.'

'Well, the Queen's recalled Essex, but he or others may have more news. Will you allow me to enquire? I have interests in shipping. I'll see if I can get letters from your family to you much faster than has been the case.' He nodded towards the worn package that had taken so long to reach me. 'Will you allow me to try?'

I capitulated, any lingering doubts dissipating with a mere brush of his hand. Our faces inches apart, I waited. For a mad moment I expected his lips on mine. But Thomas retreated, holding me at arm's length.

'I must leave you now. It may be a while before you receive any word from me. Urgent business calls me to London. I'll strive to bring you news as soon as I can.' With one last searching look, he was gone.

I listened to his footsteps fading away on the stairs. Left alone with my thoughts, the weight of silence in the empty room pressed down on me.

I did not see Thomas again at Modbury, as on the next day we rose early to return home. The children were all abuzz with the delights of Christmas. It was Richard who stood at the door to wave us off. His last ominous words.

'I will be in touch.'

Chapter Twenty-Four

The Waiting Time

1593, Dartington Hall

On a freezing afternoon at the end of January, Clotilde huddled over a crackling fire in my chamber. With a weary groan, she levered herself from her seat and moving like a crab, she crossed the room, took the book from my hands, and closed it with a sharp snap.

'You don't fool me, Mistress Roberda! You have not turned a page since Alice took our platters. My rumbling stomach tells me that was long ago! Ever since you came home, you've not been yourself. What is it?'

'Perhaps it's the bad news from France that has upset me, Clotilde.' I could almost hear her joints creaking as she lowered herself into the seat beside me.

'This cold weather makes me cease up. Old age brings unwelcome companions.' She rubbed her hands together, then settled herself, and I felt the rough skin of her palm as she gave my hand a comforting squeeze. 'Hmm – such a shock to hear about poor Giles. Such a fine young man. I remember his antics in the nursery and later... always climbing up to the rooftops. I used to be terrified he'd fall.' We sat for a time, locked in our memories of the bright boy who had met his end on a battlefield.

'My mother will grieve his loss, though she'll applaud the cause he fought for. There never was a more devoted soldier for the Protestant faith than my mother. Oh, Clotilde, she can't even pick up the pen herself any more. To think that my imperious mother had to dictate her letter to a scribe!'

'It must irk Madame la Comtesse beyond endurance, and it's unsettling for you.' Again, she peered into my face. 'But I think perhaps there is more? You've been home for weeks, but you haven't yet told me how matters stand with Master Richard. Is it that? Or is it something to do with that man, Harte?'

She wouldn't give up, not until she had it all from me.

'Richard has written to the Court of Wards. I can see no way to thwart him. Perhaps it would be better for Arthur to join the Modbury household.' I still didn't trust myself to look at her, so I turned to look out of the window. Overnight, snow had blanketed my garden in a cloak of dazzling white, so bright in the afternoon sun, it almost hurt my eyes. Familiar trees stood out as eerie black shapes, like sombre mourners in a funeral procession. I shuddered as a lone black crow swooped down from a tall tree, its caw carrying in the still air. 'At Modbury, he'd have music and company. He wouldn't be stuck here in this dreary place with his mother.'

'Arthur does well enough here with you. He's a sensible boy, and Dartington is anything but dreary. These English courts grind slow. If Richard's only raised the matter, by the time it's all agreed, Arthur will be his own man.' She peered at me, judging my reaction.

'In truth, I think Richard has other things on his mind,' I said. 'They say he'll be appointed High Sheriff of Devon this year. That will please him! At Christmas he spent most of the time with the other men. They were locked in deep discussions they preferred to keep private. Something about the spoils from a ship taken near the Azores, I believe. Oh, and some talk of Sir Walter. He's been let out from the Tower where the Queen sent him for marrying Bess Throckmorton. Mistress Raleigh will be so relieved to hear he's free.'

'What of Harte?'

'He hardly spoke to me, but he and Richard seem close as two peas in the same pod. Harte's not to be trusted.' I fiddled with my cuffs, smoothing out the fine needle-lace trim, until Clotilde stilled my restless hand with hers.

'I have been at your side since you were born. May I speak my mind?'

'Oh, Clotilde, of course you may!'

'Hmm! Well, I will be direct. It's that faraway look, all the sighing and drooping about... and I overheard something Miss Lisbeth said.'

My head went up. 'What's she been saying? Did you know about her obsession with everything medical? She spent all the holidays quizzing a physician! It was embarrassing, to say the least.'

'Don't try to deflect me. We are not discussing Miss Lisbeth. Did you meet someone else? A man, perhaps?'

And then the damn broke, and I spilt it all out, words tumbling over each other as I tried to explain all my confused thoughts about Thomas Horner and his offer to help me.

Clotilde looked me in the eye. 'Your best hope of securing dowries for your girls is indeed your family,' she said. 'Once your brother Jacques has his wealth restored, not just his title and ruined estates, he may pay over your own unpaid dowry. Until that time, speedy communication with them would be a boon. There's no harm in accepting help from this man. But have a care. Everyone makes mistakes in their time on this earth. The wise amongst us learn from them!' I felt as though her sharp eyes could see into my soul.

'What do you mean, Clotilde?'

'Simply this – you let one man rule your life, convinced yourself of his tender feelings for you, and look where that has left you. It's far too soon for you to even think of another marriage, or to fool yourself that there lies the path to happiness. I doubt this man has even hinted at it. Has he?' I shook my head. 'The festive season can cast things in a rosy hue, especially when you've been lonely. You looked for solace in Master Horner's kindness. That is all. Best that you now get on with managing this estate and forget him.'

Days turned into weeks, and then months passed with no word from Thomas. I convinced myself that Clotilde was right. A surfeit of Christmas wine must have addled my brains. He was just being polite and cared no more for me than would any gentleman who came upon a lady in distress. I tried to banish him from my thoughts, to concentrate on making more economies to stretch our meagre funds even further. Yet, in the still hours of the night in my lonely bed I remembered the glint of candlelight on silver hair, soft grey-green eyes, a gentle smile and a strong arm supporting me. Only then did I allow myself to ache a little for what might have been.

On Lady Day I took Arthur with me as William and the burly bailiff heard complaints and took in the rent money. It was time for Arthur to learn more about the estate he would soon inherit. He basked in the respectful looks the tenants cast his way, but after they had gone turned to me with a frown.

'I had not realised how bad things were. Many will struggle to meet the increase in their rent, but without charging them more, I can't see how we'll manage. I see now why you dismissed my fencing master. How could Father have thought he could afford to pay him?' He tidied a pile of papers and looked away. I bit my lip. I had known there was a risk he might lose faith in the father he had idolised when he realised the full extent of our problems.

'Your father sought to equip you as an able soldier, a man who would hold his head high amongst the best of Devon and acquit himself well should he ever be called to fight. Pray God, that will not come to pass, my boy. You've no more need of a fencing master. I've seen what an able swordsman you've become, a credit to the name of Champernowne. Your father would have been proud of you.' He gave me a weak smile, and beneath his new assurance I glimpsed the young boy still within. I returned his smile, wishing I could do more to smooth his transition from boyhood into a frightening adult world.

'Can I go to the mews now, Mother? I think we can still afford to keep my hawk, for she brings down birds for our table.' The mews were still his favourite bolthole.

'Of course. I would relish some pigeon pie if you fly her on the morrow. You have done well today, Arthur. Enjoy your sport.' I watched him go, hoping he could enjoy a few more years before the burdens of his birth fell on his shoulders.

Hay time passed and harvest too, but still I heard nothing from Thomas Horner. I persuaded myself I must forget him and fight my own battles. With no news from France I was in limbo, struggling to make ends meet, with no hope of even opening negotiations for my girls to wed. Richard was busy with his duties as sheriff, which perhaps delayed his pursuit of matters with the Court of Wards. Arthur and I had a little longer to manage the estate together.

Autumn came early that year. Past noon on a misty day in late September, cobwebs still hung from the clipped hedges of my physick garden, as I sought solace in a brisk walk. I scrunched through fallen leaves, making a mental note to find one of the kitchen boys to sweep the paths. I could no longer afford to pay an extra garden boy for such tasks.

By the time I reached it, the bench in the arbour was warmed by the sun. It was the one place where, even in difficult times, I felt most content. The worn wooden seat welcomed me amidst the fading heads of late roses, bowing down under the weight of moisture they carried.

Lisbeth did not pause as she hurried past me, carrying a massive basket full of hazel nuts, some still green, and bright clusters of orange-red rosehips. Spotting Agnes bustling along in Lisbeth's wake, weighed down by a similar burden, I called out to her.

'Come, sit with me. You work too hard, Agnes. Lisbeth will manage without you for a while.' Agnes put her basket down on the gravel path and rubbed her back before she joined me on the bench with a grateful sigh.

'A good yield this year and early too,' I said, pointing to the brimming basket.

'Yes, indeed! Best we harvest the nuts before the birds have them. There's enough to dry and set by… they are good to close the stomach after a feast. I'll make the hips from the dog roses into a cordial or a syrup. Good to cool heat in a fever, and for coughs and those spitting blood. Our young rector, Master Jones, has much need of it.'

'How is he, Agnes?'

'The poor man is fading away despite the efforts of all in the parish to restore him to health. I have tried everything I know. His fate is in God's hands. He brings up blood. It may not be long.'

'I'm sure you've done all you can, and I'm grateful for everything you do to keep us well supplied with medicines and cures, Agnes. But tell me. How is your new assistant doing? I see little of Lisbeth these days. She spends most of her time with you in the still room.'

'She is an able pupil and a great help to me,' Agnes replied. 'Any woman, nay any lady, should be proud to know how to use nature's bounty to brew cures and treat ailments.'

'But she seems to be obsessed. It can't be healthy. No woman will ever rival the physicians.'

'Hah! Physicians!' Agnes snorted. 'They are ever resentful of women's knowledge! Tongues have wagged about me before now. They call me a wise woman, but they suspect I dabble in dark arts.'

'I'll hear of none of that! You use your knowledge for good. Everyone here knows that. But Agnes, I wish I knew how to deal with my daughter.'

She sucked her teeth for a moment, then cleared her throat. 'She was at a difficult age when Master Gawen took her from you all those years ago,' she said. 'About the same age as I was when my father died. It was sudden. He was a thatcher, and he fell from a roof one day. My mother said he had too much cider. It turned my world on its head until I didn't know which way was up. But my grandmother saved me by teaching me everything she knew about plants and such. So, I'm happy to help Miss Lisbeth find her way if I can.'

'Thank you, Agnes. Better than her sitting around like a listless rag as the years go by and she is no nearer to finding a husband.' She nodded and gave me a steady, considering look.

'And you, ma'am?' Her voice dropped low. 'May I enquire how you fare in these hard times?'

'As well as may be, Agnes. I am concerned for my children, of course. I fear matters will soon slip beyond my control.'

'The servants talk of it. They say Master Arthur must go to Modbury.'

'Perhaps he will go in time, but not yet,' I said. 'I live in hope...'

Agnes cocked her head to one side as a blackbird struck up a warning. We both smiled to see one of the kitchen cats stalking beyond the clipped hedge as the bird, a young male in his first black plumage, fluttered away.

'Blackbird's staking out his territory,' Agnes said. 'Cook's cat has missed his chance. My sister Margery sends her good wishes.'

'She's seen me through many hard labours. I can't say I'm sorry to have no more need for Margery's services. All those years of childbearing wore me down. Tell her Bridget thrives.'

'You will find the strength to face whatever may come, ma'am,' she said as she stood up and gathered her basket. Her light footsteps left no mark on the path as she headed off, leaving me to enjoy the sun for a little longer.

I must have dozed, for the shadows had lengthened when voices startled me. Marie panted out her news. 'A visitor, ma'am! I've shown the gentleman into the parlour. Joan says it's someone you met at Christmas.'

My mouth went dry, and I nearly fell off the bench.

'Please serve refreshments while I tidy myself. I'll be there directly.' Marie waddled away to do my bidding, and I flew round the garden paths, kicking up a cloud of dust behind me. Once through the back door, I hitched up my skirts and dashed up the stairs to summon Clotilde to help me put on a prettier gown.

'I'll come down with you, shall I? For propriety's sake?' However much I might wish to say no, to meet him without her prying eyes on me, I knew it would not be wise.

'Yes, you had better join me,' I said, taking a quick look at myself in the glass. Ignoring Clotilde's tuts and warning looks, with my best cap set over upswept curls, I descended in a flurry of rustling silk. Clotilde followed me down, keeping up a steady stream of complaints about her aching knees with every step.

All of a flutter, I pushed the door open, and there he was.

Chapter Twenty-Five

News from France

Autumn 1593, Dartington Hall

I burst in with a warm, welcoming smile on my lips, but Thomas's grave face stopped me in my tracks. Without a word, he crossed the floor in just two strides. I couldn't suppress a shiver of anticipation. It danced up and down my back as he took my outstretched hand and bent his head.

He did not release his grip, nor did he return my smile, but stood motionless, his handsome features set in stern lines. The quip I had prepared about him having forgotten me froze in my throat. My mouth went dry. All my excitement at seeing him again fled as an unnatural stillness fell. The atmosphere was taut as a bowstring, the only sound Clotilde's laboured breathing.

'Come… sit,' he said, his sombre tones breaking the silence. 'I have news about your family in France.' For the first time, I noticed the leather pouch he had brought with him lying on the chair beside the court cupboard where Sir Arthur's silver salt sparkled on top of a rich red turkey rug. How strange to notice such unimportant details – the white circle on the oak tabletop where a wet mug had rested; the spent roses spilling from the vase still adding a hint of drowsy fragrance to the air; the fine blackwork embroidery on Thomas's cuff protruding from his sleeve; the cool feel of the ring set with a blood-red ruby on his finger as he kept hold of my hand. It felt as if I was trying to capture the scene in my memory forever.

'My brother Jacques? Is it Jacques?'

He swallowed and summoned his courage to break whatever bad news had caused his handsome face to set in so severe a mould.

'It's not your brother. My dear Roberda, it is your mother. It is my sad duty to tell you that Madame la Comtesse de Montgomery has died of a fever at her home at Pontorson.'

I gasped, and a loud crash came from behind me as Clotilde dropped to the floor.

'No, no! Not Maman!' My voice shook as I squeezed my eyes tight shut, trying to block out the truth. I gaped at him, oblivious to the groans and words of encouragement as a patient Marie coaxed Clotilde onto her feet and helped her to a seat. The sound of wine pouring from a flagon into a mug rang loud in my ears, but I refused the drink Marie offered. Before I had recovered my senses, Clotilde spoke, her voice crackling with emotion.

'I pray you will forgive the weakness of an old woman, sir, but this is the worst of news.' Suddenly aware that he was still holding my hand, I took a step back, withdrawing my fingers from his grip. At last, I found my tongue.

'This is Clotilde. Clotilde, may I introduce Master Thomas Horner? Clotilde has been at my side since the day I was born. She is more a friend than a servant to me and she loved my mother well.' I reached out and found her cold, bony old fingers as they scrabbled to clutch a thick woollen shawl round her shaking shoulders. 'Thank you for bringing us this news. We are both beyond consoling.'

Thomas ran his finger around the inside of the ruff at his throat.

'It pains me more than I can say to bring you such distress. When you feel able, there are letters from your family here.' His words were formal but softly spoken, reaching into the depths of my soul. 'I regret it has taken so long for me to visit you. It took me a while to track down my Lord of Essex and others at court, to gather all I could about your family's situation in France. Not wishing to raise false hopes before I had the whole, I waited. That delay means I am now the bearer of these sad tidings. By all accounts, she was a remarkable woman.'

The shock settled like a block of ice, chilling me to the bone.

Thomas nodded to Arthur, who sat white-faced, his knuckles tense as he gripped the edge of the hard bench beneath him.

'Your mother will have need of your support in the coming days.'
Arthur stood up, extended his hand to Thomas in a most grown-up
way, gulped and nodded his assent. 'Good lad!' Thomas said, taking
Arthur's hand. He turned to me again. 'I will leave you now to recover
a little. I have business in Totnes. You'll wish to send a response to
your brother. I can arrange for letters to get there safely. Perhaps I
may return in a few days?'

'Of course... and thank you.'

Before I realised what was happening, he was on his way.

Marie had been helping Agnes and Lisbeth make rose-hip syrup
in the still room. She must have wiped her hands on her apron, for a
sweet smell hung round her as she fussed around us. That delightful
fragrance – apples, roses and almonds all mixed together – would
forever remind me of the day I heard Mamam was gone. As my
faithful maid offered drinks and what comfort she could, I let my
mind dwell on it, picturing the glossy autumn fruits bobbing in the
breeze. It was easier to think of that than to accept the enormity of
the new Thomas had brought.

Supporting Clotilde, who seemed to have lost the use of her legs,
Marie puffed and panted as she guided us both from the room. As
the heavy door swung open, its creaks all but blotted the sound of
scuffling feet. Alice's retreating figure disappeared, heading for the
kitchens. She had been eavesdropping, and it wouldn't be long before
news of Maman's death spread throughout Dartington.

'Shall I bring the letters, ma'am?' Marie asked. They lay on the
settle, tied up in a fat package bursting with its own importance, red
seals dangling. I heaved a great sigh. They could hold their secrets for
another day.

'I don't have the energy for more. Leave them until tomorrow.'

We struggled up the stairs to my bedchamber with Clotilde
clutching her chest. Agnes came and pushed open a window, allowing
the cool breeze to freshen the air. Steam rose from the cup she carried,
an infusion of camomile and poppy seeds. As Clotilde swallowed
the last dregs, I, too, drank of Agnes's potion, savouring the taste
on my tongue. It was pungent yet calming. I lay down on the soft
feather bed and found oblivion in sleep.

I woke with a start to find the room as black as pitch. In the hour before moonrise, when the darkness becomes most impenetrable, dreams, nightmares, and reality blur together. In that darkest hour, we may imagine the dead can walk among us. Clutching at the bed sheet so hard my fingers hurt, my pulse raced.

Tap... tap... tap. Click... click... click.

The eerie tapping echoed though the silent house. It was just like the sound Maman's shoes used to make as she paced in the nearby room, the one that would forever be called the Countess's Room. In that room she had waited for word of my father. There she had received the evil tidings of his death on the scaffold in Paris.

Tap... tap... tap. Click... click... click.

I hid under the covers, trying to block out the terrifying idea of her spirit returning to Dartington, the place of her deepest sorrow. Perhaps she would haunt that room forever more. It was a long time before sleep claimed me again.

When I woke the sun was streaming in from a clear blue sky. The terrors of the night seemed foolish. However, I soon discovered I had not been the only one to hear strange sounds in the dead of night.

Marie pinned my hair up and handed me the glass so that I could admire the effect.

'There now, you look much better this morning, ma'am. It must have been such a shock for you. I can't believe the old lady's gone. She seemed indestructible.' Leaning forward, she pushed a curl back from my forehead. 'I'll never forget that day she came and released you after he'd treated you so bad.' Her face flushed. 'Begging your pardon – it's not my place to remind you of such a time. Did you sleep at all?'

'I did, at least for part of the night.'

'Ah, then mayhap the commotion woke you? Cook was spitting nails this morning. He said there'd been such a ruckus last night that nobody got any sleep. Just afore moonrise that simpleton maid Alice came bolting down the stairs, shrieking like a stuck pig.'

'Whatever was she doing on the stairs at that time of night?'

'Well, she said she'd come up to check if the candles were all snuffed out. The stupid chit claimed she heard footsteps, in the

Countess's Room, ma'am. It's all stuff and nonsense. Everyone knows we've kept that room locked up for years. But now Alice's saying the old lady has come back to haunt us.' My face, reflected in the glass I still held, turned chalk white. As I set it down, my hand shook. I took a deep breath to steady myself.

'As you say, Marie, it's nonsense. Trust Alice – she's full of fanciful notions. I do not expect to hear any more of it. Tsk! We don't want to frighten the little ones.' Brave words, yet goosebumps pricked my skin as I hurried past the firmly closed door as I went down.

Clotilde rallied much faster than I expected. I found her later that day, sitting in the arbour.

'I hope she's reunited with him, for he served her well,' she said, pointing to Alain 's memorial. 'And with your father too.'

'Alain served us all well, dear Clotilde.'

We stayed there, side by side on the sun-warmed bench, each lost in our memories. Fallen leaves still covered the paths, creating a rich mosaic of reds, russets, browns, and gold. The sun dipped out of sight behind a cloud and a chill wind brushed my face, a reminder that winter would be upon us. Clotilde pushed her kerchief up her sleeve and hauled herself to her feet. As we strolled towards the house, I felt her weight hanging heavy on my arm, while the sound of the leaves rustling beneath our feet sounded loud in my ears.

'What's our life any more than those leaves?' Clotilde said. 'All of us must wither and fade away, just as they do. Your mother led a good life. Her time had come. To truly honour her memory, strive to be as strong as she was. You have more battles to fight.' She gave me a sideways look, and I saw that the twinkle had returned to her eye. 'And joys to come too. Best read everything before he returns, *ma petite*.'

'I will.' I knew I must, though I did not relish it. As I left her, Clotilde called out.

'He seems an honourable man.'

Chapter Twenty-Six

Matters at Home and Abroad
Autumn/Winter 1593, Dartington Hall

Another night passed. This time no ghostly footsteps disturbed my sleep. Early the next morning, I spread the contents of the leather pouch across the polished surface of the high table in the Great Hall. Shafts of glittering sunlight streamed through the twinkling glass in the elegant windows, casting patterns onto the scrubbed floor. A ride through the woods would have cleared my head, perhaps even eased my grief. I hated to pass up the gift of a bright autumn day to be confined to this task inside. But it must be accomplished.

I tapped my fingers on the tabletop as I considered the muddle of papers. Dissatisfied, I shuffled the documents along the board, attempting to follow the order of events they covered. No matter how hard I tried, I couldn't make sense of it. Mixed in with meticulously scribed copies of reports of battles were dog-eaten letters addressed to me, lost in transit until now. The yellowing pages spanned years of events that had changed the fortunes of my family.

I looked up when Arthur wandered in, bringing with him the mouthwatering smell of one of cook's famous meat pasties. Pushing the last morsel into his mouth, he asked what I was doing.

'Don't speak with your mouth full, Arthur,' I snapped, then, realising it wasn't fair to take my frustration out on him, I gave him an indulgent smile. 'It's not good for your digestion.'

He grinned. 'Cook's pasties are the best, and I was hungry after my ride this morning. I couldn't resist sneaking one while he had his back turned.'

'Alice will be after you for spilling crumbs on her newly swept floor! But to answer your question, I'm trying to make sense of what Master Horner brought.' I waved my hand over the disordered pages. 'These missives are in such a muddle.'

'Can I help, Mother?' Without waiting for my reply, he picked up an ink-stained sheet and read. 'See, here's the day this was penned,' he said, jabbing a greasy finger at the foot of the page, setting the red wax seals swinging. Without waiting for my reply, he took another from the pile. 'If I can decipher dates on all of them, then it will be easy to set them in order.'

'Go to it, my son. For I'm in despair to complete the task!'

The cramped, spidery writings had him scratching his head, screwing up his eyes and holding them to the light. Even worse, most were in French, one or two in Latin, which tested his learning to the limit. Yet he went about it with dogged determination, and before I had downed the cooling draft of new ale Alice brought me, he had them in neat piles, ordered along the length of the board.

'It's lucky none are in cipher,' he said, setting the last one down with a flourish.

'Indeed it is. Well done, Arthur! Now let us read.' Arthur gave me a knowing grin and stood tall, basking in my praise. As he read aloud, his voice breaking a few times, as was to be expected in a boy of his age, Clotilde, who I had thought to be dozing, perked up. She reminded me of a blackbird searching for worms in the herb garden as she set her head on one side. Now and then, she nodded, as if adding some weighty truth to her store. We were all so engrossed in the unfolding story, none of us noticed Lisbeth slinking in.

'I'm not sure your French is up to this task, little brother,' she said, not unkindly, as he hesitated over a word. 'Let me help too.'

'By all means, Lisbeth.' Watching the two of them working together, sometimes disagreeing over translating an unusual phrase, I felt as if the air was bottling up in my chest. In that moment I almost believed my perplexing eldest daughter had not quite slipped beyond my reach.

When they reached the last document, Arthur raked his fingers through his abundant hair.

'Even now, I can't understand everything. I would love to have been there when my uncles tried to seize Mont Saint-Michel! Armed men disguised as women breaking in, stabbing the guards and opening the gates! What a ruse!' He smacked his lips in appreciation. 'How brave was that!'

I clamped my mouth shut. Such tales of daring deeds had, of course, stirred a sense of adventure in my son. He saw only the glory, none of the suffering. I closed my eyes and drifted back to my childhood. An image of the abbey, perched on its craggy mount, danced into my mind. I heard again the glorious singing in the chapel.

'It's a pity indeed such a holy place should be the scene of such acts of war, its sacred stones defiled by blood! Oh, you think it fine sport, young Arthur. But war's a deadly business and many innocent people suffer.' He looked crestfallen and muttered an apology.

'Look, it says here they did not hold Mont Saint-Michel for long,' Lisbeth cried, pointing wildly at a scrap of paper covered in spiky writing. 'One of them was captured – I can't make out if it was Uncle Jacques or Gedeon or Gabriel – and does this say they were released in a prisoner exchange?'

'To think all this was happening, and we knew nothing of it,' I said, glancing at Clotilde as unspoken words hung between us. Why had Gawen not told me? I was certain he had received some reports. Arthur's brow furrowed.

'Well, it was just after Drake drove the Spanish up the Channel. My father had other things on his mind,' he said. Arthur would hear nothing bad about his father.

'So, Charlotte is married!' Clotilde piped up, deftly turning the conversation.

'Yes, she was left a wealthy widow after Christophe died at the battle of Jarnac,' I replied. 'Goodness! How many years ago is that?'

'Too many to remember,' Clotilde chuckled. 'I never thought she would marry again.'

'It seems he's a young man named Daniel de la Touche,' I said, puzzling over another letter. 'Hmm... Charlotte's provided him with a wealthy income from her lordship of Plessis-Bertrand. Do you think that's why he married her?'

'Perhaps! I've heard that name before. He's an adventurer. A bit like Sir Walter, I should think. Wants to sail the seas and discover fortunes in foreign parts.'

'Anyway, there's more,' I said. 'They have a daughter and I'm glad of it! Charlotte deserves her slice of happiness.'

Arthur picked up another paper.

'My uncle Gabriel seems to have won great acclaim. It says here he's going to marry a wealthy woman, and he's appointed Governor of Pontorson.'

'Yes, that is good news. Suzanne de Bouquenot brings him a dowry of 10,000 crowns!'

Relief was only just sinking in. Knowing my family's fortunes were improving went some way towards assuaging my grief at Maman's death. It was just possible that now they might be able to help me. If they could pay over some of the dowry outstanding from my marriage contract with Gawen, I could look for husbands for my girls. I took the last letter from Arthur. It was signed by my brother Jacques, dated only a month before.

'This spells out the sad news of your grandmother's passing. Your uncle Jacques says it will take some time to set her affairs in order. I must go to France.'

A few days later, I waited for Alice to take his drenched cloak. Thomas had returned as promised, as I knew he would. The look we exchanged said more than our formal words of greeting. A moment of mutual understanding, of recognition, of certainty and hope, passed between us. Clotilde gave a discreet cough from her seat beside the sputtering fire. Only then did he tear his eyes from mine. Sniffing, I became aware of the musty smell of damp logs and invited him to sit.

'Did your business go well?'

'As well as it could in this weather.' With a rueful smile, he looked down at his wet boots. 'The roads are awash.'

'I'm grateful that you braved such conditions to call on me again. We often get storms at this season.' Thomas took the mug Alice offered.

'I would do anything in my power to assist you,' he said. The girl eyed him with curiosity and pretended to mop up non-existent spills from the jug.

'Thank you, Alice, that will be all.' With some reluctance, she shuffled off. When she was out of earshot, I laughed.

'Alice will have anything we say all over Totnes before we know it. We may speak free before Clotilde. And of course you know Arthur and Lisbeth.' Arthur grinned, then looked at his boots, bashful and respectful, while Lisbeth locked eyes with Thomas in an insolent stare. I rushed on.

'We've read it all, yet we still can't make sense of everything that has happened. I thought my mother was safe in Pontorson. Now it seems her life was on a knife's edge while they fought over the town.'

Thomas drained the cup and frowned, as if considering his response with care.

'Indeed! There was heavy fighting in Pontorson. They appointed your brother Gabriel as the governor there. But it's all one now. Henri of Navarre has embraced the Catholic faith.' I let out an audible gasp and blinked rapidly.

'What's that you say, sir?' Clotilde's sharp exclamation gave voice to my astonishment. 'How can this be? Did he not say that we cannot change religion as easily as a shirt? Are you saying he has given in to the Papists?'

'He's had enough of war. He can't afford to pay his soldiers. It's a pragmatic solution,' Thomas said. 'I understand that, given your father's role in the wars, this comes as a shock. But, believe me, it may also help your own cause.'

His words did not satisfy Clotilde. Her chin shot up, and she let out a French oath, then blazed at him.

'How can he have given in to the Catholics? After all the years Madame la Comtesse dedicated to the Protestant cause, all the bloodshed! Is this the best Henri de Navarre can do? If you ask me, it's what brought my lady to her end! His own mother, Jeanne D'Albret, must be spinning in her grave.'

It had come as a shock, but I didn't share Clotilde's indignation.

'I, for one, am glad to hear it! Anything is better than the vicious wars that have divided my country since I was a child. You're right,

Clotilde. My mother was staunch in her support of the Protestant cause, to the last breath in her body, no doubt. But I am not my mother.'

'What does the English Queen say to it then?' Clotilde was like a dog worrying at a bone.

I found I didn't care at all what Queen Elizabeth thought.

'Let us not concern ourselves with high politics. Thomas, you said you could get a message to my family?'

'I have opened a secure channel for your communications. Essex kept in touch with Gabriel. If you wish to send a letter, I'll see it gets there.'

'And can you help me arrange a passage to France?' All the colour drained from his face, and he opened his mouth to interrupt me. But I pressed on. 'I must go to settle my mother's affairs. I am a beneficiary of her last will. There is no other way.'

With his eyebrows drawn together, he studied me for a moment. Then, as though satisfied, he gave a curt nod.

'If that is your wish, I can arrange it for you.'

'Thank you. Will you take refreshment while I bring letters to you?'

He nodded assent, and Clotilde, still huffing and puffing, went in search of Alice and food for our guest. Arthur followed, with Lisbeth flouncing along behind him. I waited until they had gone, then paused at the door. 'Someday, I hope to repay your kindness.'

'It is my fervent hope there will one day be much more between us than kindness,' he said. The warmth crept into my cheeks as I nodded. 'But first you must settle your affairs.'

The weeks dragged by as I waited for a response. I had written to Jacques advising him of my intention to visit Pontorson in the spring, and to my sister Charlotte expressing my sorrow at Maman's passing. I went about my duties, managing the household and estate, keeping a close eye on economies that would help us through the winter.

Agnes came to me on All Souls' Day, shooing a group of ragged children towards the kitchen

'Boys from the hamlet of Week – they're good lads. They help with scaring crows, collecting firewood, and such like,' Agnes said. 'They've come begging for soul cakes. Keeping up the old ways, though of course in these times no one believes in purgatory. But they mean no harm. Cook will find some cakes for them. Ma'am, I'm come on a sad errand.'

'What is it, Agnes?'

''Tis about poor Sir Griffin, the rector; I've done all I can. It will be any day now. Churchwarden says it's time you thought who may replace him.'

'That is sad news indeed. But you may assure the warden it's in hand, Agnes. I've consulted the Bishop. Master Robert Bruxham's on his way from Exeter. Arthur and I will stand together to present him.'

Not two weeks later, the day after Martinmas, we laid our young rector, Griffin Jones, to rest. The new man I'd recommended couldn't have been more different in appearance, being broad in the girth and rosy in the face. I'd shared the task with Arthur; another milestone in his education. The right to nominate a minister for the church of St Mary would fall to him in due time; one of the many responsibilities he would assume when he came to his majority and was master of Dartington Hall.

We prepared for a quiet Christmastide, less lavish than in times past, but with a good supply of hams. As soon as the weather turned cold, William ordered the pig killing to begin. In the damp air in the kitchen courtyard, the smell of burnt straw and singing hair often caught our throats. The kitchen boys wiped the sweat from their foreheads as they went from carcass to carcass, setting light to piles of straw. The flames licked and crackled around the pigs' flesh. In no time, the fires died, and all hairs removed, the butcher's knife could have full play. Everyone worked hard to set joints to salt and smoke, while we ate well of all the parts that our skilful cook could not preserve.

Lisbeth watched in fascination until I sent her away.

'It's unseemly in a young lady, Lisbeth. Go and practise your lute playing or sewing.' My rebuke provoked one of her disdainful glares and did nothing to improve our relationship.

Arthur was keen to play his part in furnishing the Christmas table. On a crisp early December morning, I found him pulling on his buckskin gauntlet, his face flushed with excitement.

'I'm off to fly my hawk. Father's goshawk hasn't taken to me, but my bird can bring down plenty of fowl for the table. Lisbeth's going to ride out with me. Did you know she's been training a little merlin? She might bring down a partridge or two.'

'Well, I never! You'll need to take two grooms with you to carry all your spoils!' He grinned and nodded, before ducking as he stepped though the doorway. Laughing, I called after him.

'Be sure to wrap up warm, the cold's biting.'

He raised his arm, and I followed to wave them off. Outside, Lisbeth was already in the saddle and held her hooded merlin on her arm, the bells jingling on the jesses as her horse pawed at the frosty ground. I smiled at her, pleased to see them spending time together.

As I watched them go, I saw other horsemen approaching. Even from a distance, I recognised Thomas and ran inside to tidy my hair and swap my everyday linen coif for a more becoming headdress.

'Back again so soon, is he?' Clotilde's knowing smile told me she approved.

'No doubt Master Horner has news for me. He's arranging my passage in the spring and I've asked if he can persuade Richard to allow Pierre to accompany me to France.'

'I wish I could go with you, to see my native land again, to see how your sister and brothers do, and to visit Alain's grave,' Clotilde said, as she dabbed her eyes with the corner of her kerchief and sighed. 'Alas, my bones are too old for such a journey. Pierre will be an agreeable companion. Let us hope Master Richard will release him. I'll leave you to greet your visitor.'

I waited, wiping my sweating palms on a napkin, which I hid beneath a cushion. Limber as a much younger man, there was a spring in Thomas's step as he came striding into my parlour.

'I have it all in hand. We must await good weather, but you'll sail from Dartmouth in the spring.'

'Won't you have a seat and tell me more, Thomas?'

Beaming, he laid out his plans for my voyage. He seemed unable to keep still, turning a small parcel round and round in his hands.

'I'm working on Richard. I think I can persuade him to allow the musician to travel with you, though he's loathe to part with him even for a short time. If you would allow me to hint that you may come to some financial settlement with your brothers concerning your mother's will, that might help. I know he's a curmudgeonly fellow, but, in his way, he wants the best for Arthur.' Thomas fidgeted, awaiting my answer. 'What is it?' he asked with gentle concern.

'I can't bring myself to trust him,' I said at last. 'He wants Arthur as his ward. I don't want to lose my son to his care. Nor do I want any money I can secure for my girls to drain into his leaky coffers.'

'I understand your concerns.' he replied. 'But Richard's not all bad; he upsets people with his meddlesome ways and quick temper, then he's surprised they aren't grateful to him.'

'Humph! What about John Harte? What axe is he grinding in this? He seemed helpful at first, but I'm not sure of him.'

'Don't distress yourself about Harte. His only concern is to secure loans that will bring him a fat profit. Has it ever occurred to you that his intention all along has been to set you and Richard at odds?'

'Do you think so?' I considered for a moment. 'I've always suspected that Gawen was in debt to him. I'm sure Harte's not to be trusted.'

A smile tickled the corners of Thomas's mouth.

'Well, then, I am flattered that you seem to trust me amongst all these other rascals. But let us be serious. Once you have matters settled in France, you can resolve it all. As for Arthur, I wonder if you've considered whether it might be good for the boy to have some different company? Most lads of his age would have left home a long time since. Would going to Modbury be so bad?'

I looked down at my hands.

'I know. You're right. I'm clinging to him when I should let him stretch his wings and fly.'

'All I ask is that you think about it.' He glanced down at the package he held as carefully as if it were made of glass. 'My dear Roberda, would you allow me to mention another matter? Something so dear to me, it is burning a hole in my heart as each day passes.' In a flurry of energy, he leapt from the seat, and for a moment, I thought he was about to kneel before me.

I turned away and patrolled up and down by the window, a fold of my skirt squashed into my curled fist as I avoided his eyes. At last I turned and looked at him. He took my hand and his eyes gave me the reassurance I needed. Those steady grey-green eyes, with their specks of gold, reminded me of sunlight filtering through leaves on a spring morning. How I longed to take the leap, to bind myself to this courteous, handsome gentleman for the rest of my days. Standing on tiptoe, I held my finger to his lips.

'Hush, Thomas. It is too soon. I must go to France first.'

With a gentle smile, he sighed and pressed the wrapped package into my hands.

'Take this then, open it when I am gone and keep it to remind you of me. I will wait in hope.' A commotion beyond the door advertised that someone was on the other side. I burst out laughing.

'Ah, Thomas! For now, we must behave with due decorum. I have cause to know the damage wagging tongues can do.' I dashed to the door and lifted the latch. As it swung open, Alice fell over the threshold.

Chapter Twenty-Seven

A Homecoming?

Spring 1594, Pontorson, France

A heavy mist hung in the air, dense and choking. Shivering, I clutched my woollen cloak more tightly, feeling the damp seeping through to my bones. As we docked in the port of Saint Malo, Pierre's face turned white and he gripped the rail, absorbing the shock of the barque banging against the quayside. It was over twenty years since we took ship for England together.

'At last!' he said with a rueful grin. Neither of us had enjoyed the voyage from Dartmouth. Throughout the journey, we had spent most of our time hanging over the side or over a bucket as we spewed up whatever we had last consumed. I offered up a silent prayer of thanks that no fierce westerlies had brought our vessel to grief.

'We'll soon be on dry land again,' I said, with an answering smile wavering on my lips. Although the motion of the ship had ceased, I still felt as though my insides quivered and lurched.

I peered into the mist but there was no warm welcome in the dark outline of the town walls. They loomed out of the mist, forbidding as a well-defended castle. The plaintive notes of bells drifted from a church tower rising tall above the fortress-like walls, almost as if they tolled our doom. As I stood on the deck, it didn't feel like we were coming home.

I swallowed my unease and gathered my composure, and with a determined step, I approached the gangplank. Pierre grunted as he picked up our bags while Joan, who seemed to have the stomach of a born sailor, trotted behind him. The adventure of being in a foreign land made her cheeks flush, and her eyes darted everywhere. For me, there was no excitement. Only the pressing responsibility of securing my just share of my mother's estate and the dread of arriving at her home to face the brutal truth that she was gone forever.

'Will they receive us well here?' Pierre asked as we walked down the gangplank onto the quayside. 'I heard Saint Malo had split itself from the rest of France and set up as an independent state. I didn't expect Master Horner to suggest we come this way.'

'Lots of people in Brittany joined the Catholic League, including the governor here. They didn't want Henri of Navarre as their king,' I said. 'He's named as king in Paris now, but they say many of the League have not accepted him yet and some may even join forces with the Spanish.' Pierre frowned and glanced over his shoulder as a sailor passed us. 'But don't worry, Pierre. Master Horner tells me the town still keeps good relations with those from Dartmouth who want to trade.'

Turning to Joan, I painted a smile onto my face.

'Anyway, here we are! It's by far the closest port to Pontorson. Master Horner has arranged for men to meet us with horses and we'll soon be on our way. With good luck, we'll be there by nightfall, though we'll need to ride hard.'

The mist had cleared, and the sun was high, glinting off a shimmering sea as we rode alongside the bay of Saint Michel. I shaded my eyes, feeling my spirits lift as I took full advantage of my lofty position on the back of a spirited black gelding.

'I had quite forgotten how beautiful it is!' The tide, high when our ship docked, had receded to reveal a vast expanse of golden sand stretching from the emerald marshes to the blue horizon. Joan's eyes were round as she clung behind Pierre on a more placid bay gelding.

'I never saw anywhere like this! With the sea and the sky so blue, it's as if there's no end to 'em.' She peered over Pierre's shoulder and pointed. 'And that island – it seems to shimmer in the air! Oh, and just look at all the sheep.' She gave an exaggerated sniff. 'What's that smell? It's salty but a bit like rotten eggs as well.'

The disgusted look on her face made me laugh.

'It often smells like that when the tide's out. But wonderful plants grow here,' I said, pointing. 'See, over there, the sheep are grazing amongst the samphire. I'm looking forward to feasting on some salt-marsh lamb.'

Pierre was studying Isle Saint Michel, which rose above the waters of the bay as if it floated in the air.

'You're right, Joan. It is amazing. It makes me think of Avalon and King Arthur. The island might be the castle of Camelot, suspended between the heavens and the sea. It's inspiring me to write a new song.' He hummed a haunting tune as we turned away from the sea, skirting the marshlands. On a slight rise in the ground, far in the distance, the sails of a windmill turned, lazy as courtiers dancing a stately pavane.

'You can see so far! Not a bit like Devon, is it, ma'am,' said Joan, squinting as she tried to take in the endless sweep of low-lying land that stretched before us. I let my eyes go out of focus as nostalgic thoughts of the rolling wooded hills round Dartington blotted out the flat landscape of France. How strange that amid what should have been a joyful homecoming, I was already missing my English home.

The light was fading when we made our way through Pontorson to the Chateau Montgomery. As the sun slipped beyond the horizon, the air grew chill and a sharp breeze nipped at my cheeks. In the dwindling daylight, I could only just make out the dark outline of the formidable towers of Eglise de Notre Dame rising above the neighbouring rooftops as we turned into the gate.

Torchlight flickered around the walls of the courtyard, and bright light flooded from every window of the ancient mansion house I remembered so well. Slipping from the saddle, exhausted after our long journey, I summoned the strength to enter the house I had not seen for so long.

I strode forward with determination, lifting the skirts of my riding gown as I climbed the short flight of steps beneath an imposing porch. Pierre and Joan trailed in my wake, like ducklings following a mother duck to the water.

A tall man with a well-trimmed beard greeted us at the door. His voice, soft and well-educated for a servant, meant I had to pay attention to recall the French words after spending so much time in England.

'*Bonne soirée*! You must be Madame de Champernon. I am Antoine de Gaillardy, butler to Monsieur Gabriel. He and Madame await you within. Your serving people will find a welcome in the kitchens.' A woman in a clean apron and old-fashioned cap appeared, ready to show them the way.

With a nod to Pierre and Joan, I made to follow the butler. I had taken only two paces before I froze. The sight of the majestic oak staircase held me spellbound. I cocked my head to one side, studying the carved finial that used to remind me of a dragon, and a shallow sigh escaped me. The flight of stairs appeared smaller than I remembered, its grandeur seemed dimmed. Yet the well-worn treads still had the power to transport me to my childhood. Surrendering to the honeyed scent of beeswax polish, memories of playing on those stairs with my sisters rushed into my mind. What fun we had swishing down the polished steps on our bottoms! As I looked up, I half expected Maman to sail down, her black gown rustling, and caution us to be careful of our fine clothes.

Antoine prompted me with a discreet cough.

'Madame? You remember the way? It's through here.' I gave myself a shake and followed him.

Gabriel had his back to me, warming his hands before a smouldering fire. When I saw the set of his shoulders, a lump rose in my throat. I was overwhelmed by the startling resemblance to my papa. I had no time to recover myself before an elegant woman dressed in a gown of rippling blue silk with the latest style of open lace ruff rose from her chair and extended her hand.

'Roberda? I am Suzanne. Welcome!' Before I could take her hand, Gabriel turned. My little brother had somehow changed from the gauche young man I remembered into a sophisticated French gentleman. With a beaming smile lighting his face, he made his way across the room with outstretched arms. I flew to him and he held me close, until at last he released me. As he stood back, I saw he had not only gained maturity but a livid scar that ran from hairline to chin.

'Noticing the badges of my military success, sister?' Hearing his rich laugh, I relaxed, thinking visiting my kith and kin might not be such an ordeal as I had imagined.

Next day I met Gabriel in one of the elegant rooms overlooking the formal gardens.

'We haven't got round to replacing all the cracked glass yet,' Gabriel said, pointing to the damaged mirrors in their ornate frames. 'During the fighting, the mob got in for a short time. Before we got things under control, they wrought havoc in Maman's best parlour! She did not find it amusing!' It was the first time he had broached the sensitive subject of Maman. 'Even though she was not so spry as she used to be, she was much in evidence during the battles here in Pontorson.'

'So, did she stay, even when the fighting was at its worst?' I asked.

'Oh yes! Can you imagine our formidable Maman doing anything else? I had to restrain her from joining the barricades.' I could tell from his smile he was only half in jest.

We had a lot to catch up on and spent hours together that morning. When the old serving woman came in with wafers and a glass jug of wine, Joan tripped along behind her, wide-eyed and clearly enjoying herself. She sidled up to me and whispered in my ear.

'This lady is showing me how they make their caps. I'd like to try that style in Devon. Can I, Mistress?' Her face lit up when I nodded my agreement, and she trotted off.

'I'm sure they're looking after your people,' Gabriel said. 'Do you think we can persuade your musician to play for us later? I hear your orphan boy has come on a lot.'

'Of course. He's been composing a new song. He'd love for you to be first to hear it.'

Gabriel drained his glass and wiped the crumbs from his mouth with a napkin of the finest linen.

'Let me return to my story,' he said.

Savouring the faint spicy taste of the wine, I spread my skirts on the window seat and gave him my full attention.

I cried when Gabriel spoke about Giles and the battles they had fought side by side and smiled when he spoke of their attempts to seize Mont Saint-Michel.

'My son Arthur thinks you are a hero. But is it over now?' I asked. 'Will they leave Henri of Navarre to rule with no further uprisings?'

'For now, at least I think so. That means we can concentrate on regaining all our lands as Papa demanded from the scaffold. Maman was determined we must regain everything they took from Papa. She made many sacrifices to help us.'

'Did she suffer at the end, Gabriel? I noticed she had to dictate her letters to a scribe. How she must have hated that!'

'She bore it all with the gritty determination you would expect. How pleased she'd be to see you here in Pontorson.'

'I wasn't always a good and dutiful daughter, Gabriel. Yet she came to my aid when I most needed her. I wish I'd seen her one last time.'

'She had not forgotten you. Her instructions were quite clear.' My mouth dropped open.

'What do you mean?' I asked, my voice rising. He laid a reassuring hand on my arm.

'You are to receive your rightful share, Roberda. Jacques and Gedeon are on their way from Lorges. The agreements are all drawn up. Maman told me how much she regretted your suffering because of the unpaid dowry. She wanted to make it right.' It seemed awful to grin when we were talking about Maman's death, but I couldn't keep the smile off my face.

'But what about my sisters?'

'They're all well provided through their husbands. You're the one in need.' I felt like running out into the garden and shouting my joy to the rooftops. It was the answer to a prayer.

Much relieved, I settled in for a few restful days before Jacques and Gedeon arrived. Suzanne kept me company, sharing stories of her childhood as she worked on her sewing or sitting beside me as we read. One afternoon, she closed her own book with a snap and looked at me.

'What is that book you read from every day, Roberda?' I flipped through the pages of the slender volume in my hands, reluctant to confess that my focus often rested on the words inscribed on the frontispiece and the folded note with his signature, rather than the poem that followed. Thomas's gift had delighted me, though it left me to mulling over the weight of his expectations upon my return to England. I couldn't deny the powerful attraction between us. With the prospect of a solution to my perilous financial predicament now within my grasp, I might be free to make my decision. However, I wasn't ready to disclose any of this to Suzanne or any of my French relatives just yet.

'It's a poem by an English woman all about the wars in France. Her name is Anne Dowriche.'

Holding her own book tight against her chest, Suzanne fixed me with an incredulous stare.

'A woman has written a poem, and she had it published? How extraordinary!' she said as her eyebrows shot upwards. 'But what can she know of affairs here, and why would she choose to write about our misfortunes?'

'She is one of the many staunch Protestants in England who hoped to persuade the Queen to do more to support the Huguenots in France. I believe she drew on conversations with French refugees who told her of the horrors of St Bartholomew's Day.' My words came out all in a rush. 'It is indeed a brave thing to have published a poem. She is the wife of a Devon vicar!' Hoping to avoid having to hand the book over for her to look at it more closely, I said, 'Perhaps I can translate a few lines for you?'

Setting her head on one side she gave me her full attention. 'Thank you, Roberda. A moving account, though I doubt it swayed Queen Elizabeth to action! But tell me, why do you sit for so long staring at the opening page?'

I swallowed and spread my fingers across my chest in a defensive gesture.

'It is a gift from a friend, that is all!'

'Ah, I see,' she said. 'I think this must be a very special friend, n'est-ce pas?'

Chapter Twenty-Eight

Family Affairs

Spring 1594, Pontorson, France

Bawling orders at the top of his voice, Jacques threw his cap aside, revealing hair shot through with a sprinkling of silver threads. He unbuckled his sword belt, letting the weapon fall with a crash. I didn't need a second glance to recognise the engraved scabbard as my father's.

Jacques offered me no warm words of welcome or loving embrace. Instead, he marched in without even looking at me. Gabriel winked, and we followed Jacques inside. As I made my way towards the door of Maman's best parlour, the thud of pounding feet made me pause. I glanced over my shoulder and saw Gedeon running up the steps. He took my hand, and bowing theatrically, planted a kiss on it.

'Don't mind Jacques, Roberda. He has the manners of a wild boar! It's good to see you!' Gedeon said, trying to lighten the situation.

'He does seem put out! What's going on?'

Gedeon responded by putting a finger to one side of his nose and patting it. We took our seats in front of Jacques like members of a Commission of Inquiry, waiting for answers. Jacques pulled up a bench behind a table groaning under the weight of great platters of biscuits and cakes, crusty bread and cheese, along with bowls of nuts and fruit.

'Fill the mug, fool!' The butler recoiled at Jacques' belligerent tone but proceeded to fill the proffered mug with ale. Taking up a knife, he hacked several slices of bread from the loaf and took a good helping of soft cheese from a heart-shaped block. The nutty tang of the cheese wafted round the room. Jacques spoke with his mouth full, spitting crumbs over the crisp linen cloth.

'Where are the papers, Gedeon? Let's sign and have done!'

I pursed my lips. I was having none of that.

'Now hold on a moment, Jacques,' I said. 'I haven't even seen these papers, much less read them.'

Breadcrumbs and spittle spattered the documents that lay scattered across the white cloth. Jacques looked at me in the same condescending way he used to when we were children.

'What would you know about Maman's lands? You've been in England all this time.'

I threw up my hands in despair. It was as if we were back in the nursery.

'That's hardly my fault, is it? You know very well my life there has not been easy.'

'Well, you're free now that fool Champernon is dead! Couldn't abide the man myself! I expect you'll marry again soon. Why should some other Englishman snap up my mother's inheritance?'

Gabriel intervened.

'Look here, Jacques! I know you're peeved that Maman insisted Roberda have her full share. Gedeon and I, well, we believe Maman was right to set it up this way. We're here to make sure it's done properly.'

Jacques crossed his arms and frowned, looking more and more like a cornered bull. Gedeon and Gabriel grinned.

'He'll start pawing at the ground soon!' Gedeon said, his face creased up as he tried to suppress a chuckle. Gabriel hugged his sides as if to hold in gales of laughter. I couldn't see the funny side at all. So much was resting on the outcome.

Jacques drained the cup and thumped it down, signalling for another. The butler, mild-mannered Antoine, scurried to do his bidding while Gedeon and Gabriel watched, not bothering to conceal their amusement. It was hard to understand how three brothers who looked so similar could have such differing personalities.

While Jacques wolfed down his food, Gabriel tried to arrange his face into more serious lines.

'I'm sorry, Roberda. We're used to seeing him like this. He's a sight to behold in one of his moods. Let me explain. We've drawn up succession agreements for Maman's properties in Touraine and Beauce for your share. It's what our parents should have paid to Champernon as a dowry.'

'In coin or bonds or what?' I asked. 'I have responsibilities to discharge on behalf of my son in Devon. French lands are no use to me at all!'

'We can raise the coin, but we'll have to sell some land. That's what's upsetting our brother.' Gabriel flashed a scornful look at Jacques, who picked up two walnuts and cracked them in his palm. Gabriel's voice was now laced with irritation. 'Then we need to complete an inventory of her goods. We can also sell off a few jewels and such like.'

Jacques slammed his mug down, spilling a fair amount of ale in the process.

'Can I remind you I am charged to regain all of Papa's lost properties? Selling off lands and sending money to England is not part of my plan.'

My anger had been simmering. Now, like an unwatched pot, it boiled over. Pushing my chair back with a clatter, I shot forwards and leant over the table, stabbing a finger towards Jacques. I locked eyes with him and my voice pierced through the chasm between us like a sharp sword thrust.

'The debt is long-standing, as you know only too well. What about my sisters? Do you intend to have their share too?'

Jacques glowered at me.

'Their dowries were paid. There's nothing owing to them!' he snarled. The mugs of ale had not improved his temper. Gabriel gave a more reasoned answer.

'Charlotte has said she'll come when she can, but to see you, not to benefit from Maman's will or her possessions.' His smile, and the thought of seeing my sister, blunted the edge of my fury as he continued. 'She has no need of anything more from Maman's estate. Her inheritance from her first husband was substantial, and she fought hard to get it all back.'

'Given it all to her second, Daniel de la Touche. Fought well alongside us, but he's too young for our Charlotte,' Jacques said.

'He's taken all her money to fund his adventures on the high seas. That rather proves my point! A widow's money's fair game for many men.'

Gabriel's eyes flicked upwards, and he shook his head, then continued as if Jacques had not spoken.

'I doubt if we'll see Elisabeth or Suzette either. As Jacques says with such eloquence, they have all had their share.' Gedeon, who had been silent during this exchange, spoke up.

'Look, why not read all the details, Roberda? Then we'll all get together tomorrow to sign everything. We'll need witnesses too. Gabriel's squire, Jules Capello and the butler will do.'

After I had wiped the crumbs from their crinkled surface with my hand, I gathered the documents up into my arms. With a withering look at Jacques that would have frozen ice on a pail of milk, I left them to it.

Joan, waiting at the foot of the stairs, pulled at a lock of hair that had escaped the linen cap she'd tried unsuccessfully to arrange in the French style.

'Is everything all right, ma'am?' she asked. 'I heard shouting.'

'All is well, Joan! Please arrange for a meal to be sent to my room. I have a lot to consider.' Leaving her open-mouthed, I stalked up the stairs.

As I passed the door to Maman's room, I paused. My fingers fluttered above the knob and I reached out with trembling fingers until I felt its cold metal surface against my skin. But, I was not ready to face so many memories. I was still seething at Jacques' ridiculous attitude. So I released my grip and moved on.

In the chamber assigned to me, I hurled the succession agreements onto the faded bed cover, where they landed in a disordered heap. I stood at the window, pressing my fingers hard against the cool glass panes. From there, I had a good view of the walled garden behind the house, a green oasis that bore a few scars from the recent fighting. Straight gravel paths divided the overgrown beds of Maman's once tidy formal garden, while beyond them, a tangle of long grass swayed in the breeze under the fruit trees. The apple buds were still furled tight, delicate blossoms hidden from view. But a few early cherry blossoms had burst, coating the branches with a froth of pale flowers.

Watching two men piecing together the damaged stonework of

the wall, I pushed the window open a crack. The metallic clink of the workmen's hammers beat out a staccato rhythm as they restored order from the chaos war had left behind. At that moment, I envied those two ordinary working men. They would soon have the wall looking as good as new. Even though Maman had arranged compensation, no one could repair the damage I had suffered. Maman's money seemed a gift from heaven to secure my children's future. I could not allow Jacques to keep it from me.

Next morning, when I woke, the sky was a canvas painted with delicate streaks of dusky pink, hinting at the promise of a new day. I stood at the open window, feeling the cool breeze brush against my face as the soft rays of the morning sun gently warmed my skin. The air carried a delicate flowery scent, mingling with the earthy smell of damp grass. Encouraged out by the joyful song of a proud robin claiming his territory, I decided to take a turn in the gardens.

Not bothering about my appearance, I donned a cloak over my plainest gown and slipped my feet into my soft leather riding boots. I let my hair fall in an untidy braid over my shoulder; no one was likely to see me at this hour. Later, I would have Joan to help me into more suitable finery in time to face my brothers.

When I reached the fruit trees, I noticed a labyrinth of slimy trails criss-crossing over the grass. The mild March weather and refreshing overnight rain had encouraged snails from their secret havens. A song thrush used a stone slab left by the masons as a makeshift anvil, busy smashing snail shells, each blow a satisfying crack. Deep in thought, I watched the bird pick up the unsuspecting creatures in its beak and bash them on the hard surface until the fragile shell gave way to yield the succulent treat within. Footsteps behind me made me whirl round to see Jacques almost on top of me, his long strides eating the distance between us.

'Determined little beggar, isn't he?' He nodded towards the bird. Startled by my brother's towering presence, it took flight, leaving a trail of broken shells and half-eaten snails behind. 'As determined as you are, sister.'

I knew he was just trying to get under my skin, but I couldn't help but round on him.

'Like any mother, I fight for my children. Arthur must have his inheritance, and my girls need dowries.'

Jacques' craggy features softened.

'I can see something of Maman in you, Roberda. Look, I'm sorry for what I said. Of course, you're free to marry as you wish.'

'Freedom? That will be a novelty to me! You'll remember I had no choice but to marry for duty as a girl. All to forge an English alliance to aid Papa in the war. I ended up shackled to a cruel and ambitious man, far from home, with no support from my family!'

'Well… I did what I could.'

'Only after our sister Béatrice traipsed all over France to shame you into writing to Walsingham. I've always wondered if, left to yourself, you'd have bothered at all.'

'Ah, our half-sister, the sainted Béatrice, the nun, Papa's little indiscretion! Yes, she found me. There was a war on, as I recall it.' He reached up and plucked a spray of rosy cherry blossom and made a show of presenting it to me. 'Peace offering, Roberda? That water has long passed beneath the bridge. Can't we meet as friends?' He put a hand on my arm, but I shook him off.

'Not if you continue to treat me like an imbecile who will sign away all her fortune to the first man she meets.' A guilty flush crept up my cheek as an image of Thomas flashed into my mind. I dismissed it with a stamp of my leather boot. 'Be in no doubt, brother, I will always put my children before my own happiness, just as I had to put family first when I married Gawen.'

I don't know where the thought came from, but standing in the orchard, suddenly my future path became clear.

'I will never take another man's name. Should I decide to marry again, I will remain Lady Gabrielle Roberda Montgomery, even to my husband, whoever he may be. If he won't accept that, I'll not be his wife.'

'Calm down! I don't even know if that's legal for a woman in England,' he said. Yet as Jacques stared at the house, all his bluster vanished. The barred and shuttered windows of Maman's room were a stark reminder of the sad task that had brought us to Pontorson. 'It's just the sort of thing she would do,' he went on. 'Remember how Papa made her his attorney all those years ago? I can't believe she's gone, Roberda.' My arrogant brother's chin actually wobbled, and his eyes misted over so that he had to blink hard to keep the tears from flowing into his neat beard. 'The thing is, Papa issued a challenge from the scaffold at Place de Grève. I must put all my efforts into regaining everything they took from him.'

'That I understand. Maman has already transferred most of what she was able to reclaim to you, Gedeon and Gabriel. She managed on a pittance for years so that you could rebuild. Surely, you don't mean to dispute her wishes now and deny me my share?' My tone was gentle now. He held up his hands as if in surrender.

'Are you sure you won't let any man get his hands on it? It will all be for your children?' I let out a roar.

'Have you listened to anything I've said?'

'All right, all right. Have you read it all?'

'I have, and I'm ready to sign. It will be best if I help prepare the inventory of Maman's remaining possessions. You may be glad of a woman's eye to judge the true value of her clothes and jewels. If Charlotte comes, we can do it together.' Deep down, I was dreading it. Yet, I was determined that the boys shouldn't sift through my mother's things without me. They would take a cursory look and might dismiss her prized treasures as worthless trinkets. The painful task would be easier with my sister at my side.

'So let's declare a truce between us. Here, take my arm. Let's walk in together and show them a united front. We are being observed.'

I glanced over his shoulder. Sure enough, Gedeon, Gabriel, and Suzanne stood in the open doorway while at an upstairs window, I saw Joan. When we entered arm in arm, they all cheered.

'I must change my gown,' I said, bolting for the stairs. Jacques' voice followed me.

'Gather the witnesses and we can soon get this business done.'

Chapter Twenty-Nine

Sisters

Spring 1594, Pontorson, France

The child's wide eyes sparkled with a mixture of exhilaration and wariness as she stepped gingerly down from the carriage. Unsteady on her feet, she wobbled, and Joan reached out to prevent her from tumbling. Supported by Joan's reassuring arm, the fair-haired child landed on the uneven cobblestones with a sharp clatter from her pretty shoes and gaped at me.

A tall elegant woman emerged from the coach.

'Charlotte? Is it really you?' I said. She dropped her bag onto the gravel and wrapped her arms round me. I felt the comforting warmth of her body, the familiar, half-forgotten scent of her favourite floral perfume. Releasing my sister, I stepped back, laughing. 'Let me look at you. Why, you've hardly changed at all!'

She took the child by the hand.

'My daughter Anne,' Charlotte said. 'She's excited to meet her aunt.'

'Tante Roberde!' the little girl chanted in her sweet, sing-song voice, beaming up at me.

I bent down to greet Anne, whose cherubic face came no higher than my knee.

'I am pleased to make your acquaintance, little one.' She giggled as I shook her hand. 'Oh, Charlotte! It's been so long, and yet you look younger than when last I saw you. Motherhood must agree with you.'

'Yes, I am so lucky to have this little one. I thought my chance was long gone.' Her bright smile faded with her next words. 'I wish the errand that has brought us together again was a happier one.'

As we turned, arm in arm, to make our way up the steps, Anne bouncing along beside us, I caught a faint flicker of movement. Someone else was descending from the coach. Her dark nun's habit caught on the door, and for a moment I couldn't see her face as she struggled to free the folds of heavy cloth. A silver cross chinked on rosary beads hung from her girdle and a crisp white wimple framed a familiar face.

'Béatrice? Can it be?' I grasped the hands she extended to me and looked into her piercing blue eyes, so like my papa's. 'How wonderful! I never thought to see you again.' When she replied, her voice was as light and sweet as it had been when first we met as children.

'May God be with you, Roberda. I am also delighted. He has granted us this opportunity to meet again.'

'I have never forgotten what you did for me. It was you who persuaded Jacques to intervene with Gawen. That must have been so hard for you, as Mother Superior of a Catholic convent. To give money to the Huguenot cause as you pleaded with him on my behalf.' A serene smile spread over her face, and with a tinkling laugh, she set my mind at rest.

'Let us say no more of it. I owed a debt. We must pay such debts. I did so. It is done, and all is equal between us and before God.'

We sisters spent several days catching up while a giggling Anne played an endless game of 'all hid' with her new friend, Joan. Charlotte's little girl had taken to my young serving maid. She found many enticing hiding places in Maman's old house, while a patient Joan counted to one hundred.

Jacques and Gedeon had left for Lorges as soon as we had signed the agreements, but Gabriel was still there with Suzanne at his side. We all enjoyed walking in the gardens together, and one sunny morning, we took a stroll through the town to the 'sermon' Maman had set up.

'I hope soon they will agree that those of our faith can worship safely again,' Gabriel said, looking up at the shuttered windows.

'Until then, it's best for everyone to say their prayers and read the word within the walls of their own home, as we do.'

A cloud crossed Béatrice's face.

'I hope I give no offence when I go to Notre Dame.'

'Not at all!' Gabriel said, tugging at his collar as his face flushed with embarrassment. I jumped in.

'Let us hope good sense will at last prevail and King Henri will agree to a formula that will allow everyone to follow their own conscience as far as religion is concerned. But howsoever that may be, you are our family, Béatrice.'

'Of course you are, and you are welcome to stay with us as long as you wish,' Gabriel said. I hoped Béatrice did not catch the concerned look Suzanne flashed at her husband.

'I am needed at my convent, so I must leave you on the morrow,' Béatrice replied, her expression bland, with no sign of any ill feeling. 'I will pass Alain du Bois' grave on my journey home, Roberda. Would you like me to lay flowers there for you?'

'Ah, that would be a kindness but do it for Clotilde, not I. A bunch of her favourite lilies, perhaps?' She smiled her understanding.

It was a wrench to say goodbye the next morning, knowing how unlikely it was that we would ever meet again.

Later that day, a messenger arrived with letters from England. I read them on the terrace, drinking in the sweet floral fragrance of roses, valiantly blooming despite years of neglect. Anne ran amongst the untidy flower-beds, chasing butterflies, Joan egging her on. The child's delighted laughter was enough to lift anyone's spirits, but I frowned as I studied the close written lines.

'Not bad news, I hope?' Charlotte asked.

'No, no indeed! Merely a dutiful report from Mary. I've left her in charge of the little ones.'

Charlotte reached over and patted my hand.

'You miss them, don't you?'

'It's not being there for those special moments. My youngest, Bridget, will turn two this summer. Mary says she's speaking in complete sentences, though she gets the words mixed up.'

With a sigh, I put Mary's tidings aside and took up the letter I had saved until the last, the one addressed in Thomas Horner's elegant hand. Feeling the heat as a flush crept up my cheeks, I reached for a mug of ale while studying his opening words. My hand stopped midway, frozen as I stuttered out a denial.

'Oh no!'

'What is it?' Charlotte asked.

I set down the page and let my head droop.

'It's Mistress Raleigh. She's gone!'

'Who? Tell me, my dearest sister,' she asked. I hauled myself up from the depths of despair, knowing I must explain.

'It is Walter's mother. You remember Walter, who came to Ducey years ago? He was there at Elisabeth's wedding.'

'Of course. An adventurer, a kindred spirit for my Daniel.'

'His mother, Katherine Raleigh, has always been a friend to me. She helped me with the refugee women. It's hard to believe a woman of such an indomitable spirit has given up her grip on life. I must write to Walter.' Stumbling up to my chamber, I called for ink and paper. But when I sat at the desk, no words of comfort came to me.

We had not yet broached the difficult subject of entering Maman's room to complete the inventory. Instead, Gabriel suggested that, the weather being fine, we might ride to Ducey.

It was one of those enchanting spring days when the world awakens, bursting with joy. I turned my face to welcome the caress of the sun's gentle rays. As I looked up, an endless sky stretched above, a vivid shade of blue, like no other. Delicate yellow primroses dotted the roadside. Fresh green leaves swayed in the breeze. The air was alive with jubilant birdsong and the air was sweet with the barest hit of salt from the distant marshes. Yet, amidst this display of nature's delights, a pang of sorrow ripped through me. On a day so radiant, it was difficult to accept that Katherine Raleigh would never again witness the beauty of such a morning. It was a reminder to cherish life's joys while we have the chance, to value each precious moment. I resolved to give Thomas his answer.

As we drew nearer, Pierre lifted his voice in song, louder and louder with every passing mile. His excitement was infectious. We were all looking forward so much to seeing dear Ducey once more, although Gabriel had warned us not to expect too much.

We clattered over the bridge, past the very spot where I had found Pierre when he was a starving orphan boy. Breaking off mid-chorus, he turned in his saddle and craned his neck.

'The house where my mother lived is gone,' he said shaking his head. 'Nothing left, not even a shell.'

Worse was to come. Even the stout walls around our old home had crumbled to rubble. The plot where a mansion house with glittering windows had welcomed us in times past was desolate, a tangle of upturned stones and brambles. There was no sign of the neat gardens where I had chased a white puppy between the hedges. A single white rose bush scrambled over the debris, the tips of new buds just visible amid the chaos.

'I warned you,' Gabriel said, shaking his head. He cleared his throat and took up a noble stance. 'I vow before you all. One day I will raise the Chateau Montgomery again here in Ducey.'

We dismounted, wandered towards the overgrown orchard, searching for landmarks of our youth.

'It's somewhere near here. It must be around here,' Charlotte said. 'This must be where we had our swing. And over there, that must be where Alain set a headstone for your puppy.' I knelt amongst the long grass, pushed it aside and there it was, the name 'Fi Fi', letters still clear on the mossy surface.

'My, how you loved that little dog,' Charlotte said, with a catch in her voice. I had a sudden yearning for the green hills of Dartington, the holy well and the yew tree, and my physick garden.

'Let's sort through Maman's things tomorrow, Charlotte. I need to go home to my children.' I did not add how much I also longed to see a man named Thomas Horner.

Gabriel gave the shutters a mighty shove and a beam of sunlight fell across Maman's bed, dust mites dancing along it like fairies. The room had few furnishings and a bleak feel, with little attention given to creature comforts. The thick hangings of bright red embroidered linen around the four-poster bed would have kept out the draughts, but that was about the limit of Maman's luxuries.

The old woman I had seen on arrival at Pontorson led us to a large chest.

'I was maidservant to Madame la Comtesse. She said I should have some of this.'

'Do not worry, Odette. We'll do everything as Maman has asked.'

'Did she expect to die? Clear everything away in her last days, thinking to spare us pain?' I asked.

'No, Roberda, this is how she lived. She gave up everything so that we could build anew,' Gabriel answered. 'I have completed the list of all the furniture.'

The maid crouched over the chest and fumbled with the catch, cursing under her breath as her aged fingers struggled to release it. At last it flew open, emitting a screech, eerie as an owl's hunting cry, as the hinges pinched. Inside was a collection of clothing, a couple of rough woollen over-gowns, another of faded red velvet and quantities of linen.

'Take all you wish, Odette. It is what she wanted. There is money, too, sufficient for your needs.' The old woman sniffed and rubbed a none-too-clean hand across her brow.

'Thank you, Madame. She was a good mistress. Just and generous to those who served her.'

Charlotte and I exchanged glances.

'This can't be all. Odette, did she have another special place where she kept things during the fighting, perhaps?'

The old woman grinned, revealing toothless gums.

'Oh, yes, indeed, she did. Called it her coffre fort. Here!' She pulled aside the curtain at the head of the bed to reveal a metal door. The maid pulled the bed frame aside so that we could see the door was high enough for us to walk through, if only we could open it. 'Blacksmith made it for her. I have the key somewhere. Now let me think.'

We waited while she racked her brains, then scurried off. We heard her footsteps on the stairs die away as she headed for the kitchen. When she returned, she carried a heavy iron key.

'It was hidden behind the bread oven, halfway up the chimney. That's where she told me to keep it, so I did.' Brushing the black soot from the metal, she gave it a rub on her apron before she passed it to me. To my relief, the key turned in the lock to reveal a small closet. We found money, silver cups, bed covers exquisitely embroidered in gold, red and black silk thread, a fine turkey rug, and all of her wearing apparel. In a smaller chest, a set of knives with fine crystal handles nestled upon a bolt of crimson silk-satin embroidered with gold and silver threads.

'Take the cloth, Roberda. Have it made up for your wedding day,' Charlotte said with a twinkle in her eye.

'I have not said I am to be wed, sister.'

Gabriel stood open-mouthed while Charlotte gave me an arch look.

'You do not need to,' she said. 'The way you constantly trace your fingers over the name at the foot of that letter and turn the pages of that little book, but seeing none of the words – well, I'm afraid it gives you away. I hope this man will make you happy.'

Chapter Thirty

A Proposal

August 1594, Dartington Hall

He offered me his arm, and together we strolled through my physick garden. Pausing along the way, Thomas plucked a rose from the briar that twined around the arbour, and grinning like a kitchen cat locked in the dairy overnight, offered it to me. With a laugh, I took a pin from my collar and fixed the fragrant red bloom to the front of my gown. The intoxicating musky scent from its soft petals brought back happy memories of my childhood home.

We wandered on past the holy well and took the path to Sir Arthur's favourite viewpoint as I shared my experiences in France. Despite Clotilde's wise advice not to bombard everyone with tales of my adventures, I couldn't contain my excitement and continued to chatter, oblivious to his growing impatience.

'It was wonderful to see my half-sister, Béatrice, again. Did I mention she's Mother Superior in a Catholic convent? It could have been awkward with my brothers still so strong on the Protestant side, but funnily enough, it wasn't. She's been in that convent since she was a girl, sent there by her mother's family. The de Tavannes have always been strong supporters of the Catholics. Her uncle fought against my father. Although Béatrice has spent years shut up behind those convent walls, if truth be told, I'm envious of her.'

'You don't mean you yearn for a cloistered life?'

'Oh no, not at all! It's just that Béatrice is at the head of that community of women. She has such independence and power. Such a contrast to the position I held as Gawen's wife, and even now, as a widow, I find my options limited.' I flashed him a playful grin. 'It is a man's world, is it not, Thomas?'

As we reached the top of the hill we paused, suddenly at a loss for words. A light breeze had sprung up, bestowing a gentle caress on my skin and teasing strands of hair from beneath my headdress. It brought a much-needed respite from the oppressive August heat. Wanting to fill the silence, I prattled on, inconsequential, short sentences spilling out of my mouth.

'This is my favourite spot on the estate. Sir Arthur loved it too. He set this seat here so he could take in the view. I often come here to think.'

He found his voice at last.

'Perhaps I should have waited, given you more time to recover from your journey. I could wait no longer. My dear Roberda, ever since I first saw your lovely face in the solar at Modbury, it has stayed with me, etched in my mind clearer than my own reflection in the glass.' He took my hand, and a shiver ran through me as he led me to Sir Arthur's weathered bench and sat beside me. 'I've rehearsed a long speech countless times, but all I need do is to ask. Roberda, will you be my wife? It would make me the happiest of men. Will you say yes?'

'Dearest Thomas! Are you sure?'

'I am. But you hesitate!' I caught a flicker of doubt in his eyes before he looked down at his boots, then continued with a sigh. 'When I came upon you that day, so distressed and reeling from the sad news of your brother's loss, my immediate instinct was to protect you. Yet when I saw the valiant lift of your chin and heard the determination in your voice, I realised you were more than capable of taking care of yourself. Your independent spirit has intrigued me these past months, fascinating me yet making me fear you may not want to share your life with me.'

Excitement and delight that he should declare his love for me fought with panic lest I put myself under the rule of another man. I sat bolt upright, feeling as tense as a coiled spring and smoothed my skirt with anxious fingers, not daring to look at him. Stung by

Jacques' suggestion that I would marry some other Englishman who would take control of the money from Maman's estate, I had made a brave pronouncement about keeping my own name. Was it too much to ask of this honourable man, this man who had done so much to help me, this man I yearned for with every fibre of my being? Could I ask him to accept such terms?

'What is it?' he asked, his voice gentle as the breeze that lifted a lock of his hair. Raising a hand, he pushed it away from his forehead with an impatient gesture. 'I was sure you had feelings for me.'

'Oh, Thomas! You are not mistaken! It would be an honour to share my life with you. But you know how my first marriage has left me bruised and buffeted. And I told my brother Jacques I would always put my children first and would never take another man's name.'

'Whether you take my name doesn't matter to me. I will support you in all your endeavours, but Roberda, I have no wish to rule over you. I've had two wives already. Like you, I married for duty. Good women both, who gave me sons. Now I am free to choose. I don't need or want a dutiful wife. I choose you, Roberda, because I love you. All I want is to have you at my side, to see your smile when I wake each morning, to sit with you by the fireside of winter nights.' As he continued speaking, at last I mustered the courage to look up. 'I'll not have you known as the widow of a scoundrel who treated you so ill,' he said. 'I will not force my name on you. To me, you will always be Lady Gabrielle Roberda Montgomery. We can find a way, can't we?'

'Yes, Thomas, I believe we can.'

It was a long time before we noticed how long the shadows cast by the trees had grown.

'We should return to the hall, or we will be missed,' I said. 'I'm surprised we haven't seen that busy-body Alice lurking behind a bush to spy on us.' His laughter rang out, as bright and warm as the summer sun on my back. Giggles welled up from somewhere deep within me in a shared moment of intoxicating joy I shall never forget.

'For once, they will put two and two together and come up with the correct answer!'

As we subsided into silence, sunlight filtered through the leaves, leaving intricate patterns on the grass at our feet. All the colours of the familiar scene appeared more vibrant and alive than ever before.

'When I was in France, my birthplace, I felt no sense of homecoming. Instead, these rolling Devon hills beckoned to me, calling from across the sea.' As I spoke, like a sudden gust of wind, the realisation struck me: Thomas would likely prefer his estates in Somerset over my cherished home. My radiant smile wavered as the enormity of my decision hit me like a hammer blow. I had fought so hard to secure Dartington for my children, but soon I would have to leave.

Thomas sensed some struggle within me. His voice rose in concern as he tried to understand what had changed my mood.

'You're not having second thoughts?'

'No, no! Never that! It is just that this place has played such a big part in my life, it will be hard to leave it behind.'

We walked on, my arm through his, and with each step, our feet kicked up clouds of fine dust, leaving a delicate film at the hem of my gown. Inhaling the earthy scent of the warm soil reminded me how long I'd been rooted in Devon. It was time for me to blossom elsewhere with the man I loved.

We turned the corner, and the hall came into view, its slate-grey walls warm and welcoming in the late afternoon sun. To one side, the black outline of St Mary's Tower rose up into a clear blue sky. A figure emerged from beneath the yew tree to hurry along the garden path. It was Lisbeth, carrying a basket, no doubt returning from some foraging expedition. The sight of my eldest daughter, still unmarried and over twenty, brought me down to earth with a jolt. I sighed. My work at Dartington was not over. Before I could move on, I needed to fulfil my obligation to administer Gawen's will.

Thomas had noticed her, too, and it was as if he could read my mind.

'Though I long to take you to my manor at Cloford, where we can live as happy and undisturbed as two birds in the nest, we can return to Dartington as often as you wish.' He took both my hands in his. 'My dearest love, nothing would please me more than to have the priest marry us today in the church down there. But I know there is much for you to accomplish to seal your family's future before we embark on our new life together.'

'If I could, I'd ride away with you today, dear Thomas. But, as you say, my task here is by no means complete. My mother's will provides the dowry they should have paid to Sir Arthur so long ago when I married Gawen. In his will, he charges me to use it to provide for all my daughters. On top of that, I have to pay off debts and finalise Sir Arthur's purchase of Dartington if I'm to pass on the estate to my son when he comes of age. There simply isn't enough money to do it all, and I'm afraid Gawen's overseers are just waiting for me to falter. I'm still not sure of Richard's motives. It's strange I've heard no more from him.'

We had reached the ornate iron gate to the formal gardens. The click of the latch sounded unnaturally loud in the stillness of late afternoon as Thomas paused and fiddled with the catch.

'I rather think Richard's had other things on his mind, matters I fear are unfit for a lady's ear,' he said.

I smiled and reached out to touch his cheek.

'Nonsense, Thomas! I'm no green and tender maid to be shielded from the ways of the world. I admit I am intrigued. Whatever can it be that makes you blush so! Let us sit in the arbour. You must tell me all.' I adjusted my skirts and half turned towards Thomas, who sat so close I could feel the warmth of his leg pressed against mine. Out of the corner of my eye, I caught a fleeting movement by the kitchen door.

'What did I tell you? There she is. Alice with her ear to the ground for some juicy gossip!' The plump maidservant held a white linen tablecloth aloft and gave it a vigorous shake, sending crumbs flying high into the air to land on the gravel path at her feet. The commotion attracted a flock of sparrows that swooped down and pecked at the unexpected bounty, chirping and squabbling. After shooing them away, Alice made a business of folding and refolding the cloth, running her fingers along the creases with unnecessary precision. Throughout this performance she stood on tiptoe, peering at us.

'Well, my Lady Montgomery,' he said, his voice filled with mirth and anticipation. 'Shall we give her something to tattle about?' With those words, he pulled me into his arms and kissed me. In that moment, all my worries, Alice's gossiping, and even the Spanish threat vanished from my mind. Within the haven of his embrace, I felt that anything was possible. After a long time, he released me, and I noticed that Alice had disappeared.

'Now, tell me this shocking story about the master of Modbury. I'm all agog,' I said.

'Don't say I didn't warn you. It's an indelicate tale! I think it must have started when the Queen sent Robert Cecil down to Dartmouth to put a stop to the rioting over the cargo of that captured Portuguese ship, the *Madre de Dios*.'

'Ah, I remember that. Loaded with spices, silks and jewels, and all sorts of valuables, and everyone rioting and squabbling, trying to get a piece of the plunder. Cecil couldn't control the men of Devon once they were roused, and Queen Elizabeth released Walter from the Tower of London to sort it all out.'

'That's it. Well, it seems Cecil visited Modbury while he was in Devon and heard one of the choir boys sing.'

'Ah, yes, the one who sang like an angel when everyone gathered here after Gawen's funeral.' The events of that afternoon were etched clear in my mind – the faces of the men surprised by my unexpected return, Richard's angry reaction, and the boy's glorious voice rising to the rafters.

'Well, Cecil wanted to take the boy to London, have him in his own household so he could impress the Queen. He tried to get Richard to part with him, but Richard dug his heels in and said no. That should have been the last we heard of it, but they've been arguing for months. Lately it seems a malicious rumour is going round. The gist of it is that Richard uses... er...' He broke off, cheeks flushing. 'Er... how can I put this? They say Richard uses unnatural means to keep the boy's voice high pitched.'

My mouth dropped open.

'What? You don't mean? I've heard they do it in Italy... but surely you don't mean they accuse poor Richard of gelding the boy?' Thomas's face was by now red as the apothecary's rose that bloomed behind our seat. I went on. 'Pierre says Richard's an excellent master who loves music above all else. He would never do such a thing.'

Thomas's face turned more serious.

'I don't believe it either. But with that going on, I don't suppose

Richard's had much time to think about Dartington. He's complaining about troop allocations for the defence of Devon. Though he rubs people up the wrong way, he's right to be concerned about that. I fear the Spanish threat remains. And, Roberda, we will have to talk about Richard's involvement in Arthur's future sometime soon. But today is far too happy a day for such conversations. Let us go in and tell them all.'

He sprang up from the bench, pulling me to my feet beside him. I stood on tiptoe, and we kissed one more time.

'At the risk of denying Alice more opportunities to spy and gossip, I want to share our happiness with the entire world,' he said.

Chapter Thirty-One

The News is Out!

Late August 1594, Dartington Hall, Devon

All was quiet when we entered the empty hall, where sunbeams streamed through the windows, casting a beautiful dance of light and shade upon the floor. The sound of footsteps broke into the hushed calm, and William appeared in the doorway. Behind him, the burly bailiff shifted a sheaf of documents under his arm. The loud rustling made Thomas turn his head.

'We hoped to discuss estate matters with you, ma'am,' William said, as the bailiff fumbled to remove his cap without dropping the papers he carried.

'Perhaps we might deal with those matters tomorrow, William. Master Horner and I have something important to share with the family.'

William blinked. He took in the line of children filing into the hall, then looked at my flushed, smiling face. Noticing my hand resting on Thomas's arm, his smile broadened to a grin, and he nodded as understanding dawned.

'Of course, ma'am. We'll withdraw.' As he turned, he bumped into the bailiff, who gawped at us with his mouth wide open.

'No, please stay. Both of you are welcome. Indeed, please gather all the servants.' William rushed off, to call everyone to come from the kitchens, the buttery, the scullery, the bakehouse, and the still room. In came the cook, and the scullery maids, the kitchen boys, crowding round Alice, who had a smug 'I told you so' expression all over her round face. They hurried in from every part of the house, the gardens and the stables, nudging each other with their elbows, pointing and casting amused looks our way, the buzz of their lively chatter louder than bees around a honey pot.

Marie braced herself to take Clotilde's weight as she helped the older woman hobble to her seat. Groaning, Clotilde took her time to lower herself down, ordering Marie to stop plumping a cushion she was trying to slip behind her head. Once settled, my aged nurse looked me up and down and nodded in satisfaction. She made a fist with her bony fingers, gave the air a feeble punch, and grinned as if she had just received news of an astounding victory. Joan, standing behind her chair, tittered to see the formidable old French woman looking so jubilant.

Lisbeth brought with her, clinging to her clothes, the faint scent of herbs, a reminder of her work in the still room. Despite her plain attire, there was a delicate beauty about Lisbeth. She looked like a willowy nymph, although her bored expression suggested she was only there on sufferance. I longed to hug her, to share my overflowing joy. When I tried to catch her eye, she turned away to talk to Agnes, who rubbed her hands on her apron, causing the herbal smell to intensify.

Next to Lisbeth, Kate and Ursula giggled and chattered, bubbling with excitement. Arthur towered above the girls, broad-shouldered and confident. Mary scolded the twins and Jane, urging them to keep still while little Bridget squirmed in the firm grip of her nurse. A surge of pride washed over me as I surveyed my children, lined up awaiting the news we were about to share.

Heads swivelled and an expectant hush fell. Thomas cleared his throat.

'We've called you all together to tell you that the Lady Gabrielle Roberda Montgomery, this beautiful and noble lady' – he paused and nodded to Arthur and the girls – 'your esteemed mother, has done me the honour of agreeing that she will become my wife.'

Gasps, whoops, and applause filled the Great Hall as the news sank in until it felt as if the walls themselves were rejoicing. My smile was so broad I felt my face might split. Arthur stepped forward and shook Thomas by the hand. I gulped to see my boy so dignified and grown up. The little girls squealed and danced for joy, while Ursula and Kate started chattering about what they would wear for the wedding. A brief smile flitted over Lisbeth's lovely face before she nodded and followed Agnes out of the hall.

Beaming, Pierre, who had not yet returned to Modbury, picked up his fife and began playing a merry tune. The old shepherd, who had wandered in from the field in his workaday smock, soon joined him on the fiddle. As the lively music filled the air, an impromptu dance began, and before long, everyone was stepping through the measures. Thomas, with a beaming smile that would have lit every beacon from Plymouth to London, took my hand and led me out, while the little ones raced around, getting in everyone's way.

Later, Alice and the kitchen staff brought out trays of hot pies, and the butler served some of Gawen's best Gascon wine from the cellar. It turned into the merriest summer evening Dartington had seen in many years.

As the sun dipped below the horizon, we slipped away from the bustling party and found a quiet moment in the garden. Holding hands, we strolled along the gravel paths, feeling a cooling breeze brush against our skin. I couldn't quite decide if it was the hint of approaching autumn in the cool air or the sheer delight of walking beside him that made me shiver. Our feet led us to the arbour, where the rose-briar shielded us from prying eyes. With a contented smile, Thomas turned to me, his face shining with happiness.

'Are you happy?' he asked.

'Beyond all my dreams.'

'Let us hold this moment, my love, for tomorrow will bring responsibilities for us both. I must return to Mells and give my family our news. There is much to discuss, much we must both accomplish, as we make plans for our wedding. For now, it is enough that we are here together.'

Stars twinkled in the night sky when at last we left the fragrant rose bower. The garden door creaked softly as we went in, and I giggled, hoping no one would discover us.

Yet at the foot of the stairs my face flushed scarlet, and I pulled away. Thomas released my hand and stood back, his smile wavering just a little.

'I must bid you goodnight now,' I said, my voice overloud. 'My reputation is precious, the more so because of the slanders spoken against me in that vile court years ago.' All the tension vanished from Thomas's face.

'I understand. Oh, my love, however tempting it might be, I agree. We must allow no hint of impropriety. Alice and her friends would have it all over the county in no time.'

'We'll be watched by people like Lady Stretchleigh, or whatever she's called – you know, that patronising matron I met at Modbury – and Richard's wife, the daughter of the famous Judge Popham,' I said. 'Women like them still suspect I was guilty, that there was more to Gawen's accusations than nonsense fed to him by evil minds. Even though they threw out the case and exonerated me, people may still believe there's no smoke without a spark!' I twisted my hands together in front of me. Thomas reached for my restless hands.

'Listen. I would have you received in every household, in all the land – aye, from the royal court down – as is your right. You must take your place among them as the Lady Gabrielle Roberda Montgomery, a French Huguenot woman of noble birth. I say this not only for you, my dearest, but for your children, too. We cannot allow any suggestion that we must rush to the altar to tarnish your name. Now I have your promise, I can wait a little longer.'

I managed a weak smile.

'You are a man of considerable honour, Thomas Horner, and I am fortunate indeed to have your love and care.' Another warm embrace, another kiss, before he tore himself away heading towards the guest chamber.

'For now, I must bid you good night and go to my lonely bed,' he called. 'Sweet dreams!'

On a clear mid-September morn, I'd much rather have enjoyed the fresh air, riding out with Arthur and Lisbeth, who had taken the hawks out. But time was pressing, Michaelmas almost upon us, and I needed to set my affairs in order. Seated at the oak desk in Sir Arthur's office, I worked on the estate accounts with William and John Blatchford, the bailiff.

'A few land transactions are still outstanding, the ones we

discussed at Lady Day, when you were away in France. Apart from that, I have accounted for everything,' Blatchford said, running a hand through his unruly mop of sandy hair.

'Yes, please see to it. Now I must give my report to the overseers of my late husband's will. Edward Denny is elsewhere on the Queen's business, or so I suppose. I'll write to him and invite the other three overseers of Gawen's will here to inform them of my decision to wed Master Horner.'

'I expect they know already, ma'am,' William said with his usual broad grin. 'News travels apace here in Devon.'

A week later, Edward Seymour stood in my parlour, hunched over the fire, drying out his wet clothes. Coils of steam rose from his shoulders, and a musty, damp smell filled the air. To my disappointment, Bess was not with her husband.

'Caught in a sudden squall. Damned roads turned to mud. Are the others here yet?' He stomped up to the fire, cursing under his breath.

'I can send Arthur for a change of clothes for you Edward, if you'd be more comfortable.' Arthur was halfway to the door before the querulous answer came.

'No need to fuss. I want to be away by noon. Are they here yet?'

'Not yet,' I said, with a hesitant smile.

His only response was a grunt. Out of politeness, I tried to turn the conversation.

'I was sorry to hear of your father's death last year. Bess tells me you have grand plans to extend his house at Berry Pomeroy and make it an even grander mansion.' Edward cleared his throat and spat into the fireplace.

'Harrumph! That's as may be – if we have enough coin. The Earl of Bath is asking us all to put our hands in our pockets so they can build up the defences in Plymouth. Drake and John Gilbert have three hundred soldiers holed up there. But the fort's not up to it, and they can't keep them fed either.'

'What's that you say? Soldiers in Plymouth?' My voice rose as a tight knot formed in the pit of my stomach. 'Are the Spanish on the move again?' Livid spots of colour flared on Edward's cheeks as he rapped out a sharp reply.

'Yes, Devon's coast is under threat again. While there's breath in his body, Philip of Spain will send his forces against us. They say his shipbuilders have been busy, and he sends his Papist priests in secret to those who will harbour them.' As Edward spoke I felt the stiff fingers of fear creeping up my arm, setting the hairs on end. Once more, I would have to prepare Dartington's people in case of an attack.

Voices and footsteps sounded outside, and Richard burst in with John Harte a pace behind him. Richard eyed Edward like a cock sizing up his opponent in the ring and stalked up to the fire, making a show of warming his hands. Edward gave him a belligerent stare.

'I suppose you've chipped in plenty for the defences in Plymouth?' he said, jabbing a finger in Richard's direction. 'Tax, tax, tax, but I doubt if we're any better prepared, and the Spanish are set to plague us again.' The two men glared at each other, making the air feel so brittle I thought it must snap, if one of them didn't snap first. Edward's voice was full of menace as he poked his finger at Richard's chest again. 'There are some who don't pull their weight.'

Richard bristled and recoiled as if he'd been struck.

'I play my part and would do more if given the chance!'

'As you did when we were preparing in '87 and you went off to Ireland and gave up your position as captain of the trained bands!' Edward smirked and Richard's face was by now as red as a cock's comb.

'I came back and was here when the threat came!' Richard said, and the two men squared up to each other. As if punching a bruise, Edward spat out another set of stinging retorts.

'Because your enterprise in Ireland came to nothing! Everyone knows that plantation scheme's in tatters. Devon needs men to step up to the plate again, not seek to feather their own nests over the water.'

As the last taunt hit home, Richard clenched his fists and planted his feet wide. Taking a firm stance between them, I placed a hand on each man's chest.

'Gentlemen! Please! This bickering aids no one.' I was desperate to keep them apart. 'Won't you take a seat?' After a bit of huffing, Edward slumped onto a bench, muttering.

To my surprise, it was Richard who mastered his anger first. With a tight nod of his head, he struggled to bite back an insult and turned to me.

'Please accept my apologies,' he said, grimacing as he sought to control his voice. 'You're right. We need to pull together in these times. Drake says they are struggling to feed the soldiers at Plymouth.'

'That's so,' Edward replied. 'But seizing all the food doesn't go down well with people trying to make a living! Remember that butcher in Dartmouth in the spring? I heard him blathering about it in the inn...' Harte spoke up at last.

'What was his name? Blackaller, was it?' Alice gave him a searching look as she brought in a tray. No doubt the butcher of Dartmouth was one of her many uncles. Harte continued, his voice clipped and impatient as usual. 'All ready to kill twenty oxen when there came a staying order; such meat to be reserved for Plymouth only. Now they want all the biscuits and beer and more taxes to be collected on top of that. People have had enough. Some say they won't pay up.'

'They'll be sorry if the Spanish land,' Edward said. 'It doesn't help when the deputies fall out with each other. Look at John Gilbert and Cary – all that squabbling about Spanish prisoners in '88.' He fixed Richard with another malevolent glare. 'Every man should do his bit and not allow fine living and singing boys to distract him.' A livid mottled flush covered Richard's cheeks as he growled through gritted teeth. I hastened to intervene.

'Gentlemen, gentlemen, gentlemen! I'm sure everyone has their own view on how best to meet the threat and will do all they can,' I said, determined to take control of the situation. 'We'll not solve all Queen Elizabeth's problems nor fight off the Spaniards today. I've invited you here for quite another purpose. I need not detain you for long. Please, gentlemen, take some refreshments, and then we can make progress.'

Alice set down a tray of wafers and a flagon of ale with a thump and handed them each a mug. Not much escaped Alice's notice. She'd tell everyone all about it, raised voices and all, as soon as she had the chance.

Richard's colour subsided, and sinking into his seat with a sigh, he accepted the document I handed to him and studied the columns of figures. Edward gave his copy a cursory glance.

'I've set out here how I've managed matters on Arthur's behalf,' I said. 'Now, I should acquaint you with the outcome of my visit to France and other changes.'

'We all know you're going to marry Horner. No doubt you'll hand over the reins so I can manage Dartington for the boy.'

I felt my hackles rising as Richard's voice grew louder. However, I remembered what Thomas had said about his manner belying his good intentions.

'We have yet to set the date for our wedding,' I said, keeping my own voice low and steady. I welcome your good counsel, Richard. However, Thomas – that is Master Horner – and I believe it is best to wait until I have more news from France.' I outlined the import of my mother's will, the need for my brothers to sell lands before I could receive the dowry money, and pointed to the set of accounts I had set before them.

'You will find everything in order, gentlemen. In the longer term, I suggest I work with Richard and we manage matters together. There's no need to formalise a wardship agreement.'

'Your new husband will deal with it all in time, no doubt,' Harte said, giving me a sly look.

'It may be the custom in this country for a husband to take charge in that way, Master Harte, but the nature of my agreement with Thomas is different. I shall follow my mother's example. In France, she had full control of my father's affairs for many years. He granted her power of attorney.'

'Well, I'm dammed!' Edward Seymour exclaimed, rubbing a hand across his brow.

I had not quite finished.

'I have the authority to administer the estate on Arthur's behalf until he reaches the age of twenty-one years. But he need not wait until then to marry. Following my marriage, I suggest that, together, Richard and I open discussions about a bride for Arthur.' Arthur's eyes opened wide, but to his credit, he remained calm as I continued brisk and businesslike. 'When he is of full age, of course, he may prove his father's will again and by then, the dowry money will be available to meet all commitments.'

Richard and Harte went into a huddle, murmuring and muttering, but I could see that the plan I had devised with Thomas's help had worked.

A bitter blast roared through Chase Grove Wood, shaking the last leaves from the trees. It cut into the cheeks of anyone foolhardy enough to venture out, bringing coughs and chills to the unwary. That November, the cold set in early.

Clotilde sat on top of the fire in the parlour, banging her feet on the floor as she tried to get the circulation moving in her numb toes. As I entered the room with a steaming dish of pottage, she slowly raised her head before letting it fall onto her chest.

'Come, Clotilde, you must keep up your strength,' I said. After the celebrations of our betrothal, she had slumped into a fit of the deepest melancholy. I could find no way to raise her from it.

'Hmm... that's as may be. You know as well as I, the grim reaper is sharpening his scythe. I can feel the ice-cold blade drawing near. Winter's a dangerous time for us old folks. Death stalks us, thinking to reap his harvest.'

'You must not speak so! Please eat this. You'll come through, as you always do.' Clotilde set her jaw and held my gaze before she spoke again, her voice low and steady.

'If I'm still here by Candlemas, then I might outrun him. If at Easter, then I'll skip for joy.' At last, a vestige of a twinkle returned to her eye, and she spooned the savoury mixture into her mouth, smacking her lips. 'You must go to Mells to meet Master Horner's family at Christmastide, my dear.'

'His sister Jane is to marry Bishop Still in December. Thomas thinks it will be an excellent opportunity to introduce me. But I'm loathe to leave you.'

'Whatever will be will be. Don't deny yourself happiness, *ma petite*! Go!'

'Are you sure?'

'Never more certain! This is your time to shine, to find happiness as a woman in your own right. Be sure to take Joan with you, for propriety's sake, *ma petite*. Go with my blessing.'

Chapter Thirty-Two

West Country Society

Christmas 1594, Somerset

My feet felt like blocks of solid ice as I sat in the country church where Thomas's sister Jane stood beside her new husband. Bishop John Still, a portly man, looked resplendent in his robes of office. I imagined that he must be wearing plenty of layers to keep warm. As for his bride, she wore a sumptuous gown of scarlet silk trimmed with fur. She gave a brave smile, though she suppressed a shiver, her breath a fine mist hanging like a cloud around her. At last, the ceremony over, the happy couple led the way, stepping out briskly over the uneven floor. In the quaint church of St. Mary at Ston Easton, the pews were packed with people, yet the biting cold air seemed to seep right through my heavy clothes, making me shiver. It was a relief to follow the crowd and make our way along the gravel path, our footsteps sounding loud in the still wintry air.

Carriages waited to whisk us to the Manor House, the home of Jane and Thomas's sister Dorothy. The smell of roasting meat met us at the door, beckoning me towards a blazing fire, where I hoped to thaw my frozen toes. Tantalising aromas wafted from the kitchens, promising warm food and comfort. But, despite the cosy atmosphere, I perched on the edge of the richly upholstered seat, crossing and uncrossing my legs beneath my skirts. Conscious I was about to meet Thomas's family and all the high-born people of Somerset, I smoothed my velvet gown and scanned the room. As the moment approached, I felt an anxious trickle of sweat run down the back of my neck.

I waited for Thomas to bring me a warming cup of wine, toes tingling as the warmth found its way to my feet. As I sat by the fire, a towering and portly figure loomed over me. Stern eyes bore into me from a pallid face dominated by a prominent hooked nose. Despite his ashen cheeks and upright bearing, his expansive girth made me wonder if this giant of a man might be overfond of good living.

'Lady Montgomery, I believe?'

'Indeed, and you are?' I asked, without rising from my seat.

'My name is John Popham. I believe you know my daughter, Elizabeth?' Flustered, I hastened to rise and make my curtsey. Richard Champernowne's famous father-in-law, the Chief Justice of the Queen's Bench, a man said to deliver harsh judgements, studied me. I held his eyes, willing myself not to flinch from his searching gaze. I'd heard that neither recusants nor felon's could expect quarter from Judge Popham.

'Yes, sir, I know her well,' I said, noticing a family resemblance. Elizabeth Champernowne's pinched mouth was very like her father's.

'Going to marry Horner, I hear? He was wed to my daughter Amy. She's gone to her grave now. Gave him plenty of sons, but I suppose a man needs a wife. You're Montgomery's daughter, aren't you? How does your family fare in France? Got their lands back from the Catholics, have they?' He rapped the questions out at me as fast as an archer looses arrows at the target. Before I had time to reply, a matronly woman took my arm. Dressed from head to foot in opulent fur-trimmed velvet, she was an imposing sight, with her steel-grey hair peeping from beneath a dark hood. Jewels caught the light as she turned to the judge. A warm smile spread across her round face, right up to her blue eyes. As I saw the warmth in those bright eyes, crinkling with mirth, I felt the tension leave me.

'Leave the girl be, John Popham,' she said, giving him a shove. 'I'm Amy, married to this one, for my sins. Now come, let me introduce you. We've heard all about you. It's terrible how they've persecuted you Huguenots over in France. My John will make sure we don't allow any Catholics to hold sway here in Somerset. Have no fear of that.'

'It's true, my family has suffered in the wars that have divided my homeland for so long.' Encouraged by her smile I went on. 'Our fiercest enemies, the Catholic house of Guise, fought in the name of religion, though it was the quest for power that drove them on.' For a moment I thought I had annoyed Judge Popham. But his thin lips stretched into a smile.

'Ah, I see you are a sensible woman. Wars are always a struggle for power,' he said with a sage nod of his balding head.

'I left my people in Devon in fear of another attack from the Spanish,' I said.

'That's why we need to keep the Jesuits out.' His eyes, keen as a hawk's, never left my face. I could understand how those who came before him accused of some crime might wilt under such intense scrutiny.

'Well, sir, I hope that will never lead to such divisions as we've seen in France. For my family's sake, I hope Henri of France's more pragmatic approach will secure lasting peace.' That set off a long diatribe from the judge about the Jesuits, Spanish spies, and the dangers of compromise. The broadside of words left me no time to respond.

Amy Popham intervened, taking my arm to whirl me round the assembled gentry of Somerset. At last we reached Thomas's sister Jane and her new husband, seated in splendour to receive the wedding guests. As we drew near, Jane rose from her seat and hugged me close. A sweet perfume of violets lingered as she released me.

'I hope soon to congratulate you on your own wedding. Thomas tells me you have matters to resolve for your family, but he hopes it may not take too long. Why, since he met you, he's a new man! I can see why!' I blushed while John Still looked on, beaming, his hands steepled across his belly, every inch the benevolent Bishop. His voice boomed out, as if he were speaking from the cathedral pulpit, and heads turned.

'You are welcome here, my dear Lady Montgomery. Let us raise a toast to Thomas Horner's bride-to-be.' Everyone smiled and raised their glasses, and I held my head high. They were receiving me as a French noblewoman and a Huguenot refugee. It was as if all the years at Dartington with Gawen had never happened. My hands flew as I chatted with Jane and the other ladies, my French accent becoming ever more marked.

'Did you hear what the Queen had to say about our marriage?' Jane said, turning to her husband. The likeness to her brother was striking, even down to her tone of voice as she went on. 'Queen Elizabeth said it was a dangerous name for a bishop to match with a Horner!' Everyone was laughing, but I was taken aback by the Queen's rude remark. I felt the colour rising in my cheeks, for even a French woman like me knew that 'horner' was the English term for a cuckold, the husband of an adulteress.

Bishop Still stroked his white beard and grinned, unconcerned to be the butt of such merriment. Jane took my arm, and we moved amongst the guests, exchanging greetings and the latest gossip as she introduced me to friends and neighbours from all over the West Country.

At last, I found Thomas beside me with a wide grin lighting his handsome face.

'I drank the hippocras myself,' he said, chuckling. 'Come, let us sit for a moment. You have been quite the centre of attention!' We returned to the fireside, and Thomas found another drink for me.

'Well?' he asked. 'How do you like Somerset Society?'

'Oh, I like it very well! Even though it was like being caught up in a furious whirlwind, with Amy Popham and your sister steering me into the gale.' I took a sip of the spiced wine, feeling its invigorating warmth spread through me.

'Amy Popham is a force of nature. Well, she'd have to be, wouldn't she? Married to the judge, I mean.' He laughed, then took the twinkling glass from my hand and with infinite care set it on the small, carved oak table beside me. The firelight glinted on the glass, making patterns leap and play on the wall behind. Thomas took my hand in his, intertwining his fingers with mine. The buzz of voices faded into the background. As if an imaginary velvet curtain encircled us, we sat together, cocooned in our own private space.

'Everyone has been so welcoming, your sister Jane especially so. I'm received as my father's daughter! It's been a long time since anyone has treated me like that.'

'It is your due to be greeted so, Roberda,' he said. 'You are the daughter of a French nobleman. You are a beautiful, accomplished woman. You should not remain shut away in Devon, no matter how much you love that place. This is your world. Are you ready to take your place in it at my side?'

I felt I had grown several inches taller and was light as air.

'Oh, Thomas, with you, oh… yes!' In that moment I pushed away all doubts about my children, the threat from the Spanish, and poor dear Clotilde. A new life beckoned.

Our stay at Ston Easton was short, and soon we were riding through the lanes to Mells to meet Thomas's children. A watery December sun lit our way as the horses splashed through deep ruts filled with meltwater. Although the snow had gone, an icy wind kept us huddled in furs as we rode along. I twisted in the saddle to give Joan a reassuring smile, then turned back, to guide my mount beside Thomas's grey, hoping the mud would not splash my riding skirt too much. I'd never seen him so animated as he chatted about his plans for our future life together. Eyes sparkling, cheeks flushed, his excitement bubbled over like a brook descending from the heights of Dartmoor.

'If the weather's good, we can ride over to Cloford. If you like it, I thought we might live there. My eldest son will have Mells, of course. I've also got a crew of builders standing ready to complete our house in Bristol. It's in St Austin's Green, near the Great House. We can spend time there too.'

'Forgive my ignorance, Thomas, but who lives at the Great House?' It was quite a challenge to keep up with his enthusiasm for our future life together.

'John Young built it and received the Queen and all her entourage there when she came on progress, years ago. Young's dead now, of course, but Dame Joan keeps a fine household. Oh, you'll enjoy the pleasure gardens and they've built a banqueting house at the top. They call it the Red Lodge.' I was silent, trying on for size the strange image of living in a newly built townhouse, visiting fine ladies to share a plate of honey cakes and a glass of wine in pleasant gardens on sunny afternoons. Though perhaps not so grand, it conjured up echoes of the life my parents lived long ago, at the royal court in France before the world went mad.

'You will like it, won't you, Roberda?' he asked. His restless hands disturbed his horse, making the beast shy at a gate post.

'Don't worry so much, Thomas. You'll disturb your horse! All will be well,' I said with a smile. However, I turned away so that he would not see me biting my lip. I hated to quench his joy, but I had matters to resolve at Dartington. Above all, I couldn't rid my mind of the thought of Clotilde, who might be lying near death in her bed while I was gallivanting all over Somerset.

Surrounded by close wooded banks, the Mells River burbled on its way. We passed fulling mills, placed to use the flowing water to finish the cloth that had built Thomas's fortune. A group of rosy-cheeked children ran out to greet us.

'Are ye home for Christmastide, sir?' one lad asked, sniffing and wiping his nose on a grubby sleeve.

'That I am, and there will be plenty for all. Come to the Manor on Christmas Day – as you always do.' Thomas smiled down at the boy and we rode on.

I looked over my shoulder to see the children running helter-skelter into the cottage, calling out, 'Ma! Pa! Here's Master Thomas, come home with a fine lady with him.'

'There, you see. Even the children recognise how lucky I am,' said Thomas.

Thomas's face shone with pride and love, but I was silent as we urged the horses forward over the last mile. The skeletal branches of winter trees stood out stark against the leaden sky when we swung into the village. Stone-built cots clustered around a church with a tall spire. Behind the church, on the other side of a high wall, was the manor house.

'They built that wall to separate the Bishop's house from the church,' Thomas said, waving his arm. 'You know that we bought the lands here, and at Nunney and Cloford, when King Henry put the Abbot of Glastonbury out?'

I nodded. It was a familiar story.

'Here we are,' he said. 'The building work's not quite done, so you'll not see it at its best yet.' As we rode through the iron gates, flung open to welcome us, I saw Mells Manor for the first time. Windows in the latest style twinkled from the many gable ends, while the walls were touched with a warm hint of honey as the sun slid away.

'I had not realised how splendid it would be,' I exclaimed. A groom helped me dismount at the block. I noticed a cloud crossing Thomas's face as he handed the reins to another boy. His brow furrowed as he took my hand.

'I hope one day you will come to love Somerset as much as I know you love Devon. The builders will start work at Cloford as soon as the weather allows. You can have anything you want there, and in the Bristol house, too. I so want to make you happy.' The sound of approaching footsteps, unnaturally loud to my ears, excused me from giving more than a fleeting smile in reply.

'Now here's my son John and his brothers come to meet us,' Thomas said, still studying my face. I wondered how I would ever remember all their names as the family filed out of the door.

I was to share a room with Thomas's eldest daughter, Agnes, who, though only a few years older than my Lisbeth, was already married with several babies. She'd left her children behind in the care of their nurses while she joined her father for the holiday.

'It's a houseful for Christmas, so we must all squash in together,' she said as she helped me lay out my best gown.

'Don't you miss your children?' I asked.

'They're too young to join in the feasting and they're well cared for at home,' she replied. I toyed with my pearl necklace absently.

'Mine are older. My eldest girl's nearly your age. I wonder what they are all doing?'

'I can see you're feeling the miss of your family,' she said with a kind smile. 'We're all so very happy to welcome you to ours.' I nodded and blinked hard before turning to stare out of the window at the row of clipped yews in the formal garden below.

Thomas's many children soon drew me into their preparations for the holiday. On Christmas Day, we went to St Andrew's Church before the customary round of feasting began. Replete and warm, I sighed, twisting the soft cloth of my gown round my fingers. I looked up as Thomas joined me, eyes shining, excited as the children who were giggling and squealing as they played a riotous game of hoodman-blind.

'Let us ride to Cloford tomorrow,' he said. 'I want to show you the manor house. It's a pretty place. You can have a garden there. We can plan it together so it's ready to welcome you.'

I couldn't meet his eye as I felt a slow tear trickling down my cheek. Thomas caught my hand as I reached up to brush it away. I tried to force a smile, but my voice sounded flat.

'I would like to see the house, Thomas... but...' His head dropped, and he closed his eyes. 'Oh, Thomas, I'm sorry. Everyone has been so kind. But I can't help but miss my children. And there's Clotilde.'

'I know,' he said, trying to smile. 'I can tell you're worried.'

'I have no doubt that my future lies here with you. But what about Arthur? The girls? And if anything should happen to Clotilde while I'm away...'

He let out a heavy, quivering sigh.

'I understand,' he said, giving my hand a squeeze. 'I can't bear to see you distressed. You won't be content until everything there is resolved. How would it be if I take you back to Dartington as soon as Twelfth Night is done?'

Chapter Thirty-Three

A Testing Time

Winter 1594/95, Dartington Hall

A lowering sky, as dark a grey as Sir Arthur's pewter platters, loomed over the rooftops as Dartington Hall came into sight. Gusts of wind whipped at our cloaks, swaying the bare trees and piling up the few leaves that remained beneath them to remind us of the warmer days of autumn.

As home came into view, Joan peeped out from her hood.

'Thank God. We're nearly there. I'm chilled to the bone. I hope they have the fire well stoked,' she exclaimed. But Thomas looked up at the sky.

'Looks like a storm brewing,' he said. 'Mark me well, a blizzard will rage before dark.' Taking charge, he signalled to the groom who had been following us with Joan perched behind him on a plodding bay gelding.

'We'll ride on ahead. Follow as fast as you may.' Seeing Joan's anxious look Thomas added. 'It's all right, Joan, you'll beat the storm, but your mistress is eager to be home.'

The groom, whose fair hair protruded at rakish angles from beneath his shabby woollen cap, nodded. There was no mistaking the authority in Thomas's voice. In any case, he could see for himself how the dark clouds might start to release their burden of snow at any moment.

So, putting our heels into the horses' flanks, we cantered on, hooves thundering on the hard ground. We soon left the bay and its double load, far behind. Glad that my leather gloves protected my hands a little from the cold, I reined in under a mighty oak. The venerable tree spread its barren branches in all directions, even over the deer park fence. All the colours seemed to have leached out of the dreary landscape; shades of black and grey were all that remained of the verdant scene of months before.

'That's odd,' I exclaimed with a frown. 'I'd expect to see men out here, repairing the ditch and pale. It's a regular wintertime task,' The heat rising from my horse's heaving flanks was all that kept me from freezing.

'Perhaps they've noticed the storm coming. It will soon close in. Come on,' Thomas called over his shoulder as he spurred his mount forward. The ice-cold air stung my cheeks and whipped moisture from my eyes as we pressed on to cover the last half mile.

We came to a sudden halt in the archway and stared, open-mouthed. There was not a soul in sight – no maids scurrying from the bakehouse with baskets of freshly baked loaves, no young boys loaded with sticks shuffling along, bringing fuel for the brewhouse furnace. There was no sign of any men sharpening billhooks or gathering tools, ready for work when the storm had passed. No stable boys rushed out to help us dismount. The eerie silence of the deserted courtyard screamed at me. Something was wrong.

Forgetting how much my legs ached after our long ride, I urged my horse forward to the mounting block. Thomas matched my urgency and the clatter of hooves skittering over frosted cobbles echoed unnervingly loud from the walls. Without a word, Thomas threw himself from the saddle, and I felt his strong arms lift me down It was only then, over his shoulder, I saw a small boy running from the stables. When he reached us, the boy slid to a halt, startling the horses. He righted himself, ran his hand through a mop of dark curls and making a grab for the reins, he got the words out at last.

'I-I-I'm sent to take the horses, ma'am. There's n-n-no one else can come. They're all s-s-sick.'

'Dear God! What is it? Not the plague or the sweat?' I took the boy by his skinny shoulders and gave him a shake. Thomas tried to hold me back but I wrenched free.

Cursing the weight of my riding skirt, I launched myself towards the porch, vaguely conscious of Thomas's footsteps ringing out as he pounded along in my wake. At the steps, I tripped on the hem of my thick cloak. Righting myself, heedless of the bitter cold, I shrugged it off and left it where it fell. It lay there, an untidy bundle of wool and fur, like a wild animal crouched at the door, ready to pounce.

My feet hardly grazed the floor of the lofty hall where the merest trace of smoke rose from a long-neglected fire. I burst into the parlour as though the hounds of hell were on my tail, then stopped dead.

Clotilde sat on the settle, surrounded by bright cushions and swathed in a warm blanket. She struggled to her feet and opened her arms to greet me. I flew to her, overjoyed to breathe in the familiar lily of the valley perfume that clung to her clothes.

'Thank God – you're alive and well!' I cried. 'But where is everyone else? The place is as empty as a rook's nest in December. The boy said there's sickness? God send it's not the plague or the sweat?' I swallowed several times to quell the fear that was making my stomach tumble like a butter churn. With infuriating precision, Clotilde settled herself back on the cushions.

'Neither of those, *ma petite*,' she said, wrapping the blanket tighter and adjusting her position with a little groan.

'Well, at least you seem well, Clotilde, – no worse than when I left. If others are ill, how have you escaped?' Her lips twisted into a grin.

'I never could abide the way the Dartington cook prepares fish.'

'Whatever do you mean?'

'I suppose I should have some sympathy with the poor man,' she said. 'He does his best. It's hard to get provisions these days, what with everything diverted to Plymouth to feed those soldiers in case we come under attack.'

'Clotilde! Please, get to the point, for goodness' sake!'

'It's simple enough. In desperation, the fool bought a day-old catch. Maybe it was more than a day past its best. For sure, the fish had gone bad. Everyone who ate it has been spewing up and voiding their bowels for a day or more. They're all struck with griping in the guts and sweating. Ugh! How they writhe about – they kept me awake all night with the noise. Now they're all stuck firm in the garderobe, and there's no one to tend me!' She gave a cackling laugh that made me tap my fingers on the back of the settle in annoyance.

'Are you sure it's not the plague or some other foul contagion?'

'Of course I'm sure! I didn't eat the fish but had a fancy for a posset instead. See, I'm hale and hearty. The fish was tainted. The sickness passes in a day or so, but while you're in its throes, it's a beggar!'

Before I could quiz the old woman further, Mary appeared, her usually serene features twisted into an anxious frown. Following closely behind her was Lisbeth, towering over her plump sister.

'I'm so glad you've come, Mother,' said Mary, as, with a weary sigh, she took off her apron and folded it carefully before placing it on the window seat. The two girls exchanged glances. There was something about the look they shared.

'Are you well, girls? Did you also pass on the fish?'

'We did, Mother, but I'm afraid the little ones didn't,' Mary said.

All this time, Thomas had stood in the doorway, turning his hat round and round in his hands. His face was anxious as he came to my side and reached for my hand. I clung to him, in that fearful moment glad to have the man I loved at my side.

'Mother, it's not only the rotten fish that's made Bridget ill.' Mary's face was grave. 'She's had a fever for three days.' A chilling sliver of dread slipped down my back.

Keeping a firm grip on my hand, Thomas prompted her, his tone as gentle as if he was coaxing a reluctant colt to take the halter for the first time.

'Go on, Mary. What ails your little sister? Should we send for a physician?' Mary chewed her lip and turned to Lisbeth for reassurance.

'I don't think so. Lisbeth thinks the fever's turned. She's been helping me to nurse poor little Bridget.'

Lisbeth cut in, surprising me with the calm authority with which she spoke.

'She's sleeping now. Her brow is cool and the sheets are dry since last we changed them. I'm sure she's turned a corner. So long as no one feeds her any fish broth, she'll do.'

I broke free from Thomas's grip and was up the stairs to the nursery in the blink of an eye. I drew up a seat beside my two-year-old daughter's bed to keep vigil until she woke. I listened to the child's regular breathing, and my pulse slowed. Lisbeth busied herself, clearing away bottles and stirring a bowl from which fresh herb-scented steam rose up.

Mary sat on the other side of the bed, her steady brown eyes watching Bridget's face.

'It's my fault. I should never have gone and left you for so long,' I said, my chin quivering. I flinched as Lisbeth scraped a stool along the floorboards and sat beside me.

'It's all right, Mother,' she said. 'We managed perfectly well.' To my amazement, Lisbeth, usually so aloof and distant, twined her fingers round mine and held my hand in her lap.

We kept silence for what seemed an eternity until the little girl's eyelids fluttered. Bridget stared at me without recognition, then turned her head.

'Mary... Mary!' she cried. I felt as though my chest was caving in. She had not asked for me.

Thomas was right about the weather. Before dark, the first flakes of snow fell, and soon a howling gale rattled the windows and cold crept under every door.

I went straight to my lonely bed, aching all over. As the candle guttered, I drifted into a fitful sleep, haunted by dreams of dying soldiers from long ago in Rouen. Next morning, as the servants emerged, some still looking pasty-faced and wan, I threw myself into a round of activity. First, I checked that every trace of the tainted fish was gone. Then I tallied our supplies and gave instructions to the cook and kitchen staff on how they might eke out what we had, that we might all survive enforced confinement while the snow piled up.

Later, William sought me out, apologising profusely for what had happened. The poor man stared at the floor and shifted from foot to foot.

'You're not to blame, William. It's all my fault for leaving you. I should never have gone. The Spanish are preparing another armada. We must prepare against attack once more, and we must replenish our stores in case we have to flee inland. Did someone polish the armour in the church?'

'Yes, ma'am... and our stores are as full as possible at this time of year,' he said, shaking his head. 'There's nothing more you or any of us can do with snow drifts against every door. The lanes are blocked, and the Spaniards won't come in this season. All we can do is keep warm and sit it out until the thaw comes.' I knew he was right, but yet, eaten away by guilt, I couldn't be still.

Thomas had no choice but to remain at Dartington, but I avoided him as much as I could. He spent long hours with Arthur, who had soon recovered, or keeping Clotilde company. I shut myself in Sir Arthur's old office, pretending I was going over the accounts. In reality, I sat and stared at the columns of figures without turning a page in the ledgers.

After a week, the constant *plip-plopping* sound as icicles melted away told us that the thaw had set in. Thomas caught me as I was crossing the hall. He stood four square before the study door and barred my way. Forced to look at him, I was shocked to see he was in a sorry state. Consumed by my own self-pity and guilt, I hadn't given a thought to his feelings. His lips turned down as he scrubbed a hand across his face. I turned away, unable to meet his eye.

'Roberda? You've been avoiding me... My dearest love, please speak to me... please...' His voice trailed off.

'Leave me be! I'm a neglectful mother. I've failed everyone. I can't marry you, Thomas. I'm needed here.'

'Come,' he said, pushing the office door open. 'Let us sit together.' I allowed him to lead me away from prying eyes but snatched my hand back as soon as the door slammed behind us. My eyes flashed as I rounded on him.

'Bridget might have died. I wasn't here.'

'Nonsense! Your girls, Mary and Lisbeth, they have managed everything just as well as you would have done. That's because you've brought them up well. They are a credit to you.'

'I'm her mother, yet she cried for Mary, not for me.'

'Ah... I see. That would sting.' Tears were pricking at the back of my eyes. Thomas reached into his sleeve and took out a kerchief embroidered with the Talbot dogs, his family crest. I took it and twisted it between my fingers, refusing to use it to wipe away the tears were now running unchecked down my cheeks.

'I was so set on sorting out Arthur's inheritance… and there's Richard… and then we must fight the Spanish.' He stilled my fidgety hand and shook out the kerchief before handing it to me again.

'Now, dry your eyes and let us talk. You've done well by Arthur so far. He's a fine boy. I've enjoyed his company these last days, though I missed yours.'

'I'm sorry, Thomas. I needed to think. Clotilde looks as though she'll last beyond Candlemas, but it can't be long. You've seen how thin she's become?'

'Yes, and I've spoken with her.'

The silence between us grew suffocating and heavy. Like an impenetrable thorn fence, it kept us apart. At last, he spoke again.

'I can see you need more time, or you'll never be content. Just promise me you'll talk to Clotilde. That woman has more good sense in her old head than the best scholars in the land. Speak to Richard, too. There's a way forward for Arthur. But you must be prepared to find it.'

I flinched and grabbed his arm.

'You're not leaving me?'

Thomas gazed at me with such adoration, for an instant, I thought I might be able to forget everything but him. I ran to his arms. But with infinite gentleness, he pushed me away. When he next spoke, he weighed his words with care.

'You have a lot on your mind, and perhaps I, too, have neglected my duties. I'm wanted in Somerset. With my fellow justices, I'm called to account for failing to deal with some matters of the Spanish. Promise me you will receive me when I return?'

Next morning, I stood beneath the White Hart badge and waved him off. My list of nagging doubts was a long one.

Chapter Thirty-Four

A Passing

Spring 1595, Dartington Hall

A small, wavering voice, laced with exhaustion, emerged from behind the embroidered hangings of the four-poster bed.

'I'm still here.'

I put a hand on the turned oak bed-post that held up the ornate tester and paused, remembering I had shared that bed with Gawen. Now it was a comfortable last refuge for Clotilde. Save for the brief period when he sent her away, she had always been with me. How could I imagine a world without her?

No longer able to walk, though never complaining, my faithful old nurse lay in my bed, propped up on a pile of red and gold pillows. The upsetting sound of her wheezing and coughing had brought me to her bedside that dismal May morning.

A floorboard creaked as I stepped up to the bed and opened the heavy curtains. I let my fingers linger to caress the soft fabric, breathing in a blast of Clotilde's favourite perfume. It was so strong it nearly overcame me. The lavender scent from the bag Lisbeth had placed amongst the cushions behind the frail old woman's head could not overpower it.

The voice grew stronger.

'Where are you, Marie? Oh, it's you! The light's so dim, I couldn't see you. How are you, *ma petite*?'

'I'm well, Clotilde. A little tired. Busy laying up stores in case the

Spanish come, but I'm well enough. What about you?' My question provoked a loud snort.

'Hmph! I've kept ahead of the reaper until now. He's not caught me yet, though I doubt I'll be skipping ahead of him like a spring chicken for much longer.'

Marie's footsteps tapped out a rhythm on the polished floorboards as she responded to her old friend's call. She approached the bed, plumped up the cushions, and settled Clotilde in a more comfortable position.

I mustered a weak smile when Marie replied.

'Nonsense, Clotilde!' she said, giving the miserable predictions short shrift. 'A spry old thing like you! You're tough as my worn-out boots. You'll outrun him for a few years yet.'

'I'll leave you with Marie for now,' I said, giving Clotilde's bony fingers a squeeze. I turned away, stifling the sob that rose in my throat as light from the window caught the translucent skin stretched over her swollen joints. As I left the room I only just caught her next words.

'When will your man be here? I'd like to see him one more time before I leave you.' Trying to raise her voice sparked a violent fit of coughing that had the bed shaking on its ropes.

Later, downstairs in the parlour, Marie whispered in my ear.

'She hasn't got long, but she's determined to see Master Horner again. Can you send for him, ma'am?'

'I have already sent word, Marie. I look for him in a day or two.'

During those last days of waiting, I found myself listening to my own heartbeat, my mind wandering, distracted from my tasks. In the room that had served so long as Sir Arthur's office, then my husband's, I sat at the desk, deluding myself I was going through the accounts. In truth, I remembered my last meeting with Thomas in that very room and disappointment in his face as he left me to grapple with my doubts.

A knock at the door disturbed me from my reverie. There was no trace of his usual cheery tone when William spoke.

'I don't know how we'll manage, ma'am. I've never known spring sowing so late. It'll be a poor harvest and wheat prices are already sky-high.'

'I know. All that snow, then the thaw, and now this relentless rain. What a dreary spring it's been!'

'I suppose there's one glimmer of hope, Ma'am. The spring gales will keep the Spanish far out to sea!' I smiled, knowing I could always rely on William to find hope amongst all the gloom. He was silent for a moment, studying his boots. Then, lowering his voice even further, he went on.

'This is a large household to feed, ma'am. We'll do our best, but it will be tight. It may not be my place, but I wondered if... er... um... no, it's not for me to say.' I noticed a sheen of sweat glistening on his face.

'Go on. You may say what's in your mind, William.'

'Well, ma'am. Could some of the young people stay with relatives to lighten the load on our kitchens for a bit?'

'Thank you – that's not a bad idea. I'll give it some thought. I'm afraid my mind is full of Clotilde at present. Master Horner is on his way. I'll discuss it with him when he arrives.' A broad smile broke across William's face, like sunrise after a stormy night.

'That's good to hear, ma'am. We all wish you and Master Horner happiness together. Begging your pardon, but I was afraid some difference had come between you.'

'No, no! It's just that I have responsibilities here and much to organise for the future.'

As the heavy door closed behind him, the latch falling with a soft click, I sank onto the worn wooden seat. I put my head in my hands, feeling the weight of my dilemma bearing down on me. How could I continue to look after the estate and my children, as was my duty, if I married Thomas Horner? On the other hand, how could I bear to live without the man I loved?

The storm clouds gathered again and sheets of rain blotted out the view over the garden before noon. Thomas's horse sloshed into the courtyard, and I ran to meet him. I didn't care that he was already soaked or that I'd soon be as wet as he was. My leather shoes slipped and slid on the cobbles until he caught me in his arms. I returned his kiss. Laughing at the drips running down my chin, we hurried inside.

'It's been too long, Roberda,' he said, with such longing I swayed on my feet. He threw off his sopping hat, sending water droplets onto the blazing logs to sizzle and spit, and pulled me into his arms again.

Alice peeked through the doorway, gasped, and scurried off to spread the news that the mistress was kissing Master Horner in front of the fire. Joan, grinning from ear to ear, hurried in, bearing dry clothes for Thomas, with William hard on her heels.

'Let me help you off with your boots, sir,' William said as Thomas threw off his wet cloak.

William signalled to one of the kitchen boys, a sharp-eyed little fellow with ginger hair. The boy stirred the ashes with an iron bar and soon had flames licking round a new log.

Thomas held me close again. Mesmerised by the firelight reflecting from golden flecks in his grey-green eyes, I felt the warmth of his love flooding through me, from the tips of my fingers to my toes. If Joan hadn't given a discreet cough, we might have stayed there forever. Beaming, she steered me from the room and helped me to change.

Downstairs again, I was surprised to find other visitors had arrived.

'Pierre! Is it you? What are you doing here?' My protégé, the musician, unfolded an oilskin that had kept his lute from the rain and set the instrument down near the door.

'Word came that Miss Clotilde is ill. You know how news gets about. I expect the miller told the baker in Totnes, he told the alewife, and she told half of Devon. We soon heard all about it in Modbury. Master Champernon here, he said I could come and see her one last time.' To my amazement, I saw Richard hanging back by the door. Thomas waved him in.

'It seemed right,' Richard said. 'The boy should come to bid her farewell. I hear she's a remarkable woman, and he's known her since he was a child. Now, is there space for someone else? I need to dry out too.'

I glanced across at Thomas, who gave me an 'I told you so' look as Richard joined him at the fireside.

'You are welcome, Richard,' I said. 'It will lift Clotilde's spirits to see Pierre, and while you are with us, there are matters we should discuss.'

Pierre strummed the lute, and the gentle, lilting songs of Normandy, echoes of my childhood, drifted round the bedchamber. A slight smile touched Clotilde's lips as she held Diane the doll, stroking the soft red material of my old plaything's gown.

'That garish yellow hair still shines.' Clotilde's voice was so soft I had to bend my head closer to catch her words. 'No living woman ever had such hair without using some dark magic.' A fit of coughing racked her fragile body. After it subsided, she went on. 'You wouldn't go anywhere without that doll. I had to tie it on a ribbon round your middle.' I'll swear the doll gave me a sideways glance from beneath a painted eyebrow as I patted Clotilde's hand.

She drifted off to sleep, each breath no more than the whistle of wind through a keyhole. When she woke, we were still there, me by the bed, holding her hand, Pierre picking out a tune on his lute. It was all she could do to raise her head to sip a little of Lisbeth's cordial from the cup I offered.

'Where's that man of yours? Bring him here. I have something to say to you both.' Marie scuttled through the door to call Thomas. He came at once to join me at the bedside.

From some last reserve of strength, Clotilde summoned a firm voice.

'Thomas Horner! Don't take no for an answer. Wed this woman and let her live the life she was born to.' He nodded. 'That won't do, Thomas. Swear to a dying old woman that you'll do it.'

'I'll gladly swear it, if she'll only have me.' Clotilde nodded, then took my hand.

'Now you, Roberda, *ma petite*, it is time for you to allow others to shoulder some of your burdens and live a little. Arthur's a fine lad and he'll come into his own. The girls will all do you credit. You've done your duty and done it well. Now take the chance that's offered. Grasp it with both hands. God alone knows you deserve it. Will you promise me there'll be no more delay, no more shilly-shallying?'

'With all my heart, I promise I will take Thomas Horner, who sits here beside me, to be my husband.'

Pierre gave a cheer and struck up a lively tune as Clotilde managed a grin. Thomas left me sitting beside the bed, listening to her wheezing. Marie kept vigil with me as Pierre played on, until in the small hours of the morning, I sent him to his bed.

'I think she may be beyond hearing now,' I said. 'You have given a gift more precious than jewels to let her hear again the songs of her homeland.' With tears streaming down his cheeks, he crept away.

A torrent of memories tumbled through my mind during that long night. Scenes from my childhood, our flight from Paris, following my father in the wars, Clotilde always at my side and Alain du Bois protecting us; Clotilde pinning up the hem of my wedding gown when I married Gawen in Queen Elizabeth's chapel; Clotilde cradling my babies in her arms and her face that day when he sent her away. Once I thought I heard tip-tapping footsteps from my mother's old room, the Countess's Room, and imagined she had come to meet Clotilde and lead her on her way.

I must have drifted off to sleep in the chair, holding her hand. I woke with a start. Dawn's light was creeping over the sill. Her hand was no longer in mine, and her rasping breathing had ceased.

Chapter Thirty-Five

The Lacemaker

Spring and Summer 1595, Dartington Hall and Honiton

With gentle hands, Pierre placed a bunch of lily of the valley flowers on the simple oak coffin, the delicate white blooms standing out against the polished wood. With a bow of his head, he made way for the girls to add their posies of heartsease and gillyflowers. They each arranged their offerings until a delicate floral scent drifted through the church, overlaying the usual musty odour.

We took our places, Thomas steadfast at my side, Richard wearing a sorrowful expression, and Bess come from Berry Pomeroy, as I knew she would. Bess had known Clotilde well during my early years at Dartington. She, of all people, would understand my grief at the loss of my old nurse.

William and the house servants crowded in behind us, Marie sniffing and dabbing her face with a kerchief. Estate workers and their wives had also come to pay their last respects to the Frenchwoman who had lived among them for so long.

A radiant shaft of sunlight filtered through the stained-glass window, making a dancing pattern of colours play on the bare wall as the rector stepped forward. It seemed fitting that Rector Bruxham, a man with a lot more presence than his sickly predecessor, opened the proceedings in French.

I couldn't take in his words when he spoke from the ornately carved pulpit, extolling Clotilde's virtues. Numb with grief, I stared dry-eyed at the coffin, unable to comprehend that it held the frail body of my faithful servant and friend. I half expected to hear her pattens clicking on the stone-flagged floor, to turn my head and see her bustling in to find out what all the commotion was about.

Blinking in the rare sunshine, we left the cool austerity of the church and laid Clotilde to rest in the churchyard under the protective branches of the ancient yew tree. Bees buzzing around oxeye daisies blooming in profusion beyond the wall kept up a steady drone as one of Pierre's most beautiful melodies rose to the skies. As the last note quivered from the lute string, I looked up. Feeling the warmth of the sun on my face, I imagined Clotilde born on angels' wings, dancing with the swifts that soared in the endless blue above us.

Thomas offered me his arm, and I was grateful for his stalwart presence at my side as we made our way back into the hall.

'I'll order a memorial stone. Not in the churchyard, but in my physick garden, alongside the one for Alain du Bois. She would have liked that,' I said with a catch in my voice.

A shadow crossed Thomas's face.

'I know it means a lot to you. After we are married, you'll be able to return and visit your garden here often. And you can make new gardens at Mells or at Cloford. Would you like that?' I nodded.

'I will come to you as soon as I have Richard's answer and all the details sorted out,' I said. 'I mean to make good on the promise I made to Clotilde.'

'So may I apply for a marriage licence now? I can't wait much longer, Roberda?'

'Soon, my dearest, soon.'

I felt detached from the hum of conversation that grew ever louder as Alice served wine and sweetmeats. Richard and Thomas had their heads together engaged in deep discussion. Lost in a fog, emotions raw, I let their words drift past me.

'...the Queen withdrew all English support from King Henri... Philip of Spain's soldiers in Brittany... they hold the port of Blavet... only a quick hop from there to the Cornish or Devon coast. Roberda, are you listening?' Concern, love, and mild irritation fought each other in Thomas' voice. 'The Spaniards have a foothold in France. Only a narrow sea separates us from our enemies. We can't rely on the wind scattering their armada this time.' I gathered my wits.

'I suppose that's why they are working so hard on Plymouth's defences and commandeering all our supplies?' I asked.

'That's right. Drake and Hawkins are making ready for another voyage.'

'Ah. Some sort of pre-emptive strike, as before?'

'Perhaps, or to break the Spanish hold on trade from the Americas. They're keeping it very quiet. A good thing, too, for the Spanish would love to know the destination.' Richard nodded as Thomas went on. 'There are reports they've captured a Cornish fishing boat and questioned the crew. The fishermen say there are enough Spanish ships in Blavet to worry us and more on the way.'

By now, he had my full attention. I felt my muscles tighten as the chilling news sank in.

'So close? Dear God, we must be prepared.'

'Indeed, and on top of that, the Queen has to grapple with Ireland. The threat from O'Neil grows daily.'

'Ireland! Gawen served there. It was when we were struggling to equip our men against the first armada. In the year that followed, the parish had to pay up to send some of our men to Ireland. Edward Seymour was complaining about it when last he was here.'

'Hmph! Seymour!' Richard spat his name from his mouth as though ridding himself of a nasty taste.

'But, Thomas,' I said, attempting to deflect Richard from his running quarrel with Bess's husband, 'there's no imminent threat to us from the Spanish, is there?'

'I hope not, but we must be on our guard.'

I was left with an uneasy feeling when Bess put an end to further conversation by announcing she must leave.

'Take care, won't you?' she said, hugging me to her well-upholstered bosom. The familiar rose perfume that clung to her clothes reminded me of times past as she released her grip.

'Even though we know it must come, a death always shocks us. Allow yourself time to grieve. Next time I see you, God send it will be to dance at your wedding.' I wished she could stay. But soon Bess was gone, leaving me even more bereft.

Later that day, after we had supped together, Richard fumbled in the leather pouch he had set down on the board beside him.

'You don't mind, do you, Roberda? They say it's a sure cure for headaches. Cousin Walter swears by its medicinal properties.' I watched, fascinated, as he took dried leaves from the pouch, rubbed them between his fingers and filled the bowl at the end of a strange-looking pipe. He held a spill of paper in the candle flame, then touched it to the leafy mixture. Placing the pipe between his lips, he drew in a great breath, then puffed smoke out through his nostrils.

'Why, Richard, you look like a fire-breathing dragon! Is this the new plant from the Americas?' I asked.

'Tobacco! I find it relaxes me,' said Richard, puffing away and looking as contented as one of the kitchen cats basking in a sunbeam. 'God knows, I need something to help me with all the rumours going round.'

The unfamiliar acrid smell, with its woody undertones, assaulted my senses, starting a tickle in my throat and making my eyes water. Thomas moved out of range of the pipe smoke and waited for a spluttering Alice to clear the pots.

'She'll have a fine story to tell about Master Richard setting himself on fire, no doubt,' I said as the door closed. 'Now, Richard, what's all this about rumours?' I went on. 'Not the old accusations again?'

'Indeed, but this time it's worse. Drake wrote to me, saying it's all over the court that I misuse my singing boys so that they keep their voices.' The contented look faded from his face and a red flush coloured his cheeks as he put down the pipe. 'I've written to Robert Cecil refuting it, of course, but when people throw mud, some will stick. My wife says she can't go amongst the women of Devon without thinking they all snicker behind her back.' Thomas sought to reassure him.

'Look, Richard, we all know it's nonsense. All because you didn't want to give up your best chorister to young Cecil. He's not a patch on his father.' Richard grimaced as Thomas went on. 'It's a nasty trick and it will run its course. Best defuse it without crossing swords with him in public, though.'

I rather wished Richard hadn't brought up this unfortunate topic. I wanted to have his full attention on Arthur's future. Glum-faced, he stared at the pipe that now lay on the board. With shaking hands, he picked it up and refilled it. Once he was puffing away at it again, he became calmer. Thomas caught my eye, and I weighed in.

'I would welcome your good counsel on Arthur's future, Richard.' That made him sit up. When I outlined the solution Thomas and I had discussed, his jaw dropped.

'I must say I'm surprised, Roberda,' Richard said. 'I thought you saw me as a sworn enemy to be kept from your son at all costs. But now you say you'd consider joint administration of Gawen's will, with both of us overseeing Arthur's choice of a bride. Do you think we can work together to help him learn enough to run the estate on his own as soon as he turns twenty-one?'

'Yes, Richard, I do. I think perhaps we've been misled into believing we are enemies, when in reality all we both want is to see the Champernowne family prosper.'

'Hmph! I'll think about it,' said Richard. 'I have already approached the Court of Wards... hmm... I've had no reply as yet.'

I pressed my advantage.

'Surely, working together, we can achieve much more for Arthur?'

'Hmm... we'll see. Oh, by the way, I almost forgot, I have a package for you from Sir John Gilbert.' He rummaged in the leather bag at his feet and drew out a small parcel wrapped in linen cloth. 'He is not in good health, you know. Been to Bath for a cure, but it's done him no good. It's his legs, I believe. I doubt he can sit a horse these days. They'll have to think about replacing him as Deputy Lieutenant soon. I'll be bidding for a regiment of my own.'

I took the package from him.

'For me? From Sir John Gilbert? What can it be?' Eager to see what was inside, I tugged at the cord binding the documents together. I unfolded a sheet bearing Sir John's signature and another in a different hand.

Richard and Thomas went on discussing musters and troop deployments. Thomas was trying to encourage Richard to choose his words with care when approaching the other deputies. I saw now that poor Richard was his own worst enemy, well-intentioned but hot-headed. Their voices droned on while I perused the unexpected message.

'Well?' said Thomas. 'It can't be bad news, for you're grinning from ear to ear.'

'Sir John found this amongst his mother's things. It's about the women we helped settle in Devon when they fled the wars in France. When you return to Somerset, as I know you must, I'd like to accompany you as far as Honiton.'

A few days later, we set off in a light drizzle that soon turned the rutted lanes into a quagmire. By the time we reached Honiton, the sky had cleared.

A frenzied hubbub assaulted my ears in the wide High Street where all manner of people milled around market stalls. The voices of those haggling for the best price combined with sellers yelling their wares to all and sundry. Groups of women gathered to chew over the latest news, occasionally administering a cuff to unruly children, looking for mischief, or a square meal.

The smell of freshly butchered meat hung at the back of my throat as dogs scrapping over discarded bones yelped and got in our way. On another day, I might have stopped to inspect the rolls of good Devon cloth. Kerseys and serges tumbled over each other on the stalls where flashes of more vibrant colours peeped from beneath piles of the sheep-coloured cloth favoured by the poor. But, on this occasion, I was keen to find the address mentioned in Katherine Raleigh's letter. I had no time for shopping.

Making our way through the chaos, Thomas steered me round a pile of stinking rotting cabbages. Next, we took a detour to avoid two brawny youths rolling barrels of ale into one of the many inns that welcomed travellers en route from Exeter to London.

'It can't be much further,' I said, craning my neck to peer at the signs swinging from timber-framed houses across the street. 'It's near the candlemaker's shop – look, it's over there.'

A young woman caught my eye as she sat in a doorway across the street, her head bowed and hands busy with her work. She was neatly dressed, with a crisp linen cap and a spotless apron over a kirtle of green wool.

'Look, Thomas. Over there, outside the tailor's shop. There she is.'

In my haste to cross the busy thoroughfare, I was almost knocked down by a horseman, careering along with no thought for others. Just in time, Thomas grabbed my arm and pulled me out of the path of the flailing hooves that splashed in puddles, spattering the hem of my gown. With Thomas's guidance, I sidestepped the squelching mud churned up by the recent rains and reached her at last.

Absorbed in her task, she didn't notice me. I waited, mesmerised, watching her hands as, with amazing skill, she worked her magic. The bone bobbins flew this way and that, clacking together in a pleasing rhythm. As they moved, finely spun flax thread twisted around pins held in a pillow on her knee. The length of gauzy patterned lace she was working on seemed to grow as I watched.

After a while, the lacemaker glanced up, and the breath caught in her throat. Putting a hand to her mouth, she half rose from her seat, scattering the bobbins which clattered onto the worn threshold. As she lifted her head, I could see how young she was, no older than my Lisbeth. A stab of disappointment shot through me, and I looked away. Madeleine, the refugee woman I'd helped, would be much older.

The girl stared at me, her pretty face twisted into a frown. She spoke in a soft, shaky voice.

'Do I know you, ma'am? There is something... I'm not sure...' She broke off and, with a sudden burst of energy, thrust her pillow to the ground and rushed into the dimly lit shop interior. Her footsteps clattered on the wooden boards as she called out in French. '*Maman, Maman, où es-tu...* come and see... a visitor.' The girl soon emerged, dragging an older woman by the hand.

I recognised her at once, though it was years since I'd last seen Madeleine at Katherine Raleigh's house in Exeter. I'd gone in secret after Gawen put an end to my efforts to aid refugee women.

'Madeleine! Is it you? Perhaps you remember me?'

'Of course. How could we ever forget what you did for us? Come inside and meet my husband.' Only a faint trace of an accent marked her out as anything but a Devon goodwife. The small ruff collar and fashionably cut gown she wore would pass in any gathering of up-and-coming townspeople.

Seeing Thomas at my elbow, Madeleine beckoned him in.

'You too, sir, for if you are a friend of this lady, you are welcome in our home.'

Over cakes and ale, Madeleine told me how she had made her living sewing and lately making lace in the tailor's shop.

'And then I married the tailor's son,' she said, smiling at her husband, who was in deep discussion with Thomas about the trade in lace. Nodding towards the girl, she went on, 'Marguerite's bone lace is much in demand. We sell some to Master Rodge, who has a flourishing business with the London tailors. And Samuel, my husband, adds lace to the gowns he makes for the Honiton merchants' wives.'

She held out a length of lace for my inspection. It felt as airy as gossamer as I turned it over in my hands, marvelling at the intricate pattern of threads. Passing the lace to Thomas, I smiled at the girl, who pushed a lock of golden hair under her cap as she refilled our mugs with ale from the flagon.

'So this is Marguerite, the little girl with blonde curls you brought out of France? She has grown into this beautiful young woman and is a skilful lacemaker?'

'Most people call me Margaret now,' the girl said with a grin. 'It's easier on the tongue for Honiton folks.' Thomas held the sample of lace up to the light.

'They usually have to import lace of this quality from across the sea,' he said. 'No wonder your work sells well. The ladies of Somerset will clamour to buy, not to mention all the court beauties.' He turned to Madeleine's husband. 'I think there may be opportunities for us to do business, sir. I'm minded to consider an investment.'

Thomas shook the tailor by the hand, promising to be in touch. Madeleine clapped her hands, then embraced me. Meanwhile, Marguerite was busy wrapping a parcel.

'Take this to trim your wedding gown, Mistress. May it bring you good luck.'

Chatting with Madeleine, for the first time since Clotilde's death, I'd felt my spirits lift. The woman who had fled France in fear of her life, and her daughter, seemed so contented in Devon. Warmth spread through me to think my actions had helped transform their lives. I almost danced around the puddles as we made our way to the inn where I would rest that night before going back to Dartington.

Thomas was bound for Mells to sort out his affairs. I could feel the strain in his muscles when he took my hand.

'I wish you were coming with me,' he said. 'I've arranged a strong escort for you. These are dangerous times. Dartington is too near the coast for my liking.'

Still buoyed up after meeting Madeleine, I made light of it.

'We are as well prepared to fight off any attackers as we were last time. I'll have my people ready with a greeting for any Spaniards who come our way!'

Despite himself, he couldn't help but smile.

'Ah, my valiant lady! Seriously, Roberda, I'd rather have you with me. Promise me you will speak to Richard. I want to see that lace on your wedding gown soon.'

'I promise,' I said as I melted into his arms for a kiss before he left me.

Chapter Thirty-Six

Resolution

Summer 1595, Modbury and Dartington Hall

Although the sun was high, an anxious shiver tickled my backbone as I looked up at the imposing battlements of the Court House looming high above me. Some long-dead Champernowne had raised those weathered walls, perhaps to keep out attackers, more likely as a sign of esteem from whichever king he served. The Champernownes were like that, good at winning favour from whoever sat upon the throne. Richard, however, was not rising in the ranks of the nobility. His quarrelsome nature forever tripped him up. Lately he had provoked arguments with the Lord Lieutenant of Devon and with the son of the ageing Lord Burghley, Queen Elizabeth's Secretary of State and Lord High Treasurer of England. With all that bickering going on, he had failed to respond to my request for a meeting to discuss Arthur's future. Taking advantage of a brief respite from the relentless rains, I had ridden through the leafy lanes of Devon to Modbury on this day in early July. I was determined to beard Richard in his lair.

A stout, red-faced servant wearing the Champernowne livery greeted me. The badge, a blue cross of squirrel vair on vivid red, looked bright and new. A man of few words, he showed me into the parlour, where I discovered Elizabeth, tight-lipped and pale. I hesitated in the doorway, watching her stabbing her needle through a piece of linen. The tension in her shoulders was clear as she bent over the tambour. With each stitch, she seemed to hope she might find some relief from a fiery anger burning within her.

'Good day to you, Elizabeth. I hope you received my note. I sent it by the fastest messenger. I need to speak to Richard on a matter of some urgency.'

'Ha! I wish you good luck with that! I haven't seen him in days. He's locked away with the musicians trying to escape the demons that pursue him, or else he's dashing off vitriolic letters.' She pushed the frame aside, thrusting her shears and shiny silver thimble into a basket already overflowing with an unruly tangle of threads of every colour of the rainbow. Raising her head, Elizabeth remembered her manners.

'I'm sorry... er... welcome to Modbury, Roberda. Come sit with me. I'll have refreshments brought in.' She rang a small brass bell. Its tinkling chimes echoing through the passages brought the same servant, bearing a flask of elderflower cordial and a tray of cherry tartlets. The pleasant aroma of the cordial made my mouth water. It was a long time since I had broken my fast and I fell upon the offerings, savouring the sharp fruity tang of the tarts.

'Hmm... these are delicious. Did you have a good crop of cherries this year, Elizabeth, despite the weather?'

'All we could salvage of an early crop before the birds got them or the gales dashed them down. I'm sorry Richard's not been in touch. He's not been himself these past weeks. This scandal is eating away at him.'

'That must be hard for you, Elizabeth.' For the first time, I felt genuine sympathy for Richard's sour-faced wife. Seeking to cheer her, I mentioned my meeting with her parents at Jane Horner's wedding.

'They have invited Thomas and me to visit them at Littlecote. I've heard it's a splendid place,' I said.

'I wouldn't know. I've never been there since my father bought the place. I believe he's rebuilt it. As you may imagine, he's not well pleased with the latest turn of events here at Modbury.' Elizabeth rubbed the back of her neck and grimaced.

'Perhaps I can distract Richard from his worries,' I said. 'I want to talk to him about our jointly managing the Dartington estate on Arthur's behalf. After my marriage, I thought we might open negotiations for a bride for the boy. I hear Thomas Fulford has a daughter who might fit the bill. She's named Bridget, isn't she? The same name as my own little one.'

For the first time, Elizabeth's ears pricked up and her face brightened.

'The Fulfords – a good Devon family – Richard knows Thomas Fulford well. But I'm amazed. I thought you were determined to do it all by yourself.'

'Although it has seemed we were at odds, we both want what's best for the family,' I said, with a smile. Elizabeth steepled her fingers in front of her face and tapped the tips together as I continued. 'You look doubtful, but believe me, I will do what is best for my boy. Arthur should have gone to some other noble house years ago, as most boys do. But, as you know, we've been through difficult times. I'm sure he'll benefit from Richard's contacts.'

The sigh that heaved its way out of Elizabeth's narrow frame held the weight of many lonely, childless years.

'I'd be glad to have him here,' she said. Frowning she picked up her needle again. 'Roberda, you are welcome to stay a day or two, but I doubt you'll make much progress. Why not leave it with me? I'll judge when it's best to speak with Richard and send word to you at Dartington.'

That was the best I could accomplish. After a few days, with Richard refusing to speak to me, I returned to Dartington as the meagre crops of wheat turned to gold under a few days of weak sunshine.

July blew in, rough winds bringing down green apples before their time and battering the ripening crops. No word came from Modbury nor from Thomas. I watched the gate, restless as a bluebottle fly buzzing about on a warm day. Everyone kept out of my way as I chivvied the servants to work harder, sparing no one my razor-sharp tongue. The children tiptoed round me. Arthur made himself scarce, out hunting as often as the weather allowed.

Later in the month, a warmer, softer wind from the southeast caressed my skin as I helped Agnes and Lisbeth gather gooseberries.

'Slow down, Mother,' said Lisbeth. 'You'll scratch your arms to ribbons on the thorns.'

'Tsk! There's no time to waste if we're to bake some of these in a coffin pie with chicken and have enough left over to preserve. We've enough sugar set aside, and we can take some with us if we have to leave.'

'What do you mean, leave?' Lisbeth's eyes widened, and Agnes put a hand on her arm.

'The Mistress means we must have plenty in store in case the Spanish come.'

'Tra-la-la!' said Lisbeth with a playful laugh. 'The Spanish? I thought it was just that you longed for Master Horner to return!'

A smile tugged at the corners of my mouth at Lisbeth's gentle teasing. Since she'd become so interested in healing as she worked in the still room with Agnes, we seemed to get on better together. We lapsed into silence, focussed on the task, until our baskets were full. Walking back to the house, we paused beside the new stone in memory of Clotilde.

'You miss her, don't you?' Lisbeth asked.

'I do. She was my best friend for so very long.' I gulped and felt a knot tighten in my throat. Memories flew through my mind like a flock of swans seeking their favourite tranquil waters. To my surprise, Lisbeth squeezed my hand and led me to the seat under the arbour in my physick garden. I brushed a tear from my eye and studied the vibrant colours of the flowers blooming in the neatly edged flower-beds.

'I hope you will be happy with Thomas, Mother. And I'm sure you'll agree with Uncle Richard so that Arthur can come into his own in time.' I recognised new maturity in my eldest daughter, whose calm presence at my side brought me unexpected comfort in such uncertain times.

'What about you, Lisbeth?' I asked. 'Once matters are settled, we could look around for a suitable bridegroom for you.'

She pulled a face.

'I'm of an age when most young men will think I'm stale goods. I'm happy enough working in the still room. Marry off my sisters first, if you must.'

I heaved a great sigh.

'I'm sorry, Lisbeth. It's not been easy. But with Thomas to help us we will persuade Richard to co-operate. Things will improve.'

She nodded, and we remained seated together in a rare moment of mother and daughter harmony as the sun's golden rays dipped beyond the moss-encrusted wall.

Wet July had slipped into sultry August, and still no news came. One afternoon, in the stifling heat, thunder rumbled from the distant hills, and the sky turned inky black. It was a sure sign a summer storm was on the way, and it was soon upon us. Huddled in the parlour, we rejoiced to be safe from the tempest as the chimneys rattled and a merciless shower of hailstones battered the glass.

The storm was at its fiercest when William erupted into the room like a cannon shot from castle battlements.

'There's riders approaching, ma'am. I can't see who.'

My book fell to the floor with a thump as I leapt from my seat. In the rain-lashed porch, I peered out as the riders dismounted and hurried through the pelting rain.

'Thomas? Is that you?'

'It is, and Richard, too.'

They crashed into the hall like a furious wave breaking on a calm shore. Thomas shed items of rain drenched clothing as he went, with Richard close on his heels. Their unexpected arrival created such a commotion that Arthur, the girls, and most of the house servants teemed in.

'We're here to warn you. The Spanish have landed in Mounts Bay.' A collective horrified gasp went up to the rafters as the children stood wide-eyed and fearful. My voice rose to a strangled squawk.

'We've seen no beacons. No alarm has been given here. You say they have landed?'

'Yes, soldiers armed with pikes and shot landed at Mousehole. Guided in by some English Catholic traitor, no doubt.' Richard's eyes flashed as the words tumbled from his mouth. 'The Spanish rampaged through the town, setting it and all the little fishing hamlets alight. Took everyone by surprise; rather than stay and fight, they all ran for Penzance.'

'Oh, those poor souls!' Marie's eyes were bulging as she put her head in her hands. Images of cottages in flames, women and children fleeing in terror, rampaged through my mind.

'Indeed! They fled rather than face the Spaniards, despite all the planning and training these last years.' Richard swished his arm impatiently as if taking a swipe at an imaginary foe. Thomas took up the story.

'Raleigh's deputy lieutenant, Godolphin, met them on the green at the west of the town and tried to instil some order. But it was no use. Walter's still away, somewhere on the other side of the world when he's most needed!' Thomas marched back and forth, his body coiled as tight as a spring.

'Dear God, those Spaniards are as tricky as a pack of foxes.' Richard's voice shook. 'After burning those poor folks out, they could see Penzance lay undefended. So they went back to their galleys and sailed towards the town, all the time firing from the decks – or so the report goes.' Everyone held their breath, hanging on every word.

'Godolphin did his best, but with few to resist them, those Spaniards laid waste to Penzance. The devils had the cheek to hold a Papist mass on the hill above the town, even threatened to set up a priory there. But Godolphin sent messengers to Plymouth, and thank God, Drake sent ships down to the Lizard. When they saw the English ships bearing down on their galleys, they took fright. But by then they were trapped and running short of water. If only the wind had not changed, we'd have had them. So they got away. Who knows when they'll be back?'

'So much for our great defensive plans!' I exclaimed, shaking my head. The horror of it was only just sinking in.

'They'll hold a great inquiry to find out what went wrong. But it's made up my mind,' Thomas said, standing straight and tall before me, chin thrust forward. 'Roberda, you can't stay here even a day longer. Richard agrees to your proposals for the future.' Richard nodded and as I looked from one to the other, I felt my mouth go dry.

A sudden radiant smile lit Thomas's face, like dawn on a bleak midwinter morn.

'Roberda, I've applied for the licence. We can be married in Exeter, or Mells, or wherever you wish on our way. Will you agree?' I gaped at him like a startled deer caught by the hounds. 'It's not safe to stay here. You and all the children can come to Somerset until things quieten down.'

I stood stock still, playing with a hundred possibilities, like a musician running his hands along the keys of the virginals, uncertain which notes to play.

William puffed his chest out, and grinned.

'If I may speak, sir,' he said. 'The Mistress here, she has everything running as smooth as one of those new-fangled clocks that measure each day. We all know our tasks. But, with the meagre harvests these last years, we've been struggling to set enough by for the winter. I hope you won't take it amiss, ma'am, if I say it… well, taking all these hungry mouths with you seems a good idea to me.'

The tension in the room broke. As sometimes happens with a summer storm, the sky cleared, and shafts of sunlight streamed into Dartington's magnificent hall. Birdsong drifted in from the garden as Thomas took my hand.

'Don't just stand there, Roberda. Start packing and get your wedding gown ready. By the way, did you trim it with that lace?'

Epilogue

16 June 1598, St Mary's Church, Dunsford

My fingertips rested gently on Thomas's arm as we strolled out of the flower-bedecked church. The hem of my finest gown, the same one I wore for my own wedding, swished over the uneven floor. As we approached the porch, I ran a hand over the shining silk fabric and felt the lightness of Marguerite's delicate lace at my throat. Satisfied that I looked my best, I smiled up at Thomas as we walked out into the sunlight.

Arthur's curls, no longer gold but darkened to burnished copper, fell to his collar as he bent his head to press a kiss onto the girl's lips. Bursting with pride, I watched my boy, now a fine, broad-shouldered young man of eighteen, towering over his beautiful bride. Only a year younger than Arthur, decked out in dove-grey damask, blonde hair tumbling to her waist, Bridget Fulford would have turned heads in any company. A pretty blush crept up her rounded cheeks as she raised adoring blue eyes to my son's face. I felt my grin would split my face in two as I watched them.

'I have high hopes that they'll find happiness in their marriage,' Thomas said, his voice brimming with optimism. 'It's a good idea to let them stay at Great Fulford House with Bridget's family for a while so they can get to know each other.' A momentary needle of doubt pricked the bubble of my happiness as I remembered that in only three short years, Arthur would be taking over at Dartington and my time as mistress of the estate would be over.

We joined the bustling throng of well-wishers lingering in the churchyard. A light breeze carried the smell of freshly cut grass to mingle with the sweet fragrance of a white rose that grew amongst the gravestones. On such a glorious summer's day, everyone basked in the sunshine, glad to greet old friends and catch up with the latest news.

My daughters stood in a line by the path, clad in a rainbow of colours, giggling to see their brother married.

I turned to Richard, who for once had a smile on his face.

'She's just right for Arthur. Her father's a good sort. You and I did well to arrange the match!'

Richard's lips twitched. He almost managed a smile before glancing around, looking as though he couldn't wait to get away. Elizabeth, hanging onto his arm, answered for him.

'It is indeed a good match. She's pretty as a picture too. And of course the dowry money helps.' I felt my hackles rising as Richard moved away, dragging his wife with him. Thomas squeezed my hand.

'Let it go, Lady Montgomery! You did well to keep Richard with you as you negotiated with Fulford. Let him have the dowry money for now.' Before I could reply, the crowd parted as Bess, sporting a fashionable wide-skirted gown, pushed her way through. Her splendid outfit, open ruff and enormous sleeves caused quite a stir.

'I'm glad to be here for this wedding,' she said. 'You cheated me out of coming to yours. Running off with this gentleman in such a hurry!' She tapped Thomas on the arm with an ostrich feather fan. 'You look well, Thomas, and you too, Roberda. That lace is beautiful.' She reached out to touch it. 'It's like a frothy cloud and sets off your outfit to perfection.'

'It's from Honiton. I'm sure Edward will order some for you! I see you've kept him and Richard apart. We wouldn't want them falling out today.'

'Don't worry, Edward's well occupied, talking to the father of the bride.'

'If you ladies will excuse me. I'd like to hear Edward's take on the latest reports of the war at sea,' Thomas said. 'Since Raleigh and Essex's success at Cadiz, you'd think Philip of Spain would give up. But there are rumours they plan another attack; Falmouth's in their sights this time. Thank God that, so far, Protestant winds have saved us.' With a nod, he wandered off.

'It seems strange when they talk about our defence against the Spanish, with no mention of Drake. It's hard to believe he's gone, lost on that last voyage. His wife didn't waste any time remarrying. But I've just heard she's died at Powderham. Her marriage with William Courtenay didn't last long.'

'Hmm… I never did take to Elizabeth Sydenham. Let's leave the warmongering to the men. Now's our chance for a good gossip,' said Bess with a conspiratorial giggle. 'Tell me all. How is your little boy doing in the nursery at Cloford?' I felt the colour rising in my cheeks and assured her the baby, whose arrival had come as such a delightful surprise to Thomas and me, was thriving.

'Little Edward's pulling himself up and he's almost walking already. It's strange, isn't it? After I tried so hard to give Gawen another son, I presented Thomas with a healthy boy. Thomas calls him my gift to him in his twilight years.'

Bess exploded with laughter.

'He doesn't look as though he's in the twilight of his life,' she chuckled, pointing to Thomas. He was waving his arms about with some vigour, demonstrating sword cuts to Bridget's young brothers.

'No! It's just his joke because he's older than me.'

'So you're content living in Somerset?' she asked. 'You're not missing Dartington too much?'

'I never dreamt I could find such happiness, Bess. Thomas's family – they've all given me a warm welcome, and Cloford is delightful. I've made a garden there and I have the running of the household too. Do come and visit us there soon.'

'And Dartington?' she prompted.

I didn't want to admit how much I missed the view from her father's favourite lookout or the arbour in my physick garden. It was a small price to pay.

'We visit often. I returned the February after our wedding to join Richard in installing the new rector. I never thought Bruxham would live to be an old man; he was overweight and always puffing. The new man, Costerd, seems reliable.'

'So you can keep your finger on the pulse while also giving

Richard reassurance that he has a say? Well done! Oh, lookout, Mrs Stretchleigh is bearing down on us. I can't stand the woman. I'll make myself scarce.' Bess skipped away, light on her feet even though she had borne several children. I steeled myself to greet the older woman. Even on a warm day, she had not forsaken her formal black attire.

'My dear Lady Montgomery! What a wonderful day! You must be so proud. Your son married and all those pretty daughters.' A string of pearls, the only adornment she wore, trembled on her bosom as she beamed at me. I had to stifle a titter, remembering her frosty words when we met at Modbury.

'Now, which is Katherine? She would be perfect for my William.'

'That's Kate,' I said, waving my hand. 'But I'm afraid we're already discussing a match next year with the Hillersdon boy.' My girls weren't getting any younger, so Thomas had agreed to put up the dowry until the money from France came through. Kate would be first.

Elizabeth Stretchleigh's face fell.

'Oh… oh… perhaps one of the other girls?'

I hadn't noticed Lisbeth at my elbow. She had lost none of her forthright manner.

'Is that William Stretchleigh you're talking about? I heard he was ill?'

Flustered, the other woman cleared her throat and gave me a stuttering reply.

'N-n-n-no, no, my son is in good health. I'll admit he is susceptible to chills, but he… no… William is very well.'

Lisbeth gave her a shrewd look.

'I have studied healing for years. Perhaps I'd be a better match for him.' A succession of emotions flashed across Mrs Stretchleigh's haughty countenance. Shock gave way to interest, and Lisbeth led her away. 'Now, tell me what ails him. Perhaps I might visit,' she said.

'What was all that about?' Thomas asked as he returned to my side.

'Only that I think we may persuade Lisbeth to marry after all! She's turned down every suitable young man you've suggested. But now I think she may have found a worthy cause, someone she can look after, in the Stretchleigh boy. What do you think?'

Thomas chuckled. 'You mean someone she can try all her salves and potions on? As in all things, time will tell. Look, they're leaving at last. I'm famished. I hope Fulford's laid on a good spread.'

A carriage drew up at the bottom of the sloping path. The girls rushed to line their way as the happy couple set off. Their feet scuffed on the gravel path as they threw handfuls of rose petals from the small baskets they carried. I watched Arthur and Bridget go, taking the first steps into their future.

The air was still; no whisper of a breeze stirred the leaves. A bright sun shone from a cloudless azure sky. A melodious blackbird, perched on a nearby elderflower bush, serenaded us while graceful butterflies danced among the dainty white flowers. Brimming with hope and joy, I took Thomas's hand and together we followed the young couple, ready to embrace whatever lay ahead.

Author's Note

Mistress of Dartington Hall is a work of fiction that draws inspiration from people who lived in Elizabethan Devon. Most of the characters in the book are based on real individuals. Yet the historical record offers us only fleeting glimpses into their lives, providing a few fixed milestones on their respective life journeys. I have respected the record, but to fill in the gaps, I have employed creative imagination, grounded in extensive research and considering the context of their time. To enhance the narrative, I added a few fictional characters, including Roberda's French maid, Clotilde, and the steward, William Putt.

The Armada

My story begins in the autumn of 1587, by which time England had been at war with Spain for over two years. The threat of invasion was real, and Devon was in the front line. It must have been a terrifying time for the people of Dartington, which lies only sixteen miles upriver from the port of Dartmouth. Several false alarms are recorded before the Spanish Armada finally sailed in July 1588.

While researching this turbulent time, I easily discovered details of the actions of Spanish commanders, naval battles, and the significant roles played by the English officers, including Drake and Admiral Howard. I read accounts of Drake's fireships and the changing wind that scattered the Spanish ships and drove them around the coast of Scotland. Digging deeper, I uncovered the last-minute efforts to shore up Plymouth's defences, the establishment of a chain of warning beacons, and musters of ill-equipped and poorly trained men. I followed the fortunes of men like Raleigh, and of Devon's Deputy Lieutenants, including his half-brother, John Gilbert. In short, I could uncover a wealth of information about what the men were doing. However, I found no details in the record to tell me what the women of England did as the invasion became more and more likely.

Some wealthy women of Elizabethan Devon may have retreated to safer estates further inland, while others, like Roberda, opted to stay at home to face the invading army alongside their tenants and estate workers. The situation in 1587/88 was much like that southern England faced during the Second World War, when a different invasion seemed imminent. In *Mistress of Dartington Hall*, I have allowed Roberda to adopt a sort of 'Blitz spirit'. She rallies the women to provide better clothing to equip their menfolk, to manage food supplies against the likely need for evacuation, and to prepare medicines to care for the injured.

Devon had a narrow escape in 1588. Choosing to sail on up the Channel to rendezvous with the Duke of Parma was a poor decision by the Spanish, made catastrophic by bad weather – what some people called the 'Protestant wind'.

The richest prize taken from the Armada was the flagship Neustra Senora del Rosario (Our Lady of the Rosary). During the first skirmishes in 1588, laden with gold coins, diamond-hilted swords, wine and munitions, the galleon collided with another Spanish vessel. The commander of the crippled ship, Don Pedro de Valdes, surrendered without a fight when challenged by Drake. Crowds from Brixham, Paignton and Torquay, perhaps even some from Dartington, gathered along the coastline to watch the Rosario as she was towed into Torbay. All those on board, nearly 400 sailors and soldiers, were brought ashore. Some were taken to London. Sir John Gilbert (Gawen Champernowne's cousin) and George Carey of Cockington, both of whom were Deputy Lieutenants, were charged to hold some 160 of the Spanish prisoners in Devon, and to pay for their keep. It seems Carey may have shown more compassion to the prisoners than Gilbert, who is said to have used them as labour to landscape his gardens at Greenway on the River Dart.

The Dartington Churchwarden's accounts for 1589 mention providing shoes, shirt and stockings for a Spaniard and the watching of him, but no further details are given. I have moved this incident to September 1588 to suit my narrative.

Even though the first Spanish Armada failed, the war continued until 1604. In 1595, Spanish soldiers raided Mounts Bay in Cornwall. They sacked and set fire to Newlyn, Mousehole, Penzance, and Paul and even held a Catholic mass. Initially, the local gentry failed to muster a strong enough force to repel them. They were only driven off when Drake's ships arrived from Plymouth with reinforcements.

Hearing of this daring raid must have struck a new terror into the hearts of everyone at Dartington Hall.

Gawen's death and its aftermath

The cause of Gawen Champernowne's death is not recorded. However, the witnesses to a codicil dated midnight, 16 March 1591, were a physician named Percival and a chirurgeon (the old name for a surgeon) named Fell. The attendance of a surgeon suggests Gawen had suffered a grievous injury. One of the most common procedures practised by a surgeon was amputation.

In his will, Gawen named his eleven-year-old son Arthur as executor and appointed four overseers. However, it was Roberda who proved the will soon after Gawen's death. The will did not mention her except in the codicil naming her as the mother of an unborn child. Richard Champernowne of Modbury chaired an Inquisition Post Mortem on July 17, 1592. I found no conclusive evidence that anyone challenged Roberda's right to represent her son until he came of age.

It is not entirely clear from the records what exact role Richard played during the remaining years of Arthur's minority. An undated document at the South West Heritage Trust (Devon Archives) appears to be an early draft or a copy of an agreement for Richard to purchase Arthur's wardship for thirty-six pounds and fourteen shillings. Wardship would have given Richard the right to manage and take the income from the estate and to arrange a marriage for Arthur, keeping the dowry paid by the bride's father. However, no signed copy of a wardship agreement bearing an official seal from the Court of Wards has come to light. It appears that Richard may have initially planned to pursue the claim for wardship but reached an agreement with Roberda instead. On 8 February 1596, Richard and Roberda jointly presented a new rector, Edward Costerd, at St Mary's Church, Dartington.

John Harte is a shadowy figure. I have found it difficult to identify him with certainty, but he seems to have engaged in money lending.

Thomas and Roberda's marriage licence, which was granted in Exeter, is dated 12 August 1595. However, the records do not show where their wedding took place.

What Happened Next?

Roberda and Thomas

Roberda and Thomas lived together happily at Cloford, with Thomas active in local affairs, sitting on several inquiries. In 1603, he was one of those required to provide light horse for service in Ireland. The birth of their son, Edward Horner, in 1597, probably came as a surprise, since Roberda was at least forty years old. Thomas died in 1612 and was buried at Cloford. He made generous provision for Roberda in his will, leaving her the use of his town house in St Austin's Green, Bristol, and the manor at Cloford.

'To Lady Montgomery, my wife, certain lands… provided she keeps seven score deer within the park, and my house situated in St Austin's Green, near the city of Bristol, and after her death to go to Edward Horner, my son…'

In his will, Thomas Horner named Roberda as 'The Lady Montgomery'. Furthermore, she is referred to by that name in every document I have found after Gawen's death. I have yet to discover the date of Roberda's death.

Roberda's daughters

Thomas also left bequests to those Champernowne girls who remained unmarried at the time of his death, treating Mary, Frances, and Bridget as if they were his own daughters. He had already provided dowries for Roberda's other daughters when they wed. Mary never married and died at Dartington in 1638. Roberda's eldest daughter Elizabeth, who I have called Lisbeth, married William Stretchleigh at Dartington in 1601. William subsequently died and in 1607 she remarried an Italian doctor, again at Dartington.

Arthur and Bridget

Arthur and Bridget had a large family, seven daughters and six sons, and seemingly a happy marriage. However, Arthur's finances became entangled in debts Richard of Modbury racked up. To boost his income, Arthur became a moneylender, and he reportedly exploited mortgage arrangements for his own gain. The name of John Harte comes up in connection with some transactions.

By 1622, Arthur's ships were also operating in the New England fisheries under licence from his kinsman, Sir Ferdinando Gorges. One of Arthur's sons, Captain Francis Champernowne, arrived in New England in 1637 to supervise his father's 1000-acre grant from the New England Company and settled at Piscataqua. He had a farm at Strawberry Bank in present-day Portsmouth, New Hampshire. Having returned to England during the English Civil War, Francis went back to New England. He died in early 1687, at age seventy-three, and was buried in Kittery, Maine.

Roberda's Daughters

With the exception of Mary, all of Roberda's daughters married. The dowry money that had been at the root of Gawen and Roberda's differences continued to cause division. In 1621, all of Roberda's daughters and their respective husbands took legal action against Arthur, accusing him of failing to pay the girls their rightful share of Roberda's dowry money from France, as set out in Gawen's will. Roberda is mentioned in the papers, suggesting she may have been still living at this time.

Bess and Edward Seymour

Bess and Edward had a large family, and continued to live at Berry Pomeroy. Edward served as a Member of Parliament and held a number of offices in the county, including High Sheriff of Devon in 1605. In 1604 he tried to claim part of his grandfather the Duke of Somerset's estate, but was unsuccessful. In 1611 he was created Baron Seymour of Berry Pomeroy, having paid £1,095 for the necessary patent. This added to his money worries, and he never completed his lavish plans at his home. He died in 1613 and a memorial to him, his father and to his wife Elizabeth, (Bess), was erected in St Mary's Church, Berry Pomeroy. although it is often assumed that Bess died in the same year as her husband, I have been unable to confirm her date of death.

The Montgomerys in France

Roberda's brothers continued to fight for the Huguenot cause in France. After her eldest brother, Jacques, died in 1610, her younger brother, Gabriel, inherited the Montgomery lands. He built a new chateau at Ducey, which still stands today.

Acknowledgements

First, a special mention for the late Miss C E Champernowne who compiled a history of the Champernowne family in 1953. Her work acted as a helpful signpost, directing me to many fascinating sources as I researched the fortunes of Roberda and Gawen at Dartington Hall for this book and for *The Dartington Bride*.

I am grateful to the Dartington Trust for allowing me to explore 'behind-the-scenes' parts of the fourteenth-century manor house in the course of my research to help me build a picture of the buildings and gardens in the late sixteenth century.

The staff at South West Heritage Trust, Exeter, where the Devon Archives are held, have been unfailingly helpful in my search for clues amongst the Champernowne papers.

I am grateful to my amazing team of beta readers for their helpful feedback and insights, to Bob Cooper for the stunning cover design and to Fiona, as ever, for her unfailing encouragement. Once again, thanks to everyone at Troubador Publishing for their support throughout the publishing process.

Most importantly, a huge thank you to my husband, David, who brings me tea and coffee and reminds me to eat when I am lost in Elizabethan Devon.

About the Author

Author and speaker Rosemary Griggs has been researching Devon's sixteenth-century history for years, with a particular focus on one well-connected family – the Champernownes. She has discovered a cast of fascinating characters and an intriguing network whose influence stretched far beyond the West Country. She loves telling the stories of the forgotten women of history – the women beyond the royal court, wives, sisters, daughters and mothers who played their part during those tumultuous Tudor years: the Daughters of Devon.

Her novel *A Woman of Noble Wit* tells the story of Katherine Champernowne, Sir Walter Raleigh's mother, and features many of the county's well-loved places. *The Dartington Bride*, published March 2024, is the extraordinary tale of Lady Gabrielle Roberda Montgomery, who travelled from France to Elizabethan England to marry into the prominent and well-connected Champernowne family.

Rosemary creates and wears sixteenth-century clothing, a passion which complements her love for bringing the past to life through a unique blend of theatre, history, and re-enactment. Her appearances and talks for museums and community groups all over the West Country draw on her extensive research into sixteenth-century Devon, Tudor life and Tudor and Elizabethan dress. An audience with the Lady Katherine includes a full demonstration of the costume of a wealthy sixteenth-century woman.

Out of costume, Rosemary leads heritage tours of the gardens at Dartington Hall, a fourteenth-century manor house. The Dartington Estate is a stunning centre of heritage, culture, entertainment, hospitality and innovative sustainability set in rolling south Devon parkland near Totnes.

You can find out more on Rosemary's website:

https://rosemarygriggs.co.uk/

Where you can also sign up for her newsletter to receive regular updates on new projects, news of her next book, historical insights, exclusive content from her research, early access to new blog posts, and book recommendations.

Or follow Rosemary on social media:

Facebook: https://www.facebook.com/ladykatherinesfarthingale
Instagram: https://www.instagram.com/griggs6176/
Threads: https://www.threads.net/@griggs6176
Bluesky: https://bsky.app/profile/ragriggsauthor.bsky.social
Twitter: https://x.com/RAGriggsauthor

BY THE SAME AUTHOR

Few women of her time lived to see their name in print. But Katherine was no ordinary woman. She was Sir Walter Raleigh's mother. This is her story.

Set against the turbulent background of a Devon rocked by the religious and social changes that shaped Tudor England; a Devon of privateers and pirates; a Devon riven by rebellions and plots, *A Woman of Noble Wit* tells how Katherine became the woman who would inspire her famous sons to follow their dreams. It is Tudor history seen though a woman's eyes.

As the daughter of a gentleman's family with close connections to the glittering court of King Henry VIII, Katherine's duty is clear. She must put aside her dreams and accept the husband chosen for her. Still a girl, she starts a new life at Greenway Court, overlooking the River Dart, relieved that her husband is not the ageing monster of her nightmares. She settles into the life of a dutiful wife and mother – until a chance shipboard encounter with a handsome privateer turns her world upside down…

Years later a courageous act will set Katherine's name in print and see her youngest son fly high.

THE
DARTINGTON
BRIDE

ROSEMARY
GRIGGS

1571, and the beautiful, headstrong daughter of a French Count marries the son of the Vice Admiral of the Fleet of the West in Queen Elizabeth's chapel at Greenwich. It sounds like a marriage made in heaven...

Roberda's father, the Count of Montgomery, is a prominent Huguenot leader in the French Wars of Religion. When her formidable mother follows him into battle, she takes all her children with her.

After a traumatic childhood in war-torn France, Roberda arrives in England full of hope for her wedding. But her ambitious bridegroom, Gawen, has little interest in taking a wife.

Received with suspicion by the servants at her new home, Dartington Hall in Devon, Roberda works hard to prove herself as mistress of the household and to be a good wife. But there are some who will never accept her as a true daughter of Devon.

After the St Bartholomew's Day Massacre, Gawen's father welcomes Roberda's family to Dartington as refugees. Compassionate Roberda is determined to help other French women left destitute by the wars. But her husband does not approve. Their differences will set them on an extraordinary path...

This book is printed on paper from sustainable sources managed under the Forest Stewardship Council (FSC) scheme.

It has been printed in the UK to reduce transportation miles and their impact upon the environment.

For every new title that Troubador publishes, we plant a tree to offset CO_2, partnering with the More Trees scheme.

For more about how Troubador offsets its environmental impact, see www.troubador.co.uk/sustainability-and-community